Invitation to Valhalla

2003

Invitation to Valhalla

Mike Whicker

Writer's Showcase
New York   Lincoln   Shanghai

Invitation to Valhalla

Writer's Showcase
an imprint of iUniverse, Inc.

For information address:
iUniverse, Inc.
5220 S. 16th St., Suite 200
Lincoln, NE 68512
www.iuniverse.com

This is a work of historical fiction.

ISBN: 0-595-20683-2 (Pbk)
ISBN: 0-595-74535-0 (Cloth)

Printed in the United States of America

FOR

Sandy,

and for
two heroes from the war,

PFC Floyd D. Whicker
of the 2nd Ranger Battalion
who was among the first men
to step foot on Omaha Beach
on June 6, 1944

and
"Rosie the Riveter"
Bertha M. Whicker née Gambrel
of the Evansville Shipyard

EPIGRAPH

One cannot be a good historian of the outward, visible world without giving some thought to the hidden, private life of ordinary people; and on the other hand one cannot be a good historian of this inner life without taking into account outward events where these are relevant. They are two orders of fact which reflect each other, which are always linked and which sometimes provoke each other.

—Victor Hugo, 1862

FOREWORD

Nearly seven years have passed since I received the email message from David Mayer. Like all writers I was happy to hear from someone who had read some of my work. Mr. Mayer had come across a piece I wrote for the University of Southern Indiana magazine *Transitions* in 1994 on the 50th anniversary of D-Day. The magazine posted the article on the Internet and from it Mr. Mayer found me. I wrote the piece in honor of my father, Floyd D. Whicker, who was a nineteen-year-old Army Ranger on June 6, 1944 when he, along with the other men of the 2nd Ranger Battalion (the outfit portrayed in the movie *Saving Private Ryan*), stepped off a landing craft and into a killing wall of machine gun fire on Omaha Beach. My father's outfit was among the first to land on Omaha early that morning. The purple heart he earned that day when a .30 caliber German machine gun bullet ripped through his flesh hangs on my living room wall.

Probably due to the participation of my father in this keystone event of the past century, I have long held an interest in the war and specifically D-Day, the Battle of Britain, the Third Reich, and now, in no small part because of David Mayer, a renewed and strengthened interest in both the Holocaust, German military intelligence, and the role my hometown played in the war.

For that is why David Mayer contacted me—location. Any writer would have jumped at the chance to record the amazing story that follows. I just happen to live in the town where an important part of the story took place. An old adage implies it is better to be lucky than to be good. Because of where I live and a small but timely article posted on the Internet, David Mayer sought me out. I acknowledge my stroke of luck. In the end, the Internet not only brought my name before David Mayer, later it produced, incredibly, a response from a woman in Birmingham, Alabama, whose aunt knew Erika Lehmann. More on that at the end after you, reader, have met Erika Lehmann.

I will always consider it my great good fortune that David Mayer contacted me from his home in Denver even though the past six years have proved to be the proverbial roller coaster of successes and failures. Pursuing dead ends (here and in Europe), attempting to coax or spark memories from aging participants, seeking access to documents both here and abroad (some to this day still classified) inspire me to a much healthier respect for both historians and gumshoes.

Someone attempting to write this story twenty-five years ago would undoubtedly have encountered even more obstacles than when I undertook the task near the close of the century. During the war, and for many years after, the FBI was reluctant to admit that Nazi spies and saboteurs had sneaked under their net. Of the 19,649 cases of possible espionage or sabotage the FBI investigated during the war years (1939-45) only a handful of these cases were ever acknowledged by the Bureau to be the work of the enemy. Reports released to the press were strictly limited to cases where the FBI made quick arrests: cases such as Operation Pastorius where eight Nazis saboteurs were apprehended within a few days after landing by U-boat on a Long Island beach in June of 1942.

Now, thanks to David Mayer, the case of Operation Vinland—the story of Erika Lehmann and the Mayer family—has come to light.

Mike Whicker
Evansville, Indiana
February 2001

PREFACE

Denver, Colorado—2000

Testament of David Mayer—July 8, 2000:

My name is David Mayer and I am a Holocaust survivor. With the death of my mother in 1993 (she too was a camp survivor) and my own rapidly approaching old age (I was fifty-five the year my mother died), I felt a strong need to record what I know about the circumstances of my mother's and my participation in this part of history.

Much work has taken place to enable an accurate account, both by myself and Mr. Whicker whom I have retained to record this history. Parts of this story were unknown even to me and my family until recently when time limits expired on previously classified information, information now available under the Freedom of Information Act. Starting in 1995 and continuing for six years, Mr. Whicker and I conducted interviews with principals who either played a direct role in my family's story or were in a position to witness certain events.

Most of this work was necessitated because of the strange events surrounding my mother's and my release from the concentration camp. My mother and I were among the very few Jews released from captivity by the Germans *before* the end of the war. Just that happenstance alone makes our story freakish indeed when compared to the stories of other survivors.

Although her role in the following written record is small, my mother, Ruth Herzl-Mayer, is the real hero of this story. For it was on my mother that the struggle fell—the everyday struggle of a Jew to remain alive in a Nazi concentration camp. It was a struggle she had to endure for both of us. Although I remember the Zählappell, I am spared memory of most of the horror. You see, I was three years old in 1941 when, holding my mother's hand, we stepped off of a cattle car onto a platform at Dachau.

ACKNOWLEDGEMENTS

My thanks to John Elliott, my well-read friend, for being both an exemplary source of encouragement and of valuable advice on this genre (John knew Charlie Pulaski better than the author knew him).

To Eric Vonfuhrmann for a most valuable criticism: thank you.

I must acknowledge Kathleen Shipley, a gracious travel partner, for her help during our mental sojourns in Paris; Dr. Susanna Hoeness-Krupsaw of Heidelberg, Germany, now of the University of Southern Indiana; and SuzAnn Hull, yet another expert I leaned on for help.

Thanks Josh for your insight and suggestions, and a special thanks to the world's most longsuffering proofreader—Sandra Whicker. And how could I speak of editing without mentioning the special debt owed Vicki Hammelman. Vicki, you are the High Mufti of bowdlerization.

Dr. Bernard Norling, professor emeritus of European history at the University of Notre Dame, offered encouragement and keen criticism. I thank him for both.

And to Dr. Walter Rinderle. Thanks Doc for your class, your book (I have opened it many times since we were last together), and for the copy of *Mein Kampf.* All three were invaluable to this story.

The influence of all of these remarkable people is evident in the pages ahead.

CHAPTER I

Terrible is the likeness of her face to immortal goddesses.

—Homer, (ca. 700 B.C.)

In Medias Res

Wales—March 1942

Opening a champagne bottle with one hand while steering a car with the other was a skill Henry Wiltshire had mastered of late. This talent could be performed even while driving at night with war-dimmed headlights. Keeping his eyes focused on the small portion of the rural Wales road that the weak headlamps illuminated, he slowed before the approaching curve. Leaning the bottle against the side of his leg, he quickly downshifted, then deftly guided the huge, black Bentley around the narrow turn. After shifting back into top gear, Wiltshire grabbed the bottle and, with his right hand on the wheel, used his left hand to expertly nurse the cork free.

With a loud pop the cork rocketed from the bottle and ricocheted off the windshield. It landed somewhere in the back seat. The champagne, volatile from the bouncing car ride, geysered out onto the blouse of the young blond woman in the passenger seat to his left. The shock of the cold liquid against her chest evoked a loud squeal. Wiltshire only half-heartedly tried to cover a laugh.

"Sorry, love," Wiltshire said with total insincerity.

"You did that on purpose, you wretch!" The blond tried to sound upset, but she had already helped Wiltshire finish off a previous bottle since they left London an hour ago so her admonishment came forth more as a giggle.

"You can't mean it," Wiltshire replied. "Would I do a thing like that?"

"Bloody right you would," the woman answered while pulling the front of the wet blouse away from her skin. "I'll catch my death because of you." With that she unbuttoned and removed the blouse and the wet brassiere underneath. Wiltshire was thankful for the moon ahead that supplied sufficient light for an acceptable view of the young woman's exposed breasts.

"I suppose you're happy now, aren't you?" the woman joked.

"Are you sure none of it got on your skirt?"

The young woman ignored the quip and retrieved a blanket from the back. As she turned to lean over the seat, her breasts brushed against Wiltshire's arm. Momentarily distracted, the middle-aged man let the car's right fender brush against a hedge bordering the road. He jerked the car back to the left which made the girl slide hard against him. She shrieked again, then sat back down.

After using the blanket to dry off and cover herself, the young woman slid over and sat next to Wiltshire. She ran her fingers through his hair then patted the noticeable paunch above his belt. Her hand then went seductively lower, but only to take the champagne bottle from between his legs. She laughed, then took a long drink.

"What a tease you are, you little scamp," Wiltshire muttered.

"You'll see what kind of tease I am, love, when we get to St. David's Head." The young blond said it with the wicked look that always raised the man's blood pressure.

✠   ✠   ✠

The young woman had been right about this place, Wiltshire thought as he leaned against a crooked fir tree on a hill high above the Irish Sea. It had been years since he had been to Wales. Wiltshire always considered it a place with nothing to offer unless your tastes were geared toward bogs and moors, but she had promised him St. David's Head was a beautiful place. On the extreme western coast of Wales, St. David's Head would be a welcome respite from the rat race in London.

Without being conscious of doing it, Wiltshire drew on his unlit pipe as he gazed out at St. George's Channel. He was far enough above the water that the breaking shore waves were barely audible. Behind the breakers, countless phalanxes of waves, their moonlit tips asparkle, marched relentlessly toward the shore like an invading army. To Wiltshire's left, the moon and an owl sat side by side in the naked branches of a tall birch. To his right and behind was the cottage he had rented for the weekend. Inside, he knew Margaret Harrison was bathing, primping, and waiting for his return. Yes, Wiltshire thought, this would definitely be worth the drive from London.

A cold March breeze ruthlessly hunted any exposed flesh, and Wiltshire pulled down his trilby hat and squeezed the collar of his great-coat tight around his neck. He glanced again at the small, ivy-covered stone cottage standing half hidden within a stand of trees and tall hedges. A thin ribbon of yellow light escaped from the edges of the blackout shades covering the windows. Wiltshire knew even that much light was not allowed; you couldn't be too careful nowadays. Stationed in London during the worst of the German blitz last year, Wiltshire took the blackout seriously. He promised himself he would fix the shade when he returned to the cottage.

He lit his pipe with his back to the sea both for the sake of the blackout and to shield the fire's life against the wind. Henry Wiltshire was careful even when it came to the small light generated by the burning tobacco in his pipe. Wiltshire cupped his hand around the pipe's bowl to block the orange glow. He took several long draws to stoke the tobacco as he contemplated his good fortune.

With all considered, this war, which now raged over a large portion of the planet, was a personal boon to him. The war transformed Wiltshire from a struggling university French professor with no tenure and a bad marriage to one of the top cryptographers of the British intelligence machine. Wiltshire handled communications with French resistance. He was proud of his work for his country's war effort, and proud also of the immense responsibility entrusted to him. Splitting his time between offices of M1-9 in London and the top-secret cryptanalysis section of military intelligence at Bletchley Park, Wiltshire was privy to almost all information concerning modus operandi and French resistance efforts involving the escape lines. These escape lines specialized in guiding downed British airmen trapped behind enemy lines and "escapers," prisoners of war who had escaped from camps or resistance personnel whose cover had been blown, to freedom.

Wiltshire's concentration broke when he heard an automobile engine start somewhere in the distance. He turned toward the faint sound. Carried by the wind, the noise came from the next cottage a couple of hundred meters down the coast. Wiltshire watched as the car, barely visible even in the full moon because of the distance, foliage, and diminished headlamps, pulled out onto the coast road and headed in the direction of the local village five kilometers inland. Probably a journey to the pub, Wiltshire concluded.

Several cottages perched as humble sentinels atop the rocky cliffs up and down the coastline of St. David's Head. The cottages were owned and rented out by a local farmer. When the blitz started a little over a year ago, business picked up. Places like this in Wales and other remote parts of England distanced from Luftwaffe targets became popular with people like Henry Wiltshire and the girl. People who, for a night or two, wished to get away from air raid sirens (and the apprehension that accompany them). The girl found out about this place and she had taken care of renting a cottage for the weekend.

Ah, yes, the girl—more of Wiltshire's great good fortune. Amid the great human suffering this war inflicted upon millions, how could his life get any better? How else but within the great drama of a world war would a situation arise that would bring him Maggie?

He met Margaret Harrison at a cocktail party the previous fall. It was a particularly dreary affair as he remembered, hosted by some mid-level bureaucrat in Sussex. Dreary, that is, until *she* arrived. At the time, she was working as a secretary/quasi-reporter at a small circulation weekly newspaper in Greenwich. During the course of her work covering war stories, she met and occasionally dated a few British officers. One had asked her to accompany him to this cocktail party.

At the party, Margaret Harrison stunned the men with her charm and beauty and embittered the women who constantly kept discovering their men glancing in her direction. Here Wiltshire's recent luck stepped in again. Amid all the young, handsome officers it was he, Henry Wiltshire, the middle-aged, slightly overweight professor, who ended up occupying most of the young beauty's time and attention. Wiltshire had stepped out onto a balcony for some fresh air shortly before she did the same (he could understand her need for a break from the gaggle of admirers). A pleasant conversation ensued. When he discovered she spoke fluent French and some German (and wasn't particularly happy with her job in Greenwich) he suggested she contact the personnel people at M1. He told her whom to contact and promised her he would put in a good word.

Three weeks later she was working as a low-security translator in Room 840 of M1-9. Wiltshire's office, Room 900, handled the high-security translations. The relationship between the two grew until one night in December, after one of several Christmas parties, he found himself in bed with this fascinating creature. They had been practically inseparable for the three months since that night, a turn of events

almost unbelievable to Wiltshire. Indeed, Margaret Harrison was someone special. The beautiful young woman ignored the office jokes about
the "beauty and the beast" and the curious stares from strangers when
the two of them were out and about.

Gazing out at the cold, foreboding Irish Sea, Wiltshire's thoughts
returned to the war. Will Hitler invade by sea? If so, when and where?
Surely never here, on this part of the western shore where cliffs rose
steeply from rocky beaches. True, this western coast was much less
guarded than the eastern, but Wiltshire still thought it made much
more sense for the Nazis to come across the short distance of the
English Channel than to swing the massive amount of men and invasion matériel around the whole of England to these western shores.

Another cold blast of air convinced Wiltshire it was time to suspend
his sightseeing and ruminations on life in 1942 England. He pounded
the burnt tobacco from his pipe, turned his back on the Irish Sea, and
walked briskly toward the cottage and the warmth of Margaret Harrison.

Inside the cottage a small fire danced weakly in the stone hearth,
lighting the room with the help of two oil lamps. One lamp sat on a
table, the other on a shelf. The cottage had no electricity. Wiltshire
retrieved a poker from a bucket beside the fireplace and pushed around
in the embers. From a small stack of wood next to the hearth he
grabbed two small logs and placed them over the hottest coals.

The cottage was small, just one room with a kitchenette and bath. A
small brown couch, two sturdy-looking wood chairs, and a small table
were the room's only furniture except for a bookshelf that held no
books. The bedroom was not one really, just a separate cubicle curtained
off from the main room by a sliding portiere. A fireplace and a cook
stove were expected to supply sufficient heat even during the coldest
weather and Wiltshire imagined that they did a fit job of it. The room
was warm and cozy at the present with just the small fire.

He heard occasional sounds from the bath.

"What's doing in there, Maggie? Making progress?"

"Soaking, love," Wiltshire heard her say from behind the door. "And since you finally decided to stop mucking about outside, would you mind bringing in the hot water on the stove?"

Wiltshire walked to the nook that served as the kitchen. On the stove sat a large kettle of water that was already steaming. He had not noticed the stove being fired when he entered the cottage. No wonder it was so warm inside. The water was hot enough to require Wiltshire to locate a couple of dish towels in order to hold on to the kettle's steel handles.

Inside the bathroom, Margaret Harrison sat soaking in the small, claw-footed tub. She reclined to a point which brought the water to her chin. The soapy water prevented any view of the female form within. Wiltshire poured the hot water into the tub at the end where Margaret's feet rested out of the water on the tub's rim.

"Thanks, Henry. You're a dear. Did you find anything interesting out there?"

"You were right, Maggie. Nice place. I bet it's even more beautiful in the summer."

"I told you," the young woman replied. "And you said Wales had only cows and cockneys. Such a closed mind for a professor."

Wiltshire laughed.

The young woman grabbed his hand which still had not warmed completely.

"Why you're chilled to the bone." She looked him in the eyes and added with the wicked look, "Why don't you get in here with me? The water will warm you,—not that there aren't other ways to accomplish that."

"I don't think we would both fit, Maggie. Why don't you finish up. I have a nice blaze going."

"Well, if you're afraid of a little water," Margaret splashed a small amount of water on his pants. She then pointed to a towel that lay atop a small hamper. "At least you can dry my back."

As she rose from the obscurity of the water, she knew Wiltshire would blush. It was something he always did (quite to his embarrassment) when the lights were on and she was undressed. She looked for this customary sign of his innate shyness and smiled when it appeared on his face. She turned her back to him and waited. Wiltshire gently patted her back with the towel.

Wiltshire's reaction to all of this was, of course, male. What man, Wiltshire mused, would not experience a quickening of the blood when called upon to do his present chore. Here was Aphrodite, he thought, or Shamhat, the seductive temple girl, from Gilgamesh. Her arms were above her head, her hands against the wall for support as she leaned slightly over. This accentuated her curves. Her skin was clear but not pale—more like a delicate, golden hue. Her body had an athletic look, very much feminine, but strong. (She had told him that she was quite the tumbler during her teenage years and even worked out for a while with the boys' gymnastics team at school.)

When he finished, she turned and took the towel from his hand, placed it against his chest to shield him from her still-wet front, put her arms around his neck and drew him to her. They kissed, then he picked her up and carried her from the bath.

A few hours later, an exhausted Henry Wiltshire awoke to the sound of the wind rattling a loose window pane directly above the bed. The fire had died so the room was cold and dark. Wiltshire pulled the covers tight. Through the rattling window came the only light in the room, furnished by the gypsy moon that had left the branches of the tree and the owl behind. The moon had tracked the Englishman and now stared down at him through the glass. Margaret was not beside him, but he heard her footsteps approaching from the direction of the bathroom.

"Ah, you're awake!" she said with glee as she jumped on the bed astraddle him. She was wearing one of his undershirts.

"Aren't you cold?" he asked incredulously.

"Never."

"I'm consorting with a madwoman," Wiltshire mumbled as he again tried to pull up the covers. She would have none of it, wrestling him and pulling away the sheets.

"Get up, Henry. I want to go down to the beach."

"What? Now? You *are* daft," he told her as he tried unsuccessfully to retrieve the covers. "What time is it?"

"It's around half past three, but who cares. Don't be such a fuddy-duddy. We're on holiday." She leaned over him and whispered in his ear: "I'll give you special attention on the beach."

"Come to bed, Maggie," Wiltshire replied as he finally managed to retrieve a cover. "We'll go in the morning when it's light."

"Well, be like that then. I'm going down to the beach, with or without you." She then goaded, "Who knows, while down there I might meet another gentleman who's not so worried about a little cool weather."

"I don't think your chances are very good to meet someone at this hour."

She rose, lit an oil lamp that she had moved to a small dressing table beside the bed, and began gathering her clothes.

"You're actually serious," Wiltshire said with exasperation. Maggie did not answer verbally but proved her intent when she began dressing.

Wiltshire sighed. He was dog tired; her energetic lovemaking usually lasted for hours and it always wore him out. But he could never be irate with this gorgeous female who had brought so much vigor into his life. He sat up on the edge of the bed and looked for his clothes.

They had to drive a short distance back up the coast road to a point where a narrow walk path led down to the shore. Margaret said she had seen the path when they drove in earlier that evening.

"It was dark when we arrived. You must be part owl to have spotted it," Wiltshire joked.

Following Margaret's directions, Wiltshire turned off the main route onto a bumpy road that led to the cliff's edge. He turned off the headlights

before the car reached the end of the trail and let the Bentley roll slowly
to a stop. He shut off the motor and engaged the emergency brake. After
getting out of the car, Margaret grabbed Wiltshire's hand and led him,
half pulling him along, down the steep, narrow path to the beach.
Wiltshire was again thankful for the moon, but still the path was dark
and it was hard to see where they stepped.

"Slow down, Maggie, we'll break our necks."

"Not to worry, I'll catch you," Margaret said happily.

As they grew nearer to the water, the crashing sounds of the breakers
grew louder. Once on the beach, Wiltshire immediately noticed it was
easier to see. The water and the pale sand reflected the moonlight. It was
a rocky shore, and not much of a beach to speak of, but there was a
small, flat area of dry sand at the base of the cliff that ran to the water's
edge. Huge, dark boulders rose from the water on either side of this
secluded mini-beach. These rocks produced large, vertical sprays when
the incoming breakers slapped their slick faces.

"How about a dip?" Margaret looked at him and laughed.

"How about a straight jacket," Wiltshire answered.

She sat in the sand and he joined her.

"The mountains or an ocean shore...I can never decide which I love
better," Margaret said. "They are both so beautiful and serene."

"Yes, they are."

"I could stay here forever," she said dreamily.

They chatted for a few minutes, then she leaned her head against his
shoulder. He put his arm around her. They sat without talking for several minutes, just listening to the symphony of water meeting land, one
of nature's operas. She looked up at him and smiled.

"Cold?" Margaret asked.

"I'm, okay."

"Well, I could stand a blanket," she said.

"You? The superwoman who never gets cold? I can't believe it."

She jabbed him playfully in his ribs and stood up. "There are a couple of blankets in the trunk. I'll get them."

"I'll go," Wiltshire said and started to stand.

"You stay here, love," Margaret insisted. "Let me have the keys. There is something else—a surprise."

Wiltshire looked at her and she grinned. He handed over the keys. She ascended the path almost effortlessly (he knew it would have taken him twice the time and he likely would have made a fool of himself by falling and rolling back down to the beach). When she safely reached the top, Wiltshire turned around and gazed back out to sea. One thing was sure, he thought, the Nazis would never land around here. The beaches were inadequate, and then there were the cliffs. He leaned back on an elbow and waited for Margaret Harrison.

"Close your eyes, Henry."

He sat up quickly. He had not heard her return because of the ocean noise and her voice startled him slightly.

"Oh, did I unnerve you, pet? I'm sorry. Here now, close your eyes like a good boy."

Henry grinned and obeyed. What in the world was she up to now? He felt cold glass against his lips and the smell of brandy. He opened his eyes and saw her kneeling beside him with the bottle. The brandy was her surprise. He heard the familiar, wicked little giggle.

"My intentions are to get you drunk and take advantage of you—again," she declared. She handed him the bottle. He took another drink then offered her one.

"Not just yet," she said. "You drink up. I have a promise to keep." She patted his stomach, then moved her hand lower.

Wiltshire took another drink of the brandy then sat the bottle in the sand. Suddenly he felt a hot sensation in his neck and scalp. He felt dizzy and faint. He tried to ignore it, but then an overwhelming fatigue came upon him. He struggled to remain lucid.

"What's wrong, love?"

Wiltshire heard Maggie's voice but it seemed a mile away.

"I don't know…something…wrong…" He never finished.

Wiltshire tried unsuccessfully to struggle to his feet. Turning, he knocked over the bottle of brandy, pouring it into the sand. He tried to make it to his feet but kneeling was as far as he got. As he faced the cliff, the last thing Wiltshire saw before he passed out was the unusually bright headlights of the Bentley, turned-on with the dimming shrouds removed, shining out to sea.

☩   ☩   ☩

Some nightmare! That was Henry Wiltshire's first thought. *I have to wake up.* He was lying on his back. Wiltshire struggled to turn, to move his legs, anything to force himself awake. Something was holding him! He struggled to open his eyes. He could not see! A panic waved over him and he heard himself yell out.

"Help!" Wiltshire shouted. Then he thought he heard something. What was that? Voices?

He heard it again. It was voices! Again Wiltshire hollered out.

"Help! For God's sake, help me!"

The voices seemed to come nearer. Wiltshire heard what sounded like a curtain being opened beside him.

"Halt's Maul, Engländer!"

It was a man's gruff voice. It was telling him to shut up in German!

"Where am I? Who are you?" Wiltshire demanded. He was now lucid enough to realize he was blindfolded and tied up.

"Halt's Maul!" The voice barked again. Wiltshire heard the curtain close.

He could now tell he was lying on some sort of bed or cot but it felt like the whole room was tipping back and forth. *It must be a boat. What the hell has happened?* Wiltshire tried to remember. *He was on the beach with Maggie…Maggie! What has happened to her? Is she okay?* The panic returned. He managed to lift his legs, which were bound. As he raised his legs, he kicked what felt like another cot above him. He kicked and yelled again.

Soon he heard the voices again approaching—all speaking German. One sounded female! *It was a female; he heard it plainly now. A female speaking German!* Again Wiltshire shouted and made noise by kicking whatever it was over him. He heard the curtain beside him open again. Wiltshire felt someone take off his blindfold. With the blindfold off, Wiltshire tried to focus on the form standing beside him. Eyes unaccustomed to the brightness and a red ceiling light behind the person's head made it impossible to see the face, but Wiltshire could tell it was a female form. The woman turned and said something in German to a man behind her. The man stood on the other side of the light so Wiltshire could see him better. Wiltshire recognized the German *Kriegsmarine* uniform of a *Unterseebootman*—a German U-boat crewman!

"Where am I?" Wiltshire screamed the words. "And where is the girl who was with me? Damn you!" He was sweating profusely and he felt he would retch. The shadowy female form standing over him spoke.

"Henry, please, you're making such a fuss."

It was the voice of Margaret Harrison.

Henry Wiltshire turned his head and vomited.

✠   ✠   ✠

CHAPTER 2

♪Wir versaufen unser Oma ihr klein Häuschen,
   ihr klein Häuschen,
♪Wir versaufen unser Oma ihr Klein Häuschen,
   und die erste und die zweite Hypothek.♪

(We are drinking up Grandma's little house,
   her little house,
We are drinking up Grandma's little house,
   and the first and second mortgage.)

—popular song in 1922 Germany
in reference to the runaway inflation

Berlin—March 1942

"So…"

Her father always began his subtle interrogations of her with that word. This latest attempt began as he sat down to his cold cuts and *Schwarzbrot*, the same breakfast he had eaten for as long as she could remember.

"…they must have something of importance on their minds."

"Or so they feel, Father," was all she offered. Erika approached the window of her father's Berlin apartment. As she neared the window, her ghost stared back at her through the shining glass pane.

Erika Lehmann was still baffled and more than a little annoyed at the premature recall from the England assignment. Covert missions were dangerous enough. Fourteen German agents working in England had already been identified, arrested, and hanged since the start of the war. Changing plans in the middle of an assignment only added to the danger. The hasty recall forced her to set up the complex escape at St. David's Head which included a secret trip to Wales to reconnoiter a location, find a suitable haven like the cliffside cottages, and establish and stick to the elaborate time frame for the U-boat rendezvous. All of this forced her to spend much additional time on the transmitter communicating with home base. Of course the English monitor the airwaves. If they had broken the code they would have been at St. David's Head waiting for her. Unexpected withdrawals are dangerous business.

The recall was so premature, in fact, that while still in London Erika considered the information she had thus far collected to be of minimal value. She felt, even while preparing to withdraw, that her mission had been in vain. Originally her infiltration time was eighteen months; she was in England less than half that time when she received the transmission *Wotan invites you to Valhalla*—the code ordering her to withdraw at the earliest opportunity. Wotan was the Germanic equivalent to the Viking's Odin, the supreme god in ancient mythology. Valhalla, or heaven, represented Germany in the code.

So of her own volition she took Henry Wiltshire captive and brought him back for interrogation. At least this way perhaps something could be salvaged from the mission.

Looking out of her father's window, Erika could not help but compare the Tiergarten across the street with Hyde Park in London. She was struck by the similarities. Both of the famous parks had trimmed shrubs, shaved lawns, and now, anti-aircraft guns. But instead of the hastily sandbagged British guns scattered helter-skelter around Hyde Park, the Germans had constructed the steel Flakturm, a massive, olive green anti-aircraft gun structure that rose high above the park's trees. The quiet peace and beauty of both famous parks had been sacrificed to the needs of war. And, although she could not see the main fountain that was blocked from her view by the lime and chestnut trees, she knew no Union Jack flew atop the fountain pole. Instead, the park across the street was flanked with dozens of flagpoles flying red flags bearing a twisted black cross in a white disk.

The temperature outside was typical for the time of year. Seldom was Berlin not a cold place in March. But the wind was slight and the usual gray cloud cover had made an error, allowing the sun to shine through an opening. On the street below, a military transport truck with a canvas canopy traveled one direction while a heavily bundled bicyclist with a large package tied to the handlebars traveled the other. They passed each other below her father's fourth floor window.

Erika Lehmann knew no more than her father about why she was ordered back to Berlin so abruptly. She attempted to change the subject.

"How did you find this place, Father?"

"A Jew banker temporarily resettled somewhere and he leased this place out to the Ministry. He must have been in some straights for money. I have these rooms for sixty Reichmarks a month. Cheap, hey?"

Indeed she knew it was. A spacious, six room apartment such as this, overlooking the Tiergarten, must be worth three times as much.

"I think they have all resettled," Erika said. "I haven't seen a Jew since I returned to Berlin."

A pause. Everyone knew the government was attempting to influence the Jews to move east. Help was needed to rebuild the war torn areas in Poland. This influence seemed to be working. The capital was now nearly empty of Jews.

"The government is offering them free land if they agree to rebuild the damaged areas," the father said. "You know the Jews, they are not going to pass up free land, and who can blame them?"

She watched her father tear the black bread and spread a pat of butter. The war made butter a frill, not easily obtained by the average

German citizen. But her father was not average. Karl Lehmann held a high post in the Reich government, he was a highly respected member of the Party, and, most importantly, her father was an old friend of Adolf Hitler.

And he was still handsome. He sat upright at the table (he had always been a stickler about posture) in neatly pressed black pants and a starched, snow-white shirt buttoned tight to the neck. The fifty-three-year-old face was unwrinkled. The dark brown hair of his youth was now silver but still full, the jaw chiseled from stone. Erika could understand why her mother had been swept off her feet by this man.

Erika always thought it a romantic story. Her mother was the daughter of a minor British diplomat assigned to Berlin before the first war. Karl Lehmann was an enlisted man serving in the Kaiser's army and for a brief time he had been assigned duty as one of the embassy drivers for the British chargé d'affaires. That is how her parents met. The beautiful British daughter of an embassy staff member needed a ride through Berlin one afternoon and Karl Lehmann drew the assignment. It was a quick and effective courtship, and they married in the summer of 1914. On their honeymoon in the Italian Alps they heard of the assassination of Archduke Ferdinand.

Against the wishes of her parents, and against the advice of the other quickly packing members of the British contingent in Berlin, her mother elected to stay in Germany during the war. She lived with her husband's parents in Oberschopfheim, a small, rural village in Baden in southwestern Germany. There the young bride felt she would at least be available to her husband during any furloughs.

The pretty young woman who now stood at the window in a light-blue chenille robe was the product of one of those brief, infrequent leaves in 1917. Erika Lehmann had her father's hazel eyes and high, wide cheek bones. The blond hair, full upper lip, and the chenille robe were gifts from her mother.

Karl Lehmann served faithfully on the western front and a moment's heroism during the Battle of the Somme in 1916 earned him the Iron Cross First Class, to this day his most cherished possession. Following the war, the Versailles Treaty not only helped shatter the German economy but also her father's plans of a soldier's career. With the German military establishment scuttled, Lehmann found himself on the streets, just one in the hordes of unemployed patriots. In 1920, with no prospects in little Oberschopfheim, the father left the family behind and journeyed the two hundred kilometers to Munich where a cousin had found work.

Karl Lehmann found a job as a printer's devil for a small publisher— a humble job for a decorated veteran and former escort to diplomats. He quartered in a flop house to save money, most of which he sent home to his wife and young daughter. But the German government's bad fiscal policy during the war and reparations to the Allies after the Treaty caused an inflation rate so fantastic that Karl Lehmann's wages were rendered practically worthless in just the short time it took the mail to deliver the money home to Oberschopfheim. This, along with the humiliation Lehmann felt was dealt his homeland with a spiteful and unfair treaty, led him, like so many others, to be engulfed in the maelstrom of discontent directed at the Allies and at the German Weimar Republic, the democratic wannabe government most Germans felt was forced down their throats.

In those early days after the war, one of the many small newspapers that Karl Lehmann's employer had as clients was entitled the *Völkischer Beobachter*. The *Beobachter* had it own press, but occasionally contracted out some of its work. That newspaper expounded the views of a small, right-wing fringe organization. In those days her father had little time for reading, but over the course of doing business he came to know the man who dropped off and picked up the printing orders for the *Beobachter*. The man's name was Anton Drexler, a short, stout man with bulging eyes. When Herr Drexler found out the young printer's devil was a struggling veteran with a family left behind, Drexler adopted an attitude of friendliness toward him and eventually talked her father into attending a speech by the new leader of his organization. Drexler told him this leader was also a struggling veteran and a man who he felt had answers to Germany's problems.

In later years, the story of how her father met Adolf Hitler would be often repeated, and it was the centerpiece of her father's conversation at social gatherings. No one ever tired of hearing it.

It was early in 1921 at the Zirkus Krone. This was the Munich auditorium that Drexler had told Karl Lehmann that the organization that sponsored the *Völkischer Beobachter* would hold its first national congress. The movement was called the National Socialist German Workers Party. Her father recognized the name, having set the letters in type many times, although he had paid it little heed.

The speech was to begin at eight o'clock that night. Drexler gave Karl Lehmann a free ticket for admission and told him to look him up after the speech. The wrinkled ticket was still kept in a place of honor in the Lehmann family album. Erika had seen it often and always noticed the small type at the bottom, *Juden Verboten*—Jews not allowed.

In those early days, shortly after the Great War, her father had remained a monarchist. Had not Germany's best days been under the Kaiser? Let the Hohenzollerns return from the Netherlands and things could be as they were before the war.

Nonetheless, a family man alone in a strange city has few opportunities for entertainment (at least not a faithful family man such as Karl Lehmann) so he decided to attend Herr Drexler's meeting. Walking through a cold sleet and January wind, her father arrived an hour early to an almost empty auditorium. But the people came. At ten minutes until eight most seats were filled with a line still outside.

The theme of the speech was "Future or Ruin." The speaker was physically not impressive but he quickly won the crowd. Her father told Erika that some of those around him seemed almost entranced. The speaker was forced to stop mid-sentence several times amid spontaneous cheering and clapping that drowned out his words. The man at the podium told of a new and greater Germany rising Phoenix-like from the ashes, and, although her father confessed he did not at the time understand many of the programs the man was promoting, he found himself agreeing with what the speaker claimed had led Germany down the sorry path upon which it now found itself, mainly the "November Criminals"—the German leaders whom many felt had betrayed the country by surrendering a war many Germans felt they had not lost—and the spiteful terms of the Versailles Treaty.

After the speech, her father noticed Herr Drexler and others joining the speaker on stage. Remembering Drexler's invitation, he approached the men. There, on the floor of the Zirkus Krone, the young Karl Lehmann shook the young Adolf Hitler's hand for the first time. Drexler told Hitler about Lehmann's service during the war and his work in the publishing business. This seemed to perk Hitler's interest. Hitler and Drexler had business to discuss and, when ready to leave the auditorium, Hitler insisted that Karl Lehmann come along.

Through the cold, dark Munich night the three men walked to Hitler's apartment, which turned out to be a small back room over a store at Thierschstrasse 41 near the Isar River. The room was no more then a small cell, eight by fifteen feet, and cold and damp. Her father always enjoyed describing the drab, rundown apartment the future conqueror of Europe occupied when he first met him and how Hitler had given him his last beer while the future Führer and Drexler went without.

The congenial host who had given up his last beer was very interested in her father's war years and his views of current events. Hitler also quizzed her father about his work in the publishing business. The men talked for several hours. Often Erika heard her father say that when he left the dingy little room that night his "heart raced with renewed hope for the Fatherland."

So her father joined the infant movement during the earliest days of the struggle, unlike the vast majority of current members who waited until the Party gained power in 1933 and then joined in droves. This gave her father his status as a Party celebrity. He had earned the *Blutorden,* an honor bestowed only on those who had taken part in the early street fighting in the twenties. Now Herr Lehmann was always in demand among the social circles of the Reich. The baronesses fought over the handsome widower who had access to the Führer.

But 1921 was twelve long, hard years from power. The young Lehmann family would continue to struggle. When the Führer went to prison after the ill-fated Beer Hall Putsch of 1923, her father had no choice but to send young Erika and her mother to England to live with her mother's family. There Erika spent her early school years. English grammar overtook her German. Finally, in 1929, she and her mother returned to Germany, and the family settled in Munich where her father now held an important position in the Party propaganda machine under Joseph Goebbels.

After Hitler ascended to power in January of 1933, life and fortune would forever change for the Lehmann family. Having learned English from his wife and daughter, Karl Lehmann was assigned to the German Embassy in Washington as press secretary to the ambassador. Erika spent her last two years of high school at the exclusive Blair School for girls in Manassas, Virginia, just outside Washington. The family lived in the United States until 1937 when her mother was killed in an automobile accident. A drunk driver ran a stop sign and broadsided Louise Lehmann's taxi. She died in Walter Reed Hospital two days later. The loss of his wife greatly affected Karl Lehmann who requested an immediate transfer home. Since then he had submerged himself even more deeply in his work.

Retreating from the window, Erika walked over and poured her father more coffee. She sat down at the table and watched him finish his breakfast. She poured herself a cup. It was the bitter German coffee and it took getting used to. English tea had always been more to her liking.

Erika thought her father looked tired. It had been nine months since she last saw him—before she left for London. At that time her father looked the picture of health and vigor. Poland, France, and the Low Countries had fallen quickly the previous summer. The last time the father and daughter were together he assured her the war would be over in a matter of months, if not weeks. Just this pesky little business with the British needed tidying.

But much had happened while she was in England. Operation Barbarossa—the Führer's attack on the Soviet Union—had bogged down after early success, and the Japanese attack on Pearl Harbor just three months ago (her father told her he felt the attack was a criminal blunder) had drawn the United States into the war. Now, as she looked at him, she could tell some of the earlier optimism for a quick conclusion to the war had waned.

"I haven't noticed much bomb damage around the city," she said. "In London I heard BBC reports of heavy damage in Berlin by the RAF. Apparently the British are doing a fine public relations job on the home front."

"Of course! Every country has public relations work to do in a war, Liebchen. The British have to confine their bombing raids to the nighttime to avoid the Luftwaffe and most of their planes cannot even find Berlin at night. Outside the city we light fires in the forest to make their trailing bombers think the first few planes have found their targets. The rest of their bombers follow the fires. Most of the British bombs end up blowing up only German squirrels and owls."

He wiped the corners of his mouth with an oversized white cloth napkin and continued: "Also, the British are not unlike us in that they rely on the flyers themselves for reports. When flying at night through the heavy flack we welcome them with, it is understandable that a twenty-three-year-old British pilot will think he has destroyed an airplane hangar when all he has really done is flatten some poor farmer's barn. Youthful optimism. We experience the same problem with young Luftwaffe pilots when it concerns damage reports."

He looked at her and changed the subject: "So, how did things go down on the Tirpitz-Ufer?"

He was asking about her debriefing. The Tirpitz-Ufer is the street where the headquarters of German Military Intelligence—Abwehr—is located. Since arriving in Berlin last week, her time had been spent in the endless rounds of question answering and report writing.

She shrugged, "As dreadful and boring as always, Father. It's the worst part of all of this. Days of answering the same questions over and over. I began to think the war would be over before I finished my reports. I think the only person who did not interrogate me was the window washer."

"Ha!" He seemed to enjoy the joke as she rose and began clearing the table.

She always avoided discussing details about her assignments, less from the desire to adhere to Abwehr secrecy rules (her father was privy to many secrets) than the reluctance to supply him with details about what means she sometimes employed to wrest information from foreign officials or military officers.

"You were wise not to let Heydrich talk you into going over to the SD," he said just before taking a last drink of coffee. "Can you imagine how long they would keep you? But at least you are finished with the debriefings now." He rose and grabbed the tie and suit jacket laying over the back of a nearby chair. "When will you find out about this new assignment? It seems if they were so eager to bring you back early they would not dawdle."

She picked up his dishes, and carried them toward the kitchen.

"I was told to report to the Admiral Friday morning."

"That *is* soon. It must be important," he said while struggling with his tie. "Well, that gives you a couple of days to relax, and you'll be available for the reception and opera Saturday night. The reception is for Count

Ciano and the Führer will attend. The Führer has not come to many social affairs lately, but Goebbels and Bormann are both making a special effort with him this time. Bormann feels the Führer needs the relaxation, and Goebbels and I both feel it will be good for the morale of the German people to see a few pictures of the Führer enjoying himself. He will be glad to see you."

She nodded.

Erika Lehmann was, in fact, a darling of the Führer's, as were most of the children of the men in Hitler's inner circle. After her and her father's return from the States in 1937, Erika spent Christmases and several summer weekends before the war at the Führer's mountain retreat near Berchtesgaden. Erika had become friends with Eva Braun who still called her on occasion when Erika was in Germany. Eva had confided in her. They had swum together in the lake below the Berghof. They enjoyed each other's company. As far as Hitler, Erika considered him an enigma. Though she considered the Führer a good man, in some ways she felt uncomfortable around him. Even after she matured, she felt Adolf Hitler thought of her not as a person, but more like a pet to be patted and played with, like his dog Blondi.

"I'll go, but only if the most handsome man in Berlin is my escort." She smiled and kissed him on the cheek while straightening his tie.

Karl Lehmann looked down at his daughter and grinned. He told her once more that he was glad she was home, put on his jacket and overcoat, grabbed his hat, gloves and pipe and left for another day's routine work with Dr. Joseph Goebbels and the Reich Popular Enlightenment Ministry.

✠   ✠   ✠

CHAPTER 3

If Hitler invaded hell, I would make at least a favourable reference to the devil in the House of Commons.

—Winston Churchill

Berlin—March 1942

The fat, middle-aged, German driver sat behind the wheel of his taxi reading that morning's newspaper. More good news from the eastern front. But, of course, the news from the east was always good, at least as reported by the Berlin newspapers. Sometimes, however, he wondered if things were really going so smoothly in Russia. A friend whose son was fighting in the east with the Wehrmacht told him the boy had written that things were not going as famously as the *Berliner Morgenpost* reported, but then again men in war tend to grumble and overreact.

The cab driver's reading was interrupted when the back door of his cab opened.

"Fahrer, zum Tirpitz-Ufer 72, bitte," the female voice directed.

When he heard the address, the driver glanced in his rear view mirror. He saw the young, blond woman take her place in the backseat and close the door. She returned his stare in the mirror and he quickly looked away. The driver knew this address to be the headquarters of the Abwehr, and he wondered what business such a young woman had with German military intelligence.

As he turned off the Bendlerstrasse and drove past the massive stretch of buildings that housed the Reichwehr Ministry, the driver considered starting a conversation. He glanced again in the mirror. She wore no lipstick and only a hint of eyeshadow and rouge. She was hatless and her long, blond hair was brushed to one side. He thought she bore the wholesome, agrarian look of a Bavarian more than the cosmopolitan look sought by most native Berlin women these days. She stared out the window and seemed deep in thought. It was a short drive so he remained silent.

The driver pulled the cab over to the curb in front of the large, red brick building that sat at the address she requested. He accepted payment for the fare with no words from the young woman.

He watched her walk to the building entrance where two armed and helmeted soldiers stood sentry, each with an MP-38 Schmeisser machine pistol slung over his right shoulder. The driver saw one of the soldiers glance at an apparent I.D. card the girl produced from her coat pocket (she carried no purse). The soldier opened the door and she disappeared inside. To the driver, she did not look like a wife or mistress of a Reichsweir official or a Party elite. He had seen such women riding in the Mercedes convertibles alongside their husbands in the parades. Some of those women were young like this one, but they looked more like overly costumed strumpets with their jewelry, furs, and heavy makeup. No, this one looked more like an office girl, though it was quite late in the morning to be reporting to work. He finally decided she was obviously some bigwig's private secretary who, because of her good looks and the fact she was having sex with her boss, was allowed special privileges. After satisfying himself with his deductions, he put the taxi in gear and pulled out into the late-morning Berlin traffic.

The young woman who had been the subject of the taxi driver's curiosity stepped off the elevator on the third floor. She walked down a short hallway and, after once again showing her identification to another young soldier who looked much like the two on the street, she passed through a set of heavy, dark oak doors and into a small reception area. Her eyes met those of a neatly dressed, pleasant looking, mid-40s woman who had risen from behind a desk.

"Good morning, Erika," said Wera Schwarte as she helped the young woman remove her coat. Erika Lehmann returned the greeting. "You are a little early, my dear; the Admiral will be with you shortly. Would you like some coffee?"

"No thank you, Wera." Erika liked this pleasant, unassuming woman who was the personal secretary to Admiral Wilhelm Canaris, Chief of Operations for the Abwehrabteilung—German Military Intelligence. Erika had known Frau Schwarte through her father even before Erika's involvement with Abwehr. Frau Schwarte had at one time served as a matchmaker, arranging for her son, Georg, to meet Erika after the Lehmann's return to Germany from the United States. Erika and Georg had a short but steamy affair consummated one night in the backseat of his father's sedan (Erika kidded Georg that making love in the backseat of a car was something she brought with her from America). From Erika's end, the relationship was strictly a physical one and it ended after a few months when Georg shipped out to submarine school. Erika knew it pleased Frau Schwarte to talk about her son so she always asked about him in her company.

"How is Georg?"

"We received a letter from Georg just two weeks ago. His ship was at Swinemünde briefly for minor repairs. They are probably back out by now. And how is your father?"

"He is fine," Erika replied as she walked over to look at a large wooden model of a schooner sitting on a black marble stand. "I think perhaps he is a little lonely. I am trying to find him a companion. Are you available, Wera?" Erika smiled at the woman behind the desk. She knew Frau Schwarte was happily married to a Naval officer but offered the question for humor.

The woman laughed as she returned to her seat. "Well, if I was available, you would not have a problem Erika, because I would have already thrown myself at that handsome father of yours." Frau Schwarte laughed again.

The women's banter ended when a loud, irritating buzz issued from a small speaker on Wera Schwarte's desk. "He is ready for you now," the secretary said and rose again from behind her desk. She led the young woman through an unmarked door a few feet away.

"Admiral, Sonderführer Lehmann is reporting," Frau Schwarte announced to the white-haired man sitting behind an immense black desk. The title *Sonderführer* was a hybrid rank given to a few non-military personnel who performed important functions within the German military complex.

Erika had been in this office many times and she never noticed any change. The room was large and seemed unremittingly dark despite several tall windows that usually had the draperies pulled back, as they were now. She thought it must be the dark woodwork and paneling that instilled the constant dimness in the room. The brown leather couch, a conference table, a few document stands, various books, and a camp bed used by the Admiral when business did not allow time to go home at night were all still there. Also still in the room was a model of the light cruiser *Dresden* and a trio of bronze monkeys from Japan that symbolized the cardinal virtues of any good secret serviceman—see all, hear all, say nothing. The *Dresden* and the monkeys sat on the desk. For a long time Erika had felt there was something unusual about this office but could not put her finger on what it was. Then one day it occurred to her that Canaris's office was the only government office she had ever been in that did not display a picture of Adolf Hitler.

The man behind the desk was expressionless as he pointed to a chair. His bushy eyebrows and ruddy complexion were the same, as was the air of impatience the man seemed to constantly emit. She took her place in the seat.

"Sonderführer Lehmann, it is good to see you again. How is your father?" Erika noticed the slight lisp had not left him.

"He is doing well, Herr Admiral. He sends his greetings."

"Yes, thank him for me and tell him I regret I must miss the reception tomorrow night. So much work lately, you know."

"I'll tell him, sir."

"Now, I've gone over your reports from your last assignment," Canaris continued. "You understand that removing your target from England was unauthorized and highly unorthodox?" The target Canaris referred to was Henry Wiltshire.

"Yes, Herr Admiral. But I decided, since my mission was being terminated prematurely, that bringing the target back to Germany for interrogation might allow us to assemble some of the information that I was originally assigned to gather but could not because the mission was called off early."

"Fräulein, you realize that as soon as the English became aware of the target's disappearance, all codes and procedures with which he worked were immediately changed."

"Yes, Herr Admiral. I told our agents who collected the target at the submarine dock at Brest that they had to move quickly. The target was not expected back in London until Monday morning. Our interrogators had over thirty-six hours. Also, if I may point it out, Herr Admiral, the British being forced to change the routes of the French escape lines because of the disappearance of the target is also to our advantage. It will take valuable time to make changes. People who use the routes will not be able to move during that time. Time in which mistakes can be made."

"Yes, yes, of course. We commend your resourcefulness, Fräulein. And I feel we have some other useful information from your time in London, notwithstanding that we brought you back early. A circumstance about which you might be a bit curious, eh?" Canaris looked blankly into her eyes searching for a reaction.

"Yes." She probably should have smiled to cover the note of agitation in her voice but she did not. Her lot as the daughter of an old friend and trusted comrade of the Führer allowed Erika Lehmann a boldness with the powerful men of the Third Reich not granted to many.

He looked her over without changing expression. "You are not the only agent recalled from England since the start of the war, Fräulein." He opened a folder that had been lying in front of him on the desk and changed the subject. "You spent much of your childhood abroad, ja?"—a question he already knew the answer to, of course.

Erika offered the information she knew he was well aware of: "Yes, Herr Admiral. As a young child I lived in England for several years with my mother, and then as a teenager I spent the last two years of Gymnasium, the Americans call it *high school,* in the United States. My father was assigned to our embassy in Washington…"

He raised a hand to cut her off. "I have scheduled a meeting for this afternoon with Major von der Osten and others to brief you. I can tell you only this now: developments in the United States have forced our department's priorities to move away from the English. That is why you were withdrawn from Great Britain, Sonderführer Lehmann. Your Fatherland wants you to return to the United States."

✠   ✠   ✠

CHAPTER 4

The power that has always started the greatest religious and political avalanches in history has from time immemorial been the magic power of the spoken word, and that alone.

—Adolf Hitler

Berlin—March 1942

Canaris ordered Erika to report back for briefing at 1330 hours that afternoon. She decided to find a quick noon meal and remembered the government cafeteria in the building that housed the Geheime Staatspolizei—the state police—a few blocks away. She distractedly walked down the Tirpitz-Ufer, not noticing the cold as she thought of Canaris' last words. What assignment had they for her in the United States? Probably something in Washington, she thought, flirting with congressmen or Pentagon officials. Getting them drunk and keeping an open ear. Letting them have their way with her if it fit the needs of the assignment, asking them innocent, well-phrased questions during the heat of the moment, then moving on to someone else. Or picking a target after she had been on the scene awhile and then latching on for an extended period, like she had with Henry Wiltshire in London. She was always a little apprehensive until she knew the details.

The street where she walked was ornate with posters. Germans love posters, Erika thought. She ignored most, glanced at some. One pictured a wholesome farm girl nursing a baby. It extolled the virtues of mother-hood and large families. Another poster promoted the Hitler Youth with a drawing of a sturdy, blond boy in a brown uniform. A ghost-like image of Hitler hovered over the boy's shoulder. *Jugend dient dem Führer* the poster preached—Youth serve their Leader. Still another poster had an image of a creature half man and half rat with the words *Die Juden sind unser Unglück*—The Jews are our Bad Luck.

Her thoughts changed as she passed by the building of the Seehaus. The Seehaus monitored foreign radio broadcasts. Not long after she and her father returned to Germany from the United States, Dr. Goebbels suggested to Karl Lehmann that his daughter's fluency in English could be of service to the Fatherland translating BBC broadcasts. It was her first paying job.

Erika's time at the Seehaus and an extraordinary gift for languages enabled her to learn French proficiently, along with acceptable Russian, and even some Danish. She enjoyed her time at the Seehaus, especially the time spent with a handsome young man who had studied at the Sorbonne and who listened in on French broadcasts. It was a busy time for Erika, but she somehow successfully juggled university studies during the day, work at the Seehaus four evenings a week, and rendezvouses with both her fun-loving Seehaus co-worker and Georg Schwarte. Neither found out about the other.

Soon she came upon the building at 8 Prinz Albrechtstrasse that housed the offices of the Geheime Staatspolizei. Erika had often joked to friends that Germans have a born need to abbreviate. As the Schutzstaffel was commonly shortened to SS, and the Abwehrabteilung just Abwehr, the Geheime Staatspolizei was more commonly referred to as the Gestapo.

Erika referred to the Gestapo as *Himmler's beady-eyed perverts,* and she had her reasons for hating them. Hated but not feared. Erika Lehmann, daughter of a friend of Adolf Hitler and a valued Nazi spy, had no reason to fear the Gestapo. She passed through the door and showed her identification to a pair of solemn men stationed just inside. The men recorded her name and identification number in a notebook. Both men wore business suits. Unlike most of the organizations along the Tirpitz-Ufer and Bendlestrasse, the Gestapo was not a branch of the military, so much of the time civilian clothing was the norm for Gestapo personnel.

The cafeteria that served the building was located toward the rear of the first floor. The room was crowded but the food line short; most of the diners were already seated. Erika found the stack of trays and followed a short man with a limp down the food line. From an obese, perspiring woman behind the counter Erika accepted a thick slice of ham, boiled potatoes and cabbage, strudel, and a large chunk of heavy rye bread torn from a loaf, not sliced. At the end of the counter another woman handed her a large glass stein of warm beer. The man in front of her was Gestapo, and not required to pay. The female cashier looked quizzically at Erika, wondering if she should ask for payment. Erika relieved her anxiety by asking how much, then paying her.

All tables were occupied. In Germany, if there are no empty tables in a public place of eating or drinking, etiquette requires those already seated to allow others to join them if their table has empty chairs. Erika spotted a table with four chairs, only three of which were occupied. She walked over to that table where sat three men.

"Gestatten Sie?" *(Would you allow?)* she said politely with a smile. The men looked up and stared at her for a long moment saying nothing. Finally one spoke.

"Natürlich, bitte," *(Of course, please)* said the one who looked to be the oldest. He opened his hand toward the empty chair. She thanked the man and sat down.

Erika guessed the man who had offered her a seat to be around forty years old. The other two looked somewhat younger, perhaps early to mid-thirties. Both of the younger men wore eye glasses—one with heavy wire rims, the other pince-nez. Erika knew that many members of the Gestapo had various physical flaws (poor eye sight a common one) that kept them from military service. The older man, despite a mangled left ear that looked like someone had dealt severely with in the past, had no obvious physical defects that could be observed across a lunchroom table.

The three men made no effort to introduce themselves or to disguise their gawking as she began to eat. She was unconcerned and ate in silence, occasionally looking up and smiling politely. *Keep your enemies close, and never let them know what you're thinking,* her father had told her. She took a drink of beer to wash down a bite of potato and decided to break the silence herself.

"They say a light snow is due us tomorrow," she said, scanning the face of each man.

The two younger men continued to stare at her and did nothing to acknowledge her attempt at table chat. Finally the older man nodded slightly and said, "Ja, that is what they are saying." He gruffly introduced the other men. "Fräulein, this is Herr Schroetter and Herr Pagel. My name is Kerling. And your name Fräulein?"

"Erika Lehmann." She offered her hand to each man and exchanged a short handshake. Although her father was well known in the Reich, the name Lehmann was a common one in Germany. There was no reason for people to make the connection to her father.

"Are you new in this building, Fräulein?" Kerling asked, forcing a smile that revealed a colorful assortment of teeth. One was silver, the rest various shades of rotting brown and yellow.

"No, I am afraid I am not lucky enough to work among such handsome men as I now sit with," Erika Lehmann was by necessity an expert actress and the ridiculous compliment sounded sincere. "I am a secretary at the OKW." The OKW stood for Oberkomando der Wehrmacht, the High Command of the German Army. The OKW was headquartered a few blocks away, down the Bendlestrasse. In a roundabout way she did work for the OKW, the only branch of the German military bureaucracy to which Abwehr was answerable. In fact, like many Abwehr agents, her identification card showed the seal of the OKW, not the Abwehr, so the secretary ruse was a common one used when someone inquired of her employment.

"Ah, and how long have you worked there?"

Erika did not have to answer these questions, but she did not mind; her answers would of course be lies anyway, and she even considered this questioning at the hands of the dreaded Gestapo a bit of comedy that took her mind off the meeting with Canaris. She did not hold back a slight smile as she looked down and stabbed a bite of ham.

"Oh, let me see…about a year or so."

Kerling glanced at the man named Schroetter, the one with the pince-nez glasses. The glance from Kerling was an obvious signal and Schroetter promptly excused himself. Erika knew why he was leaving.

"And what is it you do there exactly?" Kerling continued.

She looked him directly in the eyes and, leaning over the table, answered sotto voce, "It is my job to give the generals oral sex, but please don't tell anyone. They are all married you know, and you wouldn't believe the complaining that goes on among their wives about my job."

The younger man's face grew dark and he started a sentence, "I suggest…" Kerling cut him off with a quick glare then turned to Erika. He searched her face for a moment, then a slight smile appeared on his lips.

"Tell me, Fräulein, do you enjoy your work?"

She smiled. Perhaps she had underestimated this one. "The hours and the pay are not bad Herr Kerling, but the job requirements are so rigid."

Kerling stared blankly at her for another moment, then he burst out laughing so loudly that it drew glances from people at surrounding tables. He looked at the other man who remained somber. Kerling leaned over and slapped the man on the back.

"Ha, a good one. Hey, Pagel?" Kerling shouted, extorting the man to enjoy the young woman's humor. Pagel's expression remained unchanged.

"The Gestapo loves a good joke, right Pagel? Tell the Fräulein a joke, Pagel," Kerling coaxed.

The morose Pagel said none came to mind.

"No?" Kerling was still loud. "Let us see…yes, I have one." He turned to Erika. "What are the four shortest books ever written?" Erika patronized him with a smile and shook her head. The man answered his own question, "*A History of Scotch Charities, Virginity in France, The Morals of the American Nigger,* and *A Study of Jewish Business Ethics.*"

Kerling roared at his own joke and even the stone-faced Pagel grinned. Erika smiled politely. She thought it humor that fit the Gestapo.

Kerling continued to laugh loudly as Schroetter returned to the table and handed Kerling a small piece of paper. Schroetter had first checked with the men at the front entrance who recorded the information from Erika's identification card when she entered the building. Schroetter then took an elevator to an office on the fifth floor. One of the Gestapo section agents on duty punched the woman's identification number into a teletype connected to the OKW clearance office. The piece of paper he now handed Kerling had come spitting back out a few moments later.

Kerling glanced at the note:

Anfang.
Es ist verboten, diese Person zu befragen.
Im Falle der Verhaftung, sofort freilassen.
Wenn sie im Ausland Hilfe verlangt, ist den Befehlen dieser Person unbedingt folgezuleisten.
Weiter Feagen ans OKW weiterleiten.
Ende.

Start.
Questioning this person is forbidden.
If detained, release immediately.

On foreign soil follow orders of this person if your help is requested.
Further questions - contact OKW.
End.

Kerling gazed at the young woman who ignored his stares while she
finished what she wanted of her meal. This note told Kerling only one
thing: this was no secretary. Further questions were forbidden and he
knew the importance of following orders in the Third Reich.

The young woman rose from her seat, thanked the three men for
their courtesy, and left them for her meeting with Wilhelm Canaris.

✠   ✠   ✠

"This way, my dear."

Wera Schwarte led Erika Lehmann a short distance past the two helmeted soldiers standing guard in the hallway. The affable secretary
opened a heavy wooden door, and the young woman stepped into a
small vestibule. When the door closed behind her, a glaring overhead
light clicked on. The door was without a knob on the inside allowing
those who passed through no means to reopen. The intense overhead
light sometimes disturbed newcomers, but Erika was accustomed. A
mirror covered one entire wall and gave the cubicle an illusion of more
size than it offered. A sign posted at eye level ordered occupants of the
chamber to turn and face the mirror.

After whoever was behind the mirror was satisfied, a sliding steel
door opened and Erika stepped into a large, windowless room where
Admiral Wilhelm Canaris sat with five other men. All six sat around a
black oak table that would easily seat thirty. Erika recognized three of
the men. Although it had been almost a year since she had last been in
this room, the woman saw no notable changes in decor. The huge maps
that hung like paintings around the high-ceiling room still obscured the
beautifully stained woodwork covering the walls. Shoes still clicked

against the shining marble floor, as Erika's did now. Canaris remained seated, the other men rose from their seats as she neared.

Canaris conducted the introductions: "Sonderführer Lehmann, of course you know Dr. Pheiffer, Major von der Osten, and Herr Kappe. This is Lieutenant Richter whom I don't believe you have met, along with Herr Wolfgang Blaum. Gentlemen, this is Sonderführer Erika Lehmann." Canaris spoke quickly, impatient to get past polite formalities. The men gave the young woman the slight bow that German etiquette demands of men upon greeting a female. Canaris asked the young woman to sit and the men followed.

"Sonderführer," Canaris continued, "Dr. Pheiffer, Major von der Osten, and Herr Kappe are aware of your English speaking background and the time you spent in the United States. The other gentlemen here have been briefed on your qualifications. Because of those qualifications, and your past achievements for the Fatherland, you have been selected for this assignment. In deference to your father's position in the Reich, you understand that this assignment is strictly voluntary on your part." Canaris waited for acknowledgment.

"Yes, Admiral, I understand," the young woman answered. Because of direct orders from the Führer, assignments offered the daughter of his old friend were her's to accept or refuse, a condition Erika knew vexed Canaris to no end. To make matters worse in Canaris' eyes, Hitler ordered Erika to discuss her assignment briefings with her father and acquire his permission before accepting. This, to Canaris, was a villainous breech of security, and another proof of what he always considered reckless meddling by Hitler and Party elites into the military's conduct of the war. Canaris, if he had been given a choice, would never have accepted this daughter of a privileged Party bigwig into the Abwehr.

But German agents who spoke English fluently enough, and with acceptable accents to pass as British or Americans, were rare and their value great. Although Canaris would use foreigners who turned on their countries for whatever information he could garner from them, he despised and distrusted traitors. He preferred German nationals for agents, especially on missions of high priority. The young woman sitting at the other end of the table had proved her loyalty and Canaris had to admit, even if begrudgingly, that Erika Lehmann had shown talent working as an "asset" on enemy soil. She had shown an innate resourcefulness on her last assignment when she captured the *Engländer,* and the fact that she refused to turn the captured man over to the Gestapo pleased Canaris to no end.

That story still brought a smile to Canaris' face. The Gestapo office in Brest, France, where the U-boat containing the Lehmann girl and her British hostage docked, had agents permanently assigned to surveil the sub docks. Two Gestapo agents on duty at the time her sub arrived from St. David's Head saw the Englishman unloaded. The Gestapo agents immediately sought to take the man into their custody.

The girl refused and when one of the Gestapo agents tried pushing past her to the drugged, seasick, and only half-conscious Englishman, the girl attacked the unsuspecting Gestapo man from behind, sending him plummeting from the dock into the water beside the moored submarine. She then pulled a Luger from beneath her jacket and placed the point of the pistol's barrel firmly between the remaining Gestapo agent's legs and asked him if he wanted to argue. All this to the delight of the U-boat crewmen and their captain who documented the incident. Before the Gestapo men could make it to a telephone to call for backup, the Abwehr people, who had been notified by the girl while the U-boat was still at sea, arrived and spirited the girl and her captive away.

Heinrich Himmler, the SS chief who also controlled the Gestapo, was furious when he got word. Himmler called Canaris who promptly hung up on him. Canaris knew Himmler could not cause him any trouble over this matter because the Gestapo had no rights to the Englishman. The two Gestapo agents on the docks in Brest probably thought they could bully the girl into stepping aside. Canaris smiled at the thought of the girl holding the point of her gun to the Gestapo man's scrotum.

Canaris looked at Erika and continued, "You will be given only a general overview of the mission now. If you decide to accept, you will receive the specifics of the assignment and undergo the necessary training." The Admiral turned to a small, middle-aged man with a pointed goatee and nodded. Dr. Erich Pheiffer, chief of naval intelligence for Abwehr, leaned forward and spoke.

"The focus of our naval intelligence efforts has shifted," said Pheiffer, who seemed to talk to no one in particular and never looked at Erika. "The United States must now be regarded as the decisive factor in the war. The capacity of its industrial power is such that it could be a decisive factor in the war, not merely for the United States itself, but for any country with which it may be associated. The most logical course at the present is to monitor this huge output of matériel closely."

Still avoiding eye contact with Erika, Pheiffer continued: "It is obvious the allies have begun putting great effort into assembling massive numbers of landing craft for an eventual assault on the European mainland. We know Churchill is obsessed with this project and has hounded Roosevelt for quite some time. The ships that interest us are the largest of these vessels. They can sail the open seas and deliver large numbers of tanks and heavy equipment directly onto beaches. It is a priority for us to learn certain things about these vessels, information that will best enable us to destroy these ships at sea or prohibit them from beaching on the shores of Europe."

Pheiffer leaned back, an apparent cue for the next man. Major Ulrich von der Osten, a chief assistant to Canaris who was considered one of Abwehr's top experts on the United States, rose and walked over to the map of that country. Von der Osten was a tall man with thinning gray hair and a beaked nose. Erika first met von der Osten at a Christmas party at the Berghof in 1938. Eva Braun introduced her to the major (then a captain) and his wife. Von der Osten was the first to suggest that Fräulein Lehmann's ability to speak non-German accented English would better serve the Fatherland in the Abwehr instead of the Seehaus.

Von der Osten told Hitler that the talents of the bilingual, beautiful young daughter of Karl Lehmann were wasted at the Seehaus, where any German *Gymnasium* teacher who taught English could be recruited to translate BBC broadcasts.

Standing with his back to the others, von der Osten flipped a switch. The light that came on illuminated a large wall map of the United States.

"Fräulein," the uniformed officer began, "the American shipyards along the coastlines are currently operating at full wartime production. This has forced the Americans to seek new locations for the construction of these new ships of which Doktor Pheiffer refers." Von der Osten looked down, picked up a pointer, and continued. "Within the past few months the construction of these ships has begun at newly constructed shipyards located far inland on the larger waterways." Von der Osten used his pointer to circle a large unspecific area of the American Midwest, giving Erika nothing more than a very vague idea of location. "Upon launching, the ships sail down the rivers to the Gulf of Mexico." Finished, the major pointed to the Gulf.

Canaris continued the briefing. "The location of these shipyards aids their security from a military standpoint. These shipyards are much too far inland for any type of attack from sea. On the other hand, the necessity to quickly find thousands of workers extends security problems for them that should allow us to establish an agent on the inside without much difficulty. That is the assignment, Sonderführer Lehmann,—to infiltrate a specified shipyard and gather specific information. You will be told the nature of the information at the appropriate time if you decide to accept the assignment. Lieutenant Richter will supervise your training under the direction of Herr Blaum and Herr Kappe."

Canaris signaled the end of the meeting by standing. The others then rose as Canaris added, "I believe you have sufficient information to make your decision concerning acceptance of this assignment, Sonderführer Lehmann. I expect your decision by Monday morning." And, with noticeable sarcasm evident in a grin, he added, "This will give you time to consult your father, ja?"

"Admiral, I have never refused…"

"Monday morning, Sonderführer," he curtly cut her off. "I have my orders. Now you have yours."

Erika had grown accustomed to these subtle, verbal boxing matches with the old man. She stared back at him without wavering and smiled. Showing him she could not be intimidated was a point of pride to her. In fact, in a way she had to respect a man who was bold enough to insult a daughter of the inner circle. She never told her father of Canaris' lack of respect for the top Nazis, including, it seemed, the Führer himself. Erika had found Canaris to be expert at his job and a fervent anti-communist faithful to his country. Even if he was not enamored with the National Socialists, she knew Germany needed competent men in high places. She saw no need to stir up trouble for this highly capable and successful head of Abwehr, especially after listening to her father complain about highly qualified men being replaced by incompetents for something no more serious than telling a harmless joke at a cocktail party about Göring's ever-expanding waistline.

Erika also understood the futility of asking Canaris further questions about the mission, questions she knew would not be answered until later. She nodded to Canaris and politely thanked the other men, acknowledging each by name, including Richter and the two civilians who had not spoken a word during the briefing. She felt the eyes of the men on her back as she returned to the steel chamber that would fetch her back to Wera Schwarte.

"What mood was he in this time?" Wera asked as she opened the vestibule door for Erika. The secretary had been alerted at her desk that the meeting was over by a short sequence of buzzes from Canaris.

"Pleasant as always," Erika answered.

Reading between the lines, Wera rolled her eyes as Erika stepped into the hallway and the women proceeded to her office.

"He becomes more impossible every day," Wera muttered.

Back in her office, Frau Schwarte helped Erika with her coat and asked the young woman about her plans for the weekend. "Young officers are probably falling over each other knocking at the door of such a pretty girl."

"Actually, Wera, the only date I have this weekend is with my father," Erika replied matter-of-factly. "I promised I would accompany him to the Führer's opera tomorrow night."

"Oh! aren't you the lucky one," replied the starstruck secretary, "rubbing shoulders with the Führer. And me, I have never met him. He was in this building last summer but I was stuck here in the office while he attended some meeting with the Admiral and other big shots in the room you just came from. Of course normal procedure was bypassed; the Admiral had to wait downstairs for the Führer to arrive. At one point, I heard people in the hall and stuck my head out in time to see just a glimpse of the Führer from behind as the Admiral escorted the entourage down the hallway. Tell me, Erika, what is he really like?"

"He has always been pleasant to me."

"Promise me someday you will work a way for me to meet him, my dear."

"With the war, I don't see him very much at all now, Wera. In fact, tomorrow will be the first time I've seen him in almost two years."

"Well, then after this awful war you will work a way. Promise me."

"Yes, Wera. After the war."

✠   ✠   ✠

CHAPTER 5

For Adolf, nothing could compete with the great mystical world
that Wagner conjured up for us.

—August Kubizek, Hitler's boyhood friend

Berlin—March 1942

He wore black pants.

And instead of the usual black jacket of the SS, a snow white tunic.
This white jacket was used by the lower-ranking SS officers when they
served at state functions attended by the Führer. This was one of those
affairs, a reception for the Italian foreign minister Count Galeazzo
Ciano who happened to also be Mussolini's son-in-law. Catching the
eye and adding a splash of color to the young lieutenant's white military
jacket was a bright red swastika arm band. On the left collar was the
emblem of his rank; on the right collar the symbol of the Schutzstaffel,
a symbol that many foreigners thought looked like two lightning bolts,
but which were actually ancient, mystic rune symbols once used by the
warlike peoples of northern Europe in pagan times. The second lieutenant was one of several young officers who stood behind a long, white
linen-covered table. The lieutenant's orders for the evening were simple
yet specific: keep the champagne glasses full and do not speak to guests
unless spoken to. Other young SS officers circulated through the crowd

holding silver platters heavy with blue crystal flutes filled with the finest French champagnes.

Etiquette demanded no staring at guests, but the young SS lieutenant found himself admiring the young woman who had walked over and picked up one of the glasses he had just filled. She wore a shining silver evening gown that bared her shoulders. In the front, the dress dipped down between her breasts, in the back, to the base of her spine. A diamond-studded hair comb entrapped the blond hair piled high on her head. An elegant, but not gaudy, diamond pendant rested just above her breasts, suspended there by a thin gold chain. White gloves covered her hands and extended up past her elbows.

Despite the young lieutenant's efforts to avoid being caught ogling, the young woman noticed his glances. She took a sip of champagne and quickly looked up, catching him looking at her chest. His face reddened and he immediately looked away.

"Good evening, Lieutenant," she said to him and smiled.

"Good evening," the young man replied tactfully.

She said no more but continued to stare at him and smile over her drink. The stockpiling of hormonal urges within the young man was finally interrupted with a shout from somewhere in the crowd.

"Erika!"

The loud voice came from behind her. The young beauty turned to see a tall man in a jet black uniform weaving his way through the crowd. He approached smiling, took her free hand, bowed, and kissed the back of her glove.

"Reinhard," said Erika Lehmann, returning his smile. "How nice to see you." Then she added jokingly, "Oh, excuse me, perhaps I should not be so familiar. I should say 'Obergruppenführer.'"

The man laughed loudly and she continued, "Really, Reinhard, every time I see you, you have moved up again in rank. Now, not yet forty years old and already a Lieutenant General. I'm impressed."

"Ah, dear Erika, as beautiful and charming as ever," said the man with a broad smile. "It is wonderful to see you again. I had no idea you would be here."

The man was Reinhard Heydrich, one of the most powerful men in the Reich. Second only to Himmler in the SS, the thirty-eight-year-old Heydrich oversaw the Gestapo and ran the SS intelligence operation the *Sicherheitsdienst,* or SD, which included one domestic and one foreign intelligence service. Nicknamed the "blond beast" by associates and enemies alike, Heydrich had eliminated thousands of "enemies of the state," either by detainment in concentration camps or execution.

His impressive height, blond hair, high broad forehead, and long predatory nose, were Nazi prototypes of "Aryan" appearance. Nervous, beady eyes, a wide mouth, slender hands with extremely long—almost spiderlike—fingers gave him a sinister appearance, but one that was not necessarily unattractive to women. In fact, Heydrich was famous for more than his merciless treatment of malcontents; despite a wife and son back home in Munich, his romantic affairs were numerous and well known.

Heydrich had pursued Erika Lehmann for years, both personally and professionally. She had let their personal relationship go no further than a friendly goodnight kiss on the cheek after dinner or an opera. Erika met Heydrich before the war when she worked at the Seehaus. One evening Erika's father asked her to serve as an interpreter at a dinner for American journalists hosted by Goebbels. Heydrich was at the dinner and volunteered to drive Erika home. Since that night he had used any opportunity to get closer to her.

"How are things at Abwehr?" Heydrich asked. "They tell me Canaris is showing the strains of war."

"I hadn't noticed."

Despite Wilhelm Canaris' and Heydrich's former association (they served together aboard the cruiser *Berlin* in the twenties) and the benefits that coordination of efforts between the two intelligence services would offer their country, the Abwehr and SD leaders functioned more as rivals than complements. Heydrich thought that by wining and dining the beautiful, multilingual daughter of Karl Lehmann, he might succeed in getting her into both his bed and the SD, stealing her from Canaris. So far the attempts at both had failed. But the "blond beast" was not one to give up easily.

"Tell me, Erika, what is the mood in England?" Heydrich nonchalantly took the empty glass from her hand and sat it on the table in front of the young second lieutenant who now, in Heydrich's presence, looked especially rigid and uncomfortable.

Erika looked at Heydrich. Very efficient, she thought. He should not have known she was in England. She ignored his question.

"Tell me Reinhard, how are Lina and your son?"

Heydrich knew she would not answer his question and he burst out laughing. He reached for two more glasses of champagne, giving her one.

"They are doing well, but I have not seen them much recently. My duties in Prague take up most of my time."

"Have you seen my father yet?" Erika asked.

Heydrich shook his head no as he swallowed a drink of champagne.

"Come then." Erika took his arm. "He will want to see you."

A cavernous structure on the Unter den Linden, the Prussian State Opera House dated back to the 19th century. Flaunting Italian marble floors and walls, imported teak archways, and glimmering chandeliers, it had served as the main venue for artistic performances since 1933 when, after the infamous Reichstag fire, the Kroll Opera House was converted for Reichstag use. The reception gallery where Reinhard Heydrich now walked with Erika Lehmann on his arm was a long, L-shaped corridor. Rembrandt's, Cézanne's, and van Gogh's, lately acquired by the Reich in their jaunt across Europe, adorned the walls.

The normally quiet gallery was now loud with prattle from the crowded assembling of German elite. A healthy supply of generals, admirals, and top Party officials filled in spaces around tuxedoed industrialists and financiers who bragged and told vulgar jokes while their gaudily bejeweled wives gossiped. The barons and baronesses huddled in cliques, breaking away only briefly to acknowledge another notable, or shake the hand and smile with condescension at one of the capitalists who sought their company.

Erika spotted her father talking to a small group of men. She recognized Robert Ley, the head of the German Labor Front, an organization Hitler formed after he disbanded the labor unions in the thirties. Alongside Ley stood Julius Steicher, the fanatical anti-Semitic publisher of the Nazi tabloid *Der Stürmer*, and Joseph Goebbels, head of the Reich Propaganda Ministry and her father's boss. Another man, whom Erika did not recognize, stood with the group.

Goebbels and Erika's father had both been with Hitler since the early days. But in fact, Karl Lehmann predated even Goebbels in the chronology of Hitler's rise to power. Goebbels did not meet the future Führer until late in 1924, after the latter's release from Landsberg prison. At that time, Goebbels' loyalty belonged to another Nazi leader, Gregor Strasser, and it was not until 1926 that Hitler succeeded in convincing Goebbels that he, and not Strasser, was the one true hope for the Fatherland.

But Erika's father had been at Hitler's side even before the Putsch. Before Joseph Goebbels had even heard of the NSDAP or Adolf Hitler, Karl Lehmann was in Munich taking part in the tavern fights with communists or whoever happened to disagree with Hitler's speech that day. Karl Lehmann had been one of the carriers of the famous blood flag on November 9, 1923. He had been there in front of the Feldherrnhalle when government troops opened fire, killing several of his and Hitler's comrades.

And now Goebbels was her father's boss. Despite this, Erika had never detected any animosity toward Goebbels from her father. Her father was a diplomat serving in a foreign country while Goebbels was home in Germany building the world's most impressive propaganda machine. Her father was a fair man who gave credit to Goebbels for his accomplishments. Karl Lehmann was also a soldier, ready to serve where needed, and if his Führer needed him as Goebbels right-hand man that is where he would serve.

Herrs Lehmann and Goebbels were now closely bound in both work and loyalties. Erika had always thought no two men could be more alike in ideology and unlike in appearance than her father and Joseph Goebbels. Her father was over six feet tall, well built and handsome. Goebbels was a foot shorter than Erika's father, a frail one-hundred pounds, and he walked with a limp. But their loyalty to their country and to the man who now symbolized it was complete and unquestionable. Goebbels and Lehmann rose with Adolf Hitler and his movement. They were there in the obscure days of the struggle—old comrades whom the Führer trusted.

Karl Lehmann spotted his daughter as she approached on the arm of the Protector of Czechoslovakia. Lehmann shouted for the couple to join him. He shook Heydrich's hand and the two men exchanged greetings. He then turned to his daughter.

"Erika, of course you know Dr. Goebbels."

"Of course," Erika smiled at the diminutive man who was reaching for her hand. "How are you, Herr Doktor?"

"Much better now, Erika," the grinning Goebbels said with a smile. "I always feel younger when I am in your presence." The other men chuckled. Goebbels offered the comment for protocol's sake, but nonetheless he seemed reluctant to relinquish her hand. Erika was aware of Goebbels' reputation for philandering. A reputation that, although not as well known among the German people as Reinhard Heydrich's, was justly deserved.

Her father proceeded, "And, of course, Herr Ley."

"You look lovely tonight, my dear," said Ley. He did not reach for her hand. His hands were busy with a drink in one and a burning cigarette protruding from a short, silver cigarette holder in the other. Instead, the uniformed, heavy-set Ley bowed and clicked the heels of the shining black jackboots that rose to his knees.

Her father turned to the next man.

"And…I am not sure, my dear, have you met Herr Streicher?" Her father glanced at her.

"Yes," Erika assured her father. "Although I am sure a man with Herr Streicher's weighty responsibilities will not remember meeting an awkward young girl of eighteen at the Olympics." Erika Lehmann's keen memory had come to her aid more than once, both in her personal life and during her Abwehr assignments. She remembered meeting the menacing Streicher in 1936 when she and her parents returned from the United States to attend the summer games in Berlin. Even the normally scowling, harsh-looking Streicher, whose looks intimidated people with dark, beady eyes, a crooked nose, and a long, jagged facial scar, smiled slightly at the fair young woman who flattered him in front of these other men.

"Fräulein," Streicher said with a nod. With that one word this gruff man seemed to be marshaling the sum of his affability.

The remaining man in the group was the one Erika did not recognize. He was a young SS officer; Erika's guess was thirty years old. His uniform was that of a captain and it displayed several medals. One medal signified that he had already served on the Russian front; another medal confirmed a wound in the line of duty. Erika considered the unknown man pleasantly handsome. He had dark hair and eyes and a broad smile that revealed a very noticeable gap between the two upper front teeth. Erika thought the gaped-tooth smile gave the man a friendly and somewhat farcical air.

"Erika," her father said. "I doubt if you have met our new friend. This is Captain Josef Mengelé. He is a doctor, no less, and just returned to Berlin from the Russian front." Karl Lehmann turned to the young man. "Captain, this is my daughter, Erika."

"I am honored, Fräulein Lehmann." Mengelé took the gloved hand the young woman offered him; he bent and kissed the back of the glove.

"You flatter me, Herr Doktor," Erika answered. "Surely I am the one who is honored. It is not every day a German girl is in the company of so many important men…and all so handsome too!"

The men laughed. They obviously enjoyed flattery from a beautiful young woman. Charming men was a craft in which Erika Lehmann was professional.

As the other men returned to speaking between themselves, Mengelé's attention was on Erika.

"Of all the important men, as you say, Fräulein," Mengelé said, "surely I am the least in this distinguished group."

"Such humility only adds to your stature, Herr Doktor," Erika said. "Tell me, what brings you to Berlin? I feel your accent it not local." Erika by necessity was an expert on regional dialects and accents: German, British, and American.

"From the front I was sent home to Günzburg to recover from a wound. My father is an industrialist who was invited to Berlin for this affair. He could not attend tonight, so I am afraid you get me as a poor substitute."

"Your injury is healed I hope."

Mengelé nodded. "I'm doing fine, thank you."

"Will you be able to return to your duties?" Erika asked for conversation's sake. A flurry of activity at one of the entrances to the hall had caught her attention.

"Yes, of course. Also, I was involved in medical research before the war and there has been some talk of assigning me a post where I can continue that work. But, of course, I will serve wherever my country needs me."

"Of course." Erika said. She smiled politely at the man with the comical gap in his teeth.

The activity that had caught Erika's eye involved a group of uniformed SS men who had entered the great hall and milled around one of the entrances. Others also noticed the activity and those who smoked looked for the nearest place to extinguish their cigarettes. No one smoked in the presence of Adolf Hitler.

As if by instinct, a receiving line quickly formed. At a trot, a plump, heavily bejeweled wife of the one of the industrialists rudely bumped passed Erika, dragging her husband by the arm and admonishing him to hurry for a better place in line. Mengelé offered his arm to Erika, but Heydrich stepped between the two and gave the lower-ranking Mengelé a beady-eyed stare. Mengelé nodded politely and backed away.

"Gentlemen, I thank you for your chivalry." Erika said to both Heydrich and Mengelé. "But I have already promised myself for the evening." She smiled, pulled away from Heydrich, and took her father's arm.

Those with daily access to Hitler, and personal friends such as Karl Lehmann, had no need to enter the receiving line. The line was a reward for the loyal German elite lucky enough to be invited to such an affair. For many of them this was a once in a lifetime opportunity. Those who shook the Führer's hand tonight would further enhance their privileged status back home tomorrow.

An SS officer with the rank of colonel entered the room and stood at the head of the line.

"Ladies and Gentlemen," the colonel announced loudly and formally. "Count Galeazzo Ciano, Foreign Minister of Italy, and Countess Ciano."

A polite applause followed as the Italian and his wife entered and walked slowly down the line. The Italians nodded politely and shook hands.

With the Cianos halfway down the receiving line the SS colonel added: "Ladies and Gentlemen, the Führer of Germany, Adolf Hitler."

Upon hearing the words, Erika noticed the attention of everyone in the receiving line turn away from Ciano and his wife. All heads stared at the entry way. Even those in line who were next to shake hands with the Italians could not keep from turning their eyes toward where Hitler was supposed to appear. There was a delay, as if the SS colonel had spoken too soon, but in a moment Adolf Hitler appeared in the doorway.

The applause was much louder and sustained much longer this time. The German guests made no pretense about whom they revered. Accompanying Hitler was his ever-present entourage. Erika spotted Martin Bormann who walked to the side and a step behind Hitler. This made her remember a time at the Berghof when she overheard Heinrich Himmler talking to her father. Himmler had referred sarcastically to Bormann as "the Führer's fat shadow."

Hitler was in uniform. He had not worn civilian clothes in public since the outbreak of the war. Like the young SS lieutenant whom Erika had caught staring at her earlier, Hitler wore black pants and a white tunic with the bright red Nazi party arm band. Pinned on Hitler's tunic was the Iron Cross first class he had been awarded for heroic duty as a corporal in the first war. It was the same type of medal Erika's father had been awarded. Hitler's shirt was white, his tie black. Expressionless, Hitler stepped toward the receiving line.

For as long as Erika had known him, Hitler had struggled with his hair. He seemed to have less trouble conquering France than an unruly cowlick that refused to be slicked down like the rest of his black hair. And many times she had noticed Hitler brushing back a wedge of hair from off his forehead. As she watched Hitler now, Erika saw him brush back that same troublesome hair before he began shaking hands.

Hitler worked steadily through the receiving line. He took little interest in the people who kowtowed as he passed. He rarely made eye contact with those whose hands he shook. When he reached the fat lady who had dragged her husband, Erika thought the woman would swoon when Hitler took her hand. Hitler seemed not to notice. When the end of the line was reached and the last hand shaken, Hitler spoke briefly to the Cianos before turning away to whisper something to Bormann and another aid.

Apparently responding to some chore assigned them, Bormann and the aid left the room. The Führer now stood alone in the midst of the crowd, his hands clasped behind his back. As Hitler slowly turned, he spotted Goebbels standing with Karl Lehmann and Erika. Goebbels came calling on Hitler almost daily with Reich business, but it had been several months since Hitler had seen Karl Lehmann and the drab expression on Hitler's ashen face seemed to change. The eyes brightened a bit. Hitler started toward them so they walked toward him in response.

"Good evening, mein Führer," Goebbels offered his hand.

Hitler nodded at Goebbels and shook his hand, but he quickly turned his attention to Karl Lehmann.

"It is good to see you, Karl." Hitler clasped Lehmann's extended right hand and shook it vigorously.

"Thank you, mein Führer," Lehmann responded. "It is always a pleasure to see you, I assure you."

Hitler turned toward Erika. She had always considered Hitler's piercing blue eyes the outstanding feature of a face quite ordinary. But the eyes—they were so blue they appeared fluorescent. Those eyes now looked into Erika's.

"Hello, Erika."

Hitler clasped Erika's hand in both of his, but before she could return his greeting he looked at Karl Lehmann.

"Karl, your daughter looks more like her mother every time I see her."

"I agree, mein Führer," Karl Lehmann said.

"Thank you, mein Führer," Erika added. She considered Hitler's comment the most sincere compliment she had received all evening because she knew the man who offered it had no ulterior motives for flattery like Reinhard Heydrich.

"Come," Hitler said to Karl Lehmann. "You and your daughter will join me in my box tonight." He offered his arm to Erika.

Operas attended by Hitler started when and only when the Führer decided it was time to start. Sometimes an impatient Hitler would enter his box an hour before the scheduled curtain time. If so, that is when the opera started and the patrons, players, and orchestra knew to be ready. Likewise, if the Führer was busy and running behind, the curtain might go up two hours late. Hitler now nodded to yet another aid who somehow knew this meant curtain time.

With Erika on his arm and Karl Lehmann and the Italian guests of honor alongside, Hitler made his way slowly out of the great hall. As they passed the other guests, some women in the crowd looked on with envy, others with contempt at the young woman on the Führer's arm. Who was this young girl who received such favor?

The same SS colonel who earlier had announced the arrival of the Cianos and Hitler now proclaimed that the performance would begin shortly. The other guests began filing out of the great hall behind Hitler. Each guest took a handful of throat lozenges from one of several crystal bowls placed on marble pedestals by the archways (it was the height of rudeness to cough during a German opera—even one not attended by the Führer).

The Führer Box at the Prussian State Opera House jutted out over the theater's main floor. As in many opera houses, several of these private boxes ringed the perimeter. The occupants of these boxes were the top echelon of the Reich. Joseph Goebbels had a private box as did Herman Göring and Heinrich Himmler. But the Führer Box was specially modified. Larger than the other boxes, it had a separate entrance. The Führer was prone to leave suddenly if the performance, or a visiting luminary sharing his box, bored him.

The opera was Richard Wagner's *Die Walkure.* Well known was Hitler's admiration for the German composer and, although Hitler had seen this opera dozens of times, he never tired of the brooding Germanic gods and Wagner's loud, crashing music. Erika enjoyed *Die Walkure,* although her favorite Wagnerian opera was *Parcifal.* Like Hitler, Erika preferred German opera, which emphasized the story and the orchestra, over Italian, which she felt concentrated too much on the voice of one lead singer and not the music and choreography.

When they reached the Führer Box, Hitler insisted that Erika sit directly on his left. Karl Lehmann sat beside his daughter. Countess

Ciano sat on Hitler's right, between the German leader and her husband. Martin Bormann sat toward the back of the box, almost unnoticeable among several SS guards who stood in the shadows.

This was the first opera Erika had ever attended with the Führer. As they waited for the curtain to rise, her father and Hitler briefly recalled a 1934 festival in Bayreuth they both attended along with Richard Wagner's daughter-in-law, Winifried Wagner. The event was a special celebration of the famous German composer's life.

"Those were the days, Karl," said Hitler. Erika felt the words were said with a certain yearning.

"Yes, mein Führer," agreed Karl Lehmann. "Those were the days."

Still ignoring his Italian guests, Hitler turned his attention to Erika.

"So, you have spoken with Canaris?"

The question surprised her.

"Yes, mein Führer."

Hitler looked at her with his burning blue eyes. She returned his gaze. He smiled and patted her hand.

"I will speak of this with your father later."

"Yes, mein Führer." She knew her father would not want her to return to America to be possibly caught and executed as a wartime spy. But she also felt her father would not use his influence and standing with Adolf Hitler to keep her from serving Germany if the mission was important.

Hitler discussed no more business. The curtain rose. On stage a wounded Siegmund, pursued by enemies, sought shelter in Sieglinde's forest hut. Erika thought briefly about asking Hitler of Eva Braun's welfare but considered it much too forward. These things were not discussed with Adolf Hitler. Moreover, the thundering orchestra did not lend itself to spectator conversation.

The scene on stage moved to Valhalla, where the god Wotan directed his Valkyrie daughter, Brunnhilde, to defend Siegmund against the vengeful Hunding. In the Führer Box, Erika glanced at Hitler and the Cianos. Hitler stared at the stage, a glassed-over look in his eyes. The

Cianos seemed bored. Most Italians considered German opera second rate to their own. Mussolini's daughter thought the pounding drums and crashing cymbals of a Wagnerian opera an assault on the senses. Also, the countess was angry that Hitler seemed to take little interest in her and her husband, instead concentrating his attention on the young German woman.

After the final curtain, Hitler drew Karl Lehmann aside and talked briefly as the entourage exited the box. Hitler shook Erika's hand then left with the Cianos and the rest of the human convoy through a special exit. The countess was no doubt glad to be rid of the young German beauty.

Outside, Erika's white fur coat guarded her against the cold Berlin night. The same Wehrmacht sergeant who had earlier driven them to the opera house now held open the back door of the black Mercedes for Karl Lehmann and his daughter. Waiting his turn amid a parade of other chauffeur-driven vehicles, the sergeant guided the car out onto the Unter den Linden.

✠   ✠   ✠

CHAPTER 6

I swear to Thee, Adolf Hitler,
As Führer and Chancellor of the German Reich,
Loyalty and Bravery.
I vow to Thee and to the superiors
Whom Thou shalt appoint
Obedience unto Death,
So help me God.

—*SS Oath*

Gestapo Headquarters, 8 Prinz Albrechtstrasse, Berlin

June 1942

Reichsführer-SS Heinrich Himmler sat at the head of the table in the meeting room connected to Heinrich Müller's Berlin office at 8 Prinz Albrechtstrasse. Müller was Himmler's chief of the domestic branch of the Gestapo. The two men were joined at the table by Günter Syrup. Syrup had served as Reinhard Heydrich's top subordinate in Prague.

Reinhard Heydrich was dead.

Three weeks ago Heydrich was assassinated by the Czech resistance. A well-placed bomb exploded under Heydrich's car as he followed a familiar route after leaving his Prague headquarters. The explosion sent fragments of the Mercedes' seat springs into Heydrich's body. Reinhard Heydrich took four days to die.

Nazi retribution was immediate. On the day Heydrich died, 152 Jews were executed in Berlin. A few days later, three thousand more Jews were shipped from the Thereesienstadt work camp to extermination camps in Poland.

In Czechoslovakia, the entire village of Lidice was wiped from the map.

Suspecting that the Lidice villagers had harbored the assassins, the SS executed all the male inhabitants of the village over the age of thirteen and shipped the women and children to death camps. The SS dynamited the homes and other buildings and brought in bulldozers to clear the rubble. The Führer himself insisted to Himmler that not a trace of the town remain.

When the news of Heydrich's death first reached Berlin, Himmler ordered Heydrich's files in Prague sealed and placed under guard. The day after Heydrich's funeral, the files were shipped to Gestapo headquarters in Berlin under Himmler's personal orders that only he have access. Here the files sat, under guard, taking up most of the large conference room.

Much of Himmler's time for the past two weeks had been spent scrutinizing the dead man's monumental files, with Günter Syrup on hand to answer questions. Going through Heydrich's files was a task Himmler insisted on doing personally for several reasons, one reason being Himmler did not trust his late second-in-command.

So here he was. The Reichsführer of the SS shuffling through files like an office clerk. Embarrassing, perhaps, but Himmler did not like surprises.

Business that needed immediate attention was dealt with first. There was a file concerning a Czech official in Plzen who had fallen under

Heydrich's suspicion. Syrup told Himmler that the man was suspected of homosexual activity. Himmler ordered the man arrested and detained until time would allow a proper interrogation. Another file contained names of suspected black marketeers in Bratislava; the arrest orders were issued. In another matter, the supervisor of a ball-bearing factory in Ostrava was requesting more laborers. Ball-bearings were critical to the war effort. Since Ostrava was a border city near southern Poland, Himmler sent down the order for workers to be shipped from the closest concentration camp, Auschwitz, immediately.

When the affairs that demanded immediate action had been dealt with, Himmler's attention turned to the other people and topics that had interested Heydrich enough to elicit their own dossier. Heydrich's files on certain well-known figures of the Reich had especially caught Himmler's attention. All were there: Göring, Goebbels, Bormann, even Hitler and Himmler had a file. The information on Hitler was strictly generic, nothing derogatory. Heydrich was not a fool. Himmler saw nothing in the file with his own name on it to get upset over, and overall nothing surfaced about top Nazis that was not already common Gestapo knowledge.

(Himmler would never find out that Günter Syrup had pulled the disparaging information on Himmler and other powerful members of the Nazi hierarchy. Heydrich had not died immediately after the attack, which was a stroke of luck for Günter Syrup—perhaps a life-saving stroke of luck. The doctors attending the injured Heydrich initially expected Heydrich to survive, so his files were not sealed posthaste. This delay in sealing the files allowed Syrup time to destroy any embarrassing details about the powerful men, details that Syrup would be called upon to explain since he had helped gather some of the information.)

There were files on other high Nazi officials, names less well known to the world but nevertheless important. Baldur von Schirach, the head of the Hitler Youth; Hjalmar Schacht, the private banker who served as Minister of Economics; the labor leader Robert Ley; Karl Lehmann,

Goebbels right-hand man and a Himmler comrade from the early days; Sepp Dietrich, another old comrade of both Hitler and Himmler who had eliminated many of the Führer's enemies during the thirties and was now a Waffen SS general.

Like the Gestapo, Heydrich maintained files on celebrities. German defectors such as Albert Einstein and Marlene Dietrich. Americans Charles Lindbergh and Henry Ford warranted a dossier; the Nazis considered both of these famous *Amerikaner* sympathetic to their cause. After checking the contents, Himmler knew he had the same information on these people.

Finally assured that the documents contained nothing negative about himself (or new and worth noting about other top echelon Nazis), Himmler proceeded to other files. Several boxes were marked *Abwehr.*

Abwehr files would be of next interest to Heinrich Himmler. For sitting at the top of the SS chief's long list of people he did not trust or like was Wilhelm Canaris.

Himmler had tried myriad times to convince Hitler to incorporate all of the Reich's covert activities under Himmler's massive SS and SD umbrellas. Abwehr did not have to be dissolved, Himmler argued, but *Mein Führer, at least instruct Canaris to brief your Schutzstaffel on Abwehr operations.* But Abwehr was a branch of the regular German military, and the Army High Command had never sanctioned Himmler as deserving their respect. Himmler had not fought in the first war and the medals the Reichsführer-SS displayed on his uniform were medals Himmler himself had commissioned for SS personnel. Keitel and some of the other generals liked referring to Himmler as "the expert on chicken shit" alluding to Himmler's agricultural training as a youth.

Hitler, always the astute observer, rightly foresaw unneeded problems if Himmler's request to oversee a branch of the Wehrmacht was granted. So in a political move to placate the OKW, Hitler refused his old comrade. The result: the espionage/sabotage work of Canaris'

Abwehr and Himmler's SS/SD/Gestapo continued to work with total segregation, neither trusting nor cooperating with the other.

But Hitler's refusal to place Abwehr under Himmler's control did not deter the SS chief from monitoring Canaris and his operations whenever and wherever he could. At Himmler's orders, an entire section of the Gestapo was assigned to gather (discreetly of course) information on Abwehr movements. In Germany and the occupied countries this snooping proved somewhat successful. The Gestapo could skulk about following known Abwehr agents as they moved about in Germany or countries under German influence. In addition, in occupied cities and towns, Himmler's men could rifle the files of local factories and government offices with impunity, a phony reason always ready. Sometimes this supplied clues as to why an Abwehr operative was working in the area.

Sleuthing out the missions of Canaris' people behind enemy lines was much more difficult. Usually the most the Gestapo could do was to judiciously monitor airfields in Germany and the occupied countries, along with the submarine docks on the Baltic Sea and the western coast of France. These were the departure points for Abwehr agents heading to foreign shores. The eyes of the Gestapo were alert for known Abwehr agents who appeared in these places. Logs could be later checked for clues to destinations (flight logs were sometimes falsified but submarine logs never). This twenty-four-hours-a-day snooping on one's own countrymen gleaned limited results and was done at the expense of massive manpower. But done nevertheless.

Heydrich's Canaris file was redundant with Himmler's own. As with the previous files, nothing new worth noting was uncovered. The main points of suspicion toward Canaris revolved around his sometimes feeble support of the Führer and his obvious lack of interest in rubbing shoulders with the Reich elite. All this information was contained in Himmler's own archives and simply aped in Heydrich's.

While studying the Abwehr files Himmler came across the thickest dossier in Heydrich's collection. The name on the dossier was *Erika*

Lehmann. Himmler knew about Karl Lehmann's daughter; he had a file on her, of course. *One of Canaris' cherished English speakers,* Himmler thought, *untouchable because of her father's relationship with the Führer.*

The bitch who had refused to hand over the Engländer to his Gestapo agents in Brest!

But curiously, Heydrich's file on the girl was much thicker than any other Abwehr file. Himmler issued an order to Heinrich Müller.

"Pull *our* file on Lehmann's daughter."

Müller had been helping Himmler and Syrup sort through the imposing mountain of paperwork (that is, of course, *after* Himmler personally checked the file that bore his own name). Responding to Himmler's order, Müller now exited the room.

While Himmler waited for his Gestapo chief to return, he opened Heydrich's bulky dossier on Erika Lehmann. Inside the folder was paperwork listing place of birth, parent background, and other vital statistics—just stock information. Several pages were allotted to family ancestry. Nothing so far, Himmler thought, that should not be in Müller's Gestapo file on the girl. Then there were photographs—hundreds of them. Many of the photographs had been separated and placed inside large manila envelopes. Some lay loose within the pages of the dossier. The unusually large number of photographs gave the girl's file its thick girth.

The official government identification photograph was inside, a swastika stamped conspicuously across one corner. One envelope contained several prewar photographs of the girl winning athletic awards: several for swimming and various track and field events during Aryan Mädchen (Aryan maid) competitions held twice a year in conjunction with the Hitler Youth Days celebrations before the war. Another envelope contained family photos. There was a picture of a teenage Erika Lehmann standing beside another, unidentified teenage girl in front of the Lincoln Monument in Washington. Himmler shuffled quickly through the family photos: the smiling girl with her mother (again in

America), with her father on a sailboat (on the back it said Chesapeake Bay), a group photo with her mother and father at the Berlin Olympics standing next to Goebbels and the famous German filmmaker Leni Riefenstahl.

Lying loose within the folder was a newspaper clipping with a photo of the girl accepting yet another athletic award. *The bitch is quite the athlete*, thought Himmler. In this photo the girl leaned over from a winner's platform while Rudolph Hess placed a medal around her neck. The newspaper caption read:

> *Deputy Führer Hess awards Fräulein Erika Lehmann the First Place Medal in gymnastics competition at The Party Day Aryan Maids' Games of 1937.*

Himmler shook his head. He could understand Hess agreeing to present the winners their medals. Hess always fancied himself a gymnast, showing off his skills for the children of high Party officials at Berghof summer picnics. *I wonder if Hess has room for his back flips in his English prison cell*, Himmler quipped to himself.

Müller had meanwhile returned with the much thinner Gestapo file on Erika Lehmann. Müller sat and read silently through the file, waiting on Himmler who continued to thumb through the thick stack of photographs collected by Reinhard Heydrich. Himmler withdrew the typewritten pages from Heydrich's file on Erika Lehmann. He handed them to Müller with instructions to compare what was there with his own Gestapo information on the girl, noting any dissimilarities.

Himmler opened another envelope of photographs. This one contained surveillance photographs taken from a distance; each was dated with locations recorded on the back. Some photos pictured the girl simply walking down a street, others getting in and out of taxis or going into buildings.

"What is all this, Syrup?" Himmler asked.

Syrup gathered himself for a moment and replied carefully, "Obergruppenführer Heydrich was very…preoccupied with the girl, Herr Reichsführer."

Himmler looked at Syrup, then returned his attention to the photographs. He came across a grainy 8 x 10 picture obviously taken with a zoom lens from a high vantage point; the photo was of the girl alone on a beach, naked, and drying herself with a towel.

"Continue," Himmler ordered without looking up.

Syrup continued: "It was standing procedure to keep the Lehmann woman under surveillance whenever possible. Those were Obergruppenführer Heydrich's orders. Of course, sometimes this was not possible. Being an Abwehr operative, this woman spent considerable time outside the Reich's sphere of influence. But, whenever possible, the Obergruppenführer wanted her movements recorded and surveillance photographs taken."

Himmler, still not looking up: "And her sexual liaisons documented."

"Yes, sir."

"Thank you, Syrup." Then Himmler added, "You are dismissed for now. Wait out in the hall." The nervous Syrup clicked his heels, then made a beeline for the door.

Heinrich Müller used the time spent waiting on Himmler to familiarize himself with the Gestapo dossier on Erika Lehmann. He had never looked it over before now; he had no reason to. And, as Himmler had ordered, Müller checked Heydrich's file on Erika Lehmann for anything that might be additional to or different from the information in his Gestapo file. When Himmler looked at him, Müller began.

Erika Marie Lehmann
 ▸ *Born: 16 December 1917*
in Oberschopfheim in Baden
  ▸ *Father: Karl Wolfgang Lehmann. German. Former Catholic.*
  ▸ *Mother: Louise Gwendolyn Minton. British. Catholic.*

Müller paused and looked up at Himmler to signify important information was coming before returning his eyes to the folder.

"As it states, the mother was Engländerin, Reichsführer, the daughter of a British chargé d'affaires stationed in Berlin before the First War. The parents married in June of 1914…"

"Yes, yes, yes, Müller," Himmler interrupted impatiently. "I know about Lehmann's wife. And I don't care how many times they screwed on their honeymoon. Move on."

Müller cleared his throat.

"After the Putsch in '23 when the Party fell on hard times the mother and the girl were sent to England to live with the mother's family. The girl and her mother returned to Germany in February of 1929. By then her father had established himself, second only to Goebbels, in the Propaganda Ministry."

Müller ad-libbed: "Apparently the girl and her mother succeeded in teaching the father acceptable enough English that when the Führer came to power, he assigned Karl Lehmann to our embassy in Washington." Müller paused to check his facts, "One moment, Reichsführer…that would be in September of 1933."

All this information was redundant and inconsequential to Himmler. He had never taken the time to read the Gestapo file on Erika Lehmann but he was familiar with the family background. He and Karl Lehmann went way back. Both joined the Party in the early days. Himmler impatiently strummed his fingers on the table while Müller read. But Himmler listened and remained silent.

"Before leaving for America in '33," Müller continued, "both father and mother passed the racial requirements of The Office of Ancestry and Racial Purity. Therefore, of course, the daughter passed the same check in 1938. No Jewish blood has been found in her ancestry line."

Disappointing, Himmler thought, but finally some important information.

Müller: "The mother was killed in an automobile accident in November of 1936…, no foul play suspected. The girl and her father returned to Germany two months later—January '37. At which time Karl Lehmann rejoined Goebbels in the Propaganda Ministry."

"Tell me about the girl, Müller. I'll have you read me the remainder of the touching family history if they invite us to their next family reunion."

Müller flipped past the next two pages which contained more family background information. Himmler's fingers continued the drumbeat on the table. It took Müller a moment to locate information specific to the girl then he proceeded.

"Now back in Germany…" more flipping by Müller. "From April of 1937 until September of the same year the girl worked for her father as a volunteer interpreter for the American and British press. In September of that year, apparently at Goebbels suggestion, the girl began work at the Seehaus translating BBC broadcasts. While at the Seehaus, she became quite proficient in French."

"Evidently the girl has a flare for languages," Müller added. "It says here she also speaks Russian and some Danish, learning these languages while mingling with other interpreters during her time at the Seehaus."

"Impressive," Himmler responded with an obvious lack of enthusiasm. "Go on."

Müller turned another page.

"The subject continued working at the Seehaus until June of 1938. Obviously it is sometime prior to that time that Heydrich met the girl. There is an entry here from Heydrich dated 12 January 1938 where he recommends her for recruitment into the SD as a possible agent. He gives her a glowing appraisal. His recommendation notes her 'impressive ability with languages,' her 'sterling Aryan background,' and the girls 'considerable athletic ability.' It looks like Syrup was right. Heydrich seems quite taken with this girl."

Müller flipped to the next page, scanned it briefly, then turned back to the one from which he had just read. The Gestapo chief summarized for Himmler.

"There are several entries from Heydrich concerning meetings he had with the girl over the course of several months, Herr Reichsführer. All document his attempts at recruiting the girl."

"Without success," interjected Himmler. "But apparently she decided, or someone decided for her, that Heydrich was correct: she could be of more value to the Fatherland than simply translating radio broadcasts."

"Correct," Müller concurred. "On 24 May 1938 she reported to the Abwehr training facility at Tegel for precursory indoctrination. Her age at that time: twenty years and five months. Three weeks later she was transferred to Quenzsee for further training."

"Just three weeks at Tegel?" Himmler was genuinely surprised this time. SD trainees also spent time at Tegel. There was not a set staying time at Tegel for the plebe spies, but an average stay was six weeks before a candidate was qualified to move on to more advanced training at the larger covert training facility at Quenzsee.

Müller checked the sheet again. "Yes, Reichsführer. Three weeks."

"What do you have about her time at Quenzsee?" Himmler asked.

Müller laid the stack of papers he had already recited from on the table in front of him, then explored and compared more papers from the Gestapo file and Heydrich's file.

"There doesn't seemed to be much here pertaining to Quenzsee," Müller apologized. "A few dates. She spent the required time there for advanced training—ten weeks. According to this, she has returned to Quenzsee other times, most probably for retraining."

Himmler smiled. Here he could circumvent Canaris. The Quenzsee training center was not used solely by Abwehr. As with the facility at Tegel, Quenzsee also trained SS, SD, and Gestapo agents in certain circumstances.

Himmler had access to Quenzsee records.

He directed Müller to send a courier to Quenzsee for the records on Erika Lehmann. Müller wrote himself a note on a small pad he took from inside his jacket pocket.

Himmler moved on. "What do we have about her Abwehr assignments?"

"Very little, Reichsführer. While I waited earlier that is the first information I looked for. We do know her Abwehr code name: *Lorelei*. As far as her Abwehr assignments, the information is lacking. She has apparently completed two missions since the start of the war. Two separate, lengthy absences from Germany point to this. We know she returned from her second mission three months ago, on 10 March. She brought with her a captured British…"

"Yes, I know," Himmler curtly cut him off. "I know all about the incident at Brest." He expected Müller's information on her foreign activities would be frugal. The Gestapo operated only within Germany, occupied countries, and neutral zones like Switzerland, Spain, and Portugal.

"Where is the girl now?"

Müller had anticipated that question. "We don't know, Reichsführer."

Himmler looked incredulous. "The girl has not been under surveillance since she returned from England?" His voice rising as he spoke.

"No, Reichsführer. Most of the information I gave you concerning the girl's movements came from Heydrich's file. There is a memorandum here in our Gestapo file. At a meeting on 18 September 1939 the list of Abwehr personnel to be place under our surveillance was discussed. It was decided at that time that the Lehmann girl would not be included. Because of her father's relationship with the Führer, it was thought to be a sensitive issue. Also, the war had just started and our manpower was needed elsewhere at the time. The memorandum has your signature Reichsführer." Müller handed the piece of paper to Himmler who glanced at it, mumbled something under his breath, and threw it on the table.

Himmler shuffled around in his chair. "Anything else, Müller?"

"Just a page on personal matters from Heydrich's file that I haven't looked over yet, Reichsführer."

"Quickly," Himmler stated. His fingers returned to strumming on the table.

"Nothing is known of her sexual activities in America," Müller began paraphrasing. He could sense his boss's growing impatience so he read verbatim from the sheet in front of him.

- apparent Bohemian attitude toward sexual intercourse

- 1937, while at the Seehaus the subject had a confirmed sexual liaison with an Edvard Hull, a fellow interpreter (French), Hull was twenty-six at the time - the subject twenty.

- 1937, during the time period the subject was involved with Hull, she had another confirmed sexual liaison with a Georg Schwarte, the son of Wera Schwarte, Wilhelm Canaris' secretary. Schwarte was twenty at that time.

Himmler's interest perked. None of this information was in the girl's Gestapo file.

- July 1939, while in Paris on holiday the subject had a confirmed liaison with a Paris museum guide, a Claude Vauzous.

- other sexual liaisons suspected but not confirmed

"That's basically the extent of the combined information, Reichsführer," Müller confirmed.

Himmler turned away and for a moment stared into space. The fingers stopped drumming. There was a slight pause.

"Your dream girl Heydrich?," Himmler seemed to be admonishing the dead man's ghost. "I thought you insisted on virgins."

Suddenly Himmler burst forth with an eerie laughter that surprised Müller. The Gestapo chief had never seen the grave Himmler laugh so hysterically.

"The great lover Heydrich!" Himmler now addressed Müller. "His Aryan princess…quite the strumpet it seems."

Himmler continued to laugh as he took the page out of Müller's hand. He adjusted his pince-nez glasses and looked the page over for himself. His laughter calmed to a chuckle. Then as abruptly as it had started, the laughter disappeared, replaced by a darkness in Himmler's face. Himmler continued to generalize about Erika Lehmann, the acid in his voice now evident.

"A Canaris embassy floozy who thinks the Gestapo is not fit to interrogate some dumb British bastard she kidnaped. It's all vintage Abwehr."

Himmler threw the report on the table in front of Müller. He was tired from hours of searching through files and was ready to call it a night. Himmler was about finished working his way through the last envelope of photographs in Erika Lehmann's file. He had carefully studied a few, quickly glanced over most.

The little white envelope was almost overlooked. It was buried at the bottom of the last large manila envelope, which itself had been stuffed full with photographs.

Himmler extracted the smaller envelope.

The small white envelope was sealed and at first felt empty. Himmler slid his fingers over the surface and felt just the slightest disparity in thickness. He opened it carefully. Inside was a delicate piece of tissue paper. The tissue shrouded three small photographic negatives. Holding the small pieces of celluloid by their corners, Himmler held each toward the light then issued an order without taking his eyes off the negatives.

"Magnifying glass."

Müller walked into his adjoining office, returned momentary and handed a magnifying glass to Himmler. Himmler rose and walked to a table lamp that burned nearby. Leaning over the lamp's shade, he used the magnifying glass to study the negatives. He looked them over for several minutes, then looked up and stared at the wall in front of him.

Thinking.

Again he looked at the negatives.

After what seemed to Müller an eternity, Himmler returned to the table, carefully placed the negatives back in the tissue paper, and returned them to the small envelope. He placed the envelope in the breast pocket of his black tunic and turned to Müller.

"Have the Lehmann girl's Quenzsee records on my desk by noon tomorrow, and use discretion when obtaining those documents. Also I want to know where the girl is by that time, Müller. I'll have further orders for you tomorrow when you deliver the Quenzsee reports. That will be all for now."

Müller clicked his heels and raised his right hand.

"Heil Hitler."

Himmler, deep in thought, distractedly returned the salute.

"Heil Hitler."

✠   ✠   ✠

CHAPTER 7

Lor•e•lei \lōr əlī *n* [German] : a siren of Germanic legend whose
singing lures Rhine River boatmen to destruction on a reef

—*Merriam Webster's Collegiate Dictionary: Tenth Edition*

Brandenburg, just outside Berlin

June 1942

The primary German training academy for the art of espionage and the
science of sabotage was located at Quenzsee in Brandenburg, not far
from Berlin. The buildings resided on a lavish old estate which included
a lake, a large park, and beautiful gardens. A high fence topped with
barbed wire encircled the grounds, belying the serene setting. Machine
gun toting guards patrolled both sides of the fence, a leashed and muz-
zled German Shepherd attack dog at their side.

The motto at Quenzsee was *"Fetch the Devil from Hell."* The goal of
the school: training agents who could carry out that mission if need be.

Quenzsee was a second home to Abwehr agents. After finishing
preliminary indoctrination at another facility in Tegel, all Abwehr agent
wannabes reported to Quenzsee for their main training. Here they
underwent a grueling ten-week training period all had to successfully
finish before being considered for the advanced training that would require
several more weeks. In addition, the elite few who were eventually

chosen for covert assignments returned to Quenzsee before each mission for retraining and acquiring any special skills needed for the specific assignment.

However, the vast majority of people who passed through Quenzsee would never see duty as an Abwehr spy or saboteur. Although prospective agents were carefully selected and screened (almost all were recruited, volunteers were rarely accepted), six out of seven washed out of the initial ten-week training course. Of those left, only one of nine would eventually see duty as an "asset"—the Abwehr euphemism for secret agent.

There were a few exceptions. Specialized cram courses gave amateur saboteurs—usually malcontents from enemy countries—a few needed skills in explosives before being dispatched back home. These traitor missions were rarely successful. Most ended with the fumbling amateur blowing himself up or apprehended, and summarily executed, before any damage was done, none of which distressed their former instructors at Quenzsee. ("If nothing is tried, nothing is gained. They were not Germans, after all.")

The preparation of bona fide, professional German agents was handled much differently. Training was extensive and no stone unturned when it came to processing a candidate. The few elites who measured up as full-fledged Abwehr agents demonstrated exceptional skill levels in both espionage and sabotage.

The espionage section at Quenzsee taught trainees International Morse Code and the use of shortwave transmitters (later they would learn how to build their own transmitter). Trainees were well versed in microphotographing documents and coding and decoding messages, along with knowledge of the chemistry of secret inks. Burglary skills were taught including gaining access through locked doors and windows without leaving evidence of entry, lock picking, and safe cracking. For specific countries, satisfactory language skills entailed much more than just proper speech. Regional dialects, mannerisms, and idioms were practiced repeatedly; syntax, grammar, and accents had to be flawless.

Classes were held on the country to be infiltrated. Knowledge of the target country's history and geography was meticulously tested; skill in map-making demanded.

Quenzsee's second branch, the sabotage section, instructed trainees in the use of explosives and fire bombs (advanced candidates learned how to make bombs of ordinary materials that could be purchased at hardware or agricultural stores). Trainees fired an assortment of pistols and rifles for a minimum of one hour each day. Pistol marksmanship was especially stressed, and before they left the school agents could make homemade silencers from readily available materials. Effective use of blackmail was an included course. Hand-to-hand combat was practiced every day, and silent killing methods studied.

Near the Quenzsee lake Erika Lehmann stood third in a line of eight young women. In front of the women was a twelve-foot-high chain-link fence topped with three strands of barbed wire. The fence was part of the Quenzsee obstacle course. A heavily muscled male instructor in a white T-shirt and navy blue short pants stood near the fence. Quenzsee's "Fetch the Devil From Hell" logo—a swastika engulfed in flames through which a very Aryan-looking secret agent ran dragging a devil—could be seen above the left breast of the man's shirt.

The women wore navy blue shorts similar to the man's. They also displayed the same Quenzsee insignia on their white shirts but in a different location. Because the womens' shirts were the sleeveless and open neck athletic *Bluse*, the swastika and flames were displayed between the breasts.

The women had worked areas of the obstacle course for most of the afternoon. In addition to the chain-link fence now in front of them, the course included a brick wall that had to be scaled using a rope and grappling hook, a descent from a three-story tower using a cast iron rain gutter downspout, belly-crawling under a set of barbed wire obstacles, and a three-kilometer run around the lake that had to be completed in (for women) less than eleven minutes. Several swimming tests were part of required Quenzsee training including a timed sprint across the lake, a marathon swim around the lake, diving and retrieving objects from the bottom of the lake, and remaining submerged for designated time intervals. The swimming tests were scheduled for the next morning.

Erika Lehmann was a celebrity to the other young women in the line. They were plebe agents—*Anlernling;* none had ever been on a mission. But the blond *Sonderführer* standing in line with them now trained for her third assignment. The two small dagger insignias above the burning Quenzsee swastika confirmed that she had already completed two assignments. Of course the others knew nothing of the particulars of these missions. They did not even know her real name. Agents and trainees at Quenzsee went by code names. The other women, and even the Quenzsee instructor standing by the fence, knew Erika Lehmann only by her Abwehr code name *Lorelei.*

The muscleman barked at the women in line: "As you know, twenty seconds maximum to touch ground on the other side."

"You! First in line! Get ready!…Go!" He clicked a stopwatch.

The woman at the front of the line ran toward the fence, stopped, then started climbing. When the top was reached, she gingerly negotiated the barbed wire then lowered herself down the other side.

"Twenty-nine seconds! Terrible!," the man shouted, then added sarcastically. "The only way you would not have been spotted is if you were breaking into the asylum for the blind. Get back to the end of the line."

"Next! Go!"

The second woman ran to the obstacle, stopped, then started the climb. She ascended the fence faster than the first woman, but at the zenith she cut the inside of her left leg on the barbed wire. On the ground the instructor showed no sympathy for her injury.

"Twenty seconds. But look at the drops of blood on the ground," the man shouted in the girl's face, veins bulging on his forehead. "A trail easily followed! You've just blown your mission, idiot! And probably gotten yourself and anyone with you killed!"

The woman stood rigidly, blood running down her leg, as the instructor continued his rebuke. One name directed at the woman was the German equivalent of the English "shit-heel" among other even more vulgar monikers. Whether from the pain of her injury or the reprimand, or both, tears welled in the woman's eyes.

Don't cry!, Erika thought as she watched the woman being castigated. She hated it when a female trainee cried. "Never cry," Erika turned and said to the others behind her. "Crying makes you look silly and weak. Just try again."

When the instructor thought the woman sufficiently harangued, he sent her, still bleeding, to the back of the line. Like the first trainee whose time was too slow, she would have to try again.

Erika was now at the front of the line. When the instructor saw who was next, he paused.

"Fräuleins, pay close attention." Then to Erika: "Go!"

Erika sprinted to the fence but instead of stopping she jumped high up the fence to save some climbing. She shot up the chain-link portion, grabbed the highest strand of barbed wire between two of the barbs, flipped herself over the top then free fell to the ground. The instructor clicked his stopwatch.

"Nine seconds!"

The other women began clapping but a sharp look from the man halted the applause.

"That, Fräuleins, is an acceptable effort." The stern man could not find it in himself to embellish the compliment further, even though he knew the word "acceptable" did not do *Lorelei* justice. Twenty seconds was the required time for a female to clear the fence, fourteen seconds for males. In all his time at Quenzsee, he had seen only four *men*, among the hundreds of men, scale the fence in less time than this young woman.

When the last woman had scaled the fence, and the instructor satisfied that the ones who failed to make the required time had been cursed sufficiently, he released the women. He reminded them of dinner in one hour, followed by the mandatory ninety-minute swimming practice, and after that their last foreign language classroom session of the day. He added that a movie of the Führer's latest speech to the Reichstag was their reward before lights out at ten o'clock.

With the training session over, the female trainees walked sluggishly toward their billets, their only goal to collapse on their beds for the hour until mess. The Sonderführer, *Lorelei,* the one with the two daggers on her chest, stayed behind. She plucked a Quenzsee swimsuit from a rucksack, changed into it inside a boat house on the lake's shore, and began crossing the half-kilometer wide lake—a full-out front crawl across, a butterfly back. She calculated the free hour would allow at least three complete crossings.

After the evening meal and the mandatory swimming practice (Erika served as an additional swimming instructor for both the men and women), the last training activity of the Quenzsee day was language instruction. The sign over Erika's classroom read *American English* (there was a separate room for the British version). Speaking in German was strictly forbidden in the classroom. Ernest Kappe, who had attended Erika's initial briefing session in Canaris' office, was one of the instructors on American English at Quenzsee. Before the war, Kappe worked as a journalist in Cincinnati and New York City. Lieutenant Richter and Wolfgang Blaum, two more men from the initial Abwehr briefings, were also now at Quenzsee supervising Erika's training. The three men were the only personnel at Quenzsee who knew *Lorelei's* real identity.

Kappe stood at the front of the room and welcomed the eight men and two women who took their seats. Fifteen minutes were spent reviewing the previous day's work and *Hausaufgaben* (homework) collected. Yesterday's homework assignment had been to write a paper, in informal American prose, describing sights that might be seen while taking a bus ride in New York City. Here again Erika Lehmann served more as an instructor than a student, and Kappe handed her some of the papers to help speed the evaluations.

The first of her classmate's papers Erika read contained some spelling errors, but not any that a true American poor speller might not make. The second paper contained a dangerous error: all the nouns were capitalized including "Seat" as in "bus seat." Erika made a note on the paper that, unlike German, not all nouns in English are capitalized. When Erika finished looking over the essays, she handed them to Kappe who made comments then handed the papers back to be corrected and resubmitted by the authors.

All of the "students" spoke fluent English, but speaking fluently was not enough. Passing for native speakers was the goal and that demanded much more than simply being well versed in a language. The remainder of the class time was spent working on accents, with Kappe and Erika listening closely for any hint of German inflections. Erika estimated to herself that half the men might succeed in passing themselves off as Americans, the other half still had work to do. The only other woman in the class, a woman around thirty with the code name "Hippolyta," was improving. *Hippolyta* had been one of the women in line with Erika at the obstacle course earlier that day, and Erika remembered her scaling the fence in twenty-one seconds, only one second from passing. *Hippolyta* had commented to the other women that she would make the time tomorrow and Erika did not doubt that she might. She was a strong, big-boned woman in trim shape.

Hippolyta was working on a New York accent, which was the easiest American accent for a German to master in Erika's opinion. (Erika thought a Midwestern accent was the toughest for a German to mimic.) *Hippolyta's* New York accent had improved over the course of the past few weeks, but Erika also noticed occasional syntactical slips in her English. The woman used the words *also* and *still* too often and sometimes in the wrong place within a sentence. The German equivalents to those words, *auch* and *noch,* were used more commonly by Germans in everyday speech, especially by Bavarians which is where Erika concluded the woman most probably hailed from. Regardless, the mistakes were enough to tell Erika the woman should not leave for America too soon.

After class, Kappe asked Erika to stay after for a few minutes. This was not unusual considering Kappe's responsibility to help prepare Erika for her mission. During these post classroom sessions, none of the mission particulars were discussed. Those top secret deliberations were limited to certain soundproof security rooms in another part of the building. Topics after class included innocuous subjects such as things that had changed in the United States since Erika left the country in 1937. Perhaps one night Kappe might have magazines with current American hairstyles, another night catalogs showing the latest fashions. Tonight Kappe gave Erika a long list of popular American dance music and several phonograph albums to listen to on the record player he had issued for her room. These subjects were addressed in a morning class designed especially to cover American culture, but Kappe, always the fussy teacher, was giving Erika an opportunity to study ahead. When Kappe finished discussing American popular music he had news.

"Your presence is requested at the Berghof, *Lorelei,*" Kappe announced (Kappe never addressed her by her real name at Quenzsee). "You leave tomorrow." He handed her the paper with her new orders.

She looked at the paper. "Does it state the purpose of the visit?"

"No," Kappe answered. "Upon completion of your stay, report back here immediately for completion of your training. Now I suggest we go listen to the Führer's speech."

Erika placed the paper between two of the phonograph records and walked out of the room with Kappe.

Before lights out each night trainees, retrainees, and Quenzsee staff were treated to ninety minutes of organized recreation, normally in the mess hall. An opera recording might be played, a Propaganda Ministry motion picture might be shown (Erika recognized some films her father helped produce), or a special speaker brought in. Erika's father had spoken here on a couple of occasions; Göring spoke once, and Hess had been a regular guest speaker before his baffling flight to Scotland.

Tonight's treat was a film of the Führer's recent speech before the Reichstag. After everyone was seated and the Führer's speech given its proper introduction with sufficient accolades from August Pampe, the Kommandant of Quenzsee, the lights were dimmed and the film rolled.

Hitler spoke for just over an hour on the war in the east and the many sacrifices the German people must ready themselves for to achieve the final victory. This was not the ranting, fist-shaking Hitler of the British newsreels Erika (aka Margaret Hamilton) had watched in England. On the screen a subdued Hitler stood with his hands behind his back moving slowly through his speech choosing words carefully. Hitler had always been a powerful orator; his ability to bewitch the masses from a podium was legendary. That ability had not abandoned him; Erika looked around the room at faces frozen in attention.

During the first few minutes of the speech Erika's mind wandered. *Why was she summoned to the Berghof in the midst of training?* Normally only the Führer invited people to the mountain retreat. In Erika's case, one other person might be responsible. Eva Braun contacted her just last month suggesting they spend some time together this summer. Was Eva behind the invitation/orders, or the Führer? Not that Erika objected, the Obersalzberg above Berchtesgaden had always been a favorite place. Besides, the obstacle course had grown boring—it failed to challenge her anymore—and much of the other training redundant.

Curiously, as her mind moved from the Berghof to the film in front of her, Erika found herself critiquing the Führer's grammar. The Lower Bavarian dialect was evident from the abundant use of little modifiers such as *denn, ja, noch,* and Hitler's favorite adverbs *besonders* (espe-cially) and *damals* (then).

I've been spending too much time in language classes, Erika mused silently. *Yes, perhaps a break from the Quenzsee routine would be just the thing.*

At the conclusion of the Führer's speech everyone stood and applauded, then the mess hall slowly emptied. Tired bodies gladly homed in on a bunk back in the barracks. Most of the trainees quartered in basic training style—several two-level bunkbeds in a large barracks room. Men billeted in a barracks behind the main chateau, the much smaller number of women occupied a similar but smaller barracks closer to the lake.

Experienced agents quartered in the same buildings with the *Anlerlinge* (raw recruits), but these agents, the ones with the dagger(s) embroidered above the Quenzsee devil, were given individual rooms. These rooms were small, the size of a jail cell, and sparsely furnished: a cot, a small table with one wooden chair, and a hanging wall picture of the Führer. Each room had one small window—a summer necessity.

Back in her room, Erika disrobed and looked through the stack of music records. Ernest Kappe included music by Cole Porter, Glen Miller, Bing Crosby, and Hoagy Carmichael among others. Erika was familiar with the names, either recalling them from her teenage years in the United States or from her more recent visit to England. Some of the music had been written years ago but was apparently still popular—Herr Kappe would not make that mistake. Erika noticed Carmichael's *Georgia on My Mind* and *Stardust* in the stack. She remembered both tunes were popular with her prep school classmates at the Blair School in Virginia in the mid-thirties. *Stardust* was especially well liked. Erika roomed and boarded at the school as did all the girls. She remembered one of her roommates playing *Stardust* over and over at every opportu-nity for days. Finally some of the girls conspired and hid the record.

On Erika's table sat a stack of folders containing briefs, maps, and engineering data concerning ship building and metallurgy. Next to the folders, and occupying the remainder of the small table, sat a record player. Erika placed an Artie Shaw record on the turntable. As the band played, the sultry Kay Grainger sang a popular Cole Porter tune.

Below, in the bunk room with open windows, seven exhausted German women were serenaded to sleep by the music filtering down from the room overhead even though most of them understood none of the English words.

> *b When they Begin the Beguine*
> *It brings back the sound of music so tender.*
> *It brings back a night of tropical splendor,*
> *It brings back a memory evergreen.*
>
> *b I'm with you once more under the stars*
> *And down by the shore an orchestra's playing,*
> *And even the palms seem to be swaying*
> *When they Begin the Beguine.*

☩   ☩   ☩

Chapter 8

Not necessity, not desire—no, the love of power is the demon of men. Let them have everything—health, food, a place to live, entertainment—they are and remain unhappy and low-spirited: for the demon waits and waits and will be satisfied.

—Friedrich Nietzsche, 1881

Berlin, Gestapo headquarters

8 Prinz Albrechtstrasse

June 1942

Behind his desk Heinrich Himmler read. On the wall behind him was a five-foot tall painting of Adolf Hitler. Hitler stood on a hill wearing a trenchcoat that flowed in the wind, the rays of a distant rising sun to his back. In the corner beside Himmler's desk, a replica of the famous Blood Flag hung limp from a standard. The authentic Blood Flag was safely stored in a Reichstag safe and brought out only for important occasions. The original was the flag that Himmler (and Karl Lehmann) helped carry during the Beer Hall Putsch of 1923. Sixteen members of the infant NSDAP were killed that day. The sixteen were now Nazi martyrs (Hitler dedicated *Mein Kampf* to them) and the Blood Flag the most revered Nazi icon. Displayed only on important Party days, the Blood Flag was used by Hitler to consecrate other flags by touching them to the original in a solemn ceremony.

Himmler was studying a list of reports from Franz Stangl, the Kommandant of the new concentration camp at Sobibor. Sobibor became operational two months ago, and Stangl was working out the "bugs" at the new camp. Among the problems: work was progressing slowly on an additional access road leading into the camp, the number of camp inmates with skills that could be of use in nearby factories was pathetically low, and the ditch that served as the latrine for a certain block of inmate barracks had been dug in the wrong location. Stangl complained in the report that the ditch could be seen from his residence. His visiting wife and children had been subjected to a panorama of Jews relieving themselves in the ditch.

Another problem that had already surfaced for Stangl concerned the camp brothel.

Although Himmler established brothels at many of the camps to serve the SS guards, select laborers and Jewish *Kapos* (block supervisors who were themselves inmates) could be rewarded with a brothel visit if their SS masters thought their work superior. Of course, strict procedures were in place to insure that the women who serviced the SS guards were not available to the Jewish inmates. Himmler wanted none of his SS to mingle with women who had previously serviced any *Untermenschen*.

The young women "workers" in these brothels were selected from the general camp population. Some starving female inmates volunteered for service, taking advantage of the extra rations and better living conditions, but most had to be forced into service. Young Gypsy girls were selected first, but their numbers were usually not sufficient, so Slavs and Jewesses were also chosen for the brothels.

The SS supplied ample reason for the brothel girls to show enthusiasm for their work. Girls who lacked the proper zeal for their duties were quickly taken to the gas chambers.

Originally, some debate had taken place between Himmler and camp *Kommandanten* about the minimum age for brothel girls. Some suggested any girl past puberty, but this might include girls as young as twelve. Finally Himmler, who had daughters himself, decided on fifteen ("We are not animals, after all.").

Stagl's problem swirled around one of the brothel girls who had already become pregnant. With the absence of contraceptives, certain policies were in place that attempted to curtail this problem. The German guards were cautioned to withdraw from the girl and relieve themselves somewhere else on her body. Most of the guards followed the rules, so brothel pregnancies occurred mostly among the girls who serviced men other than the Germans. Standard procedure in these cases was to send the pregnant brothel girls to the gas.

In this case, however, one of the girls who serviced the SS guards had become pregnant, meaning the fetus was half-German. To complicate matters further, this girl, although a Slav, had blond hair, blue eyes, and other Aryan features such as detached earlobes and acceptable skull measurements. Stangl was therefore asking Himmler for guidance.

Himmler decided the girl would have to be sent to a *Lebensborn*. (Himmler established these maternity homes, scattered throughout Germany, in 1935 for unwed, pregnant German women in order to boost Aryan birthrates.) After the child was born, the brothel girl would be returned to the camp and the child raised in a state-run orphanage until a time when it could be determined if the child was suitable for assimilation into the Reich. Himmler also ordered the guards to be disciplined. Since Stangl could not determine who was the father among so many (Stangl wrote that the pretty blond girl was "much used by the men"), Himmler instructed Stangl to determine the time period of the impregnation and to deduct a certain amount of money from the pay of all guards who had frequented the brothel within that time period. This money would go toward funding the girl's stay at the *Lebensborn*. Also, these same men were to be banned from further brothel visits for sixty days.

Himmler was moving on to Stangl's next concern when the door to his office opened.

"Herr Müller is here, Herr Reichsführer."

The announcement came from Ursula Ziegler, Heinrich Himmler's secretary. She stood at his office door awaiting instructions.

Himmler did not look up. He pointed a finger to a seat in front of his desk, a familiar signal to Frau Ziegler who turned and announced to Müller that he might enter.

Müller walked briskly into the room, papers wedged under his left arm, his cap in his left hand. He stopped in front of Himmler's desk, clicked his boots, and stuck his right hand in the air.

"Heil Hitler."

Himmler switched his focus from the papers detailing Franz Stangl's difficulties at Sobibor to the man standing in front of him. Himmler returned Müller's salute then directed him to be seated. He knew Müller was here with information about Karl Lehmann's daughter.

Himmler began.

"I presume discretion was used in obtaining the girl's Quenzsee records?" Himmler did not want to tip his hand to Wilhelm Canaris.

"Yes, Herr Reichsführer. I ordered all the reports from a certain time period—a time period in which we knew the woman was at Quenzsee. With so many records there will be no way for anyone to determine which report we sought."

"Good. Now I take it you have had a chance to review the reports. Anything of interest on her?"

"Hard to say, Herr Reichsführer," Müller was not quite certain what information Himmler deemed important. "It seems she is a bit of a celebrity at Quenzsee. When she is there the instructors use her to help give language lessons to other English speaking agents. Also, the girl has set all the female records in the obstacle course, and she serves as a swimming instructor for trainees when she is at the facility. Works out with the men in hand-to-hand combat because none of the women can give her any competition. Even holds her own with some of the men during hand-to-hand according to this."

Müller handed the Quenzsee reports to Himmler who looked through the papers. The girl's Abwehr code name, *Lorelei,* headed each page. Dates in residence at Quenzsee were there, a list of the types of training undergone, instructor evaluations and comments, and the glowing athletic records Müller mentioned. As Himmler thumbed through the dossier, Müller made an announcement.

"I do have some additional information about the Lehmann girl's missions, Reichsführer."

Himmler glanced at Müller over his glasses and put the Quenzsee folder down on the desk.

"Proceed."

"She has completed two assignments since the start of the war. The second mission you are somewhat familiar with. On that assignment she spent seven months in England where she infiltrated M1-9. As you know, M1-9 is the cryptography section of British Intelligence. We have now found out that Canaris brought her back from England prematurely. Why? We do not know yet. While in England the girl apparently gathered her information by seducing some middle-aged M1-9 cryptographer who decoded messages from the French resistance. When Canaris recalled her, she somehow kidnaped the man and brought him back to France. That's when the conflict on the pier in Brest—the one you referred to last night—occurred. Our agents had the submarine docks under surveillance, as they always do, when they spotted the bound and blindfolded Engländer being unloaded from the submarine. Our agents moved in to take control of the hostage. That's when the girl attacked them."

"Not *our* agents, Müller," Himmler interrupted scornfully. "*Your agents.* One ends up being tossed in the drink and the other with the point of a Luger held to his balls! All by a girl! How embarrassing for you."

Müller turned red but said nothing.

"Go on," Himmler ordered.

Müller gathered himself. "Her first and only other Abwehr mission, Reichsführer, was an assignment in Lisbon soon after the outbreak of the war. Posing as an American college student on sabbatical, she charmed an American diplomat and gained access to various embassy functions: parties, receptions, etc. She made no mention of the fact she spoke German, but she eventually convinced the embassy staff that she could be of use to them translating French cable traffic. Her claim was she learned French at college in America. She used this access to monitor sensitive French communiques, sending anything of value on to Abwehr. The girl had the fools at the embassy so enamored with her that they allowed her almost totally free passage within the building with the exception of one or two areas where the most sensitive documents were stored. The girl used this access to reconnoiter the place. She later burglarized the embassy and microphotographed several sensitive documents."

Himmler was taken aback at the girl's apparent skill. *Karl Lehmann's daughter?* "Where did you get this information, Müller?"

"Walter Schellenberg, Reichsführer."

Schellenberg was a protégé of Reinhard Heydrich. Schellenberg was the SD's top sleuth; a man who could uncover things no one else could. But Schellenberg's main job was to gather information on subversives. *How and why did Schellenberg have this information on Karl Lehmann's daughter?*

"Why was this information not in Heydrich's file on the girl?" Himmler asked.

"I asked Schellenberg that same question, Reichsführer. He did not have the answer. He informed me that he gathered the information at Heydrich's request and turned it over to Heydrich personally. After that, Schellenberg had no control over what the Obergruppenführer did with the information."

"Anything more?"

"We have located the girl's whereabouts, Reichsführer."

Himmler waited for him to continue.

"She is at Quenzsee."

"How long has she been there?"

"Almost nine weeks."

Makes sense, Himmler thought. Canaris would not abort a mission prematurely unless he had a more important one looming. She was obviously at Quenzsee preparing for her next assignment.

Heinrich Müller, Himmler's chief of the Gestapo, had done his job well.

"You're to be commended, Müller."

"Thank you, Reichsführer."

"That will be all, Müller."

Heinrich Müller rose, offered his *Heil Hitler,* then turned to leave. As he opened the office door to exit, he heard Himmler's voice behind him.

"Oh, and Müller."

Müller turned toward the voice.

"Where is Axel Ryker?"

"In Budapest, on assignment, Herr Reichsführer," Müller answered.

"Pull him off the assignment and have him report to me as soon as possible. No train—fly him in."

As Müller closed the door behind him, Himmler retrieved a large envelope from a drawer in his desk. The envelope contained the 8" x 10" photographs that Himmler had ordered processed from the negatives he found in Heydrich's file on Erika Lehmann. Himmler had studied the black and white photographs earlier; he now looked them over again. The pictures were not of Karl Lehmann's daughter or anyone else Himmler could identify.

In the first photograph a dark-haired girl sat rigidly in a wooden chair in a room that was obviously an office. The girl looked to be Italian, or perhaps Spanish, and in her late teens or early twenties. She wore a simple, light-colored work dress—the type a maid or kitchen girl might wear. The girl's head was turned, her eyes looked directly into the camera. The look of extreme fright on her face obvious.

The second photograph was of the same girl but now in a different room. The girl was standing naked except for a blindfold. Her arms stretched high over her head, bound to an overhead pipe. The marks across her breasts were clearly from a flogging.

In this second photograph the girl was not alone. A woman and two men stood near the girl. All three wore civilian clothing; all three ignored the camera. Both men were looking at the naked girl, one with an obvious smile on his face. The middle-aged woman's gaze was directed more toward the smiling man and she too was smiling, as if the two had just shared a joke. Both the smiling man and the woman held a riding crop.

The third and last photograph showed the naked girl turned around to expose her backside to the camera so the flogging marks across her buttocks could be seen.

Although Himmler did not recognize anyone in the photographs, he identified their purpose immediately. He had seen hundreds like them. They were photographs of a Gestapo interrogation; the two men and middle-aged woman were obviously Gestapo agents conducting such an interrogation. A mandate from Himmler himself in 1940 decreed the written and photographic recording of every step of Gestapo questioning. These photographs were clearly taken during the early stages of a Gestapo interrogation of an uncooperative subject.

It was obvious the agents followed procedures. If mental and emotional intimidation failed to elicit satisfactory responses, the subject, regardless if male or female, was stripped and paraded in front of Gestapo personnel; this applied pressure by humiliation. Then the Gestapo's euphemism for torture—*physical persuasion*—was called for; men were to be flogged on the buttocks and penis, women on the breasts, and buttocks, and the vaginal area. A riding crop was the officially suggested tool although a plain leather belt was acceptable. If this scourging failed to convince the suspect to talk, there was a second level of physical persuasion approved for the very stubborn. Second level techniques included electrical shocks to the scrotum or vagina among other procedures, but a suspect was not to be subjected to higher levels of physical persuasion unless the initial scourging failed. Himmler was always a proponent of logical sequence.

Interrogators were trained to not get carried away. A dead suspect was a poor supplier of information. In the case of scourging, agents were expected to halt before the subject was rendered unconscious. Hence the order to photograph; it served as an incentive to follow the rules. All interrogation photographs were to be sent directly to 8 Prinz Albrechtstrasse in Berlin. An agent downstairs sole responsibility was to look over all such photographs and tag any that suggested procedures might have been compromised. Tagged photographs would then be sent up the chain of command. If it was determined that Himmler's guidelines were not followed, the agents who conducted the interrogation were disciplined.

Himmler could find nothing amiss in these photographs. The first photograph was clearly taken upon the girl's arrest. She was stilled clothed and obviously ordered to look directly into the camera for a good facial view. The other two photographs were obviously taken to prove the flogging had been administered to the prescribed areas of the body. It looked like the agents had shown good discipline. No whip marks other than on the breasts and buttocks were visible and it looked to Himmler like the girl was still conscious (the blindfold hid the girl's eyes, but her head was still up). Also, the fact that the interrogators had allowed themselves to be photographed with the girl was a strong indication to Himmler that the agents were confident all procedures had been followed.

Himmler concluded the photographs presented nothing to be concerned about.

So why had Heydrich placed—no, hidden—the negatives of these photographs in the Lehmann girl's file?

Earlier that day, after the developed photographs were delivered to his office, Himmler summoned Müller and showed him the pictures. The Gestapo chief agreed they were standard interrogation photographs. Müller, after studying the faces closely, thought one of the men looked familiar. A man named Schwartz, Müller thought. It was checked out downstairs in personnel and Müller was correct. A Gestapo personnel file photograph of a Hans Schwartz matched. Schwartz was currently the chief investigator for the Gestapo field office in Rome.

Günter Syrup, Heydrich's aid, had been called back in, shown the photographs, and questioned about why the negatives were in the Lehmann girl's file. Syrup could supply no information on the matter claiming Heydrich never allowed anyone access to the Lehmann file. This was confirmed (luckily for Syrup) by a phone call to Heydrich's former secretary who was still in Prague, now working for Heydrich's successor.

When it came to Karl Lehmann's daughter, Himmler thought, many people knew nothing. But Heinrich Himmler had ways of getting answers to questions. At his disposal was the iron umbrella of the Gestapo and the SS, an umbrella that canopied the entire European continent.

The job of answering those questions would not be given to Heinrich Müller. Himmler learned long ago (learned it from watching the Führer in fact) to not put all your eggs in one basket. Do not rely on any one individual too heavily. Do not let any one individual know too many of your thoughts. Keep those close to you at least partially in the dark. Yes, the Führer had taught these lessons.

So no, this job would not be given to Müller, nor to Heydrich's top sleuth Walter Schellenberg who supplied Müller with most of the information about the Lehmann girl's covert exploits. Schellenberg was a talented investigator, but, in the end, Himmler considered him Heydrich's flunky. Moreover, Schellenberg now knew that the information he garnered for Heydrich had not been handled properly. Copies should have been sent to Gestapo headquarters in Berlin and not squirreled away in Heydrich's private files in Prague, or even worse, totally left out. Schellenberg, although not responsible for what Heydrich did with the information once he turned it over, would nevertheless be wary of repercussions from the procedural gaffes. Schellenberg would be looking out for himself.

Axel Ryker was the man for this job.

✝   ✝   ✝

CHAPTER 9

In physique and general appearance the boys and girls of Germany are now the finest in Europe.

—G. Ward Price, English Journalist, 1936

Below the Berghof on the Obersalzberg near Berchtesgaden

July 1942

The surface of the lake at the base of the Obersalzberg reflected the surrounding mountains like a living eye. The mightiest of these mountains, the magnificent Untersberg, was still white-capped even now in July.

Suddenly, a few yards off shore, the calm, glittering veneer of the water broke. Eva Braun exploded from under the surface and gasped for air. Standing in chest-high water, Braun pushed the wet hair from her face and spun frantically.

Looking.

Suddenly from under the water she felt a forceful pull on her ankles. Braun fell backward and again disappeared under the surface. The ripples caused by the woman's splash had not traveled far when she again launched herself out of the water, this time alongside another woman. Braun coughed out a mouth full of water. The other woman laughed.

"You're a rat, Erika!" Braun coughed again. Braun launched herself at her swimming partner and attempted to place her hands on Erika's shoulders and force her under water, but Erika pivoted sideways and dunked Braun again. Even though Eva Braun prided herself on her athleticism, in a wrestling match she was little competition for Erika Lehmann. After a third dunking, Braun headed to shore.

"I wish we would have brought something to eat," Braun struggled to say, still coughing from the dunkings as she and Erika left the water. "I'm starved."

Braun perched herself on a large boulder that lay half-submerged at the lake's edge. Erika lay down on one of the towels the women had stretched out on the shore before they entered the water. Neither woman dried herself. Both were naked. Braun turned toward the other woman and for several moments looked silently at Erika who lay on her back shielding eyes from the noon sun.

"This reminds me of some of the wonderful days you and I spent here before this war started," Braun said wistfully. "Remember, Erika, you were just recently returned from America. You would tell me of America and all your boyfriends!"

Still shielding her eyes, Erika smiled.

"Yes, Eva, I remember. I was only nineteen when you and I first came here together. It seems like an eternity ago."

Braun playfully chastised her.

"Oh, you sound like an old washwoman. How old are you now, an ancient twenty-four? twenty-five?"

"I'll be twenty-five in December," Erika smiled at the teasing.

"My, we better find you a wheelchair. I'm the one who should be complaining. I'll turn thirty my next birthday."

Braun sat on the rock with her legs pulled tight to her chest. An old man rowed a small, rusty fishingboat to within fifty meters of the two women. Erika looked up briefly then laid her head back down. Braun waved at the old man. Neither woman was concerned about their nudity. The old fisherman glanced their direction but kept rowing, eventually disappearing around a point in the shoreline.

Braun turned and looked out longingly over the water.

"Tell me about Hollywood."

"I have never been there, Eva. I told you before."

"I can't believe you were in America all those years and you never visited Hollywood. That would be first on my list."

"America is a very big country, Eva. Much larger than Germany. My father was stationed in Washington; it's on the Atlantic coast. Hollywood is on the Pacific coast. It's not like driving from Berlin to Bavaria for a weekend. It is over five thousand kilometers across that country. If you live in Washington, you don't just get in your car and take a Sunday drive to Hollywood."

"I don't care," Braun declared. "Hollywood is the first place I'm going after this war is over. Adolf promised me he would take me to Hollywood."

Adolf. Whenever Eva Braun referred to the Führer by his Christian name, it struck Erika as more than just an oddity. It somehow bordered on bizarre. It would be judged a gross breech of etiquette and respect coming from the tongue of any German besides the young woman who sat on the rock. But to Braun's credit the only time she referred to Hitler by his given name was with her younger sisters, Gretl and Ilse, or with a friend she felt especially close to—like Erika. With staff and servants Braun knew this familiarity would be inappropriate. With those who were not close enough for her *du*, Braun always referred to Hitler like other Germans. He was *Der Führer.*

For a few minutes both women were silent. Braun continued to stare out over the water. Erika lay on her back with her eyes closed. Eventually Braun announced her hunger could wait no longer.

"I'm always starved after swimming. Let's go back up and have lunch."

Both women stood and retrieved articles of clothing which lay on another large rock nearby. They dressed, then began the journey back up the mountain. They walked slowly, arm in arm, up the long, twisting path to the Berghof.

Braun directed Erika's attention to a falcon swooping down the mountain, crossing the path ahead. Without moving its wings, the tan and white bird rocketed toward the lake like one of Hitler's Stuka dive-bombers descending on Warsaw.

"A fisherman," Braun said, referring to the bird.

The two women continued up the steep dirt path. Occasionally Braun would stop and pick a wildflower from among the vast assortment offered by the Bavarian Alps. A clump of Alpine forget-me-nots failed at camouflage within a copse of birch; the flowers sweet fragrance and blue color betrayed its presence. But Braun was dissuaded from picking an offshoot of the rare flower by a heated battle taking place over the plant between a bumble bee and a wasp. A few steps more and Braun noticed yet another species of wildflower.

"Oh! look, Erika. Edelweiss."

Braun pinched off two of the woolly, white herbs and handed one to Erika.

"Now you'll have good luck with love," Braun promised. She retook Erika's arm and they continued walking. Eva Braun was always curious about her sisters' and friends' love lives.

"Tell me, darling, about the men in your life. Anyone special right now? And don't leave out a single detail."

"No one right now, Eva."

"Oh, really? Well, we might have to do something about that."

Eva Braun and Erika Lehmann took their lunch in the main chateau, then spent the rest of the afternoon in the teahouse, a round, stone structure a twenty-minute walk back down the Kehlstein mountain. The six large windows of the teahouse provided a wide vista. From one window Erika enjoyed a superb view of the Ach River roaring down a mountainside. Beyond, she could see the baroque towers of Salzberg.

The two women spent a pleasant afternoon talking of personal matters, both serious and trivial. Knowing that Erika was an accomplished pianist, Eva always insisted that Erika play when they were together. The teahouse included an expensive white Beckstein, rarely touched except by cleaning ladies. Erika played a song inspired by a performance of Shakespeare's *MacBeth*—the *Watchman's Song* by the German composer Edvard Grieg.

Hitler was not at the Berghof. The business of conducting a world war limited Hitler's visits to his beloved mountain while Eva spent more and more time there. Alone. For the past three days Hitler had been at Werewolf, his headquarters on the Eastern front. In the woods a few miles north of Vinnitsa in the Ukraine, Werewolf was a dreary place. Eva told Erika that Hitler's return to the Obersalzberg would brighten the Führer's spirits. He was due that night.

Braun preferred spending her days in Bavaria. Here, on the top of a mountain—freedom. Here Braun wasn't forced to hide, at least not from the people of Hitler's inner circle. In Berlin she remained in the shadows, never seen in public with Hitler. He insisted on this without giving her a reason. She accepted it placidly.

"Great men require great sacrifices from those around them," she told Erika. "It is my place to be there for him when he needs me. This I do for him and for my country."

By six o'clock, the two women had walked back up the mountain to the main chateau. Blondi, Hitler's Alsatian, met them at the bottom of the stone steps and escorted them into the chalet. Once inside, the German Shepard was handed over to a servant before the women proceeded to their rooms.

The private rooms were on the second floor, at the top of a wide, oak stairway. Other stairways, in other parts of the chalet, led to rooms reserved for high-ranking officials of the Third Reich or foreign dignitaries. This particular set of stairs led to a hallway with four rooms, one of which was Hitler's private chambers. Only a very special few ever walked up these stairs. At the bottom of the stairway, two fully-armed SS privates stood at attention. Only Hitler and Eva Braun could ascend these steps without an escort. Even the maids who cleaned the rooms were escorted by, and never out of sight of, the SS. If Erika had not been with Eva Braun, an SS escort would have followed her up the stairs and stood sentry outside her room. But Eva was the undisputed mistress of the Berghof, and with Braun on her arm, Erika was allowed to pass without an escort.

The two SS men stood like (and looked like) statues. Both were Aryan epitomes: tall and muscular, blond, blue eyes, granite jaws.

As the two women passed the soldiers, Eva Braun leaned over and whispered in Erika's ear.

"One of those might make for a pleasant interlude for you tonight."

Erika grinned: "Yes, they are beautiful."

Both women knew the other was joking. If not about the sex, at least about the location. It would be too dangerous at the Berghof. Eva had told Erika that Hitler was an enigma when it came to these matters. In the past, Eva had seen Hitler ignore the indiscretions of men like Joseph Goebbels and Reinhard Heydrich. But in general he disapproved of liaisons between unmarried couples, and once Hitler ordered Goebbels to break off an affair with a Czechoslovakian actress when the propaganda chief's philandering threatened to break up his marriage. This was one of the many confidences Eva Braun had shared with Erika. Karl Lehmann's daughter would be in no danger if caught, but it would not be worth the risk for the man. A night of passion with a Berghof guard might get the soldier shipped to the Russian front.

They walked down the hallway to their rooms past walls covered with paintings from the old masters and exquisite pieces of sculpture. On a marble stand sat an exotic vase.

The pair stopped in front of Braun's room and Erika was invited in. When Braun opened the door, two black Scotch terriers raced yapping toward Eva. Braun gathered both of them in her arms.

"Staci and Negus, my darlings, Mama is home." She let the dogs lick frantically at her cheeks for a moment before returning them to the floor.

The room was spacious and nicely decorated but not opulent. A small boudoir and bath adjoined the bedroom. An antique dresser and bed table sat along one wall but there were no famous paintings or sculptures. A full body nude charcoal sketch of Eva, done with artistic good taste, hung next to a tapestry of a mountain scene. The signature at the bottom of the nude was Hitler's. It was dated *'30.*

"Adolf sketched it not long after we met," offered Braun pleasantly. "I was eighteen."

A large window offered a view from the front of the villa. The vehicle road that allowed visitors up the mountain could be seen along with a sweeping panorama of the neighboring mountains. In the wall separating Braun's room from Hitler's was another door which was open.

Sensing that Erika was curious to see the Führer's quarters, Braun took her hand and led the way through the door and into a passageway. In this vestibule to Hitler's rooms was a private bath that Hitler and Eva shared.

Hitler's chambers included a bedroom and a studio. Erika was surprised at the austerity of Hitler's studio. The walls were bare save for a map of the European continent that hung over an aged rolltop desk in need of varnish. A wooden file cabinet occupied a corner. A small, framed picture of Klara Hitler, his mother, sat atop the desk. Even though the woman's picture was black and white, anyone would immediately conclude where Hitler got those staring, guileless eyes. In another corner of the studio sat one overstuffed chair beside a small table and reading lamp. The bedroom was even more spartan. A single bed with no headboard sat opposite a chifforobe and a wooden chair. There was a window similar to Eva's but the heavy drapes were closed making Hitler's bedroom gloomy in comparison. The women returned to Eva's room.

"Erika, I'll eat dinner with Adolf. It might be late. You eat whenever you wish, no reason to wait for us. Just give a valet your order. You can eat in your room or downstairs, wherever you like."

"Then I'll excuse myself and see you later," Erika said. The two women exchanged a brief, friendly kiss on the cheek before Erika departed.

Back in her room across the hall, Erika bathed then put on a pink, satin robe Eva lent her. Erika's room was much like Eva's: simple good taste with a breathtaking view from one large window. After quickly combing her damp hair, Erika withdrew a healthy stack of folders and maps from a brown leather satchel pregnant with papers.

Homework from Wilhelm Canaris.

Her mission had been codenamed *Operation Vinland,* Vinland the Viking name given to the land that would eventually become the United States by Leif Ericson after the Norwegian explorer and his crew wintered there around 1000 A.D.[1]

Among several folders all marked *Geheime Reichssache* [Secret Business of the Reich] one was of particular interest to Erika. Inside was a picture of and information on an American metallurgical engineer just recently assigned to the U.S. Naval installation Erika would infiltrate. The man was a Jew and had relatives in Germany. He had come to Abwehr's attention before the war when he sent communications to the American Embassy in Berlin, the International Red Cross, and the German Immigration Office in Berlin seeking exit visas for his German relatives. Most of those relatives never left Germany and now this American scientist was suddenly an excellent candidate for blackmail. Thirty years old and unmarried, he was a prime target for *Lorelei.*

---

1   Author's note: Vinland, or "wine land," was chosen by Ericson because of the
    success the Vikings enjoyed in cultivating grapes in the new land.

Erika ordered dinner to be later delivered to her room and settled in to study.

Hours past and she was still going over the Abwehr paperwork when she heard the bustle outside. Hitler had arrived. It was almost eleven. An hour later, just after midnight, someone knocked. Still in her robe, Erika opened the door and recognized Otto Günsche, an SS officer who was one of Hitler's personal adjutants.

"Yes," Erika said to Günsche who stood rigidly outside her door.

"Fräulein, the Führer has asked for you to join him in the main study," the man said without really looking at her.

"Thank you, Major. Please inform the Führer I will be there directly."

There was a sharp click of his boots and the man left without comment.

Erika dressed, then proceeded downstairs. The study was on the second floor but in another part of the chateau. From her room, Erika had to descend to the main level before going back up a different stairway.

No one was in the study when Erika entered. Among the rooms in the Berghof, this was Hitler's favorite. Although Erika had visited the Berghof on several occasions before the war, she had been in the study only once, during a Christmas visit with her father in 1938. This room had served as the venue for some of the century's most famous, and infamous, discussions. Hitler and Neville Chamberlain sealed the fate of Czechoslovakia in this room. In this room, Mussolini gave Hitler advice about how to handle relations with the Vatican. Göring, Himmler, Goebbels, and Rudolph Hess: all had spent hours in this room discussing the world's fate.

A small fire burned in the stone fireplace. The fire was not solely for aesthetics. Even in July, at night and at this high altitude, the fire was pragmatic.

Several paintings adorned the walls, all painted by German artists— some well known, others not. On one wall a portrait of Bismarck hung beside one of Goethe. Over the fireplace, Frederick the Great (Hitler's favorite German Emperor) was next to Frederick I the Holy Roman Emperor. Erika noticed the bright red beard that Frederick I was famous for. Like most Germans, Erika was familiar with the legend of Red Beard, or *Barbarossa,* who began the Third Crusade in 1189. The legend has it that Frederick never died, but was merely sleeping beside a huge table in the Kyffhäuser Mountains. When his beard grows completely around the table, Barbarossa will arise and conquer Germany's enemies.

The room had two windows, both on the same wall. Curtains were closed. Between the windows, on a beautifully ornate cherrywood base, sat an enormous world globe. Against the wall opposite the windows, two couches sat side by side beneath Bismarck and Goethe. Four over-stuffed wing chairs sat in opposing places around the room, each with its own small side table and reading lamp. Two of these lamps, along with the fire, supplied the light for the room. Heavy walnut bookcases and a matching cabinet of drawers covered the fourth wall. The shelves held some books, an assortment of porcelain figurines, and several antique cuckoo clocks of various sizes. The doorway to the room was near the corner of this wall. Covering most of the varnished wood floor was a large, oval-shaped, burgundy rug.

Erika was eyeing the portrait of Frederick I when a voice from behind surprised her.

"Do you believe in the legend?"

Erika spun around and brushed against Adolf Hitler who stood directly behind her. Hitler ignored her sudden jerking motion; he did not take his eyes off of the painting.

"Mein Führer, you startled me," Erika breathed. She took a second and collected herself. "I'm embarrassed," she continued pleasantly. "Abwehr agents should not allow themselves to be surprised from behind."

Hitler now looked at her with Klara Hitler's eyes and grinned. He took the comment as flattery.

"Well, do you?" he demanded as he looked back up at the painting. "Do you believe Barbarossa will return someday and destroy our enemies?"

"The people think you are doing that, mein Führer," Erika answered then added. "And I agree."

Hitler stared at her again, then offered her a seat on one of the sofas. He sat in a chair nearby.

"Have you eaten, Tschapperl?" Hitler asked. *Tschapperl* was a nickname Hitler sometimes used for Erika in close company. It was a Viennese diminutive meaning *little thing* (although Erika never quite knew why he used it to refer to her, she was almost as tall as Hitler).

"Yes, mein Führer, earlier. Thank you."

"Your father will be here tomorrow. I sent a message to Berlin earlier today."

"Wonderful. Thank you, mein Führer."

Hitler nodded to acknowledge her thanks then rose from his seat and walked across the room. He opened the door, summoned the always near Otto Günsche, and issued orders that Erika could not hear. Erika wondered where Eva was.

"I told Günsche to have some tea brought up. Tell me, have you enjoyed your holiday?"

"Yes, mein Führer. Eva and I went swimming today. It was very relaxing."

Hitler made no comment.

Suddenly his demeanor changed.

Eva had told Erika that Hitler displayed two distinct auras. Around close friends, family, and even servants, Hitler could be the manifestation of kindness and grace. Eva thought the fact that his mother had worked as a domestic probably was a major influence on Hitler's congenial treatment of servants. Eva told Erika that Hitler once kept his generals waiting for the start of a critical meeting because of a crying kitchen girl. The young girl, whom Hitler had probably never spoken to, had lost a boyfriend. Somehow Hitler overheard her sobs. The assembly of generals, which included Rommel, waited for over an hour while Hitler sat in the kitchen holding the servant girl's hand and offering solace.

Around his generals and top Nazi officials Hitler could offer quite a different facade. This was where the Hitler of the Allied newsreels surfaced: the maniacal ranting; the loud, endless harangues; the shaking fists. The noticeable change in Hitler's demeanor came just before the following question.

"Tell me what you think of Canaris," Hitler said somberly. "And I want you to feel free to be completely frank with me."

The question was a bombshell. The grave way he asked the question and the "feel free to be completely frank" phrase was the tipoff. Erika thought: *My God, he doesn't trust Canaris!*

She chose her words carefully.

"I consider the Admiral a patriot, mein Führer." Erika paused, then continued. "I know nothing of his politics or personal convictions. My only dealings with him have been at briefings or debriefings concerning my assignments. I have never talked with the Admiral socially. I have never attended a social function where he was present. My only relationship with the man is on a professional basis, where he impresses me as extremely efficient."

Hitler watched her closely without comment. For Erika, a tense moment. Hitler continued as if his first question was never asked.

"So, Canaris wants to send you to America. What does your father think of this?"

"My father is always apprehensive when I leave Germany, mein Führer. This is natural, of course, toward a daughter. But if I were a son fighting at the front, as you and my father both did in the first war, I doubt if it would be different for him. But my father realizes how important the gathering of information is to our war effort."

As she spoke, Hitler stared at the fire. His brief, suspicious mood when he referred to Canaris vanished as if a switch was thrown. Now, once again, his ambience was that of a concerned uncle.

"I'll speak to your father about this tomorrow," Hitler declared. "Speaking English has been your burden, Tschapperl. Perhaps I should keep you here in Germany. Your father has already lost a wife in America—and you a mother."

Erika was speechless. This was totally unexpected. Was this the reason she had been invited to the Berghof? For a change of plans. Was the decision already made? or would it depend on her father? She had already trained for ten weeks for this specific assignment; why wait until now?

Probably for the best, a reply on Erika's part was made impossible with a knock on the door. As soon as Hitler gave his okay, an elderly woman wearing an apron opened the door. Behind the old woman was a young girl (Erika guessed she could not be over sixteen) carrying a silver platter. On the platter was a pot of apple-peel tea (Hitler's favorite) and three ornate china cups.

"Ah, Greta," said Hitler pleasantly to the gray-haired woman. "I've been impatient for your tea for weeks."

Greta Morgen smiled broadly. Hitler always bragged on her apple-peel tea, a priceless accolade in the old woman's mind. She moved a small table from the other side of the room, placing it between Hitler's chair and the sofa where Erika sat. The young girl stood quietly, holding the platter. Erika could hear the clinking of cups. The girl was trembling.

Hitler heard the clinking also. Suddenly his attention turned to the young servant girl whom he did not recognize.

"And who is this, Greta," Hitler asked.

The answer would have to wait. As soon as Hitler's attention turned toward the young girl, Erika saw the girl's eyes roll back and her knees buckle. Erika flew from her chair and almost caught her, but the collapse was too quick. The platter of tea crashed to the floor just a split second before the girl.

The old woman screamed and lifted her hands to her face, her concern more for the Führer's spilled tea than for the girl. Hitler rose from his chair and hovered over Erika who knelt beside the girl.

"She is all right, mein Führer," Erika reassured. "Apparently she just fainted. She seems to be coming around."

Hitler went to the door and ordered Günsche to bring towels and cold water. Erika and Greta helped the girl to a sofa. The old woman was mortified.

"Mein Führer," the old cook prattled. "This is so embarrassing. She is a village girl from Berchtesgaden. She just started working in the kitchen yesterday. We will replace her immediately, of course."

"You'll do nothing of the kind, Greta," Hitler said without rancor. "She will stay and work here as long as she wishes."

Günsche arrived with the cold water, but by then the girl was lucid. The girl saw the mess on the floor and began crying.

"I…am sorry," she said between sobs. "I will clean…"

Hitler patted the girl's hand and consoled: "Nonsense, it is nothing, my dear." Then to his adjutant: "Handkerchief, Günsche."

The SS major set the bowl down and retrieved a handkerchief from a jacket pocket. Hitler took it, handed it to the girl and issued orders.

To the girl: "There now, no more of this crying."

To Günsche: "Have someone clean this up."

Twenty minutes later, the spilled apple-peel tea was gone along with the girl who had swooned in her Führer's presence. Greta had delivered more of her tea. Before the old cook left, Hitler reminded her to not chastise the girl.

Eva Braun had now joined Hitler and Erika in the study. On the sofa beside Eva sat the two Scotch terriers. "Fräulein Braun's hand-sweepers" Hitler told Erika, referring to the dogs, because, he added, they looked like something a maid would use to wipe dust.

It was now past one o'clock in the morning. Hitler spent the next hour-and-a-half dispensing tales of the early days to the two women. (Hitler enjoys recalling the old days, especially lately, Eva had told Erika at the lake.) Because of Erika, Hitler focused mostly on stories that included her father. Hitler told the women a poignant tale about Erika's father going without heat for one entire winter so he could save money to buy Erika's mother a dress. It was before the Putsch. No one, it seemed, in Germany had much money, including Hitler. Karl Lehmann worked in Munich while poverty forced his wife and small daughter to stay behind in Oberschopfheim with his parents. Instead of buying coal for the stove in his rundown apartment, Erika's father saved his money so he could buy Erika's mother a dress for her birthday. When Hitler found out what his friend was doing, he offered to help. But Erika's proud father would not accept charity. It took Karl Lehmann an entire, icy winter to save enough money for the dress, Hitler told Erika.

Erika appreciated the story and thanked Hitler. She told him she had never heard it before. Hitler replied that her father never told his wife what he had to do to save the money because she would fret over him and not want the dress.

Other stories were humorous.

It must have been the summer of 1922, Hitler recalled. He was scheduled to speak in a Munich beer hall, one of myriad beer hall speeches he gave in those days. The tavern crowd was especially rowdy that night and Anton Drexler had tried unsuccessfully to call the crowd to order so Hitler could speak. Finally Erika's father jumped onto a table and loudly demanded the raucous throng's attention. Around this table sat Hitler, Drexler, Heinrich Himmler and several other of the earliest members of the Party. As the crowd started quieting, the table upon which Erika's father stood collapsed, sending Karl Lehmann plummeting backward into Himmler's lap. Both men crashed to the floor, exploding the crowd into laughter. There was no quieting the mob after that, Hitler told the women. No speech was given that night.

Hitler told stories until nearly three o'clock. He then gave a brief lecture on the perversions of American jazz in response to a comment Eva made about a new song she recently heard on the radio. The lecture on the evils of jazz lasted only fifteen minutes—very brief for Hitler who could deliver harangues that lasted for hours on such innocuous subjects.

When Hitler finished, Eva and Erika discussed plans to visit Berchtesgaden the next day. Their plans including returning to the Berghof in time to greet Erika's father when he arrived. When Erika glanced at Hitler, his head was resting backward on the chair and his mouth was slightly open. He was asleep. Eva's eyes followed hers. Eva reassured Erika that everything was fine, the Führer often slumbered in his chair. Not to worry, Eva said, they could go on talking, but Erika thought it a good time to retire and bade Eva goodnight.

Eva Braun accepted her friend's departure reluctantly, but finally wished Erika a goodnight in return. After Erika closed the door of the study behind her, Eva Braun settled back in her chair with her two sleepy dogs at her side. She would be there in the morning when Adolf Hitler awoke.

✠   ✠   ✠

CHAPTER 10

There is strength in the union even of very sorry men.

—Homer, (ca. 700 B.C.)

Berlin, Gestapo headquarters

8 Prinz Albrechtstrasse

July 1942

Axel Ryker sat down heavily in the chair facing Heinrich Himmler's desk. Ryker, a repatriated German from Lithuania, was a man called upon by Himmler from time to time for "special" tasks. Ryker possessed several qualities that augmented his usefulness to Himmler and the Gestapo. He spoke fluent Russian (his native tongue), acceptable Slovak and Czech (most speakers of Slovak had few problems with the similar Czech), and German. Ryker even managed to stumble his way through English, although his English consisted of a strange mixture of Russian, Czech, and German accents.

He could also snap a man's neck as easily as a chicken bone, which he had proved on more than one occasion. For Axel Ryker, liquidation and torture were job skills honed sharp, and sometimes even pleasant diversions.

Ryker was a full six-foot tall but a wide, heavily muscled torso gave him the appearance of being shorter. Jet black hair and dark, pitiless eyes under a protruding brow gave him a caveman countenance. On the brow grew thick black eyebrows barely separated in the middle. Adding to his already grisly genetic features was a nose that had been mashed flat against his face and never repaired. The mashed nose was a souvenir from the twenties, courtesy of a pipe swinging communist who crept up on him during a street brawl. Ryker was a teenager at the time.

To frighten women and intimidate men, Axel Ryker simply had to enter the room.

But Ryker was no mindless automaton dusted off only during the Gestapo's murder and maim hour. In addition to the impressive afore-mentioned language skills, Ryker possessed an innate craftiness, including an almost supernatural ability to discern when someone was lying to him. These qualities allowed him to ferret information when others failed.

A week ago, Ryker had been in Budapest investigating a break in at the Rumanian Embassy. Some sensitive papers detailing Nazi plans to arrest a popular, but pro-resistance, Catholic priest in Oradea were stolen. Ryker was ordered to Budapest to take over the case. His first task would be the apprehension of the embassy thieves; his second the eventual arrest of the priest.

A suspect to the burglary, under torture, had failed to implicate others. That is until Ryker had the man's wife and four small children brought in. The youngest child was still nursing; the oldest not yet seven years old. As the family stood in front of the bleeding, half-conscious father, Ryker transferred the infant from the mother's arms to the oldest child, took out his Mauser and shot the woman through the head in front of her husband and children. Ryker was preparing to do the same to the children, one by one, when the man gave Ryker the information he sought on condition the children be released. The man's associates were arrested and the papers recovered before being circulated. Ryker had all the conspirators shot, of course. The parentless children were released on the streets of Budapest. Axel Ryker kept his promises.

Ryker did not complete his mission. The Rumanian priest had yet to be disposed of when Ryker was recalled to Berlin by Heinrich Müller on Himmler's orders.

That was six days ago. When Ryker first reported to Himmler in Berlin, the Reichsführer handed him copies of three photographs. In one photograph an unidentified girl sat in a chair. In the other two the same girl was shown being tortured. A run-of-the-mill Gestapo interrogation Ryker knew immediately. The second photograph pictured three other people who were obviously the girl's questioners. Ryker was given the name of one of the men in the second photograph along with his assignment: to identify the others in the photographs, the dates the photographs were taken, location, and any other pertinent information that Ryker might procure, especially any specifics to this interrogation that might make it other than usual. The job required some leg work on Ryker's part: a flight to Rome then on to Portugal before returning to Berlin. All-in-all, however, the assignment had not been difficult. Five days after beginning the investigation, Ryker now sat across from Himmler prepared to supply the details.

"What do you have?" Himmler asked.

Ryker withdrew his copies of the photographs and several pages of notes from an attache case. "The photographs were taken in Portugal at Gestapo field headquarters in Lisbon on 10 April 1940. The girl undergoing interrogation was a Portuguese national named Isabell Machado Santos, age nineteen at the time of the photographs."

Ryker continued to read from his notes as Himmler looked over his own copy of the photos.

"The other people in the second photograph are Gestapo personnel who were assigned to the Lisbon station at the time the photographs were taken. They were on duty the day the girl was brought in, and the assignment of conducting the interrogation fell to them. The name of

Hans Schwartz, the man on the far left, you supplied to me during briefing. I flew to Rome and questioned this Schwartz. At the time the photographs were taken, Schwartz was lead investigator assigned to the Lisbon field office. He remembers the girl and the details of the interrogation clearly. Schwartz also identified the other Gestapo agents in the photograph."

Himmler again looked at Schwartz' image in the photograph.

Ryker resumed talking. "The other man's name was Hanneken; he was killed in a British bombing raid on Hamburg eight months ago. The woman's name is Frieda Gretler. Gretler, because she speaks Portuguese, has remained with the Lisbon office."

Himmler scanned the photograph as Ryker talked. Hanneken was the man holding the riding crop who stood smiling in the direction of the naked girl. The smiling woman with the riding crop was now also identified.

Himmler was now doing the interrogating. "Who is this Santos girl and why was she being questioned?"

"She was a local peasant girl who worked as a maid at the residence of the German chargé d'affaires in Lisbon. It seems a necklace belonging to the chargé d'affaires wife came up missing one day, and it was suspected that this maid, this Isabell Santos, stole it. The Santos girl was questioned by the diplomat's wife and members of the household staff but the girl kept insisting she was innocent. The diplomat's wife was quite insistent that her necklace be returned, so she called her husband who in turn called Schwartz, who was an acquaintance. The two men had met at a social function at the German embassy. Schwartz sent an agent to the diplomat's residence where a description of the necklace was recorded. According to Schwartz, the whole affair was over some type of pearl necklace of only medium value. The wife seemed convinced that this maid, the Santos girl, was the thief, so as a favor to the chargé d'affaires, Schwartz ordered the girl brought in for questioning."

Himmler was disappointed and even more confused. Such a trivial matter. Still the question survived: *Why would Heydrich bury the negatives of this insignificant interrogation in the Lehmann girl's file?*

Himmler: "Was Schwartz sure of the identity of this Santos girl? Was he sure she was just a maid?"

"I asked Schwartz that, of course," Ryker answered. "He told me a check later revealed the girl's entire family worked as domestics around Lisbon. Schwartz was sure she was a maid and no more."

"After questioning Schwartz in Rome," Ryker proceeded, "I flew on to Lisbon and questioned the Gretler woman. Like Schwartz, she also clearly recalled the girl and the details of her interrogation. Gretler's questioning corroborated what Schwartz revealed."

Himmler raised his hand to signify he was about to speak. "You say this Schwartz and the Gretler woman remember everything clearly. This questioning on such a unimportant matter took place over two years ago. Schwartz and Gretler have probably taken part in a score of interrogations since. How is it they recall this one so clearly?"

"It seems there were unusual circumstances surrounding the girl's release," Ryker answered.

"Such as?"

"Shortly after the girl was brought in to the Gestapo office someone from OKW arrived seeking the release of the girl. Apparently quite an argument followed between the OKW envoy and Gestapo personnel. This quarrel continued for some time."

Now we are perhaps getting somewhere, Himmler thought. *Someone from the High Command shows up seeking the release of an insignificant Portuguese peasant girl suspected of pilfering a piece of jewelry from some spoiled diplomat's wife. Very interesting.*

Ryker knew many of his facts by rote and only referred to his paperwork occasionally. "The OKW representative did not have the proper paperwork authorizing the girl's release so the request was denied. The OKW representative finally left—very unhappy according to both Schwartz and Gretler—and the agents on duty proceeded with the girl's interrogation."

Ryker went on.

"Schwartz told me he tried to resolve the matter quickly. He had no interest in the girl besides recovering the necklace as a favor to the diplomat. Schwartz said if the girl had revealed where the necklace could be recovered he would have released her and let the chargé d'affaires deal with the matter, but the girl kept insisting she was innocent. Schwartz reasoned that having a high-ranking official in the German embassy indebted to the Gestapo might serve some future purpose, so he ordered the interrogators to proceed with the standard scourging which is pictured in the photographs."

"Schwartz," said Ryker, "assigned the man Hanneken to administer the scourging. These scourgings always took place in a room in the building's basement. The Gretler woman showed me the room when I was in Lisbon. The room is soundproof and one wall has a one-way glass so interrogations could be viewed privately from outside the room."

Ryker now looked down at a page in his report.

"Schwartz stayed in the room to oversee. It was his custom to do so if he was not too busy. Hanneken did most of the work. The Gretler woman's main job during interrogations, Schwartz recalled to me in Rome, was to serve as a translator, but Schwartz said she frequently volunteered to help with the scourgings. The Gretler woman was especially masterful with female subjects, according to Schwartz, so he allowed her to assist Hanneken with this girl."

"If scourging failed to get the suspects to talk, as in this case," Ryker continued, "suspects were informed of further steps, which were the same for men or women. Frau Gretler told me she would translate, telling the subjects the next level of interrogation could include such unpleasantries as objects inserted into body orifices and electrical shocks to the most sensitive areas. Then, unless time was a factor, which it was not in this case, standard procedure under Schwartz was to leave the subject bound as pictured and given time to think it over. This was usually one hour according to Gretler, perhaps longer if the office was busy."

Himmler was growing bored of hearing about the modus operandi of the Lisbon field office. Nothing Ryker had told him so far was out of the ordinary or of any interest except the part about the mysterious OKW envoy. "Get to the part about the girl's release," Himmler ordered. "You said unusual circumstances surrounded it?"

Ryker glared back at Himmler and growled, "I'm getting to that." Ryker was a man not vexed with human emotions like apprehension. No one intimidated Axel Ryker, not even a menacing character like Heinrich Himmler. Ryker had found his niche in life, he did his job well, and he was detached from concern over accepted formalities. No one's superior status or rank was ever recognized by Axel Ryker; he included no titles of respect such as *sir,* or in Himmler's case, *Reichsführer.* Axel Ryker did not give a damn.

Ryker restarted.

"With the scourging of the girl completed, Schwartz and the others left the room. Schwartz said when they left, the girl was whimpering but fully conscious. Schwartz informed me it was at that time he concluded that the girl was telling the truth. Schwartz believed no one, especially not a naive peasant girl, would suffer through a flogging for a simple necklace of suspect value. It was Schwartz' judgment that the girl would not still be maintaining her ignorance unless she in fact knew nothing about the matter."

"It was now getting late, sometime in the evening according to Schwartz. Schwartz telephoned the chargé d'affaires at his residence and informed him of his conclusions. The man seemed anxious to drop the entire matter, but Schwartz could hear the man's wife in the background objecting loudly. The chargé d'affaires told Schwartz he would have his driver transport him to the Gestapo office immediately where the matter would be resolved."

Ryker checked a fact in front of him. "Thirty minutes later the diplomat, with his wife in tow, walked into the building and asked for Schwartz. Schwartz met with the couple in his office. The husband seemed quite embarrassed by the entire matter according to Schwartz, but the wife kept insisting the maid was the only person who could have possibly stolen the necklace."

"According to Schwartz, the diplomat's wife questioned the competency of the Gestapo and it was at that point Schwartz grew impatient with the woman. Schwartz assured her of the Gestapo's proficiency with such matters. He offered to take the couple to see their maid. Schwartz told me he suggested, quite tongue-in-cheek, that perhaps the lady could get the truth out of the girl if the Gestapo could not. Schwartz ordered Frau Gretler to escort the couple to the room in the basement. Schwartz followed. The couple got cold feet at the last second and refused to enter the room, so Schwartz directed them to the one-way glass. The girl was as they left her, but by now long red welts, easily noticed even through the glass, had risen on her breasts. According to Frau Gretler, the husband looked quite prepared to vomit. Gretler, on Schwartz orders, entered the room and turned the girl around. Similar long welts crisscrossed her buttocks. Some of the welts were bleeding according to Gretler."

"Schwartz said the husband quickly headed to the stairway and the wife followed. The entire entourage returned to Schwartz' office. To Schwartz surprise, the diplomat's wife suggested that the interrogation continue until the girl told the truth. Schwartz informed the woman, in graphic detail, of the next steps in the process. The woman did not flinch, instead telling Schwartz she saw no reason not to proceed if it would bring out the truth. The diplomat scolded his wife then offered to buy her a more expensive necklace but to no avail. She countered by reminding him that it was the principle that mattered. She told her husband that he, as a high-ranking official of the German embassy, should have more pride than to allow a cheap peasant girl to steal from his wife."

"The husband shook his head and threw up his hands, according to Schwartz. Finally the diplomat asked Schwartz to continue with the interrogation."

Ryker now interjected his own thoughts: "Schwartz was wise enough to foresee the eventual problems if this situation was not resolved. He realized he was now in a no-win situation. If the girl never revealed where the necklace was, and Schwartz knew she wouldn't because she didn't know, the diplomat's wife would harp loud and long and generate as many problems as she could for Schwartz. If he proceeded with the interrogation and the girl died it would only complicate matters. The diplomat's shrew would still not be happy and there would be sensitive political issues to deal with if the girl's death ever came to light. Portugal is a neutral country."

Himmler understood. Lisbon was in fact a key location in one of the few neutral countries left on the continent. Intelligence agencies on both sides referred to Lisbon was a "twilight zone," an important European city, still neutral, where both sides slinked in the dark, made deals in smoky backrooms, and took great pride in playing dirty tricks on the other side. In Lisbon, the stakes were high and loyalties suspect.

"But in the end," Ryker said, "Schwartz had little choice except to order Hanneken and Gretler to resume the interrogation. Schwartz sarcastically suggested to the diplomat's wife that she watch the proceedings but she refused. The woman was adamant about proceeding, Schwartz complained in Rome, but she wanted no part of watching it being done."

Ryker stopped for emphasis. "This is when the bizarre developments of the case started happening in earnest."

Himmler was listening.

"Approximately a half hour after the interrogation resumed, Schwartz received a phone call. Since the diplomat and his wife were sitting in his office, Schwartz took the call in another room. His secretary identified the caller as Reinhard Heydrich. Schwartz had never met Heydrich, nor spoken to or communicated in any way with such a high-level member of the Reich. Schwartz' secretary was new, having been on the job for only two weeks, so Schwartz at first thought she had made a mistake. But after picking up the phone Schwartz realized he was indeed talking to Reinhard Heydrich."

Himmler remained still. Ryker now had his full attention.

"Heydrich called Schwartz from Berlin about the maid," Ryker said with a slight grin. He studied Himmler's face for shock. Ryker apparently got what he wanted, then moved on.

"Heydrich ordered the interrogation of this peasant girl to stop immediately. Heydrich then informed Schwartz that the OKW envoy who had earlier sought the girl's release was headed back to pick up the girl. Heydrich ordered Schwartz to release the girl to the envoy, and send the written reports and any photographs, including the negatives, of the girl's interrogation to him—Heydrich—by way of special courier."

Himmler's eyes focused on Ryker without looking at the man. Himmler's mind raced, trying to fit square pegs in round holes.

Himmler sought answers to his thoughts. "Does Schwartz know why Heydrich ordered all this? Why Heydrich would involve himself with this foolishness?"

"No idea," Ryker seemed pleased to announce. "To finish Schwartz' story, he told me he had barely hung up the phone and returned to his office when the secretary buzzed again to tell him the OKW envoy had returned. Besides Schwartz, Hanneken and Gretler were the only agents in the building at the time and both of them were in the basement with the girl. The interrogation room had no intercom so someone had to go down to the room to deliver messages. Schwartz ordered his secretary to go tell Hanneken and Gretler to discontinue the questioning and report to him. Schwartz planned to instruct the woman Gretler to clean the girl up as much as possible and release her to the OKW envoy."

"While this secretary went to summon Hanneken and Gretler, Schwartz stayed in his office to explain to the chargé d'affaires and his wife that the girl was to be released. Apparently the wife was furious but Schwartz could not care less; he was off the hook. His orders were from Heydrich himself."

Himmler thought the sordid story was finished, and was preparing to ask questions when Ryker started again.

"Since Schwartz remained in his office, I had to question the Gretler woman for a first hand account of what happened next."

"Gretler told me that instead of telling the OKW envoy to wait in the outer office, Schwartz' twit of a secretary allowed the envoy to follow her downstairs to the interrogation room. Evidently, as the secretary and the envoy passed the one-way window the envoy saw the girl bent over and bound to a chair. Hanneken stood behind the girl with his pants down. The Gretler woman sat in a nearby chair waiting for Hanneken to finish."

"When I questioned the Gretler woman in Lisbon, she stressed that Hanneken's actions were done with Schwartz' sanction. She said it was not uncommon for Hanneken to include this as part of the second level of interrogation with some of the female subjects. I have no reason to doubt her word. Schwartz told me in Rome that Hanneken and Gretler made a good team; they had a good record of extracting information so Schwartz more or less let them have a free hand at the second-level."

"After viewing what was happening through the window, the envoy burst through the door and went after Hanneken. Gretler testified things happened so quickly she and Hanneken had no time to react. Hanneken struggled with his pants as the envoy delivered a hard blow to the back of Hanneken's head with the butt of a dagger. Then the envoy went after Gretler, sticking the knife to her throat and threatening to give her the same treatment the maid had received. Gretler said she tried to explain to the envoy that it was just normal interrogation procedure. The envoy struck Gretler across the face hard enough to break her nose then kicked Gretler in the ribs sending her flying over the chair."

"The rest is from Schwartz," Ryker explained. "He told me he heard his secretary run screaming up the stairs. Schwartz started to the basement with the diplomat on his heels. Before Schwartz got to the stairs, the envoy came through the stairwell door helping the maid walk. The envoy had found a trenchcoat to cover the girl. The envoy cursed Schwartz and threatened to kill him. Schwartz said he heard the diplomat, who stood a few paces behind Schwartz, gasp when he saw the OKW envoy. Schwartz said the diplomat then uttered the words 'It's you!'"

Himmler had his chair turned sideways to Ryker. He swivelled to face Ryker as the man finished his report.

"The envoy left with the girl and both Schwartz and Gretler told me they never saw either again. Schwartz was curious about why Reinhard Heydrich and the OKW would concern themselves with a Portuguese peasant girl. It was at this time he checked the Santos girl and it was verified she was in fact just a maid. Of course, at the time, Hanneken and Gretler thought the OKW representative should be found and punished for the attack on them, but when trying to run a simple verification on the envoy it was learned that the OKW identification papers the person used were fictitious. Schwartz included all this in the report to Heydrich. Heydrich personally called Schwartz a second time and told him that as far as the Lisbon Gestapo was concerned the entire episode never happened. Schwartz had his orders so the case was closed."

Himmler looked astounded. "What's this? You say this envoy was a fraud?"

"The name on the OKW papers was fictitious," Ryker was enjoying this. "That's what I said."

But Himmler had paid close attention to Ryker's story. "You said the diplomat apparently recognized the envoy." It was a statement, not a question. Himmler waited for Ryker to verify.

"Yes," Ryker affirmed. "The diplomat had dealings with this person in the past."

"So who was this envoy," Himmler asked. "Did the diplomat identify him to Schwartz or Gretler?"

"Him?" Ryker asked with a touch of mockery. "I never said the envoy was a man. The diplomat told Schwartz the envoy was really an Abwehr agent who used the German embassy to courier top secret information out of Portugal. The agent was a *woman,* and the diplomat could identify her only by her code name."

Ryker closed his folder and threw it on Himmler's desk, unconcerned with decorum.

"Her code name was *Lorelei.*"

Himmler stared into space, his chair swivelled slowly around. The chair stopped turning when its back was to Ryker.

Axel Ryker could not see Himmler over the high-back leather chair. Ryker did not care and spoke to the back of the chair.

"One humorous detail of the affair remains," Ryker was grinning. There was no sound from the other side of the chair. "It seems the necklace was found a week later. The diplomat's wife had accidentally knocked it off a boudoir dressing table herself. They found it wedged between the piece of furniture and the wall. It had been there for five or six months, since the last time the woman wore it."

Ursula Ziegler, Himmler's secretary, sat in the outer office and cringed at Axel Ryker's growling, unearthly laugh heard even through the heavy walls of 8 Prinz Albrechtstrasse.

✠   ✠   ✠

CHAPTER 11

Hitler's voice sounds tremendously sincere and convincing.

—William Shirer, 1935

The Berghof in Bavaria—July 1942

Karl Lehmann stood next to his daughter on the Berghof veranda.

This was Lehmann's first summer trip to the Obersalzberg since before the war. His only other sojourns to Hitler's mountaintop chalet since September 1, 1939, were brief visits around Christmas time. Lehmann noted the two different worlds which were Bavaria in winter as opposed to summer—both beautiful, but Lehmann preferred the summers. In winter just getting here from Berlin was an adventure, or a time-consuming headache, depending on your outlook. Lehmann, and other important and busy men in the Reich, could rarely spare the time for the all-day drive from Berlin, so a flight to Munich (more often than not a rocky one in the winter) was normal procedure. After arriving in Munich, the drive to the Obersalzberg, a pleasant ninety-minute jaunt in the summer, could in wintertime take hour after nerve-wracking hour on snow-packed, snakelike Bavarian roads. Then, upon reaching the base of the snowbound Berghof access road, guests had to endure a bone-jarring ride in an Army halftrack up the mountain. On most winter days an Army halftrack was the only vehicle that could make it up the icy Alpine road. *Might as well ride up on one of Rommel's panzers with the cannon stuck up your ass,* Hermann Göring had complained to Karl Lehmann once.

But July. Lehmann enjoyed the drive from Munich earlier this morning. He ordered the driver to put the top down. The sun was warm and the mountain air cool. The weather was perfect and a welcome respite from the current heatwave that had descended on Berlin.

The idyllic setting, however, was not enough to free Karl Lehmann from his anxieties.

Erika's involvement in the high-stakes and extremely dangerous game of covert activities behind enemy lines troubled Karl Lehmann. He did his best not to plague his daughter with his fears; nevertheless, Karl Lehmann seriously contemplated asking his daughter to resign from Abwehr. This he had mulled over since she left for England on her last assignment. Karl Lehmann worried about the dangerous games his daughter played.

The father knew his daughter was both smart and clever (two very different traits in intelligence work). He knew she served for the right reason: love for her country. He knew she was not reckless, the worst trait for a spy. But he also knew something else.

Karl Lehmann had two daughters. In one body perhaps but two Erikas nevertheless.

Karl and Louise Lehmann's only child was a prodigy. Walking at nine months. Complete sentences at two years. An accomplished pianist before her tenth birthday. A champion at just about any athletic endeavor she cared to try. An uncanny ability with languages. *How many is she fluent in now?*, Lehmann asked himself. Sometimes he lost track. All this, plus Erika had always been a sweet and loving child to all around her.

Most of the time.

It had shown itself early and caused her mother great anxiety. The daughter of Karl and Louise Lehmann had a dark side, an alcove in the recesses of her psyche where something menacing lurked. Many might call it simply a temper. But this temper was different. When Erika's temper surfaced it was never accompanied by a red face, shouts, or a tantrum. *If only it were so easy,* her parents had commented to each other. Erika's temper was a viper that lay in the grass and bit those who stumbled across it. Thankfully the episodes were infrequent; in fact, the episodes he knew about were years apart, but when his daughter's temper reared its head it was always cruel and somebody always got hurt.

The first incident involved a baby-sitter. Erika was four years old; Lehmann was working in Munich. His wife and small daughter stayed behind in Oberschopfheim with Karl's parents. During the winter of 1921 all adult inhabitants of the village were required to register for the census. Erika's mother and his parents were given a date and time to report to the courthouse. It was winter and an influenza epidemic had spread through the area. Louise Lehmann worried about taking Erika outside in the cold and then standing with her in a crowded courthouse where surely some would be infected with the flu. A teenage girl who lived down the road was recruited to watch Erika for the brief time the family would be at the courthouse.

Little Erika calmly told her mother she did not want to be left with the baby-sitter. There was no crying: no tantrum. Louise Lehmann consoled her daughter and assured her she would not be gone long. When they returned an hour later, the teenage girl's furious parents sat in the Lehmann's parlor tending to their sobbing daughter who had a two-inch gash on her forehead. Blood was everywhere. Pieces of a broken ceramic figurine lay on the floor. Four-year-old Erika sat quietly in a corner of the room playing with her dolls, ignoring the shouts and sobs. The baby-sitter told of Erika picking up the figurine as if to play, then smiling and asking the babysitter to hold her on her lap. While on the teenager's lap, Erika suddenly turned and smashed the figurine against the girl's forehead.

And the boy in England. Erika was eleven and now living in London with her mother. Their daughter was a model student praised by her teachers. There had been no incidents of concern since that day in Oberschopfheim.

Lehmann remembers getting the letter from his wife.

The boy liked Erika. (Louise had written before that the boy had been by the house.) The boy teased Erika one day at school—like eleven-year-old boys do to eleven-year-old girls they have a crush on— and challenged her to a foot race which the boy won. More teasing followed. Erika in turn challenged the boy to a dangerous climbing contest involving scaling a heavy tile drainage pipe to the roof of the three-story school building.

Erika went first and waved to the boy when she reached the roof. The boy was hesitant but he had no choice but to attempt the climb. An audience of classmates had gathered and a girl had already made it to the top—a girl who now leaned over the edge of the roof smiling down at him. He would be branded a coward if he backed away. Halfway up the pipe the boy lost his grip and fell. He was knocked unconscious and suffered a broken collar bone and broken right arm when he attempted to cushion his fall. Panicked classmates fetched the schoolmaster and the nurse. Louise had written that the schoolmaster told her that as they attended the injured lad, Erika descended the pipe (against the orders of the schoolmaster) and stood over the unconscious boy giggling while the other girls wept and the boys worried.

One other incident stood out. The Blair School for Girls in Virginia was not the first American school Erika attended after her father was assigned to Washington. Her first American school was a private girl's school in Maryland not far from Annapolis.

Hazing of newcomers during the first week of classes was a tradition at the school. The administration frowned on such antics but over the years the hazing had become a revered tradition to the point that wealthy alumni objected to attempts by school officials to put an end to the ritual *(We endured hazing and we turned out just fine, let kids be kids)*, so school officials turned their heads.

Like the other new girls, Erika endured the week-long hazing good-naturedly, even allowing herself at one point to be stripped to her underwear, tied to a chair, and covered with flour like the other new-comers. The very white girls were then forced to sing the school song which they better know by heart or be prepared to endure a spanking on the bare bottom with an old and treasured paddle passed down through school generations for that purpose.

Erika sang the school song and should have been finished like the other girls, but one of the senior girls decided it would be appropriate for the German to also sing *Deutschland uber alles* and give them a few Heil Hitlers. This girl took an eyeliner and painted a Hitleresque mous-tache on the tied up Erika. Erika refused to sing any more or Heil Hitler for the crowd's amusement, so the girl pulled down Erika's underpants and paddled her bottom with the revered paddle. Other girls claimed later that Erika took the paddling without a whimper and even turned and smiled at the girl who wielded the board. This irked the senior who increased the vigor of her strokes. When a welt appeared on Erika's bot-tom, good judgment finally prevailed among some of the other girls who insisted the paddling stop.

Two days later the venerated paddle was noticed missing from a glass trophy case. The next day the senior girl who had shown so much special interest in Erika was missing. When the girl failed to return to her dorm that night, the police were called in and a search mounted. The girl was quickly found the next morning tied to a tree deep in the campus wood. She was stripped to her underwear and in shock, her buttocks covered with welts. The paddle, neatly broken in half, lay on the ground beside her. The girl had spent the better part of a day and an entire night tied to the tree. The welts on her buttocks, large clusters of mosquito bites, and dehydration required a hospital stay of two days.

The girl identified Erika, of course, who calmly admitted to school officials that she was responsible. A simple revenge paddling then releasing the girl might have been dismissed as a case of the senior girl getting what was coming to her, but the severity of the retaliation was shocking. Erika had abandoned the gagged and securely bound girl in the wood and gone serenely about her business. The girl's parents pressed charges but Karl Lehmann's diplomatic immunity also protected Erika. After an investigation, and the testimony of other girls who admitted that Erika's hazing had gone too far, the matter was quietly closed when Karl Lehmann agreed to remove his daughter from the school.

The psychiatrist found nothing wrong with Erika. Neither did the next one. Just a case of youthful bad judgment and a bad temper, they concluded. Karl and Louise Lehmann succeeded in rationalizing these strange incidents of aggression. The episodes were so infrequent—years apart—and Erika such a wonderful, loving daughter that her parents gladly accepted the psychiatrists' findings. The psychiatrists helped the parents immensely.

But the incidents were never forgotten despite how hard Karl Lehmann sometimes tried. He worried that if one of these episodes— episodes that seemed to indicate to Karl a loss of control—happened at the wrong place and wrong time on an Abwehr mission it might get his daughter killed.

He now looked at her as she stood beside him taking in the sublime Alpine vista.

"This is the best time for Bavaria, hey Liebchen?"

"It's beautiful, Father," Erika agreed. Her thoughts had transported her away and her answer was perfunctory. She realized this and turned her attention back to her father. She put both arms around his waist and embraced. Lehmann sensed his daughter's distraction and he knew its cause. She had told him about Hitler's comment the previous night— the comment about canceling her mission and keeping her in Germany.

His daughter did not know that he had already discussed that very notion with Hitler. A few days after the opera for the Cianos, Karl Lehmann and Goebbels were in Hitler's Reichstag office discussing plans for handling propaganda concerning the setbacks on the Russian front. After the meeting, Hitler called Lehmann aside and they talked briefly about Erika and her oversees assignments for Abwehr. At that time Karl related to Hitler his reservations about Erika's involvement. Lehmann mentioned nothing about Erika's history with her temper. With her mother dead, only Karl was left to worry about that. Hitler told his old friend that the final decision on Erika's involvement with Abwehr rested with her father.

Lehmann never told his daughter about this conversation with the Führer, nor did he tell her she was now at the Berghof at her father's request. Lehmann called Hitler a week ago requesting the opportunity to talk with his daughter before her training at Quenzsee was completed. Pulling her out of Quenzsee would look improper if done by her father, Lehmann told Hitler, so Hitler had Eva Braun request Erika's presence at the Berghof which Eva was most happy to do.

Karl Lehmann knew he would have to decide soon; his daughter's training for the mission to America was near its end.

"You should be pleased that the Führer is concerned about you, Liebchen," Lehmann assured his daughter, referring to what he knew was now on her mind. "We'll talk about it later."

Since the number of guests was few, lunch was served on the Berghof's garden patio. Open to the air but covered by a gazebo-like copper roof and surrounded by flawlessly manicured shrubs, the patio was a favorite place among Berghof regulars during the warmer months.

Hitler and Eva Braun sat facing Karl Lehmann and Erika around an oval concrete table. Too heavy to move regularly, the table had become a permanent fixture on the patio.

An unexpected guest sat between Karl Lehmann and Eva.

Heinrich Himmler.

The caravan containing the SS chief and his entourage arrived at the steps of the Berghof less than an hour ago. Now, as they waited to be served, Hitler entertained his guests by putting Blondi through her paces. She sat up and begged, rolled over on command, and sang when her master gave the prompt.

SS orderlies poured everyone but Hitler a Württenberg red wine. A few moments later they delivered the meals. The guests were served Saurbraten with *Salzkartoffen* (potatoes boiled in salt water then coated with butter) and cooked carrots.

Besides being a teetotaler, Hitler had been a vegetarian since September 18, 1931. On that day Hitler's favorite niece, Geli Raubal, killed herself in Hitler's Munich apartment. Hitler was inconsolable. At breakfast the morning after Geli's suicide, Hitler could not bring himself to eat a piece of ham on his plate. "It looks like a corpse!" Hitler told Göring that morning. Except for an occasional liver dumpling, Hitler had not eaten a piece of meat since Geli's death.

Hitler's meal was the *Salzkartoffen* and a pasty gruel he ate almost daily. This thick porridge consisted of oats and assorted liquefied legumes. Prepared under the vigilant eye of Dr. Werner Zabel in his Berchtesgaden clinic, Hitler's gruel had been warmed in the Berghof kitchen by Greta Morgen.

Hitler looked over Eva Braun's skimpy helpings and shook his head. He had criticized Eva's dieting for years.

"When I first met you," he teased Eva, "you were pleasingly plump and now you are too thin." Turning to Erika: "What do you think, Tschapperl?"

"Women watch their figures, mein Führer," Erika replied, "only to make our critics envious."

At the table Himmler was somber and his interest in Blondi's performance and the idle table chat repressed.

Erika Lehmann loathed Himmler. Originally, when she first met him before the war, her only reflections of the Reichsführer was that he was a paradox. A paradox that started with his looks. Erika felt Himmler's pinched face and round, pince-nez eyeglasses that clipped to his nose with a spring seemed more suited to a schoolmaster than the ruler of both the dread Gestapo and the SS. Like her father, Himmler had been with Hitler from the beginning. But regardless of the long association between Karl Lehmann and Himmler, her father distrusted the SS chief and Erika was well aware of that distrust. Although Karl Lehmann kept his public relationship with Himmler amiable, privately he considered the SS chief a meddler and worse an opportunist. Her father's misgivings concerning Himmler was an important factor in Erika's original resistance to Himmler's right-hand man Reinhard Heydrich's attempts to recruit her into the SD. Later, Erika would have her own reasons to despise Himmler and his Gestapo henchmen.

On Himmler's part, he was completely unaware of Karl Lehmann's less than sterling notions of him, or of the daughter's hatred. Himmler mistakenly considered Karl Lehmann naive and had given his daughter no thought whatsoever until the surfacing of Heydrich's puzzling file on the girl. The Lehmann's had spent much of the thirties in America ("Out of sight, out of mind," Himmler told Heydrich during a conversation about Karl Lehmann shortly after Lehmann returned to Germany in 1937). He told Heydrich then that Karl Lehmann would be no threat. To the supercilious Himmler, Karl Lehmann was just another crony from the early days that the Führer kept around so he could reminisce.

But always suspicious of conspiracies, Himmler was now at the Berghof. The SS guard shack at the base of the Obersalzberg records the coming and going of Berghof workers and visitors. That information is relayed to 8 Prinz Albrechtstrasse daily. Heinrich Himmler always knew who was at the Berghof. When Himmler was informed that Lehmann's daughter had checked in at the guard shack two days ago (it meant she left Quenzsee in the midst of training which was unheard of), Himmler had his schedule altered. When the Reichsführer arrived and discovered Karl Lehmann was also at the Berghof, his paranoia mounted.

After lunch the Lehmanns decided to take a walk. Erika took her father's arm as they slowly strolled down one of the mountain walk paths. Blondi followed as they disappeared into the softwood forest.

Karl Lehmann spoke first.

"I wonder what brought the distinguished Reichsführer down from Berlin on such short notice? It must be yet another Gestapo screw up."

An agreeing smile was Erika's only reply. She had not given Himmler much thought. Neither spoke for a few moments as father and daughter continued their meander through the pines.

"So, Liebchen," Lehmann again began the conversation, "how is your training coming along at Quenzsee?"

"Fine, Father," Erika replied. "The physical training is still the same as always. The language classes are different, of course, from my last training before going to England, but after a few weeks it all becomes boring. I'll be glad when it's over."

"Tell me again about your mission." His daughter had briefed him about this upcoming assignment after her initial briefing by Canaris, but details are always sketchy at first. Now, after weeks of training, Lehmann knew his daughter would know more.

"I am to establish myself within an inland shipyard that produces a special type of large landing craft. They have not told me the exact location yet, but in briefings I've learned that all of these shipyards are located either on the Mississippi or Ohio Rivers about mid-continent— *Midwest* the Americans call the area."

"Yes," Lehmann interjected. "I am familiar with that part of America. You'll remember when we lived in Washington I once traveled to Chicago on embassy business. I was gone from you and your mother for three weeks."

"I remember," Erika affirmed, then continued. "These are large vessels, not the small amphibious troop carriers that drop a platoon of men on a beach. These ships are the size of many German destroyers. The Americans are supposedly designing them so they can sail across the ocean, ground themselves on a shore, disgorge a vast number of tanks, trucks, troops and supplies directly onto the land, then somehow extract themselves back out into the water. Our navy wants to know how this will be accomplished with such a large vessel, but the mission idea originated with the Wehrmacht High Command. Because of the size of these ships and the fact they will be forced to land on beaches that offer certain characteristics, such as access to roads and bridges for the tanks and other vehicles, the OKW feels they will be able to identify possible landing points of an invasion. With these possible landing points known, our Army needs certain design and draft characteristics of these ships to allow decisions to be made on the best shore defenses."

"That's my assignment, Father. To gather that information."

"What is the scenario for gaining access to this American shipyard?" Lehmann asked.

"The people preparing me at Quenzsee feel it will not be difficult to establish myself on the inside. The Americans are famous for their lax security; they still have not enacted blackouts on much of their eastern coast. As you know, our U-boats are using the lights at night from the American coast to silhouette merchant ships, sinking them just a few miles off shore[2]."

"And," Erika added, "these new inland shipyards are springing up so fast that there is a tremendous worker shortage. It is felt I should have few problems getting a job inside the facility. Some sort of secretarial position like I had in England would be preferred. That kind of job would at least give me some kind of access to paperwork even if it was limited to low-level information. Plus it will enable me to reconnoiter

2   In the first six months of 1942, over five hundred merchant ships were sunk by German U-Boats in or near American coastal waters. The German submarines used the light from the American coast to silhouette their targets at night. Inexplicably, the United States Navy failed to mandate blackouts along the eastern coast until late summer of 1942. This inaction on the part of the U.S. Navy led to a maritime disaster that dwarfed the loss at Pearl Harbor in both tonnage and lives lost.

the facility. If a secretarial position is unobtainable the plan will be to secure another job, perhaps as a welder or riveter. These war jobs are being filled by women just as they are here in Germany."

Karl Lehmann did not like what he was hearing. Making a mental list as his daughter outlined the assignment, he already knew his list on the negative side was much longer than the positive.

Rounding a turn they surprised a small doe that stood frozen a few yards off the narrow path. The deer remained motionless until Blondi barked it away. Father and daughter continued on, stopping when they reached a rocky point jutting out from the path. Here they could watch the Ach River race down a neighboring mountain. Yesterday Erika viewed the river from the teahouse with Eva Braun. Today the Ach was just as impatient, refusing to rest until it reached the Danube.

Karl Lehmann finally responded to his daughter's briefing. "It is a dangerous mission, Liebchen," he warned. "After a U-boat drops you on some God-forsaken beach in the middle of the night, you will be forced to travel over a thousand kilometers behind enemy lines before you even reach your specified destination. Even worse is the possibility of being forced to cover the same distance under fugitive conditions if something happens and you are discovered. I had dealings with the FBI when I was in Washington. Regardless of what Abwehr tells you about the lax security of the Americans, I found the FBI to be quite capable. When the FBI takes to somebody's trail they are like hellhounds and not easily eluded."

"My darling," Erika put her arms around her father's waist. "I know you worry about me. I know it must be hard for you when I am away. I miss you too, you know." She rose on her tip-toes and kissed his cheek.

"Sometimes I have reservations myself," she confided. "When I see men like Himmler with such important positions…"

She paused in mid-sentence knowing her father could finish the statement himself. Karl Lehmann and his daughter silently embraced for a long moment.

"Yes, I know, Liebchen. I sometimes wonder what would happen to Germany if something was to happen to the Führer before this war is won. But we must have faith. Faith in Germany and faith in the Führer. He has brought us up from ruin."

Karl Lehmann brought the conversation back to its original focus.

"You know you do not have to accept this mission," Lehmann reminded his daughter. "I would prefer your work with Abwehr be limited to the occupied or neutral countries. This is something we need to talk of further."

His daughter's first assignment in Lisbon carried with it much less danger for Erika and much less worry for her father. Portugal was a neutral country. If a cover is blown and an agent identified in a neutral country, it was a simple matter of that agent's embassy spiriting the agent out of the country. Then, of course, the ambassador would deny everything. Behind enemy lines there was no such safety net. No embassy to offer sanctuary. A firing squad or hangman's rope ended behind-the-lines missions for many agents on both sides.

"Yes, of course, Father," Erika responded on reflex. They took a last look at the angry Ach before turning to retrace their steps back to the chalet.

✝   ✝   ✝

Heinrich Himmler rose when Adolf Hitler entered the study twenty minutes late—on time for the Führer. Hitler sat down in the chair he slept in the previous night. Hitler knew that Himmler's sudden appearance on the Berghof doorstep could indicate something important had surfaced, or, just as likely with the fussbudget Himmler, he might have come to complain that the toilet paper in his headquarters was too abrasive.

"Sit down, Heinrich." In private, Hitler usually referred to the men in his inner circle by their first names. Himmler took the chair directly opposite Hitler. As soon as the SS chief sat down Hitler cut to the chase. "What is it we need to discuss today?"

Himmler began. "After Obersgruppenführer Heydrich's assassination six weeks ago, for obvious security reasons I ordered his files transferred from Prague to Berlin. I then ordered Müller to cross-check Heydrich's files with the Gestapo files. Because of the bulk of these files, this has been a lengthy process which is still ongoing."

Himmler paused for a second to see if Hitler had any questions. Apparently not so he proceeded.

"Most of the files mirror our Gestapo files. So far only one important exception had been found. This exception was an Abwehr file that I discovered personally." Himmler again paused, this time to allow his boast time to be fully noted. Hitler remained silent.

"After investigating this file, mein Führer, evidence has surfaced that proves a direct conspiracy between Heydrich and Abwehr. A conspiracy that led to a direct and intentional circumvention of a legitimate Gestapo investigation, an investigation, I might add, conducted at the behest of our embassy in Lisbon. To make the matter even more serious, this interference was done under false pretenses and covered up on the orders of Heydrich himself."

Hitler was now looking directly at Himmler whereas before his eyes pointed in the general direction of the painting of Frederick the Great. Himmler proceeded to tell Hitler about the thick file on the Abwehr agent (without naming Erika), then he gave Hitler an abbreviated version of Ryker's Lisbon story: the maid's interrogation, the phony OKW envoy, and the bizarre phone call from Heydrich ordering the maid's release. Himmler told Hitler about the phony envoy's attack on the Gestapo interrogators and the eventual cover up of the entire affair by Heydrich.

"This conspiracy perhaps might have never been uncovered," Himmler concluded, "if not for the unusual dossier discovered among

Heydrich's files. This dossier was on the Abwehr agent who posed as the false OKW envoy in Lisbon—Karl Lehmann's daughter."

Himmler paused for effect, then handed Heydrich's thick dossier on Erika Lehmann to Hitler.

✠   ✠   ✠

That evening Hitler was not at dinner. Karl Lehmann sat at the head of the table in the small dining room (the Berghof had a much larger dining area for sizable parties). Erika sat at her father's right, Eva Braun to his left. While they ate, outside they heard Heinrich Himmler's entourage slamming car doors and starting engines. Berlin beckoned.

Eva bragged on a chicken in a wine sauce entree so Erika ordered it with her. Herr Lehmann ordered *Rindsrouladen* (a stuffed beef roll), his favorite dish. Everyone was served a delicious bean soup and *Gurkensalat* (cucumber salad). Dessert was *Kirschtorte,* a cherry cake warm from Greta Morgen's oven. The *Kirschtorte* was delivered to the table by the teenage girl who fainted in the study the night before.

During dinner, Eva talked of plans for a trip to Munich and the theater for her and Erika. Erika reminded Eva that the length of her stay at the Berghof was unknown but, "If I am here, Eva, it will be lovely." After dinner, the trio adjourned to the veranda for coffee and brandy.

Erika loved star gazing on a clear night. The Alpine stars overhead seemed several times larger than city stars—like a different set. *They switch the stars when you get to the mountains, Liebchen,* her father use to tell her when she was little. In the mountains it seemed the bright white stars hung closer to the ground, as if suspended by strings from a black ceiling.

Herr Lehmann lit a cigar. The orange glow at the end pulsated bright as he pumped breath through it. Erika knew her father agonized about her dangerous work, but a conclusion to their afternoon talk would have to wait. A cool mountain breeze persuaded Eva Braun to grab a blanket and curl up beside Erika on a small divan.

The brandy was warm. The chat idle. Both were pleasant, and both interrupted when Otto Günsche appeared on the veranda.

"Herr Lehmann," Günsche clicked his heels and stood rigid. "The Führer has requested your presence, and the presence of Fräulein Lehmann, in the study immediately."

"Very well, Major," Karl Lehmann accepted. Günsche clicked, turned, departed.

✠　　　　　　✠　　　　　　✠

Hitler had spent a few hours mulling Himmler's latest conspiracy theory. Himmler came to him often with these anxieties. Sometimes the conspiracies turned out to be simply figments of Himmler's paranoid mind. Other times the tales demanded action.

In the past, Hitler had been forced to have old comrades arrested and even executed for conspiracies (whether real or imagined) and it left him despondent for days or even weeks depending on how close the relationship. Ernst Röhm, an old friend from the early days and Hitler's head of the Stormtroopers, forced Hitler's hand in 1934. Röhm's challenge to Hitler's power ended when Hitler purged the SA leadership, liquidating Röhm and several other old friends. The *Night of the Long Knives* weighed on Hitler for months.

He now stood with his back to Karl and Erika Lehmann. Hitler had been in the study when the Lehmanns arrived, very unusual for Adolf Hitler who usually forced people to wait on him, sometimes for hours. At Hitler's Reichstag office in Berlin sometimes the time period was not hours but days. It was not uncommon for some lower-level official with an appointment on Monday to be forced to wait until Thursday to see Hitler, the official reporting back each morning to wait all day.

The Lehmanns had no knowledge of Himmler's concerns nor of his conversation with Hitler earlier that afternoon. When summoned by Günsche, they assumed Hitler wanted to talk about Erika's latest assignment.

Father and daughter sat together on a sofa. Hitler stood gazing out a window with his hands clasped behind his back. He remained that way as he began speaking.

"Tell me what you thought of Heydrich, Karl."

It was not the subject Karl Lehmann had prepared himself to discuss, but Hitler was famous for getting sidetracked or changing the flow of a conversation without transitions.

"Basically I knew him only socially, mein Führer," Lehmann said. "He tried to convince my daughter to join the SD, and once he spoke with me on that subject at a dinner function we both happened to attend. That was before the war. Besides that conversation, my only exchanges with the man were cordial greetings if we happened to see each other at an official function. I last saw him at the opera you attended for the Cianos in March."

Hitler's mind was razor sharp when the subject was important enough to warrant his attention. The Führer of Germany had dealt often with conspiracies. The man with the hypnotic blue eyes who stood gazing out the window was perhaps better skilled than anyone in the world in this situation.

Hitler was probing.

"Ah, yes," Hitler said coyly. "I remember he did want your daughter in the SD. He came to me complaining when she decided to enter Abwehr training instead. Heydrich asked me to intervene. I think I spoke with you about it at that time."

"Yes, mein Führer," Lehmann verified. "You called me in and asked me about my wishes on the matter. By then my daughter's mind was made up to serve so I informed you I preferred military intelligence over the SD. You were gracious enough to honor my wishes."

Hitler turned and looked at Erika.

"And your thoughts on Heydrich, Tschapperl?"

"I met the Obergruppenführer when I worked at the Seehaus, mein Führer," Erika recalled for Hitler. "Socially, he asked me to dine with him on a few occasions. I knew Obergruppenführer Heydrich was married and our personal relationship went no further then these occasional dinners where he tried to convince me to join his SD. After discussing these matters with my father, I decided to join Abwehr instead."

Hitler did not have to ask why. The astute Hitler had always sensed a slight tension between Karl Lehmann and Heinrich Himmler, and he knew Lehmann would not want his daughter under Himmler's thumb.

"I was sorry when I heard of Herr Heydrich's assassination, mein Führer," Erika continued. "On one occasion the Obergruppenführer came to my aid."

Erika knew she would have to explain.

"In Lisbon, on my first assignment for Abwehr, a situation arose where I was forced to call on the Obergruppenführer to intercede in a matter with the Gestapo." Erika paused.

"Go on, Tschapperl," Hitler ordered. He knew this was Himmler's Lisbon story. Hitler knew the Lehmann's knew nothing about his earlier conversation with Himmler, or even that Himmler knew about the Lisbon affair at all. Heydrich had covered it up. Hitler was pleased the girl was volunteering the information.

Erika related a story with many of the same details that Himmler covered that afternoon: the German diplomat's wife and her lost necklace, the Gestapo interrogation of the innocent maid, Erika's attempt to secure the maid's release by posing as an envoy from the High Command.

"I was on assignment at the time and I could not use my real name," Erika explained. "When my attempt to bluff the Gestapo into releasing the girl failed, I called Obergruppenführer Heydrich in Berlin. I explained the situation to him and he agreed to contact the Gestapo office in Lisbon and order the girl's release."

"What exactly did you tell Heydrich, Tschapperl," Hitler asked. "That you believed the girl to be innocent of stealing the necklace?"

"No, mein Führer. I did not know if the girl was innocent or not and her innocence or guilt had little to do with the situation. The girl's father worked as a butler in the American embassy that I infiltrated. I got her father that job in fact. I met the maid during the course of my business for Abwehr. The information I gathered I delivered to the chargé d'affaires whose wife lost the necklace. He was my embassy contact and the person in charge of sending any information I gathered back to Germany via diplomatic courier. I knew the German embassy would be under surveillance. It was safer to deliver the information to the chargé d'affaires residence. That's where I met the maid. The girl and I were on friendly terms. One day she informed me her father had just lost his job as a butler for some rich British financier living in Lisbon. So I used my influence with the people at the American embassy to win the maid's father a job."

"The father," Erika went on, "had worked at the American embassy for only a short time when he came to me extremely distraught. He babbled in a frenzy about his daughter being taken to Gestapo headquarters."

"Why did he come to you?" Hitler asked. "Surely this man did not know you were a German agent."

"No, he did not know," Erika vouched. "He and his daughter knew me only by my cover as an American student. The trips I had made to the German chargé d'affaires residence, where I met the daughter, were beyond suspicion because on two occasions the Americans themselves sent me there as a courier. Remember, mein Führer, this was 1940 and we were not at war with the Americans yet. In fact, just a week before this happened, the German ambassador and members of his staff attended a dinner party at the American embassy. The father came to me simply because I knew his daughter, and he hoped I might be able to do something."

Hitler nodded for Erika to continue.

"I saw an opportunity here. I told the father I would see what I could do, then I went about getting the girl released. It took the phone call to Obergruppenführer Heydrich before that was accomplished."

Hitler: "What was this *opportunity* you speak of?"

"A few weeks after I obtained his daughter's release from the Gestapo, I convinced the father, who as a butler had access to the American ambassador's private quarters, to procure the keys and combination to the embassy safe. I knew where these were kept but I had no access to the locked and guarded quarters. With the keys and combination the girl's father obtained for me, I obtained photographs of several sensitive documents which I sent back to Germany."

Erika concluded: "It matters little the reasons why the butler decided to help me. Whether he was simply grateful that I secured his daughter's release, perhaps saving her life, or if he thought he better cooperate or the event might repeat itself, I don't know. But it all worked out to the benefit of Germany. Instead of a meaningless interrogation of an innocent peasant girl over a ridiculous necklace, an exercise that attained nothing, in the end Germany acquired useful information from the Americans."

Hitler had remained standing throughout the conversation. He now sat down in his familiar chair. He had two more questions.

"Was this girl—the maid—a Jew?"

"No, mein Führer," Erika assured.

"One more thing, Tschapperl. You never answered my question about Heydrich," Hitler stated calmly. "This matter with the maid and the necklace was ridiculous and inconsequential but still a Gestapo interrogation done at the behest of the German embassy. Heydrich's involvement in this matter was highly irregular, he knew this or he would not have bothered to cover it up. What exactly did you tell Heydrich on the phone to induce him to come to your aid so quickly?"

Erika hoped to avoid the question because she knew the answer would sound ridiculous, but she had told the truth about everything so far and felt anything but the truth to Hitler would be identified a lie immediately.

"I told him I would go to dinner with him when I returned."

The blue eyes stared at Erika for a long moment. Then Hitler realized Himmler's dark conspiracy did not exist. The girl told the truth. Lies would have been more complex and more feasible. It was obvious from Heydrich's file on the girl that Heydrich was enamored with her and it clouded his judgement. Hitler was relieved. He sincerely liked Karl Lehmann and his daughter.

Hitler was satisfied with her story except for one detail that seemed not to fit. Himmler complained that Erika Lehmann attacked the Lisbon Gestapo agents when she returned to take custody of the maid. The Lisbon office had already received Heydrich's orders to release the maid and the Gestapo agents would never dare disregard such orders from the very top. If Erika sought the girl's release simply for professional reasons as she stated, why such an unnecessary attack?

Hitler had one more test.

"So when you returned to get the girl," Hitler sounded casual, "the Gestapo people had received the phone call from Heydrich and they released her to you without further incident I'm sure."

"Yes, mein Führer," Erika said. "That is they had received the orders from the Obergruppenführer as you stated, but when I followed a secretary to the room where the girl was being held the interrogation was still proceeding."

Erika paused hoping enough was said. Hitler waited for more.

"The girl was bleeding from being beaten and she had just been raped by one of the interrogators. I must admit my emotions entered in. I put an end to the interrogation myself."

Hitler needed no elaboration. Himmler told him that she gave the male agent a severe concussion and the female agent a broken nose and three broken ribs. Hitler had heard enough.

"A strange story, Tschapperl," Hitler commented. "I must commend you on your cleverness for turning a trivial affair into profit for your Fatherland, and I will speak to the Reichsführer about Gestapo interrogation methods such as liberties taken with young women by male interrogators. But for your sake I worry about your impetuous attack on our Gestapo people. We must remember that severe and unpleasant things happen in war. You must make yourself hard, Tschapperl. You must bury your emotions."

"Yes, mein Führer."

Karl Lehmann sat rigidly and felt apprehensive during his daughter's story. He remembered discussing the Lisbon assignment with his daughter after she returned home. She told him something about getting a butler at the American embassy to acquire a safe combination for her, but she gave no details and said nothing to indicate there had been any problems with the Gestapo or that she had enlisted the aid of Reinhard Heydrich. So his fatherly curiosity and questions at the time had been directed more to other areas such as the danger his daughter was in when she burglarized the American ambassador's safe. His daughter never lied to him, of that he was confident, but she exasperated him with her tendency to downplay and offer no information about her Abwehr activities unless asked specific questions.

Hitler now turned and addressed his old friend as if Erika was no longer present.

"Karl, your daughter is a special treasure to the Fatherland and a credit to the Aryan race. I wish all my generals had her devotion and resourcefulness…and her courage. But we all have an Achilles heel. Speak to your daughter about her sentiment. That is her weakness. We must not let it destroy her."

Suddenly Hitler paused and his eyelids drooped. For a moment it seemed he was in the process of dropping off to sleep. Just as suddenly the eyelids reopened and the blue eyes ignited.

"Karl, after talking to your daughter, I feel we must also guard our sentiments. I know how you feel old friend, but the assignment your daughter is training for is a critical one. The future of your Fatherland could hang in the balance. I think perhaps your daughter is the person who can accomplish it."

The fire again left Hitler's eyes and without speaking he rose from his chair, walked out of the room, and closed the door behind him.

✠   ✠   ✠

CHAPTER 12

Since it is difficult to join them together, it is safer to be feared than to be loved when one of the two must be lacking.

—Niccolo Machiavelli, 1514

Brandenburg, Germany

July 1942

The man lay on his stomach, his arm twisted painfully behind his back. A stiletto lay beside him on the mat. An instructor wearing a black eye patch knelt beside him and held the man's arm in the awkward position. Wehrmacht Sergeant Peter Hotzel had just demonstrated the proper way to disarm and neutralize an assault by a knife-welding attacker.

Hotzel was an expert at hand-to-hand combat and, for the past year, had been assigned to Quenzsee as an instructor. Hotzel was at Quenzsee thanks to a homemade grenade tossed in the general direction of his Wehrmacht platoon by a sixty-year-old Greek farmer during the German invasion of the man's country in April of 1941. The explosion removed Hotzel's right eye and ended his expedition to Greece.

It was a freak accident.

The old farmer had several bullet holes in him before the homemade bomb hit the ground, and the weak explosion should have caused no damage. Hotzel was not even the closest German soldier to the explosion which fired the jagged piece of metal into Hotzel's eyeball.

Peter Hotzel released the man on the mat and looked around at the seven men and lone woman who stood watching. Hotzel told the group to pair up with one partner acting as the attacker. Several pairs of men practiced, one pair at a time, under the watchful eye of the sergeant. Each agent drilled against two separate attacks. The first attack was from an overhead position stabbing downward; during the second attack the knife was to be held low and swung upward.

Finally it was time for the woman. Hotzel was familiar with her, having trained her soon after he arrived at Quenzsee a year ago. He had not seen her since then because she had been on assignment. Hotzel knew this because of the second dagger on her Quenzsee *Bluse.* Last year there was only one dagger.

The woman, *Lorelei,* worked out with the men during the hand-to-hand combat sessions. It had been decided that training Lorelei in hand-to-hand with other women agents was counterproductive. Lorelei made such short work of the other females the Quenzsee tutors deemed the training of no benefit to Lorelei and detrimental to the morale of the other women. There was no other solution. She would drill with the men.

Lorelei was strong. Although of only average height and weight for a young woman Lorelei was stronger than most women larger and heavier than she. But her strength was not the reason she trained with men. Nature could not be denied. Men were bigger, heavier, and more powerful. The traits that made Lorelei such a skilled combatant were quickness, agility, and flexibility. These gifts allowed Lorelei to hold her own with some of the male Quenzsee agents and even defeat many average men in real life situations, especially if she got the jump on them.

When it was Lorelei's turn, she took her place on the mat and faced the first attacker. The man took a step toward her and slashed the knife downward. Lorelei sidestepped the knife, grabbed the man's wrist, and, using his weight and forward motion against him, tripped him with her leg and hip and flipped him to the mat. When he was on his back, Lorelei placed her foot on the man's chest and twisted the weapon from his hand using her body for leverage.

"Next attack," Hotzel barked.

Lorelei released the first attacker who jumped up and trotted off the mat. She picked up the knife and handed it to the second designated attacker. He was a new trainee Hotzel had not seen before today. The man looked at Lorelei, then turned and flashed a smirk at the other men who laughed. Hotzel looked at Lorelei and saw her countenance change. *Oh, shit!* thought Hotzel. *Here we go.*

When Hotzel gave the signal the man brandished the knife and stepped forward. Instead of first blocking the slash of the knife like Hotzel had demonstrated, Lorelei immediately dropped to the mat and, on her back, delivered a hard kick to the attacker's scrotum. The blow doubled the man over. With the attacker's head lowered, Lorelei grabbed the knife hand in both of her hands, and with an acrobatic move flipped over and scissored the man's head between her thighs. The weight of her body toppled the off-balance man face first to the mat. She released the man's head from between her legs and quickly spun around and positioned herself on top of the attacker. She reached around the man's face, placed a finger on each eye, and applied pressure. The man growled, released the knife, and tried ripping her hands away from his face. Lorelei increased the pressure on the man's eyes and bit down hard on his ear. He bellowed loudly, cursed, reached back and grabbed a handful of her hair and pulled. She bit down harder on the ear. Several drops of blood dribbled to the mat.

Hotzel stepped in and ordered the two to release each other immediately.

When the two uncoupled, the man jumped to his feet and swore at the girl, calling her a whore and a pig. Lorelei spit in the man's face, the spittle tinged pink from the man's blood. Enraged he made a menacing move forward. Lorelei retreated and gathered herself for the attack, but Hotzel stepped in and took the man to the mat. Hotzel called an end to the session and ordered Lorelei out of the room while he held the man down. Before she left, Lorelei walked over to the still cursing man, kneeled down and stroked him seductively under his chin. The top of his left ear was purple and already ballooning. Hotzel felt the man fight even harder to get up. Lorelei laughed in the constrained man's face. Hotzel, still holding the infuriated man down, cursed and ordered her once more to leave. She walked out of the room smiling back at the man on the mat.

It was Erika's last day of training. Tomorrow morning she would check out of Quenzsee for a three-day furlough then report to Wilhelm Canaris for her final briefing and instructions.

✠   ✠   ✠

Lisbon—July 1942

Frieda Gretler sat behind the desk in her office writing out yet another interrogation report. Unlike the interrogations which she enjoyed, Gretler hated writing the reports which she found tedious, but she did it without complaint because Gretler was now the Lisbon Gestapo field office's lead interrogator. She was proud of her recent promotion. It was a job Gretler had worked hard to get.

The report detailed the recent questioning of a Spanish fisherman who worked the waters off the southern Portuguese coast. The fisherman was suspected of being a cog in the O'Leary Line—one of the secret escape routes the French Resistance used to smuggle fugitive members of the Resistance or downed Allied airmen out of German occupied Europe. Evidence suggested this Spanish fisherman used his fishing trawler to help transport some of these fugitives from Gibraltar to Lisbon where they could gain sanctuary in the British or American embassies and eventual safe passage to England.

Gretler had to admit the Spaniard was a tough nut to crack. She had flogged his penis until it bled. Bled so much in fact she had to suspend the questioning and get the man treatment for fear he would bleed to death before revealing the names of his Resistance associates. But the Spaniard eventually gave Gretler what she wanted; Gretler's blow torch to the man's scrotum did the trick. Now they had names and more arrests could be made. All this was meticulously detailed in her report to 8 Prinz Albrechtstrasse.

A secretary opened the door and interrupted Gretler's train of thought.

"Frau Gretler," the secretary said. "There is a Herr Ryker in the outer office to see you."

Ryker. Gretler recognized the name. He was the gruesome man who showed up in Lisbon a couple of weeks ago and questioned her about that bizarre, two-year-old affair with that embassy maid *and the blond bitch who broke my ribs and nose. What I wouldn't give to interrogate that blond bitch.* Gretler had fantasized about the scenario.

What does Ryker want now? Gretler wondered. She remembered feeling apprehensive and intimidated in Ryker's presence when she first met him, and Frieda Gretler was not one to be easily intimidated. Gretler looked at the secretary.

"Show him in."

The secretary disappeared and a moment later Axel Ryker entered the room.

"Ah, Herr Ryker," Gretler forced out a pleasantry and rose from her chair. "It is good to see you again."

Ryker reached inside his jacket, pulled out his Mauser, pointed it at Frieda Gretler's left eye, and blew her brains out on to the wall behind her desk.

"The pleasure is all mine, Frau Gretler."

✠   ✠   ✠

8 Prinz Albrechtstrasse, Berlin

Ursula Ziegler, Heinrich Himmler's secretary, walked on egg shells. It started with the Führer's phone call to her boss the day after Himmler returned from Berchtesgaden.

Since that phone call the Reichsführer had been impossible to live with: the ranting and raving unchecked. Himmler's wrath had been felt by not only Frau Ziegler but by any underling who happened to cross the Reichsführer's path. Frau Ziegler did not know the specifics of the Führer's phone call, but it was quite evident the discourse was not to Himmler's liking. Frau Ziegler knew someone would eventually pay dearly.

Ziegler put it off as long as possible but now it had to be done. She did not look forward to delivering the daily reports but knew if she did not it would give Himmler even more reason to tirade.

Ursula Ziegler knocked on Himmler's door and opened it slowly.

"What is it?" the voice impatient.

"The daily reports, Herr Reichsführer," Ziegler said gingerly.

Himmler did not reply. His chair was turned and he sat staring out the window, deep in thought. It was the same brooding pose Frau Ziegler had seen Himmler assume several times since the Führer's phone call.

"The reports are on your desk, sir." No acknowledgment came and Ziegler did not wait. Silence was better than a loud, bitter diatribe. She turned and made a hasty retreat back to her outer office.

The mid-day traffic on Prinz Albrechtstrasse flowed past Himmler's fifth floor window like blood coursing through a vein. Himmler saw but did not watch.

The phone call from Hitler stupefied Heinrich Himmler. Himmler had traveled to Berchtesgaden with undeniable evidence of a conspiracy to circumvent Gestapo authority. Making matters worse, Reinhard Heydrich was behind the conspiracy, a man entrusted to safeguard

against just such criminal acts, *along with one of Wilhelm Canaris'*
embassy sluts. It made no difference to Heinrich Himmler that the
Führer related some outlandish tale about the girl using the situation to
the Reich's advantage. Himmler saw an analogy between this case and
the case of the good Jew. People had come to Himmler and said, *Oh,*
let's not get rid of this Jew, he is a good Jew! A Jew is a Jew, just like a crime
is a crime, like in this case.

Fear fueled the elaborate Gestapo machine. Without this fuel the
machine sputtered and died. It was a healthy necessity from enemies
and yes, even required from important people within the Reich. Fear of
the Gestapo was the pesticide that eliminated more than one conspiracy
before the vine could be damaged. This fear insured compliance with
Party manifesto from both strong and weak. Any actions—by anyone—
that displayed a lack of this fear weakened the Gestapo's effectiveness
and should be dealt with harshly. The Führer himself had said as much
in the past. In Himmler's mind, the Führer's judgment was clouded by
his misplaced fondness for an old comrade. Karl Lehmann took advantage of that fondness. It was up to Himmler to protect the Führer from
himself and protect the integrity of the Gestapo.

There could be only one finale to this conspiracy. Reinhard Heydrich
had already paid for his sin courtesy of the Czech resistance, but there
remained one conspirator. But this was a very sensitive situation and
highly political. Heinrich Himmler was many things but certainly no
fool. He would not openly defy the Führer's wishes. Because of Karl
Lehmann's relationship to Hitler, the daughter was untouchable on
German soil: beyond detainment or prosecution. But no one could be
allowed to interfere with the Gestapo, and *she* had done it at least
twice—in Lisbon and on the U-boat dock in Brest.

Heinrich Himmler could not suffer himself or his Gestapo to be
made to look foolish, so there was one certainty in his mind. Karl
Lehmann's daughter must join Heydrich.

Somehow the girl must die.

Himmler wheeled his chair around. He thumbed through the daily reports Ursula Ziegler had delivered. Again there was something from Stangl at Sobibor. *More whining,* Himmler concluded and moved Stangl's business to the bottom of the stack. Next was the report from the SS guard huts at the Obersalzberg containing the names of Berghof guests. *What the hell is Göring doing there besides feeding his fat face? Probably showing the Führer his latest uniform.* Göring was of little interest so Himmler also buried the Berghof report for the moment. Next was a memorandum from Axel Ryker. Himmler threw the remaining paperwork on the desk and opened the envelope containing the note.

Rome and Lisbon orders carried out.

The memo told Himmler that Hans Schwartz and Frieda Gretler, the Gestapo agents pictured in the negatives hidden in Heydrich's dossier on Karl Lehmann's daughter, were dead.

It was the first step.

✠   ✠   ✠

CHAPTER 13

The new moon is black as ink
off Hatteras the tankers sink
While sadly Roosevelt counts the score
some fifty thousand tons—by Mohr.[3]

The Atlantic Ocean

Tuesday, August 18, 1942

At first light of dawn a wave crashed over the bow of U-boat 260. Behind her stern the sun finally ignited but remained hidden under the ledge of the eastern horizon. In the western sky ahead only Deneb and the brightest star of Pegasus lingered, stranded alone when stars less bold scurried at the first sign of the new day. The sky suffered no cloud and was the same deep-violet color of the water it canopied. Standing atop U-260's conning tower, Kapitänleutnant Eric Bauer cupped his hands to shield a match from the stiff breeze. He lit a cigarette. Flanking Bauer stood two lookouts, their faces obscured by binoculars held tight to their eyes. Bauer tossed the spent match over the side.

---

3   During a single voyage in March, 1942, U-124, captained by Johann Mohr, sank eight oil tankers off the American coast. As U-124 returned home across the Atlantic, Mohr radioed this poem to Dönitz.

The captain was not happy. His current orders to transport yet another German agent to America were the reason.

Having been assigned a similar mission earlier this summer, Bauer was beginning to fear the High Command's intentions were to relegate him to these tasks permanently—a sort of cross-Atlantic ferryboat captain.[4]

In June, Bauer and his crew transported a group of eight saboteurs to New York, landing them on a secluded Long Island beach in the middle of the night. This time 260's cargo was a lone woman—a girl. When Bauer's orders came through three weeks ago, the Naval officer who briefed him mentioned only that the mission concerned delivering an Abwehr agent to one of four unspecified locations on the coast of the United States. Naturally Bauer assumed the agent to be male. Two weeks ago, when the young Fräulein boarded his submarine at the U-boat pens at Lorient, Bauer knew then that what he had suspected for quite some time was true: someone in Berlin was *verrückt*—crazy. But the captain's evaluation concerning the mental stability of the powers-that-be back in Germany was not based solely on the fact the Abwehr agent below deck was female. That was just added proof.

There were other misgivings.

Bauer was of the old school. He fought in the First War, earning the Navy's Cross of Bismarck for heroic service. Bauer rose through the ranks the hard way, earning promotions with deeds, and not by writing essays on naval strategy like the young officers who now served under him on 260.

---

4   Before dawn, in the early morning hours of June 12, 1942, a German U-boat delivered eight Abwehr saboteurs to a secluded beach on Long Island, New York. Code named *Operation Pastorius* by Abwehr, the mission included sabotaging certain aluminum works plants in the Tennessee Valley. Apparently losing his nerve, one of the saboteurs turned himself over to the FBI. By the end of the month the remaining Abwehr agents were apprehended. All were tried and later hanged with the exception of the informant who received a prison term. After eventually gaining his release years after the war, the man returned to Germany.

Eric Bauer was a warrior.

That's where the real rub lay. These ferrying missions included orders to avoid engagement with the enemy at all costs. Because of this girl on board, Bauer and his crew could not do what they were trained to do, and what their ship was built for—sink enemy ships. Yesterday an unescorted American tanker appeared in the crosshairs of 260's periscope. Bauer could tell the tanker was pregnant with oil from the ship's low ride in the water. It was a fat turkey Bauer had to let pass. Because of this girl on board that fuel would now reach England.

But the same pride, honor, and sense of duty to country that enables men like Eric Bauer to avoid madness when they see the horrific results of war, also compels them to remain silent and complete the tasks assigned to them, however distasteful. The men of U-260 knew nothing of their captain's disdain of spies, saboteurs, and missions that involved him with them.

A horn sounded next to Bauer. He opened a watertight box mounted just under the lip of the conning tower and extracted a telephone-type receiver. It was the navigator below reporting the ship's current latitude and longitude. Bauer had ordered this information to be relayed to him every fifteen minutes. The American coast was not far. When he finished listening to the navigator's report, Bauer returned the receiver to the box and snapped the lid shut.

So here was another of Wilhelm Canaris' spies, Bauer remembered thinking when he first met the girl on the dock in France. The captain of U-260 had met Canaris before the war. Bauer was stationed at Swinemünde when the Admiral toured the U-boat shipyard there. One evening Bauer and several other U-boat captains dined with Canaris in the base officers' club. Like Bauer, Canaris was an old sailor experienced in war. The commander of U-260 respected that, but wars, Bauer felt, should be fought by men in uniform, not by civilians like the men he had dumped on the Long Island beach. And especially not by young girls.

However, Bauer begrudgingly admitted that the Fräulein now below deck had accepted the severe conditions aboard a U-boat without complaint. She had not asked for anything. This was surprising, in Bauer's opinion, for a woman enduring the harsh conditions of life aboard a submarine. Since they left France two weeks ago, the girl had made no demands for the sake of her own comfort. And this was a long voyage; it normally took fifteen to seventeen days for a U-boat to cross the Atlantic, depending on how much time had to be spent submerged.

The life of a *Unterseebootman:* Bauer knew the life was not for the pampered.

Crewman joked that the weather inside a U-boat was always the same: it was always raining. A continual mist permeated the ship's interior, fogging gauges and condensing on pipes. This condensation created a constant dripping from overhead.

The reek of diesel fuel hung ever present within the boat and lingered in the nostrils for days after returning to port.

Bathing was a luxury not afforded crewmen aboard *Unterseeboote.* Fresh water could not be spared. Like the men, the girl washed herself with seawater when the opportunity arose, and she had used the cramped privy and not complained if a crewman entered unexpectedly.

Like most of the crew she slept in a hammock; an extra one had been installed for her near the galley. The twenty-four-hour-a-day banging of pots, shouting, and the ribald vocabulary of the galley mates had failed to perturb her, not perceivably at least. A blanket suspended in front of the hammock afforded the only privacy from the young male crewmen, many of whom made no effort to hide their gawking when the girl walked past. But the dank air, cramped quarters, soggy bread, and lack of privacy had failed to elicit the customary grumbling from the girl that even most veteran submariners felt was their right.

She was a strange one, Bauer thought. Very quiet. Most of her time was spent reading, or perusing road maps of the United States. Oh, she had been polite enough to the crew, but she had remained mostly to herself during the voyage, which was fine with Bauer. No sense asking for trouble.

On the third day out of Lorient, Bauer invited the girl to dine with him, a tradition for a ship's captain with a stranger on board and Eric Bauer valued tradition. During the meal, taken in Bauer's cramped quarters, only generalities and small talk were exchanged. Bauer never asked her name and she never offered it.

But all things considered, this voyage had been a smooth one. Except for the mandated twice-a-day underwater runs for training purposes, U-260 had been forced to submerge only four times: once because of weather, mid-ocean winds generated six-meter-high seas one evening; twice to avoid Allied reconnaissance planes; and yesterday when the American oil freighter appeared on the horizon. Besides that, only the half-day delay when the refueling ship was late for rendezvous had slowed 260's race across the Atlantic. Since most of the voyage had been spent on the surface, 260 made good time. The powerful diesel engines used when on the surface propelled the ship much faster than the battery-powered electric engines that had to be used when submerged. Bauer estimated 260 should reach her destination sometime that evening, fifteen days after leaving the Bay of Biscay, and the sooner the better as far as Bauer was concerned. At least on the return trip to France the no-engage orders were rescinded. Heading back they could do what they were trained to do—fight the enemy.

With the advent of dawn, and the American mainland less than a hundred nautical miles to the west, Bauer knew much of 260's remaining voyage to the American coast must be spent underwater. Bauer threw the cigarette butt overboard. He ordered the lookouts below, took a last, deep breath of fresh ocean air, then called below and gave the order to submerge.

✠   ✠   ✠

Two miles off the North Carolina coast, U-260 rested quietly in the sand one hundred and thirty feet below the surface of the Atlantic Ocean. Due west was the second of four dropoff locations Eric Bauer had to choose from. He would have preferred the first location, "Point A," just south of the Cape Hatteras lighthouse. The waters there were famous for their treachery and therefore perfect for dropping an agent on shore. Because of the dangerous waters, the presence of other ships would be minimal. But through 260's periscope earlier that evening, Bauer spotted a disconcerting amount of shore activity and he was forced to navigate his ship farther down the coast. Like a tired leviathan, 260 now slept on the ocean floor just north of Cape Fear. For Eric Bauer, this was the worst part of these covert missions. Waiting. It mattered little if the reason for that waiting was to extract someone from shore, or drop off. Hours spent sitting on the bottom off some coast were interminable.

The captain sat in the sub's cramped control room. In the middle of the room, a periscope ran from floor to ceiling, the centerpiece of a compartment decorated with gauges, valves, and levers. As always, water from the dank air condensed on overhead piping and plopped to the floor, the endless dripping made even more vexing with the stillness of sitting on the bottom of the ocean. Four crewmen and an officer sat near their captain. The officer was the ship's navigator. Two of the crewman wore headsets, listening intently for any sound from above that might indicate activity on the surface. Another crewman manned the mid-ship ballast levers, and the remaining man was one of the ship's radio operators. The rest of the ship's crew manned their various stations fore and aft throughout the ship. As they had done for the past two hours, all sat or stood quietly. Waiting.

There was one other person. Bauer turned his head and looked across the room at the young, blond woman sitting on a waterproof canister. She was leaning back, resting her head on a metal grate that covered a fire hose. Her eyes were closed. She wore baggy men's clothing.

Bauer thought her hair was strangely cut. Suddenly, as if sensing eyes upon her, the girl's head rose. She looked at Bauer without expression.

"Almost time, Herr Kapitän?" asked the only female voice at the bottom of the ocean.

"We will wait one more hour then check the surface, Fräulein," Bauer answered gruffly.

One hour earlier, at midnight, Bauer had taken 260 to periscope depth. A check on the surface at that time revealed rain with extremely poor visibility. Bauer had mixed feelings about the rain. The cloud cover negated any lumination from the half moon. This lack of visibility was both good and bad. 260 would not be seen from shore when she surfaced, but it also made it impossible for Bauer to see the beach through the scope. Bauer knew where the beach was, and how far. His landing party could get the girl to the beach. The real difficulty with such poor visibility would be for the landing party to find the sub on their return. Bauer had decided to wait. 260 returned to the bottom.

Where had Canaris found this one? Bauer asked himself as he again glanced at the girl. With the immediate prospect of entering an enemy country as a spy—a condition Bauer would wager (and give odds) that will most likely get her shot or hanged—this female Sonderführer sat calmly on the bottom of the ocean resting her eyes.

At 0200 hours, Eastern War Time, Bauer gave the order to again take 260 up to periscope depth. The young German seaman who manned the mid-ship ballast controls waited for the Captain's order to be relayed to the aft ballast mate. The officer of the deck nodded to the young seaman who immediately pulled the four long handles protruding from the floor. A loud hissing noise followed—the sound of pressurized air replacing seawater in the ballast tanks that encompassed the hollow core of U-260.

The ship groaned, then briefly listed to starboard, forcing standing crewmen to grab hold of anything fixed for balance. A moment later, 260 regained her composure and began the slow, vertical ascent to the surface.

At periscope depth, Bauer pulled down the scope's two opposing handles. He turned his hat (originally white but now a sweat-stained gray) so the bill faced backward. Bauer then leaned forward and placed his eyes on the viewfinder.

The rain had stopped but the cloud cover kept visibility poor.

"May I, Kapitän?" Again, it was the only female voice on board.

Without speaking, Bauer motioned to the periscope. The young woman stepped forward and peered into the viewfinder. Like Bauer, Erika Lehmann could see little in the darkness other than the black shadow of the nearest swell. The shore could not be seen.

Erika moved away from the periscope without comment and the captain took back the viewfinder. Bauer sidestepped in a tight circle, spinning the metal column 360 degrees one way and then back again. A Lieutenant Weir broke the silence.

Weir, the only crewmember who understood English, had been looking over the shoulder of the radio operator. When 260 reached periscope depth and the ship's antenna was out of the water, Weir ordered the radio operator to scan for local weather reports.

"Kapitän, a commercial radio station that identifies itself as broadcasting from a place called Wilmington reports that sporadic rain is forecast to last most of the night. The weather system is expected to move out to sea around dawn."

"How far is this 'Wilmington' from our location, Weir?" Bauer asked.

The young lieutenant scrambled for a map of the Carolinas, but Erika interjected.

"Wilmington is fifteen kilometers from the coast, Herr Kapitän," she informed. "Approximately thirty kilometers north of us. That weather forecast would include this area."

Her initial destination for a train connection had been Jacksonville, North Carolina. But when Bauer relocated the submarine farther south, all that changed. If she landed at this location, Wilmington would now be her "melting in" spot before heading to her target area.

Bauer paused for thought only briefly.

"Then I see no advantage in waiting. The deliverance is on."

With low visibility, Bauer's biggest concern was still for the crewmen who delivered the girl to the beach. He did not want to be forced to maneuver his ship through the water searching for lost men paddling wildly around trying to locate a ship they could not see, and he could not send more men out to look for a landing party that was late reporting back. That was against orders and with good reason. If the first men were captured instead of lost, he would be sending more of his men to suffer the same fate. Bauer knew the safest strategy in this poor visibility was to give his landing crew as short a trip back to the sub as possible. Guiding the ship close to shore under these conditions would be extremely dangerous but it would have to be done. It would require experience and boldness on a captain's part. Bauer was perfect for the job.

"Fräulein," Bauer said tersely. "I assume you are ready."

"Yes, Herr Kapitän."

"Weir, inform the deliverance personnel."

Weir relayed the information aft to three crewman who had been ready for hours.

Bauer issued more orders, and 260 rose from periscope depth to "stealth" position—a partial surfacing which brought only the conning tower and two feet of the deck out of the water. Bauer donned rain gear then ordered lights out in the control room. He then led three spotters up the conning tower's metal ladder. Surprisingly, a weak ray of moonlight entered the control room when Bauer lifted the hatch. The captain scampered spryly onto the conning tower deck.

The half-moon winked on and off behind heavy, fast moving clouds. This allowed Bauer to see the distant North Carolina beach, if only in sporadic intervals. The view through his binoculars revealed a narrow beach backed by forest. Helter skelter near the shore a few large boulders jutted from the water. Bauer decided it was a good enough spot for a landing but he wanted to get his boat closer to shore.

It was time.

Powered by its quiet electric motors, U-boat 260 turned its bow westward and slowly edged its way toward the American coast.

Every few seconds a five-foot breaker joined Erika Lehmann and the three men in the small boat, inviting itself over the edge of the low-floating, inflatable raft. The weight of the water took the boat even lower until the four knelt in the water, seemingly supported by some invisible platform mounted just below the surface. Erika crouched in the front of the raft and acted as the spotter. She could see nothing. The moon had once again fled behind a dense cloud, but she knew the beach could not be far. She tried to listen for the sound of water dashing against land.

Kapitän Bauer was a gruff old sea dog, Erika thought, but one who knew his business. Bauer guided the submarine to within a mile of the shore, grounding the boat on a shallow sandbar. This would keep the boat from drifting and allow the three crewmen in the raft to easily find the ship after delivering her to the beach.

Now Bauer's three crewmen rowed vigorously as Erika tried to find America through the murk.

Erika's ears located the shore before her eyes did. Water crashing against rocks had always sounded to Erika like the cymbals at a Wagner opera. She heard that sound now but still saw nothing. When her eyes finally focused on something, it was too late. There was no time to react. The giant boulder materialized and rushed' toward them like an attacker, and almost as if it conspired with the boulder, a breaker lifted up the dinghy and hurled it against the unforgiving rock. All four of the

Germans were thrown out of the raft. The wave catapulted Erika toward the top of the boulder and the side of her lower left leg slammed against the peak of the unyielding rock. Her momentum carried her over the top of the boulder and she splashed down in the frothing water on the leeward side of the rock. The water she landed in was shallow and the side of her hip and right elbow slammed into the sea bottom. Fortunately, the four feet of water and a sandy sea floor cushioned her fall.

When she righted herself, her feet touched down on the sandy bottom and she stood up. The rush of adrenaline kept any pain in her leg from registering. Her first thought was to locate the raft. She must not lose her gear! She was suddenly very glad she had tied the container to the raft.

The water was calmer on the shore side of the rocks, and the shallow water indicated to Erika that land could not be far. The flirting moon again blinked on as the cloud that shrouded it raced away. Erika turned and saw the beach about fifty meters away—*or rather yards now,* she found herself bizarrely reminding herself even during the midst of this chaos.

Behind her she heard one of the U-boat crewmen calling out loudly to his mates.

In German! The fool!

Erika spun around and scampered up the large boulder that ended her voyage to America. The rock was polished slick from the millennium dance with the ocean and she slipped and almost tumbled off. Catching herself, she worked her way around to the ocean side of the huge stone. The crewman who had called out was struggling to climb onto some smaller rocks thirty yards away. Erika did not see the other crewmen. She jumped into the water and began working her way to the man. The powerful, incoming breakers on the ocean side of the rocks closed on her like steel gates, threatening to once again rag doll her against the stones. Twice she dived under and allowed the waves to pass overhead.

Finally reaching the crewman, Erika quietly but sternly ordered him not to speak. He was dazed and injured badly. When she grabbed his arm he cried out. His nose bled profusely and blood flowed from both corners of his mouth indicating internal injuries. Apparently going into shock, the crewman began babbling incoherently and much too loudly. His jabber persisted despite Erika's attempts to quiet him. She had no choice. Erika put her hand on the man's forehead and rammed his head against the rock he leaned against. Even over the ocean clamor Erika heard the blunt clap of the man's skull against the rock.

Now the water would be of use. Instead of carrying the unconscious crewman, Erika used the water to support most of the man's weight as she dragged him by the collar around the rocks and toward shore.

Forty yards from land, Erika spotted the other two crewmen standing on the beach. When they saw her pulling their crewmate through the surf, they rushed back into the water to help. The beach was narrow, a thick forest near. Bauer picked a good spot, *except for the damn rocks.* Erika looked for the raft and did not see it. A sudden panic washed over her. *Where is the raft and the container? What if it had been taken back out to sea?* Her identity papers and money, twenty thousand dollars, were in the container, along with a change of clothes she would need in the morning, and several critical components she would need to build a transmitter. It would all be lost!

And these men would be stranded! Erika knew Bauer would not send a rescue party. When they failed to return in the allotted time, Bauer's orders were to presume the landing party had been captured and to withdraw his ship from the coastal area as quickly as possible.

Abandoned, these men would be quickly captured. None of them spoke English and they were wearing German military clothing. They would sooner or later crack under interrogation and the hunt for her would be on.

Procedure in this scenario had been drilled extensively at Quenzsee: she would be expected to eliminate the three U-boat crewmen and bury the bodies. When the bodies were eventually found (and hastily buried bodies were always found), the authorities would put two-and-two together and hypothesize that someone had been dropped off here. Liquidating the crewmen would not solve her problems; it would simply buy some time. It would give her the opportunity to put some distance between herself and the coast. To her advantage, the Americans would assume an enemy agent would be a male and focus their search with that assumption. But in her heart Erika knew she would not kill three of her countrymen. She would simply have to abandon them to their own devices and put as much distance between herself and them as she could, and as quickly as possible.

And problems remained if she lost the container. She would have no change of clothes and be stranded in a black, German issued jumpsuit. She would somehow have to procure money for clothes, travel, and steal parts for a shortwave transmitter. Extreme risks.

When the two crewmen reached Erika and the injured man, she asked about the raft. She was relieved to find out that one of them had retrieved the boat and dragged it into the forest's fringe.

Reaching the woods, Erika used a knife to free the container from the raft while the two crewmen tended to their unconscious crewmate as best they could. Besides the likely internal injuries, the man's injured arm was obviously broken. Swelling had already doubled the arm's size, and he now had a concussion. Erika noticed that one of the other crewmen bled from an ear, but otherwise they appeared in good shape.

The two other Germans looked at Erika. One of them asked her if there would be anything else.

"Nein," she said in a low voice. She just wanted them and the raft back on the submarine and away from her before there were any more problems. The crewmen wanted the same. One of the men dragged the raft to the edge of the water then both men carried the injured crewman to the raft. From the edge of the forest, Erika watched her countrymen row vigorously back out to sea. Despite the strong incoming surf, the raft disappeared quickly into the darkness beyond the rocks.

Erika inspected the metal container. There was a noticeable dent along one side; the waves had tossed more than just Erika and the men onto the rocks. But the dent was not on a seam and the waterproof integrity of the container appeared to have survived the rough landing.

The rain returned, slight but steady.

Erika picked up the container and walked further into the blackness of the forest. She wanted to put a little distance between herself and the beach without going too far before daybreak when she could orientate herself. Erika hoped to find a rocky ledge or overhang that might provide some shelter, but visibility in the forest proved to be even worse than on the beach. The base of a large gum would be her only shelter tonight.

As Erika sat down and leaned back against the tree, she was suddenly very aware of her left leg. The adrenaline rush which had masked the pain was now subsiding. She pulled the leg of her pants up and pushed the soaking wet sock down. Probing with her fingers, she felt the lump on her ankle and the warm liquid that could not be rain. There was a small first aid kit in her suitcase inside the container, but the laceration did not seem severe. The rain convinced her to not open the container and get the clothes wet she would need in the morning. Doctoring the wound could wait until then. She was more concerned about walking out of the forest. She tested the ankle by working it in all directions. Doing so was painful but the mobility of the joint did not seem to be affected. Erika recalled what the rocks had done to the crewman and she concluded she was fortunate. She regretted injuring the man further, but she had no choice. She rationalized, thinking she might have saved the three crewmen and herself from capture by silencing the injured man. *You must make yourself hard for Germany, Tschapperl,* the Führer told her. She forced thoughts of the crewman out of her mind.

Suddenly she heard a low, rumbling sound in the distance. It was faint and far away, but nevertheless a distinctive sound Erika recognized.

Three quarters of a mile offshore, Captain Eric Bauer was forced to use the powerful diesel engines of U-boat 260 when the electric engines failed to extract the submarine from the sandbar. After two full-throttled roars from the diesels, U-260 broke free and backed away from the American coast. The submarine disappeared below the waves as the rain intensified.

Erika Lehmann, daughter of a personal friend of the Führer, leaned her head against a North Carolina gum tree, closed her eyes, and let the rain wash away the sea.

✠　　　　　　✠　　　　　　✠

PART 2

CHAPTER 14

The die is cast.

—Julius Caesar (100—44 B.C.),
upon crossing the Rubicon

A North Carolina coastal road

Wednesday, August 19, 1942

The bed of the old man's rusted pickup truck was overloaded with discarded tire rims, broken pipes, bent sections of rebar and metal fencing. The engine sputtered and belched a bluish cloud as it strained to make it up the hill. The tires were bald, so the old man was glad last night's rain had finally moved out to sea. The sun breaking through was welcome. It burned off some of the morning fog, although pockets of the thick mist still appeared and disappeared across the highway—specters who could not make up their minds. These fickle pockets of fog appeared suddenly and without warning, around this curve or that, as the old man's truck wound its way through the forest over the twisting North Carolina coastal road.

The old man was making his weekly sojourn to collect and drop off scrap metal for the Friends of Freedom Metal Drive. It was his contribution to the war effort. He collected the scrap during the week from neighbors, mostly fellow farmers, and businesses located in small towns up and down the coast.

He had lived in this area all his life. Who would want to live elsewhere? As a boy he swam and fished in the ocean as well as the numerous streams and small lakes of the many forests near the North Carolina coastline. Now, since the death of his wife four years ago and the start of the war last December, his time not spent working on his small farm was spent doing occasional favors for neighbors and collecting scrap metal for the war effort.

He had driven this road many times and knew that when he reached the crown of this hill the road fell off sharply and curved to the right, winding through several more miles of dense coastal forest. The road was still damp and slick in spots from last night's storm so when the truck crested the hill and dropped toward yet another of the low lying pockets of mist the old man braked to slow down. When his truck emerged from what he hoped would be the last of the fog, the old man was forced into a double take to convince himself what he saw was genuine. A young woman stood on the shoulder of the road just ahead. She was excitedly waving for him to stop.

The young woman wore dark green slacks (slacks had been popular among American women since the thirties, but the old man was still not willing to accept pants on females) and a light gray blouse. Her blond hair was cut in the familiar American *bob,* a popular style of the day. Beside her sat a medium-sized canvas suitcase. The old man applied the squeaking brakes, pulled over, and leaned across the seat so he could roll down the passenger side window.

"Lord, Missy. What ya doin' out here miles down this ole road." The old man's accent and dialect rang of this region of the American South.

The young woman's accent was also Southern. "Oh, sir, it's a long and sordid story. Thank you so much for stopping. You just have to save me."

"Come on ahead and jump in, Missy," the old man said.

She climbed in the truck, held her suitcase on her lap, and proceeded to satisfy the old man's curiosity. She oozed with Southern Bell innocence.

"I am trying to get to my sister's house in Norfolk. That's in Virginia. I left early this morning from my mama and daddy's house in Kure Beach. The Reverend Wilson's teenage son, Tyler Wilson, was to drive me to the train station in Wilmington. He promised Mama and Daddy responsibility for me."

She put a hand high on her chest, just below her neck, and seemed embarrassed but proceeded with her story.

"Sir, we weren't gone but a few miles when I could tell Tyler Wilson had what you might call...other intentions. My, I never thought him such a one like that, and so early in the morning! When we got on this lonely old road he pulled over and stopped the car on three separate occasions. I never saw a boy with so many hands. Well, I resisted his advances of course, but he persisted. The third time he pulled over, when it was quite obvious to me he was of a set mind, I slapped him across the face as hard as I could and quickly exited his daddy's Ford."

"Good Lord, Missy! The boy drove off and left you?"

"Can you believe it? Wait til I tell the Reverend Wilson about his son. And I'm going to tell him too, don't think I won't!"

Erika Lehmann almost grinned at the silliness of the story, but she concluded it would suffice for the half-hour ride to Wilmington. She had waited beside the remote coastal road for over an hour before the old man's truck appeared. As Erika waved the truck down, she quickly evaluated the driver. If the driver had been a younger man she would flirt, but she considered the old man a stroke of luck. Flirting might prove quite comical under the circumstances. She had not had a real bath in over two weeks, and Erika suspected she smelled like wet dog. She would not have to flirt with the old man, simply play the lady-in-distress. She knew of Southern customs from her time in Virginia. Southern men considered themselves noble, especially the older ones.

The old man would be glad to help a young Southern virgin who had just defended her honor.

The old man would have to drive her to the train station in Wilmington.

✠   ✠   ✠

8 Prinz Albrechtstrasse—[that same day]

Heinrich Himmler had been forced to wait until Erika Lehmann left the Reich. Karl Lehmann's daughter was untouchable inside Germany or any of its occupied lands. Eliminating the girl could only be done on enemy soil where Canaris, or Karl Lehmann, would never be able to investigate the circumstances behind the girl's demise. When the communications from her stopped, they would have to assume the worst: that she had been uncovered as a spy and killed while trying to escape, or captured, which meant sure execution. Regardless, there would be no way to learn the girl's fate.

So Himmler had waited.

At least he had been right about where Canaris was sending the girl. Himmler surmised all along it must be America and he just had that guess confirmed.

Himmler's conjecture about the girl's destination was simply common sense. Lehmann's daughter spoke fluent English and French. Occupied France held no need for an Abwehr foreign agent. Himmler knew the girl's destination had to be England or the United States, and it made little sense to pull her out of England prematurely, as Canaris had done, then send her back to the same country. That would have engendered unnecessary risks; the focus of an agent's operation within an enemy country can be changed without extracting the agent.

Gestapo agents monitoring the sub pens in Lorient, France, spotted the girl boarding U-260 on the third of August. With that information Himmler went to work.

U-boat orders were top secret and records sealed until completion of the mission. To find out where the submarine was heading with the girl on board, Himmler had two options. He could simply order the records sent to him, he had that authority, but that was out of the question. This was a very sensitive and politically volatile affair. Sending for the submarine's orders would make it obvious to everyone that Himmler was on the trail of Karl Lehmann's daughter against Adolf Hitler's wishes. The second option was to wait until the U-boat returned to its home dock and check the captain's log. This would not raise undue suspicion if the logs of several U-boats were simultaneously requested as a facade. But that meant waiting until the U-boat returned home which would be at least a month and perhaps more. Heinrich Himmler was not a patient man; waiting for the girl to depart had been hard enough.

So Himmler sent out Axel Ryker. Ryker's check of German Naval surface ship records revealed a German supply ship refueled and resupplied U-260 on August 11 at 45N latitude and 38W longitude, over half way across the Atlantic Ocean. Himmler was right about America.

But much work remained. Himmler had no clues to the girl's mission objectives or target location within the United States, and obtaining that information would not be easy. Canaris took great pride in refusing all requests from Himmler to share information; *the old fool guards his secrets like a miser his gold.* That, along with the extraordinary restraints Himmler was under in this case (forced to wait until the girl left the German sphere of influence, the need for total secrecy while trailing the daughter of Karl Lehmann, and the fact she would be outside Himmler's SS/Gestapo umbrella) all added up to a demanding chore ahead for Himmler. But the girl's fate was sealed in Himmler's mind. She must be eliminated and when her target location was finally pinpointed there would be only one way to do it.

Although Axel Ryker did not know it yet, he was going to America.

✠   ✠   ✠

CHAPTER 15

You know, we are told that not a sparrow falls without God's care; I am not being light when I say this—that not a person 'fell', fell ill or in need, lost his job or his house, without the [Nazi] Party's caring. No organization had ever done this before in Germany, maybe nowhere else. If you lose your job or your house in America, will your political party come to your rescue? Believe me, such an organization is irresistible to men. No German was alone in his troubles. It was the best time of our lives.

—Heinrich Kessler, baker,
German citizen during Nazi regime (interview 1953)[5]

Wilmington, North Carolina

August 1942

Erika Lehmann opened the door of the old man's pickup truck and stepped out. He had delivered her to the train depot in Wilmington, North Carolina, and he now gave her a warning: "Be careful now, Missy. There are lots of niggers traveling on those trains now, what with all the war jobs in the big cities and all. Don't you be talkin' to any niggers or traveling salesmen now, trouble is all they'll get ya', ya' hear?"

---

5   from *They Thought They Were Free* by Milton Mayer.

She nodded thoughtfully at the fatherly advice and with the accent she thought should be acceptable anywhere in the American South, Erika Lehmann thanked the old man for the ride. She closed the passenger door and bid the old man farewell.

Erika had spent hours practicing various American accents. The South had many and they were quite varied. Erika knew most Americans did not realize this, but to the trained ear a Carolina accent sounds much different than an Alabama drawl which, in turn, sounds not at all like a Kentucky or West Virginia twang.

During her teenage years in Virginia, Erika discarded any vestiges of her German accent when speaking English. By the end of her first year in America, it would have been practically impossible for even a skilled linguist to discern any remnant of the brusque Teutonic inflections.

In fact, when her family first arrived in the United States, Erika's main difficulty when trying to fit in with her American classmates was discarding the British accent she had parroted while learning English from her British mother. Erika commented at Quenzsee while teaching English to other German agents that when speaking English it had been harder for her to jettison her aped British accent than her original German one.

Erika settled for a generic Southern accent which utilized a grab bag of various regional dialects. Remember, she reminded herself, lots of double negatives and string out those vowels.

Inside the train station a blackboard with the schedules written in chalk hung on the wall behind the ticket counter. Erika initially planned her first stop to be Atlanta, Georgia, but the first train to Atlanta did not depart until 6:40 that evening. She glanced at a clock on the wall beside the schedule. It was not yet two o'clock. Too long. Erika wanted to put some miles between her and the coast.

Departing at 3:15 was a train to Charlotte, North Carolina, with a final destination of Chattanooga, Tennessee. She walked up to the clerk's window and purchased a round-trip ticket.

Chattanooga was not her final destination, of course, but neither was Atlanta. It would be a grave breech of procedure, and downright foolish, to buy a ticket to her final destination. Tickets must be purchased in stages. This would make it much more difficult for anyone attempting to track her journey. She felt confident no one from shore had seen the landing party last night. The same rain and poor visibility that made her landing a rough one was an advantage in that regard, but still it was a good idea to follow procedure, just in case.

The round-trip ticket was another ruse. She would not use the return ticket; however, if tracking an enemy agent on the move, the FBI would initially ask to examine records for one-way tickets. The FBI was good. Erika's father assured her of that. They would eventually get around to checking round-trip tickets also, but anything that might make their job a little more time consuming was an advantage for her.

Everything had to be carefully thought out during these first few hours after landing. No detail could be overlooked. Careless spies hanged from gallows. *Leave false clues, if you have to leave any.* This was a Quenzsee commandment.

There was the business of the waterproof canister from the submarine. It contained the traveling suitcase which she now carried. Even the one-in-a-million chance that someone, perhaps a hunter, might stumble across (and be curious enough to investigate) the freshly dug earth in the coastal forest where she buried the canister had to be considered. She hoped the canister was never discovered, but if it were the landing clothes she had worn ashore and buried with the canister were all male clothing articles, and two sizes too large for Erika Lehmann.

Some decisions could not be made in advance because they included variables. At other times procedures were standard.

Quickly putting some distance between the agent and the landing point was critical. Hitching a ride was risky but unavoidable, and this time it worked fine. The gullible old man was a bit of luck.

Small towns are dangerous. Strangers are too obvious and the towns-folk too nosey. Get to the nearest big city as quickly as possible. There an agent would melt in. Decisions on travel to the final destination could then be made and plans adjusted if necessary.

The first decision an agent on foreign shores was forced to make was when to proceed on to the final destination.

The decision depended on the landing.

If the agent was spotted during landing (or he strongly suspected as much), Quenzsee taught agents to abort the landing. If spotted, get back to the submarine and proceed to another location. Preferably a much distant one. Eliminating witnesses usually served no purpose. Dead bodies found on the beach (or hastily buried ones which were always quickly found once a search party was organized) immediately conjured suspicions of spy landings during wartime.

If for any reason an agent is not positive but suspects he has been seen coming ashore, Quenzsee training instructs the agent to get to the nearest large city and lie low. If the authorities (in America it would be the FBI) were notified, their first move will be to check public trans-portation leaving the area, so do not use it. The FBI would be forced to fan out when an initial, concentrated sweep of public transportation reveals no leads. Traveling will be safer after a few days.

If the landing went well, and there seemed little chance that anyone from shore had seen or heard anything, standard procedure was to pro-ceed on. This is the situation Erika considered herself in.

The problem for Erika Lehmann, or any agent, is this decision usu-ally banks solely on intuition. Unless an agent sees with his own eyes that he has been spotted (perhaps bad fortune placed a moonlight walker or a pair of lovers somewhere on the beach), the agent can only guess if the landing has been secret.

Erika decided to put some distance between herself and the coast as quickly as possible. All in all she considered the landing a success. She doubted if anyone saw the raft come and go. Last night's visibility was amply bad; she had the injuries to prove it. The ankle throbbed, especially when she stood, but she didn't think anything was broken. She could walk without a limp if she concentrated mightily. Yes, all in all, she thought the landing a success.

Erika Lehmann sat down on a bench in the Wilmington, North Carolina, train depot, placed her suitcase beside her, and awaited the boarding call for the 3:15 to Chattanooga.

✠   ✠   ✠

"Naaaashveel!"

The black porter announced the name of the city as he entered the car from the forward door.

"Folks, please take all your carry-ons with you. Don't forget nothin'."

As the train slowed, people in the seats began rising. Erika Lehmann retrieved her suitcase from the niche overhead. She had not checked her bag to storage. If the bag was somehow lost, she would lose items critical to her mission. It was a risk that was unnecessary. Quenzsee knew how large a bag a passenger was allowed to carry with them on American trains. The maximum size suitcase allowed for carry-on happened to be the size suitcase Erika Lehmann now carried in her left hand.

The train ride from Wilmington proved uneventful except for an incident in the Chattanooga train depot earlier that day.

The over-night trip from Wilmington to Chattanooga ended early that morning. Erika's first night's sleep in America and her first real shower since she left France over two weeks ago had been on the train. In Chattanooga, Erika purchased her ticket to Nashville then sat down to wait for the boarding call. There were a dozen rows of benches for passengers awaiting departures or for people waiting to meet arriving travelers. A large sign was posted nearby:

COLORED IN BACK TWO BENCH ROWS ONLY.

Erika sat in the white section. The last two rows of benches—the black section—were crowded with women and young children. With nowhere to sit, the black men stood behind and alongside these rear benches. The remaining ten rows of benches, the ones designated for whites, were half empty with the rear three rows of the white section completely vacant.

As she sat waiting in the depot, Erika noticed a black soldier escorting a very pregnant woman and young child buying a ticket at the counter. After purchasing the ticket the soldier guided the woman and child to the benches. Not finding a seat in the black section, the soldier sat the heavily burdened woman and the child in the last, vacant row of "white only" benches. The soldier stood to the side.

A few minutes passed before one of the ticket clerks, a thin, middle-aged white man with a twitching eye, spotted the black lady and child sitting in the white row.

"Gal!…Hey, Gal!" the clerk yelled, making sure the black woman could hear. "You can't sit there. That row's for white folk! There's the sign." He pointed emphatically.

The black soldier spoke up.

"Mister, all the seats in the colored section are full and all these empty," he pointed to the white seats. "I thought my wife might sit here for just a few minutes."

"There's the sign!" the clerk repeated almost frantically. "We all have to go by the sign! If you're goin' to make trouble, boy, I'll have to call the poe-leese."

An old woman sitting in the "colored" seats stood up and said something to the soldier and his wife. The soldier, embarrassed, watched as his wife stood, took the child's hand and moved back to the designated section, taking the old woman's seat.

Another white man, obviously overhearing the exchange, appeared from an office behind the clerk.

"Any trouble, Clyde?" the man asked.

"I took care of it, Mr. Jordan," the clerk bragged, then shot a dubious look toward the black soldier. "The niggers back there can't read, but I explained the sign to 'em. I don't think there will be any more trouble."

Satisfied, Mr. Jordan disappeared back into his office.

Erika was relieved there wasn't real trouble. She wanted no part of perhaps being asked to give a witness statement to the police.

At the Chattanooga station that morning Erika decided Nashville would be the second leg of her journey. The wait to board would be only two hours. It was mid-afternoon of the second day after departing U-260 when her train pulled into Nashville.

The breaks squealed as the train crawled to a stop. The porter once again reminded the passengers not to forget their belongings. Behind a frazzled woman trying to keep three small children in tow, Erika Lehmann stepped from the train onto the Nashville depot platform.

She would now head north. A check of departures revealed that a train to the next city in her original plans would not pull out until late the next morning. Erika picked an alternate city in the same general direction. That train departed in less than an hour but after checking with the ticket clerk she was informed that all seats on that train were taken.

"Soldiers have most the seats, ma'am, and they're first priority you know."

Erika decided to spend the night in Nashville. It was part of good procedure anyway. At some point, stop and let the trail cool. If an agent were followed, this delay would complicate the tracking of mass transit tickets. She walked out to the street and hailed a taxi. When one pulled up to the curb the driver started to get out but Erika told him not to bother. "I have only this one suitcase." Erika placed the suitcase in the back seat and followed it.

The heat and humidity of the August afternoon was magnified inside the cab. The sweating driver turned and looked at her. Erika guessed him to be in his late fifties, perhaps early sixties.

"Where to, ma'am?"

"I need to buy a dress for a nice dinner," Erika said. "I'm just in from Atlanta and I don't know this city. I also need to find a nice hotel. Can you help me?"

"Umm…let's see," the driver answered slowly. He looked her over in his rearview mirror.

Erika could see the man was suspicious. She thought it best to satisfy him that she was not a prostitute.

"My husband is in the Army, stationed at Fort Campbell, not far from here in Kentucky."

The driver nodded. "Sure, I know where it is. We see a lot of Fort Campbell boys around these parts." The driver waited for her to continue.

"Well, my husband found out yesterday that he's shipping out three days from now. He was given a forty-eight hour leave that starts tomorrow, so instead of him wasting most of his leave traveling back and forth from Atlanta, I am meeting him here in Nashville. After I find a room, I'm supposed to call him at the base tonight and he'll come down tomorrow. I had such sort notice, but here I am."

"I understand, young lady," the driver winked knowingly. "I was young once myself."

The driver delivered her to a downtown department store and waited while his passenger went in. Erika told the teenage sales girl what she was looking for, then promptly selected a navy blue dinner dress from a rack and another, more everyday outfit. Erika quickly tried on the clothes and told the girl she would take them. She also purchased a large tote bag with a shoulder strap and a small hand purse. Everything was paid for with cash.

Back in the cab, the driver told Erika about an area on Lafayette Boulevard referred to as "Hotel Row," a four block section of downtown Nashville with several nice hotels. She told him it sounded fine. The driver dropped her at the door of a hotel called the Arbor Arms where she paid him and thanked him for his help. A black hotel doorman opened the cab door for her and a black bellhop rushed to take her suitcase (the weight of the suitcase surprised the man and he had to adjust his grip). Erika followed the bellhop into the hotel, then looked back through the glass to see if the cab had pulled away. It had. She immediately stopped the bellhop, told him she had made a mistake, took back her suitcase and walked back out the door she just entered.

Lafayette Boulevard was busy with mid-day traffic. Heat radiated from the pavement like someone had forgotten to turn the stove off under an empty griddle. Overhead the hazy Southern sun seemed much too close, its rays an ultraviolet weight pressing the flesh. Despite the heat, numerous shoppers, mostly women, strolled in and out of the numerous small shops and larger department stores that lined the street and separated the hotels. Carrying the suitcase in one hand and the large shopping bag in the other, Erika walked a few blocks then boarded a city bus. She asked directions of the driver, and after making a couple of transfers arrived at the Greyhound bus depot.

Inside the bus depot, Erika rented a locker and purchased a ticket to New Orleans; the bus departed later that evening. It was a ticket she would never use but purchased to avoid suspicion when she rented the locker. She placed her suitcase in the locker, turned the key, and made sure it was locked. In the ladies room Erika dawdled until a young woman finished helping a toddler use a toilet. After the mother and child left, Erika stored the newly purchased clothes and the small purse inside the canvas tote bag. She tore up the ticket to New Orleans, then threw the pieces into the shopping bag which she wadded up and disposed of in a trash can.

Two soldiers sitting on a bench in the bus depot watched the pretty blond with the tote bag hanging from her shoulder walk past. One of the soldiers whispered to the other, then both men grinned. They continued to watch the blond until she disappeared through the door to the street outside.

CHAPTER 16

It is indeed a desirable thing to be well-descended, but the glory belongs to our ancestors.

—Plutarch, (ca 100 A.D.)

Nashville, Tennessee

August 1942

This was the ninth day in a row Dorothy Nolan waited tables in the bar of Nashville's Excelsior Hotel. *When are they going to get some more help in this damn place?* she asked silently. Dorothy theorized the hotel management took advantage of her because she had no husband *(and I don't want one!)*, always calling her in to work when another barmaid called in sick. *The bastards think I have nothing else to occupy my time, so why not work? My next day off I'm not answering the goddamn phone.*

But Dorothy admitted this was not the worst place she had worked. She hated working tables at the honky-tonks and dive bars of her past, and especially hated the vulgar, groping drunks she had to put up with night after night. At least the Excelsior was an upscale hotel and the bar frequented mostly by well-to-do hotel guests. That was not to say drunks and gropers were non-existent, but here at the hotel that group was made up mostly of traveling businessmen striving to cheat on faraway wives. They were easier to put in their place than the rowdy riffraff of the honky tonks.

With tray in hand, Dorothy approached a table where two men sat. She placed a double bourbon on the table in front of a middle-aged man in a gray suit, and a bottle of Hamms beer and an empty glass in front of a younger man, also in a suit. She loaded the empties on her tray. At the bar, Dorothy added the cost of the drinks to the older man's tab.

The waitress looked at her image in the large mirror behind the bar. She would be thirty-nine next month, only one year from forty. People did not consider her ugly. She had been groped enough while working tables to rest that thought, but she was not a beauty. She was flat-chested, too tall, and her nose was just a little too big (her mother had always fretted about her nose). She wore glasses because of nearsighted-ness and recently a wrinkle appeared at the corner of an eye. *Isn't thirty-eight too young for wrinkles?* But all this was insignificant in the end, she concluded. Dorothy Nolan held no interest in attracting a potential husband. For her, life would be lived alone with her books. Her books were her escape.

Still gazing into the mirror, the waitress's attention was drawn from her own image to that of a woman who had walked into the room. The woman found a seat in a booth toward the back of the bar. Dorothy grabbed up a coaster and a menu and went to wait on the new customer.

"Menu, ma'am?" Dorothy asked.

"No, thank you," the woman answered. "Not just yet."

"Can I get you a drink?"

"Yes, a brandy, please."

Dorothy walked back to the bar and gave the order to the bartender. She discreetly watched the woman in the mirror.

This one was a real looker. She was young; Dorothy guessed mid-twenties. Her blond hair was combed oddly, somewhat of a wild look, but Dorothy had seen the hairdo somewhere, perhaps in a magazine. The woman had already drawn the attention of the men in the bar. The bartender placed the drink in front of Dorothy; the waitress moved it to her tray, and took it to the woman.

"That will be thirty cents," Dorothy told the young woman. "Or I can start a tab?"

"A tab will be fine."

Dorothy Nolan found it hard to take her eyes off this woman. Her lipstick was a dark burgundy with matching eye shadow. The dark lips and eye shadow gave her a tawny, exotic look, despite the wild Viking blond hair. The navy blue dinner dress dipped just low enough in the front to beguile without being tawdry.

Suddenly, and probably because of the slight delay in the waitress leaving, the young woman looked up and caught Dorothy staring. The waitress turned away embarrassed and walked back to the bar.

As she wrote up a tab for the woman's drink, Dorothy again used the mirror to glance at the woman. Again the woman caught Dorothy looking, their eyes meeting in the mirror. Dorothy's face turned crimson and she felt like hiding; *she probably thinks I'm a pervert.*

Dorothy waited on other tables, all the time making a conscious effort not to be caught staring again by the young woman. Finally, after Dorothy delivered martinis to a man and woman at a table near the woman, she heard the voice behind her.

"Waitress."

Dorothy turned and approached.

"May I have another drink?" the woman smiled pleasantly.

"Oh, of course. I'm sorry, I'll get it right away," the waitress said abashed. Dorothy realized she had taken such pains to avoid staring that she had ignored the woman as a customer.

When Dorothy sat the brandy on the table, the woman smiled and thanked her, then suddenly took notice of a bracelet Dorothy wore on her right wrist.

"I like that," the young woman said. "Very pretty. Is that turquoise?"

"Thanks," the waitress now was forced to act casually. "Yeah, turquoise and silver. I've had it forever. Bought it in Memphis."

"May I see?" The woman gently took Dorothy's hand and drew it close to her so she could inspect the bracelet. The heart in Dorothy Nolan's chest picked up its pace.

"Yes, very pretty," the woman repeated as she let go of Dorothy's hand. The woman asked for the time. Dorothy looked at the watch on her left wrist.

"Almost half past eight."

Suddenly the woman looked irked. "I think I'm being stood up."

Dorothy could not imagine that happening to this woman.

"My boyfriend and I split up last week," the woman continued. "We were supposed to meet here for a drink, then go to dinner and talk things over. I guess it's not that important to him."

Dorothy was unsure of what to say. "I'm sorry to hear that, but I'm sure he'll show up."

"I'm not sure I want him to. Men! I'm beginning to think they're not worth it. I keep telling myself one of these days I'm going to swear off all of them." The woman smiled at Dorothy and offered her hand.

"My name is Helen."

Dorothy delicately shook the woman's hand. "I'm Dorothy."

"I noticed you're not wearing a wedding ring, Dorothy," the woman commented. "If you're single, maybe you can give me some tips on how to keep a boyfriend happy. Apparently I'm doing something wrong."

"I don't have a boyfriend." The women locked eyes for a brief moment. Nothing more was said and the waitress went about her business. Dorothy told the bartender she would be right back. She retrieved her purse from behind the bar and went in the ladies room. Dorothy looked herself over, quickly combed her hair, touched up her lipstick, and straightened her waitress dress. Dorothy Nolan hoped the boyfriend would not arrive.

After a few minutes, the waitress walked back into the bar.

The woman was gone. The money for her drinks left on the table.

Dorothy Nolan was experienced at shrugging off let downs; in her life disappointment was a close colleague, never far away. Dorothy figured the boyfriend arrived and, running late, the couple left right away to dine.

"Hey, girlie," a man at a table across the room sang out. "Does it take an Act of Congress to get a drink around here?"

Hearing the man's loud remark, many of the other patrons in the bar laughed.

Five long hours later Dorothy Nolan cleaned the last table and sat the last chair, legs up, upon it. She transferred her tip money from her dress pocket to her purse, had the bartender sign the sheet that recorded her hours, then left the Excelsior Hotel for home. The Nashville night was still muggy. Coming to work she rode the bus but now it was too late; the buses finished their runs hours ago. Each night Dorothy walked the twelve blocks home. Her feet and back ached as she walked; it was a familiar ache always there after her nine-hour shift. She was glad her journey was not farther as she stopped on a corner to check for traffic before crossing another street. Most of the route home was along the well-lighted boulevard, only the last couple of blocks were off the main drag but she had never had any trouble.

Dorothy Nolan lived in a small utility apartment in the basement of a large building of many similar dwellings. One room only: the bed pulled down from the wall, and she shared a bathroom down the hall with three other apartments. Even the refrigerator was shared with her apartment building neighbors: it sat in the hall. Dorothy minded sharing the toilet facilities less than she did the refrigerator. Several times she had discovered someone's lipstick on her milk bottles.

The only things that were her's alone were her books.

Finally home, the tired waitress walked down an outside stairwell and through an unlocked door into the hallway. Her apartment was the first one to the left. She found the key in her purse and let herself in. After flipping on a small lamp near the door, Dorothy locked the door and fixed the chain. The exhausted woman dropped her purse on a table by the lamp and collapsed into the room's only chair, thankful to be home. She turned on a box fan that sat nearby on the floor. *At least my ground level room is cooler than the sweat boxes on the upper floors.*

Dorothy kicked off her shoes and rubbed her sore feet. *If I just had some nylons, they would help my legs.* But nylons were a war casualty. She rose from the chair and removed the hotel furnished dress, leaving on her brassiere and half-slip. She pulled down the bed, then sat back down in the chair to let the fan cool her.

Then she heard the knock.

It was a soft rapping and she ignored it. *Probably some drunk who had the wrong apartment.* It had happened before. If she ignored him, he would eventually figure out he had the wrong door, or simply just give up and go away.

The knock was repeated and this time a voice followed.

"Dorothy?" It was a question, and it was a hushed female voice.

"Dorothy…are you in there?" It was asked softly, from someone not wanting to frighten or disturb, but it failed. Dorothy was unnerved.

She could not tell if it was a familiar voice or not. *Who was it at this hour?* Dorothy Nolan was a loner who people did not call on in the middle of the night. She was frightened, notwithstanding the delicate voice that knew her name.

She rose from the chair and went to the door.

"Who is it?" She spoke through the door. Her words held an obviously worried tone.

"It's Helen…the girl from the bar earlier tonight. We spoke briefly."

Dorothy stood by the door frozen, not knowing what to do. Earlier she had been attracted to the woman, but now Dorothy was afraid.

Again the soft voice: "Dorothy. I know it's late but I felt better after talking to you and I was hoping we could talk some more."

After another moment of silence, Dorothy gathered herself to answer.

"Just a minute," said Dorothy finally. She retrieved a robe from a small closet. Covering herself with the robe, she held it closed with one hand and unbolted the door and turned the knob with the other. She opened the door a few inches until the chain clicked taut.

It was her. The blue dress was gone, in its place a light green sleeveless blouse over a darker green skirt with a wide black belt, the hair and makeup the same as earlier.

As they looked at each other through the small opening neither woman spoke. Dorothy Nolan's heart raced as she closed the door and removed the chain.

When Dorothy Nolan awoke, her eyes fixed on the clock by the bed. It was almost noon and the apartment was bright with the level of sunlight that is never checked even by drawn curtains. Dorothy's curtains covered one small, ground-level window—the only window serving her tiny apartment.

Dorothy felt like one feels when just awakening from a pleasant dream. What was it Thoreau called it in *Walden,* one of her books. *The Awakening Hour.* That was it. When for an hour or so, just after awakening from a pleasant sleep, humans were at their best, or their most powerful. Something like that.

Then Dorothy felt a slight movement in the bed behind her and remembered that her euphoric feeling was not the result of a dream. When she turned over the woman beside her was looking at her.

"I was wondering when you were going to wake up," Helen teased. "C'mon, lazy bones, I'm starving. Let's go somewhere and get something to eat."

Dorothy sat up and moved to the end of the bed, covering herself with the sheet. Helen put on her brassiere and buttoned up her underpants then began gathering her other clothes. Dorothy sat for a moment and admired the young woman who walked unashamedly back and forth past her. In the light of day, Dorothy noticed the woman's left ankle was cut and swollen.

"What happened to your ankle?" Dorothy asked.

"Oh, I scraped and twisted it coming down some stairs a couple of days ago. 'Clumsy' is my middle name. It's okay; it feels a lot better today."

Dorothy spent another moment watching the woman move around the room.

"What really made you follow me home, Helen?" Dorothy was curious.

Helen looked at her and smiled. "What do you think? You told me you didn't have a boyfriend, remember? And your tone when you said it. Well…it sounded somewhat final. So when you disappeared for a few minutes, I asked the bartender about you. He said you lived alone. All that…and the way you looked at me. I just took a gamble."

"Why did you disappear so suddenly from the bar?"

"I really wasn't waiting for a boyfriend, but a girl has to say that or fight off the men. And a girl can sit alone in a bar only so long until the bartenders think you're a prostitute looking for a customer."

(The truth was that Erika Lehmann had originally gone in the bar looking for a man. Spending the night with a businessman in his hotel room was practically untraceable. Although she had several false I.D.s—all with very common names like Helen Gray—and Erika would have rented a room if she had not found someone suitable, renting a room was not as safe as not renting one. But finding the right man many times had variables unknown. Some might simply be local married men looking for something quick in the backseat of their car. Others might be looking for a real relationship or living at home with mother. When Erika concluded that the waitress was a lesbian, she quickly adjusted her plans. Instead of spending hours flirting with different men until the one most appropriate for her purpose was identified, Dorothy provided a quicker conclusion.)

"Will you stay for awhile?" Dorothy asked.

Helen stood up. "If I don't get something to eat soon, I'll be staying in the hospital."

Dorothy ignored the joke and continued to wait for an answer.

"Yes, I can stay for another day or so. You'll be bored with me by then."

"That will never happen," Dorothy said seriously.

(Last night in the apartment Erika admitted to the woman that she was not a local. She was passing through on her way to college in another state, stopping off in Nashville only for a day or two. This fabrication was to put the waitress off from later trying to find a *Helen Gray* locally when she disappeared. And perhaps even notifying the police from concern when Helen Gray, or the right Helen Gray, could not be found.)

"Let's get dressed," Helen said cheerfully. "I'm buying."

The women ate at the lunch counter in a Woolworth's department store on Lafayette four blocks from Dorothy's apartment. After lunch they spent a couple of hours browsing in the stores and shops up and down the boulevard. At a jewelry store, Dorothy insisted on buying Helen a delicate silver chain necklace with a ruby-colored stone. The chain was only a partial silver alloy and the stone was glass, but still it cost the waitress four dollars—almost a day's pay.

By late afternoon they were back at the apartment. Dorothy reluctantly readied herself for work as Helen scanned the large selection of books on the shelves opposite the bed. Genres and topics varied from the classics like *The Iliad* and *Dante's Inferno,* to dime-store paperbacks. The *Holy Bible* and several anthologies of poetry occupied one shelf: Milton and Baudelaire were represented along with the Americans Dickinson, Poe, and Whitman. *The Complete Works of Shakespeare* weighed heavily at the end of one shelf.

Several stacks of magazines were neatly arranged by publication date and included *Time, Life, The New Yorker, Reader's Digest,* and *Vanity Fair* among others.

There was even a small section of political works on the bottom shelf. Agitators were well represented: Thomas Paine's *Rights of Man* sat next to Marx's *Das Kapital.* More accepted by American society, but still controversial, was *Notes on the State of Virginia* by Thomas Jefferson; Jefferson's book lay on its side underneath his colleague Ben Franklin's *Autobiography.* The last book in this section, also laying on its side, was *Mein Kampf,* a bookmark jutting from its pages.

"Have you read all of these books, Dorothy?" Helen asked. Dorothy sat on a stool using a small table mirror to fix her makeup.

"Yeah," Dorothy answered while applying lipstick. "Well, most of them." She finished and put the cap back on the tube. "Probably surprises you, huh?"

"No, it doesn't surprise me. It's just that a few of these would be considered, oh…out of the mainstream, like Hitler's book. You've read it too?"

"Not all of it," Dorothy admitted as she stood and straightened her dress. "It's a tough read. Jumps from one thing to another. I don't get most of it. And all that stuff about the Jews…I mean, they look just like us as far as I can tell. I guess some of it makes sense, but most of it I don't understand."

"Really?" Helen responded. "You'll have to tell me about it."

Dorothy was more interested in other matters; for the first time in a long time she was not lonely. She wished she did not have to leave for work. "Will you wait up for me?" she asked Helen who was still scanning the bookshelves.

"Sure," Helen assured her automatically without turning around. Feeling the woman's eyes on her, Helen turned and smiled. Dorothy Nolan left for the bus stop anxious to finish her shift at the Excelsior.

After her hostess departed, Erika Lehmann took the copy of *Mein Kampf* from Dorothy Nolan's shelf. Erika had never read an English translation of the Führer's famous book.

Erika decided quickly the translation was a poor one. *Mein Kampf* was required reading at Quenzsee and Erika was familiar with many long passages. The English sentences were much shorter than Hitler's original, the substantives and German particles altered or left out altogether. The translation read like it was written by a poorly educated street merchant. Erika put the book down.

The Americans—what hypocrites. They treat their Negroes like dirt, then castigate us for relocating the Jews. Like Father said, at least we give the Jews land! The Americans write about our "nefarious Nazi propaganda" while themselves concocting wild stories about mass killings of Jews by Germans.

But like her father told her, all leaders have to convince their people that they fight an evil foe. Otherwise the masses will find the sacrifices demanded in wartime intolerable. "*'Heaven is on our side!' Both sides in every war ever fought make that claim, Liebchen,*" her father liked to say.

Father. Erika wondered what he was doing at that moment. *Right now it is past midnight in Berlin. He's in bed by now. Probably lying awake worrying about me.*

"Will I see you again?" Dorothy Nolan asked as she stood beside Helen Gray. It was mid-afternoon of the third day since Helen knocked on her door. Helen had just finished packing, needing only a few minutes to assemble her things. Her suitcase was still in the bus depot locker and her few personal items fit easily into one of Dorothy's surplus shopping bags.

"So you're not bored with me after all?" Helen smiled.

"Oh, yeah," Dorothy made an effort to kid. "But I was hoping you could stick around and bore me for a few more days."

Helen took the woman's hand. "I wish I could stay longer too, Dorothy, but my classes start in a few days, and I have to get registered and checked into my dorm."

"You never answered my question, Helen." Dorothy reminded. "Will I see you again?"

Helen tried to make the woman smile. "I have to come back. You never explained *Mein Kampf* to me."

Helen squeezed Dorothy's hand, released it, then picked up the bag.

"Give me a kiss." Helen ordered. Dorothy said nothing more. If there was one thing Dorothy Nolan understood, it was goodbye. The two women kissed.

"Goodbye, Dorothy."

✠   ✠   ✠

A gentle rain splattered the bus window beside Erika then angled down the glass in little streams as the Greyhound bus crossed a wooden bridge over the Big Sandy River. Already over an hour since leaving Nashville, the bus had not yet made its way out of Tennessee. Faithful stops in small, sleepy towns slowed the journey: Dickinson, Waverly, Black Center. Trains covered miles much faster, but Erika had the time to spare and varying the manner of travel was good procedure.

The driver bellowed out the next stop loudly enough for those in the back of the bus to hear.

"Next stop, Paris! Fifteen minutes!"

Erika smiled. She had noticed the name on the Tennessee map. The French capital was Erika's favorite city. For a brief while before the war she was very happy there.

She thought of Claude…and Sophie…and the loft on the Left Bank….

CHAPTER 17

There is no avoiding war; it can be only postponed to the advantage of others.

—Niccolo Machiavelli, 1514

Paris—July 1939

"For you, Mademoiselle."

The young Parisian boy looked to be seven or eight. He had just run up to Erika and handed her a flower as she strolled the Luxembourg Gardens. The Luxembourg Palace loomed behind her.

Erika took the flower and knelt beside the boy.

"Thank you, Monsieur," Erika smiled and kissed the boy's cheek. The little boy blushed then ran back to his mother who sat on a park bench nursing an infant. A small girl, surely the boy's little sister, sat beside the woman and watched the baby suckle with great interest.

Erika smiled and waved at the mother who smiled back and nodded, her hands busy with the baby.

Erika put the flower to her nose.

A sweet vermouth.

To Erika, the flower smelled like the sweet wine.

Erika had been to Paris before, briefly passing through with her parents in 1936 when the family returned to Germany to attend the summer Olympics, then again as the family returned to the States after the games. She also spent a spring weekend here in '37 with a girlfriend, a fellow translator Erika befriended while working at the Seehaus, but this was Erika's first trip to Paris by herself and her first visit of any length.

Another tediously long training session at Quenzsee had just been completed. Erika signed on with Abwehr the previous summer and had been at Quenzsee intermittently since then. Originally she was under the naive misconception that when her initial indoctrination at Tegel and the required ten-week Abwehr training session at Quenzsee was completed her training would be over. But since last summer Quenzsee recalled her on three separate occasions and sent her to other locations in Germany on practice operations.

In October she was ordered to Nuremberg on a practice mission. Her assignment was to burglarize the office of a doctor, his name chosen randomly from the telephone directory. Erika was expected to accomplish this without leaving any traces of the illegal entry. There could be no broken glass from a window, no damaged door lock. That night Abwehr supervisors waited in a car down the street for Erika to return with a letterhead of the doctor's stationary to prove her success. Checks with the police were made the next day to insure Erika's entry had been discreet. If someone from the doctor's office called the police the next morning about an apparent break in (even if nothing of value was taken) the mission was a failure. No such police report was made.

In January she was in Stuttgart. Her orders: to follow a local government official (like the doctor, this man was chosen at random by her Abwehr supervisors) and record the man's daily routine for two weeks without the man suspecting he was followed. Erika doubted the man's wife knew of the young woman whose apartment the man visited on his lunch hour each Tuesday and Friday.

April found Erika in Dresden and now she was the one stalked. This time other agents were assigned to follow her. The location was chosen because Erika had never been to Dresden, and her task was to walk around in different parts of the strange city during various times of the day and night never told when she was followed. Her test was to spot the tails and lose them. It was an exhausting two weeks.

The combination of the training periods at Quenzsee and the ersatz missions in various German cities kept Erika busy for most of the past year. There were occasional weekend passes and a one week leave at Christmas, which she spent with her father and Eva Braun at the Berghof, but never enough time for any type of extended relaxation. Now, in July, over a year since she cast her lot with Abwehr, Erika was finally granted an extended furlough. Her next scheduled training was at a special radio school near Potsdam where she would learn to assemble a shortwave transmitter from individual parts. Reporting date for the Potsdam school, however, was not until mid-September. For two months Erika was free, her only orders were to keep her Abwehr supervisors back in Berlin informed of where she could be contacted.

She started her furlough by spending four days with Eva Braun at the Berghof, then three days alone bicycling in the Alps. Two days ago Erika boarded the Orient Express in Munich; she arrived in Paris yesterday morning. At a salon on the Rue de Grenelle she bought a yellow summer dress. (It was especially tight and the hemline probably a bit too short, but it was July, the dress cool, *and this is Paris after all,* she reasoned.) In the yellow dress she had spent a pleasant day walking the Champs Élysées and wandering the gardens and parks near the Seine.

Young children ran about the Gardens taking advantage of the carousel, donkey rides, and juggling acts staged for their amusement. On the walk ahead a small group of puppeteers entertained a crowd of young children. Erika approached and stood behind a group of children at one of the puppet booths. Two marionettes sang and danced on strings, the puppeteer hidden behind a curtain. When the presentation ended, the children scattered quickly, looking for the next diversion.

Erika too started to move on. Turning away, she again placed the little boy's flower to her nose when she heard someone call out behind her.

"Pretty flower. Pretty Mademoiselle. Pretty flower."

It was a high-pitched staccato. Erika looked back. All the children were gone. One marionette still skipped on stage.

"Pretty Mademoiselle. May I smell your flower?" the marionette was addressing Erika.

Erika smiled, walked over to the puppet and held the flower to the wooden nose.

"Ah-choo!!!" the toy sneezed. Erika laughed.

"My name is Chi Chi," said the puppet. The string from the overhead stick moved and the marionette's hand reacted, reaching out toward Erika. Erika shook the little wooden hand.

"Hello, Chi Chi. My name is Erika. It is very nice to meet you."

"What part of Germany are you from, Fräulein?" the puppet questioned.

"Is my accent that noticeable?" Erika asked surprised. She thought she did a pretty good job stifling her German accent when speaking French.

"No, your French is fine," the toy answered. "Your handshake is German."

Of course, thought Erika. She made a mental note.

"You are very wise, Chi Chi. Yes, I am from a little town in Baden originally. Now I live in Berlin."

"Ah, Berlin," the toy sang out. "A beautiful city, Fräulein." The marionette began dancing across the stage and singing a popular German cabaret song. *"Das ist Berlin, Berlin, Berlin…"*

Erika laughed and asked: "Are your talents endless, Chi Chi? What else can you do?"

"I can offer the pretty German Fräulein a guided tour of Paris."

"I thank you for your chivalry, Chi Chi, but I will manage. Adieu." She walked slowly away. Erika made her way along the Boulevard St. Michel and eventually crossed the Seine near the Île de la Cité. At a sidewalk cafe that looked like it had materialized directly off a Parisian postcard, Erika found a shaded table overlooking the river. She ordered a glass of port and had just taken the first sip when Chi Chi hopped up on the table from behind.

"May I sit with you, pretty German Fräulein?" The marionette's high-pitched voice had not changed.

Erika turned. A young man held the marionette sticks. He smiled and blushed slightly when Erika swivelled to face him. About Erika's age, his hair was dark and needed combing. He had green eyes and sun freckles across his nose. The smile was that of a little boy who had just been caught with his hand in the cookie jar. Not on assignment, Erika let down her guard. She had no reason to be wary of a tail so she had not spotted the young man following her.

"Your little friend is a rascal," Erika addressed the young man. "You should teach Chi Chi it's not proper to follow strange women around. Does he do this often?"

"Only if they forget their flower," the young man said, his voice normal now. He handed Erika the flower the little boy gave her. She forgot it on the puppet stage. Erika smiled, thanked him, and took the flower. After an awkward moment, Erika let the young man know it was alright for him to sit with her.

The young Frenchman's name was Claude Vauzous, and he had ambitions to be a great painter. But he joked that his work did not yet hang in the Louvre where he worked as a tour guide to support himself. He told Erika he also raised a little extra money putting on puppet shows in the gardens and parks. After he asked, Erika told him she was a student at Berlin's Conservatory of Music.

The struggling French artist and the German spy-in-training ended up sharing a bottle of wine and an afternoon of pleasant conversation. The Frenchman had an amazing sense of humor, most of it self-depreciating; he succeeded in keeping Erika laughing for a large portion of the time they shared. He was also clumsy. He spilled a glass of wine and used the clothing covering Chi Chi to soak some of it up. He was obviously embarrassed by spilling the wine, so Erika stifled the laugh as she watched him use his puppet to clean the table. She handed him a napkin and helped him daub the spill. Finally, with the wine-soaked Chi Chi keeping another puppet company in his master's shoulder bag, Claude escorted Erika back to her hotel on the Rue de Rivoli where they said goodbye.

Erika's plans the next day included a tour of Notre Dame. On her way out of the hotel, while checking her room key at the front desk, the clerk informed her a package had been dropped off earlier that morning. The clerk handed Erika a large, flat package covered with brown paper, obviously a poster or painting. Erika found a chair in the lobby and removed the paper. It was a watercolor portrait of Erika holding the little boy's flower to her nose. Scrolled at the bottom was "The Flower of Germany" in red paint. The small signature in the corner: Vauzous. *He must have been up most of the night painting this,* she thought.

There was a note.

I have to work today. The Mona Lisa frowns if I do not report to her at the museum, so too my landlady frowns when I am late with the rent. My prayers are that the Flower of Germany will meet me for lunch today at our cafe. I can be there at noon and happily wait forever.

Erika wondered if all Frenchmen were such effective charmers.

She met Claude Vauzous for lunch and again for dinner and a cabaret that evening. They left the nightclub early. Erika suspected their reason for leaving the cabaret so soon was that her date was out of money, but she did not embarrass him by offering to pay. It was on a bridge over the dark Seine where the politically odd couple shared their first kiss before heading to the Frenchman's flat.

Claude told Erika that he shared a studio loft with two other young artists: a male sculptor and a young woman who studied theater and hoped to be an actress. The attic flat sat over a bakery on the Rue Monge on the Left Bank. After climbing a long flight of stairs, Claude Vauzous unlocked the heavy steel door leading into the flat and followed Erika in. The first thing Erika saw was a naked, ample-breasted young woman sitting on a stool under a bright light. A man sat a few feet away working on a sculpture of the naked woman, his hands and apron covered with wet gray clay. Captivated by his work, the man seemed not to notice the couple. The woman turned to Erika, smiled and offered a cheerful greeting, displaying no reaction at all to the fact she was naked.

"Sit still!" the man covered in clay yelled at the woman.

"I've been sitting here for hours," the young woman yelled back. "My bottom is going to sleep!"

The surreal sight and the woman's comment struck Erika as hilarious and she started to giggle. Erika had entered the room ahead of Claude who, when he saw the naked woman, turned red and looked frantically around the room for something to cover the woman. Finding nothing suitable, in desperation the Frenchman grabbed up a pair of shoes, handed them to the woman, and ordered her to cover herself. The woman threw one of the shoes at Claude, hitting him in the chest.

"As you can see," the girl turned to Erika and shook her head, "I live with idiots." Erika laughed, then assured Claude she was not offended by the naked woman; her assurance seemed to lessen his anxiety.

"Sit still!" the sculptor bellowed again, still ignoring Claude and Erika. The naked woman threw the other shoe at the sculptor who ducked at the last second.

"Be careful!" the sculptor screamed. "You almost hit my work!"

The woman ignored the young man's rebuke and offered her hand to Erika.

"Since the idiots won't introduce us, my name is Sophie."

Erika, finding it hard to stop laughing from the absurdity, walked over to the woman and shook her hand. "Nice to meet you, Sophie. I am Erika."

To the sculptor's exasperation, Sophie insisted on a break. She rose from the stool, walked to the far end of the room and disappeared behind a curtain. She reappeared wearing a short, white cotton robe, loosely tied in front.

Claude introduced the intense young sculptor. His name was Sebastian. Sebastian did not offer his hand since it was covered in wet clay, but he nodded and smiled pleasantly.

The studio was one large room that stretched the length of the building. Sleeping quarters were located at the end of the room—three cubicles separated only by curtains. From behind one of these curtains Sophie had fetched her robe. At the near end of the room there was a toilet and metal bathtub that looked more like a cattle trough. The plumbing fixtures sat openly in the corner and looked comically out of place in the large room. Exposed pipes led Erika to conclude the bathroom was probably hastily installed as an afterthought so the room could be rented for more money. Here again a sliding curtain, now pulled back and tied open, offered the only privacy. Cluttering the rest of the room were easels, paint, canvases both blank and with drawings in various stages of completion, sculpting tools and supplies, and books stacked helter skelter on the floor in the absence of book shelves. Several posters adorned the walls, most advertised various Parisian theatrical productions or American movies. The furniture was sparse: a well-worn divan; a lopsided chaise lounge; three stools of varying heights; two wooden chairs; and two battered, persnickety pedestal fans that clanked as blades whirled. Along one long wall sat an old-fashioned ice box in no need of a block of ice because it contained no food to cool. In general the decor was chaos but surprisingly clean.

Sophie, noticing Erika looking around the room, offered: "You should have seen the place before I got here. They lived like pigs."

Sebastian brought forth a bottle of wine that was only half full while the gabby Sophie gave Erika brief biographies.

Sophie was twenty-three, Sebastian one year older. Claude was twenty-two. Claude and Sebastian had shared the apartment for almost a year before Sophie moved in. Sophie told Erika she was an orphan, originally from Lyon, and had come to Paris to pursue a career in the theater. Sophie's acting career had so far failed to pay the bills so she made ends meet posing as a nude model for photographers, painters, and sculptors. She met Claude and Sebastian last spring when they hired her to pose.

"When I walked in here," Sophie rolled her eyes, "I found out they had pooled their money. Claude wanted to paint while Sebastian worked his clay. I told them they would each have to pay the going rate, but they didn't have the money. Of course me being the soft-hearted fool, I felt sorry for them and posed for one fee."

Sophie moved in a few days later. The two starving artists became three. Although Sophie was the same age and in the same dire financial straits as the men, she made it her duty to take care of the young men, adopting the role of mother hen to the two struggling males. Erika could tell it was a role Sophie enjoyed despite her light-hearted complaining.

Sophie's acting work was practically nonexistent and her modeling work sporadic except for one regular job at a private art school in the Latin Quarter. The school held its class in the instruction of the painting and sculpting of the female form on Tuesday evenings, so for four hours every Tuesday evening Sophie and two other girls modeled at the school. Other than Tuesday evening, Sophie never knew when she would work. She was on the list with several modeling agencies around Paris, but these lists contained hundreds of names of young female models. The hard times of the worldwide depression were still very much concrete and the extra pay for nude modeling proved irresistible for many struggling actresses/models like Sophie. Sophie told Erika that competition from girls willing to do more than simply model made it hard for the honest girls. According to Sophie, many girls were quite willing to service the male personnel at the modeling agencies in order to keep their names at the top of the modeling job call lists.

When it was Erika's turn to tell of her journey through life, she was the student of music on vacation until classes started again in September.

The half-empty bottle of wine disappeared quickly. A second bottle was not on hand and no one offered to go get one (Erika supposed they could not afford it). With the wine finished, Sebastian seemed impatient to continue his work. Sophie removed the robe and retook her position on the stool. Claude, Erika, and Sophie continued to chat while Sebastian again delved into his work. At one point Erika asked to see some of Claude's work and he led her to a stack of canvasses. A few were nature scenes, but most were of various Parisian landmarks: the Eiffel Tower, Arc de Triomphe, the Place de la Concorde, Notre Dame. Most of city's famous landmarks were there and very well done Erika thought. Some were oils, some watercolors, a few charcoal or pencil sketches. There were two nudes—one pencil, the other watercolor. The watercolor presented the woman sitting stoically and facing a Grecian urn that sat atop a marble pedestal; in the pencil sketch the woman was reclining. Both works obviously modeled by Sophie.

Eventually Claude and Erika retreated behind Claude's curtain. Sophie continued to pose and Sebastian continued to mold into the wee hours of the morning. When Sebastian's artistic inspiration had finally waned, the two retired for the night—Sebastian behind his curtain and Sophie behind hers.

It was late morning, and Erika and Claude Vauzous were still sleeping when Sophie pulled back their curtain.

"Wake up love birds," Sophie ordered. "Claude, this is your only day off work until next week. I won't let you sleep the entire day away. We must show our German friend Paris."

Erika awoke to the sound of Sophie's beckoning and the pleasant aroma of freshly baked bread permeating the loft from the bakery below. Erika and Sophie exchanged good mornings. Sophie, wearing the white cotton robe, leaned over to shake the still sleeping Claude. Claude mumbled something unintelligible and turned over. Sophie told

Erika it was up to her to rouse the sleepyhead, then walked out of the small room and closed the curtain behind her.

Erika threw the cover off both of them and quickly succeeded in opening Claude's eyes by caressing him. When he focused on Erika's face, he smiled and drew her to him.

It was well past noon by the time everyone dressed and was ready to leave the studio. Sunday was also Sebastian's day off work. (He toiled at a job he hated as a cobbler's helper.) Among the three young friends, Erika received an expert tour of Paris, at least the part that can be covered on foot in one afternoon. Sebastian especially displayed detailed knowledge of the history behind many of the famous landmarks. The walking tour took them near Erika's hotel and she stopped in for a change of clothes. Money was scraped together by the Parisians for American hot dogs purchased from a street vendor. Erika offered to buy everyone's lunch but male pride would have none of it.

The next several days developed a pattern. The loft sweltered in the afternoons so little time was spent there from noon until early evening. ("No wonder Sophie runs around naked," Erika kidded the group.) Both Claude and Sebastian worked during the weekdays so Sophie acted as Erika's afternoon escort around Paris. In the evening a pot luck dinner, usually some sort of soup or stew Sophie could throw together for a pittance, was followed by chat and perhaps a short stroll, then back to the loft. The evenings usually ended with Sebastian working his clay (he finished the nude and was now working on a bust of Napoleon using a portrait in a book for a model) while Claude and Erika made love behind Claude's curtain.

✠　　　　　✠　　　　　✠

Time passed quickly during Erika's idyllic summer of '39. July became August. Erika now lived with the three artisans full-time, all sharing the carefree Bohemian lifestyle of the Paris loft.

Sometimes friends stopped by. Most were fellow artists and, like Erika's three new friends, young and notably poor. One evening a young man, a Jewish friend of Sebastian's, came calling and the group talked until the wee hours about the volatile political situation in Europe. *Would Hitler start a war?* Since Erika was German the visitor thought she would have the answer.

"I'm sure your opinion would be much better informed than mine. I have to admit I'm frightfully ignorant of politics," was the extent of Erika's reply.

Then came the unforgettable visit from Maud.

Maud was a friend of Sophie's who modeled at the art school with Sophie on Tuesdays. Erika concluded that the art school must seek varying female forms. Maud was tall and lanky; Sophie short and big busted.

It was the first time Maud visited the flat so, like Erika, Claude and Sebastian were also meeting Maud for the first time. There had been no wine in the flat since the half bottle that disappeared so quickly Erika's first night. Sophie produced a few coins she had squirreled away and was calculating if she had enough for an inexpensive bottle. Erika had offered many times to buy some food for the apartment or to pay for a lunch or dinner for the group but the men always refused so everyone went without. When Erika saw Sophie counting coins she spoke up.

"The wine is mine to buy tonight," Erika said firmly to Sophie and the men. "I eat your food and live here. No one's pride should be hurt drinking my wine."

The men stayed behind while the three women walked to a small market three blocks away. Maud was twenty-six and had been modeling for five years. Like Sophie, Maud found modeling work sporadic so on weekends she danced in an unrestrained floor show at the Moulin de la Galette. As they walked, Maud told Sophie about a job she was hoping to get modeling for an amateur photography club. These clubs consisted of amateur photographers who hired young women to pose, usually with the models starting out in flimsy negligees and eventually taking them off. Maud promised to put in a good word for Sophie if she got one of the jobs.

At the market, Erika picked out two bottles of wine and told Sophie and Maud to each choose a couple of bottles. Erika also purchased a wheel of cheese, some fruit, sardines, a bottle of cognac, and a bottle of vodka.

"Are you sure you can afford all this?" Sophie asked wide-eyed.

"I've been saving my money," Erika said. "Germans have that reputation, don't they?—tight-fisted savers."

Each woman carried a sack. During the walk back to the flat, Maud remembered a question she had for Sophie.

"So which one do you want me to make love to?" Maud asked it matter-of-factly. Erika was not quite sure she heard the woman correctly.

"Sebastian," answered Sophie.

"He's the thin one, right?" Maud was making sure.

"Yes, Maud" Sophie laughed. "The only one with any energy. Erika here is wearing the other one out. But make sure Sebastian doesn't find out it was my idea."

Sophie turned to Erika. "I'm worried about Sebastian. More and more all he talks about is politics and that there's going to be war. His friends are all a bunch of radicals and they have him all confused. I figure Maud might help him."

Erika wondered why Sophie did not take care of Sebastian herself but did not voice the thought. That first night, when she and Claude retired behind his curtain, Erika thought Sophie and Sebastian might spend the night together. But even though Sophie had no qualms about being naked in front of her male roommates, as far as Erika knew Sophie had not been with either. Now Sophie had lined up a friend to take care of Sebastian. A Bohemian lifestyle indeed, thought Erika.

Back at the apartment the men were flabbergasted by the bags of liquor and food.

"Erika lied to us," Sophie joked to the men. "She said she was a student of music but she is really a German heiress. Her family owns one of those castles on the Rhine."

Sophie knew whom to choose in her search for someone to make Sebastian and the rest of the group forget the dire political situation of Europe for an evening. Maud was a woman who required no instruction in the science of how to get a party going, and no prompting in the art of letting her hair down. The tall dancer requested music so Claude turned on the radio and adjusted the dial. Maud drank her wine straight from the bottle, the first of which was empty in thirty minutes. An hour had not yet passed before Maud voiced her supreme puzzlement at why in the world did anyone in the room still have their clothes on. Apparently thinking it up to her to set the example, Maud rose, took off all her clothes and started slowly dancing to the scratchy music emitted by the old radio, her second bottle of wine in hand. Sophie applauded. The men looked.

Maud insisted that Sophie dance with her and since dancing unfettered was a rule with Maud, she helped Sophie out of her clothes. The two women danced for a few minutes when Sophie whispered something to Maud. Maud turned to Erika who knew immediately that thanks to Sophie it was now her turn to strip, but Claude interceded and Erika's clothes stayed on.

Maud tried to convince the men to remove their clothes but both Sebastian and Claude skirted the issue. Sophie quietly reminded Maud that her job was to take care of Sebastian.

"Which one is he again?" the inebriated model/cabaret dancer asked for the second time.

"The taller, thinner one," Sophie whispered and rolled her eyes.

"Right, I got it now," Maud slurred and took another swig of wine. "The taller, thinner one. Aim me in the right direction."

Sophie shook her head in exasperation and turned Maud around to face the men. Both men stood beside each other just a few feet away talking and gazing at the naked Maud. Maud looked back and forth at each man several times apparently still having trouble identifying Sebastian who was clearly several inches taller than Claude. Maud turned back to Sophie.

"Give me something to measure them with," Maud said seriously. "I can't tell which has a taller and thinner one. They both still have their pants on."

Sophie's face reflected her frustration. Erika burst out laughing and almost choked on her drink; even Aryan blood is not immune to heavy doses of alcohol.

"I'm not talking about their...!" Sophie had to lower her voice.

"Okay, okay," Maud said. "What do the Americans say? Oh, yes. Keep your pants on, Sophie." Maud realized what she said and laughed hysterically. "Never mind, you don't have any pants on!" Still laughing, Maud leaned on Erika, then straightened up and took another drink. "Okay, ladies, I'll get it right this time." Maud again looked the men over, then turned back to Sophie. "Are you sure we don't want to just have an orgy? It would be less complicated."

As if reading the other's mind, Sophie took one of Maud's arms and Erika the other, then they walked her over to Sebastian.

"Sebastian," Erika said, "Maud likes you a great deal but she is too shy to make the first move."

Maud reached down between Sebastian's legs then slurred: "Yes, I'm too shy to make the first move."

Sophie shook her head as she walked away. "Now I definitely need another drink—something strong," she told Erika. "Where is that vodka?"

✠   ✠   ✠

It was a Thursday morning, the twenty-fourth of August, when Sebastian exploded through the doorway. The young sculptor left the flat early that morning heading for work when he heard a newsboy on the street shouting that morning's shocking news. Instead of continuing to his workplace, Sebastian purchased a newspaper from the boy and then ran back to the loft.

When Sebastian burst into the room, Claude and Erika were sitting at the small corner table that served as the loft's dinner table and main meeting place. The young lovers chatted over a cup of morning coffee. In another corner of the loft, Sophie bathed behind a curtain. Sebastian threw the newspaper on the table in front of Claude and pointed frantically at the headline.

Hitler Signs Non-Aggression Pact With Stalin

Claude looked at the words. He realized the importance of the news but failed to comprehend the significance for his country. He looked at Sebastian, waiting to be enlightened. Erika too saw the headline.

"What does it mean for us?" Claude asked his excited friend.

For a moment both Claude and Erika expected to be illuminated on the ramifications of Hitler's strange political move. Both were disappointed. After a pregnant pause, the state of excitement left Sebastian like the air from a balloon. He collapsed in another chair at the small table.

"I don't know," Sebastain admitted with a mood of defeat. Then, realizing a German sat with them, both Sebastian and Claude looked at Erika as if on cue and awaited her input.

Erika was perhaps more puzzled than the young Frenchmen beside her. *A pact with the communists!* On the surface it struck her as unbelievable. Perhaps the newspaper was wrong. Hitler spent the bulk of his energy in the 1920's fighting the Bolsheviks and blaming the German communists, along with the Jews, as being most at fault for the loss of the first war and the sorry conditions in postwar Germany. The Führer outlawed the German Communist Party within weeks of his appointment as Chancellor in 1933. Cooperation with the communists ran counter to everything the Führer had written in *Mein Kampf*. Now, if

Sebastian's newspaper was accurate, all that was forgotten? It did not seem possible. Was this news, if true, good or bad? No one in the room knew, including Erika. Her first thought was to get to a telephone and try to contact her father.

Sebastian and Claude kept staring at her, waiting for a comment.

"I don't know what it means," Erika answered their silent question. "Could the report be an error? It doesn't seem possible."

"It's possible all right," answered Sebastian. "Read the story. There is no mistake, Erika, it tells all about it, and on the next page there's a picture of your foreign minister standing behind Stalin as he signs the paper."

Erika took the time to read the account. Details were sketchy but indeed the following page pictured a standing Joachim von Ribbentrop leaning over the shoulder of a seated Joseph Stalin, both men's gazes directed at papers on the table.

While Erika read, Sophie opened the curtain that hid the bathroom plumbing fixtures from the rest of the open loft. Standing beside the bathtub drying herself with a towel, she had heard Sebastian make his noisy entry and was curious as to the goings-on.

"What is the excitement?" Unanimously ignored, Sophie wrapped the towel around her and joined the three at the table.

"What is it?" Sophie again asked as Erika read and the men contemplated.

"The Germans and Russians signed a non-aggression pact," Sebastian answered impatiently, irked that his concentration was interrupted. Sophie looked around at the faces on which expressions ranged from concerned to totally stupefied.

"Hey, wait a minute here," the still damp Sophie admonished. "'Non-aggression' sounds to me like another word for 'peace'. Correct me if I am wrong."

All three of Sophie's roommates looked at her. They had to admit on the surface the words sounded positive.

"But what does it mean for France?" It was the key question and uttered by Sebastian. It was a question left unanswered by the four young people. It was a question that would not be answered until June of 1940 when the Germans marched into Paris. Finally, the ever exuberant Sophie interrupted the heavy thinking taking place at the table.

"Peace sounds like a reason to celebrate to me," Sophie said. "Erika, I think the occasion calls for a party!"

Erika Lehmann looked at the happy French girl and smiled. She too hoped the news was good but for some reason, despite her roommate's glee, Erika could not shake a strange awareness of gloom.

"Yes, Sophie," Erika agreed, "a party."

That afternoon Erika Lehmann took a walk. Although she moved into the loft shortly after meeting Claude Vauzous, Erika kept her room at the hotel on the Rue de Rivoli. She was under orders to keep Berlin informed of her whereabouts and she kept the hotel room for that purpose. Even after moving into the loft, she checked at the hotel desk daily, either in person or over the bakery telephone, for messages.

Erika entered the lobby and identified herself at the front desk. She was surprised but nevertheless relieved that there were no messages from her Abwehr overseers in Berlin. In this matter, no news was good news as far as she was concerned and she had no intentions of contacting them. She had followed orders; they knew where she could be contacted. Perhaps even more surprising, there was no message from her father.

Erika took the elevator to her room (which she had not stepped foot in for almost a month) and placed a call to her father's apartment. The loft had no telephone and just as well; Erika wanted to speak to her father in private. Not wanting to talk to him at the Propaganda Ministry, she had waited to call until it was late afternoon in Berlin. Hopefully, he would be home. He was not and her call went unanswered. She would try again tomorrow. With no messages from Abwehr and unable to contact her father, Erika returned to the loft.

That night the attic flat on the Left Bank filled to overflowing with friends and acquaintances of Claude, Sophie, and Sebastian along with some people no one seemed to know but who were welcome regardless. It was Sophie's party to celebrate the peace agreement between Germany and Russia. A crowd most notably young and left wing centered their talk around that day's news and its implications for France. The French communists in the room (most were Sebastain's friends) mostly applauded the German/Russian accord. Others were perplexed or of no opinion. All that mattered to them was they were young, tonight there was no war, and some naughty cabaret dancer named Maud had removed her clothes.

No one in the crowd suspected that in one week Adolf Hitler would end peace in the world.

✠   ✠   ✠

Chapter 18

The Volkswagen is the car of the future.[6]

—Adolf Hitler

St. Louis, Missouri

August 1942

A few minutes before midnight on the day she left Nashville, Erika Lehmann stepped off the bus in St. Louis, Missouri. St. Louis would be her last stop before continuing on to her target destination. Two things needed to be done right away. First, she would drop the Southern accent and adopt a Midwestern one. No need to draw attention; the regional accent is always preferable for blending in.

Second, she would find a place to stay for a few days; a place of her own. Much had to be done. There would be no time to deal with a lover just for a convenient place to stay, plus she would need privacy. Erika took a cab to a downtown hotel and rented a room.

---

6 In 1933 Adolf Hitler sketched for Ferdinand Porsche a beetle-looking body style of automobile which would become the KDF (Strength through Joy) car and eventually renamed the Volkswagen (People's car). The Volkswagen designed by Hitler would go on to become the most popular single body design in automobile history worldwide.

She awoke mid-morning, showered, then breakfasted in the hotel restaurant. The next item of business was buying a car. Erika considered American cars bulky and hard to maintain, unlike her simple and reliable *KDF Volkswagen* back home. After checking out of the hotel (she would stay in a different one each night), Erika had a taxi drop her at a large dealer of new and used vehicles on the west side of town. Erika could easily afford the brand new '41 Chevy Master Deluxe two-door coupe that caught her eye. The price tag on the new Chevy was 743 dollars. But new cars drew attention, especially when driven by a twenty-four-year-old girl, so she passed on the Chevy. She looked seriously at a '38 Oldsmobile convertible, but here again convertibles draw attention, and the trunk of the Olds was too small. A car with sufficient trunk space was a necessity for Erika Lehmann. Finally she settled for a 1936 Ford Coupe. It had low miles and looked in good shape. The Ford should give her dependable transportation. Six years old and plain looking it should not draw undue attention. Erika haggled the fat, perspiring salesman down from $200 to $180 because she knew American car salesmen expected to haggle.

"Good choice, little lady," the salesman praised as he wiped his sweating neck with a handkerchief. "That V8 engine purrs like the cat that just swallowed the mouse, and check out those pressed steel wheels—no more wires, and it's got almost a half tank of gas." (The latter was an important selling point with wartime gasoline rationing.)

Erika followed the salesman into a building. She handed him her Missouri driver's license when he requested it. Erika sat by the salesman's desk while he left to assemble the necessary paperwork. When he returned, Erika signed a few papers with the name that was on her license, paid the man cash, accepted the title and keys, and thanked the man for his help. The salesman wiped his neck again and watched her drive the car off the lot.

It would be weeks and dozens of customers later before the salesman would notice several temporary license stickers missing from the bottom of the stack in his desk drawer. He would shrug and think little of it.

Erika drove the car to a garage and ordered four new tires installed and a complete engine tune up. All the mechanics were busy but Erika said she would wait. She tarried patiently through most of the afternoon while the work was completed.

With the work finished, Erika drove around to several gas stations and filled the tank. She had a forged 'C' ration card which allowed unlimited gasoline purchases but that card would not be used except in an emergency. 'C' cards were normally relegated only to VIPs or people who traveled on behalf of the war effort. A twenty-four-year-old woman flashing a 'C' card would raise suspicion.

'A' cards were the common gasoline rationing cards held by most Americans. This 'A' card allowed a purchase of three gallons of gasoline a week. Erika held several forged `A' cards so it was a simple matter of buying three gallons of gasoline then moving on to another station and purchasing three more gallons until the tank was filled—time consuming, but safe.

Erika spent five days in St. Louis. A different hotel each night: one night a decent place, the next night a flea bag. She had much to do before heading to her final destination. The next business after buying the car had to be her shortwave transmitter. One of the major hurdles to overcome with this assignment would be communication with Abwehr via radio. On her previous mission the distance between her location in London and the Abwehr communication sub station near Calais, France was barely one hundred and fifty miles. In London a very small and lightweight transmitter/receiver was more than adequate.

A German spy in America had two options for communicating with home: via a U-boat patrolling the eastern coast or by the *Bolivar* network. *Bolivar* was a string of German communication relay sub stations that stretched from Mexico to South America. When Erika reached her target location in America she would be over six hundred miles from the Atlantic and the nearest U-boat, and twelve hundred miles from the nearest Bolivar sub station in Ciudad Juarez, Mexico. Either way—U-boat or Bolivar—Erika would need a much more powerful radio than was required in England. A transmitter of such power was much too bulky and heavy to fit into Erika's lone suitcase. She would have to build her own. The only components for the transmitter Erika brought with her were the ones she could not buy in America without raising suspicion such as the metal plates for the variable capacitor, the converter for the superheterodyne circuit, the crystals, and a few other special, smaller components. The remaining parts she would have to procure and assemble herself, but they could be purchased separately or cannibalized from everyday home radios without raising suspicion.

It took her the better part of three days. Instead of buying the parts individually (she felt that might look suspect), Erika bought several home radios, all from different locations. From these radios she stripped and used the parts she needed: vacuum tubes, circuit boards, wiring jacks, among other parts. A few tools were purchased: a soldering iron, resin core solder, needle-nose pliers, assorted screwdrivers. She also bought a piece of plywood and a handsaw. Most of the work was done in the hotel rooms. When Erika felt she was finally finished, she tested the reception.

Silence.

It took three hours, but she eventually found and mended a loose solder connection and tried again.

At first the speaker gargled softly. Erika adjusted the frequency knob and suddenly the static cracked loudly. She hurriedly turned down the volume. Spinning the knob she finally tuned into some Morse Code. Erika listened and deciphered. The signal was coming from a freighter in the Gulf of Mexico, somewhere off the coast of Louisiana. The operator was chatting with his pregnant wife in New Orleans. The wife was giving her husband an update on her condition. Erika concluded an operator, probably at the merchant line headquarters near the docks, was sending the woman's message.

Erika continued to eavesdrop.

The man at sea informed his wife that his ship was two hundred miles off shore and due to dock in New Orleans the next day.

Erika checked her map and estimated the minimum distance the ship could be from her present location in St. Louis was eight hundred miles. Reception seemed sufficient.

Checking transmission would have to wait. Receiving a signal involved no risk; all the risk was in sending them. Only during transmission could a radio's location be discovered.

When finished, Erika smuggled the blanket-covered radio from her room to the car and drove several miles outside the city. In a secluded spot, she installed the radio at the front of the Ford's deep trunk. Already prepared was a false partition Erika fashioned from the plywood she purchased. The wood was covered with a piece of cloth cut from the front of the trunk. With the radio all the way to the front of the trunk, Erika placed the false wall into place behind the radio and secured the phony panel with two bolts and wingnuts. She considered it a pretty good camouflage job. The radio's hiding place would never survive a full scale search, but anyone glancing casually into the trunk should not notice the false compartment.

Erika Lehmann's target location was only a three hour drive from St. Louis.

She would leave tomorrow, after a visit to a cemetery.

✠   ✠   ✠

CHAPTER 19

The last time I saw Paris,
Her heart was young and gay.
No matter how they change her,
I'll remember her that way.

—1940 song lyrics by Oscar Hammerstein

Paris—September 1940

Erika's first Abwehr assignment, the infiltration of the American Embassy in Lisbon, had just ended. With some measure of pride she considered her work in Portugal efficient. Several bits and pieces of important information had been gleaned from the American embassy, all without the knowledge of the Yanks. Among the Allied secrets she turned over to Abwehr included the discovery that the supposedly neutral American Navy was secretly (and illegally by international neutrality standards) ferrying British saboteurs in and out of German occupied Norway hoping to disrupt shipments of Norwegian iron ore to Germany. The information Erika uncovered was particularly helpful to the German contingent in the city of Narvik working to stifle the problem of sabotage in that Norwegian port.

But, as happens, the information well eventually ran dry. The last two months of her mission failed to garner any intelligence worth the time and risk of her presence inside the embassy. The Abwehr powers-that-be decided it was time for their Lisbon asset, who had conducted her first mission commendably, to move on. There were bigger fish to fry. Erika received word that her mission was complete and she was ordered home.

The message was delivered to her at her Lisbon apartment by a young Portuguese boy on a bicycle. Hired to deliver a message by a stranger on the street, the young peasant boy knocked on her door early one morning and handed her the sealed envelope the stranger paid him to deliver. The envelope contained a folded piece of paper with one typed sentence.

Wotan invites you to Valhalla.

She reported to the German embassy in Lisbon to await extraction to Berlin.

Three very boring weeks were spent camped out inside the German embassy building. She was not allowed to leave for any reason. Being spotted on the street by someone who knew her as an American student (her mission cover) could not be risked regardless of how slight the chance of that happening in a large, overcrowded city like Lisbon might be. While confined to the embassy, only once did Erika encounter the henpecked chargé d'affaires whose wife caused all the trouble over the lost necklace. He avoided her piercing stares during their accidental encounter as earnestly as he avoided her during the remainder of her time there.

Finally Erika's orders came through to report to Ernest Kappe in Paris for initial debriefing. The Wehrmacht marched into the French capital on the fourteenth of June, and Kappe had been stationed in that city since shortly after the occupation to help establish an Abwehr field office. Under cover of darkness, *Lorelei* was spirited out of Lisbon by automobile and driven to the Portuguese border town of Baixa da Banheira where she boarded a train. After being cooped up inside the German embassy for three weeks, the train ride across Spain was most enjoyable. Trains heading east toward the Reich were not overcrowded like the ones leaving the Reich packed with refugees. The train ride through Vichy France was likewise pleasant.

Stepping off the train in Paris, Erika was greeted by both a beautiful late summer afternoon and an Abwehr driver who immediately took her to Ernest Kappe. She spent the rest of that day and the bulk of the next three undergoing debriefings on her first mission. When Kappe finally finished with her, she was ordered to report to Abwehr headquarters in Berlin but not before being granted a one week furlough. Erika chose to spend a few days in Paris.

There were friends to see.

It had been a year since she last saw Paris. Because of the war between their two respective countries, there had been no contact between her and Claude, Sophie, and Sebastian. It was evening when Kappe released her, so she decided to get a room for the night then go by the loft the next morning. Chances of catching someone at home should be better then.

Erika took a cab to the same hotel on the Rue de Rivoli where she had reserved a room the previous summer. There were changes. Red bunting and long red flags with a black swastika in a white circle now festooned the entrance of the hotel. The four-star establishment had been taken over by the Germans for the billeting of high ranking Army officers. This was one of several Paris hotels taken over by and for the German occupiers, including the Hôtel Ritz a few blocks away which served as headquarters for the Wehrmacht.

In the lobby a uniformed German colonel sat reading a newspaper distanced from two standing majors who laughed at a shared joke. Separating the laughing majors from the reading colonel was the fountain dolphin that still spewed water from its bottle nose. Erika recognized only the dolphin. At the desk she asked about a room and was informed by a nervous French clerk that only German Army officers above the rank of captain were allowed in residence. She produced her OKW credentials which identified her affiliation with the Wehrmacht High Command. The flustered clerk grew more nervous and called for help. Another Frenchman, obviously the clerk's supervisor, appeared from an office. Seeing the crest of the German High Command on Erika's badge, he apologized for his underling and issued orders to the clerk to assign a room.

Once in her room she tipped the bellman and asked him to bring her a newspaper. Exhausted from nearly four days of questioning, Erika took a very long bath, put on her mother's light-blue chenille robe, then settled into an overstuffed chair with the newspaper and a glass of brandy. The Parisian newspaper was still written in the native language, but the French viewpoint was glaringly absent. The newspaper had been taken over by the German propaganda machine run so efficiently by Joseph Goebbels and Karl Lehmann.

The headline proclaimed yet another "mutual" agreement between the Germans and the "host" French concerning the administration of the Paris city government. Other articles named and showered accolades on local gendarmes who realized that cooperation between the visiting Germans and the local police served French interests. Opening the paper to the next page, Erika's attention was instantly drawn to a photograph of a very familiar face. The caption and accompanying story vaunted the presence in Paris of the very high ranking German official who had arrived just yesterday to inspect local operations concerning the security and safety of French citizens. The article analogized the man to a knight in shining armor arriving with the interests of the French people uppermost in his mind.

Reinhard Heydrich was in town.

✠   ✠   ✠

It was a beautiful midmorning when Erika left the hotel. Instead of ordering a cab, she decided to walk the two kilometers to the bakery on the Rue Monge. Strolling the Rue de Rivoli, it was hard to ignore the changes brought by the German occupation. Very noticeable were the swastika flags festooning certain buildings, and the men standing sentry on select street corners wearing the uniform and distinctive flared helmet of the German Army. Besides these obvious signs of occupation, overall the German presence seemed unobtrusive to everyday Parisian life. French women still shopped, French men still took their morning coffee alfresco at the many cafes up and down the Rue, and because it was Saturday, out of school French children still chased each other about, stopping regularly to throw rocks into the Seine.

A third of the city's inhabitants fled south before the Wehrmacht entered the city. Thankful that their initial fears of rape and pillage went unrealized, most of the Parisians who stayed took care not to ire their conquerors[7]. Some went even further. At cafes passed during her walk, Erika noticed young French women enjoying a coffee with gray-uniformed Germans across small, white linen covered tables. The intermingling made Erika think of a comment she overheard between two maids in the hallway of her hotel that morning. "Before long there will be little Germans running the streets of Paris," one maid said to the other.

Anxious to see Claude, Sophie, and Sebastian, Erika turned a corner and walked briskly down the Rue Monge. Anxious and a little apprehensive. Would it be like old times? Or would the fact she was German dissolve the happy relationships of a year ago? They knew her only as a German student of music, but still her country had invaded theirs. How would they react to her now?

---

7   Author's note: The French had anticipated the worst when the Germans entered their capital in June. Journalist William Shirer observed that Parisians "believed the Germans would rape the women and do worse to the men." Instead he wrote that the natives who did not flee the city "are all the more amazed at the very correct behavior of the troops." The Germans acted mannerly to the French women and civil to the men. They demanded nothing free, paying for everything. John Toland, in his definitive biography of Adolf Hitler, wrote about the German troops in Paris: "They stood respectfully bareheaded at the tomb of the Unknown Soldier, armed only with cameras. They acted more like a horde of tourists on holiday than the fearsome creatures who had just humiliated the French armies."

She remembered the last time she saw them as clearly as if it were yesterday. It was a year ago: September 1, 1939.

The week before had brought the news of the German peace treaty with Russia. Erika recalled how puzzled everyone in the loft was upon hearing the news of the agreement—including her. Later that day Erika tried unsuccessfully to contact her father, but she finally caught him at his apartment early the next morning. He told her the accord with Russia should pose no immediate concern for France, but confidentially her father told her he thought the agreement spelled changes for Poland which sat sandwiched between the two according nations. But, her father added, because of the German/Russian accord, he was optimistic that the Poles would come to their senses about the corridor, and these changes would come through negotiations, not war.

Tragically for the planet, Karl Lehmann's hopes for compromise went unfulfilled. In the early morning hours on the very first day of that September one year ago the world began a lesson in *blitzkrieg*. The second world war of a murderous century had left the blocks.

Erika, and the three struggling French artists she shared so much with during that idyllic summer, learned of the invasion later that afternoon. Around a scratchy old radio the four friends sat rapt. Listening. The atmosphere in the room was weighty. After the broadcast, words came sluggishly. They knew enough of the French and British accords with Poland that Hitler's latest move might be the last straw. The three French in the room realized, like most of their countrymen, that there would most likely be no more appeasement; no more backing down. Sooner or later, and most likely the former, France and Germany would be at war.

To her French friends' credit, the news changed none of their feelings for Erika. To them, they had by now simply become a foursome.

But the next day Claude, Sophie, and Sebastian would return to the loft to find only notes from their German friend—one note to Claude, another to Sophie and Sebastian. Their German friend Erika was gone.

A year bursting with history passed, and Erika now stood again in front of the bakery. She ascended the flight of outdoor stairs leading to the loft and was not surprised when no one answered her first knock; all three were notorious late sleepers. Her second knock was harder and followed by a third. Finally she heard the bolt unfasten and her pulse quickened. It would probably be Sophie, the mother hen, whom the knocks wrested from bed.

It was not Sophie.

The door opened to reveal a woman with gray hair and an apprehensive look. Erika greeted the woman in French and asked if Claude or Sophie were home, but the names were obviously meaningless to the woman who told Erika she and her family had lived there less than a month.

After a brief pause, Erika thanked the woman who seemed most relieved to say goodbye and close the door. Erika paused for a moment's thought before descending the stairs and entering the bakery. Erika had purchased bread from the bakery several times during her stay in the loft last summer and remembered the elderly lady who stood behind the counter. She knew the woman and her husband owned the bakery and were landlords of the apartment above.

"Good day, Madame," Erika greeted the old woman who seemed not to recognize her. Thinking the young woman before her a customer, the old woman nodded and waited for Erika to place an order.

"I'm not here for bread today," Erika continued, "but I did come in several times last summer. You might remember me."

After studying the face of the young woman a tinge of recognition appeared on the woman's face. She did seem to remember this girl.

"I'm from out of town and I'm looking for Claude Vauzous. When I was here last summer, he and another young man were the renters of the room overhead."

As soon as Erika mentioned Claude and Sebastian, a shadow fell across the old woman's face. Erika noticed it immediately. The woman said nothing, then turned and left the room through a door behind the counter. The door led to the bakery's kitchen and in a moment the old woman's husband appeared. He too recognized the young woman but did not acknowledge the fact.

"What do you want?" the man demanded impatiently. Erika repeated the reason she was there. The old man became surly.

"They are gone and we know nothing of them. Now please leave." The old man hoped that would dismiss the young woman.

Instead of leaving, Erika reached into a pocket and brought forth a small black leather wallet. She flipped it open and showed it to the old baker. Inside was a photograph and credentials identifying her as a member of the German OKW. Her friendliness and her French now gone, she irritably uttered a few sentences in German. Not caring if the old man understood, she used the German simply to seal in the old man's mind that her credentials were in fact valid.

"Tell me what you know of their whereabouts," Erika demanded firmly, switching back to French. The color of life had left the old man's face. His demeanor changed immediately from cantankerous to alarmed.

"It is the truth." The old man's voice was jittery. "We do not know where they are. Just a few weeks after you Germans arrived in Paris your Gestapo showed up looking for Sebastian. He was not home but Sophie and Claude were. The Gestapo took both of them away for questioning while others waited here in the bakery for Sebastian to return. He returned later that night and the Gestapo men arrested him. They questioned me and my wife about Sebastian's activities but we knew nothing, thank God. We have not seen any of them since that day. We held the room for a while, hoping they would return, but finally we had to rent it out to someone else. I am a poor baker."

Beads of sweat bubbled on the old man's forehead. Erika had one more question.

"Did the Gestapo tell you why they were looking for Sebastian?"

"No, they told us nothing," the old man's nerves were finished. "I swear by the Virgin we know nothing more."

✠   ✠   ✠

[that evening]

It was Saturday night and business boomed at the nightclub Moulin de la Galette. Then again business had been especially good since the Germans marched through the Arc in June. All summer the cabaret filled to overflowing with German enlisted men stopping in to investigate the nightclubs reputation for staging one of the more revealing floor shows in Paris. Sometimes the girls of the Moulin de la Galette wore G-strings, sometimes nothing at all. The German men seemed to appreciate the French women's efforts immensely.

On the center stage, surrounded on all sides by uniformed German soldiers, six women performed a naked ballet while, on a separate nearby stage, an attractive, middle-aged woman in a dark red evening gown sang and smoked a cigarette. The smoke from her cigarette quickly blended with the heavy cloud generated by the German audience.

One of the dancers was Maud. When the song ended she, along with the other naked women, retreated to a dressing room to don a frilled G-string and sequined bra. After performances the dancers mingled with the crowd. Patrons could request a certain dancer's visit at their table by bestowing a gratuity that was given to a waiter and later divided between the girls. The visits were brief. The girls had only a forty minute break between shows and by the time they dressed and made their way to the table the time was much less, but still the requests were popular and a lucrative source of income for the dancers. The dancers' guardian, an old woman named Eloise who fussed over her girls like a overwrought grandmother, gave the girls the number of the table that requested their company.

Maud's table sat at the back of the overcrowded room. Because of the influx of business from the Germans, the owners added more tables. Now, because of the packed crowd, to cross the room the scantily dressed cabaret girls had to work their way through a virtual gauntlet of groping patrons. And regardless of their straitlaced behavior on the streets of Paris by day, the Germans in the room were men, and under the influence of alcohol and the cabaret's bawdy atmosphere the Germans were no different than men of other nationalities. As Maud worked her way to the table designated by Eloise, a German sergeant took one of Maud's breasts in hand as she passed. Not to be outdone, another soldier at the same table grabbed the other breast while unseen hands behind her quickly fondled other parts of her body. Maud joked with the men, few of whom understood her French but laughed with her nevertheless, while she paused for a moment to let them enjoy themselves before moving on. This scene repeated itself several times before she reached the back of the smoky room.

Maud's table was in the "balcony." Not a balcony per se, this was a small area at the back of the nightclub raised a few feet off the main floor. Five small tables outfitted the balcony which was reserved for couples who did not wish to mingle with the rowdies on the main floor.

Finally through the crowd, Maud straightened her bra and walked up the four steps of the balcony. At four of the five tables German soldiers and French women drank champagne. At the fifth table, the one Eloise indicated had requested Maud, instead of a couple a lone woman sat with her back to the wall. When Maud, approached she was surprised when the woman greeted her by name.

"Hello, Maud."

It took a moment before the cabaret dancer recognized the woman in the darkness.

"Erika!" Maud shouted the name as she slid into a seat at the table. The attention of the men and women in the balcony was on the near-naked showgirl who had just entered their little island, but after a few moments of staring, the people turned their attention back to each other and the champagne.

Maud's initial elation at seeing an old friend lasted but a moment. Maud's mood suddenly turned somber as her mind and emotions quickly associated the woman beside her with her missing friend Sophie.

Erika Lehmann knew where Maud's thoughts had suddenly traveled. It was the reason Erika was there.

"Do you know where she is?" Erika asked. Sophie's name was unnecessary.

"No." Maud answered sadly.

"Claude or Sebastian?" Erika continued. "Have you heard anything of them?"

Maud slowly shook her head. The tears welled in her eyes just before the thought struck. Maud suddenly remembered Erika's nationality.

"Erika, you're a German. You can find them!" Maud blurted out with naive enthusiasm.

Erika could have revealed her real identity but considered it wiser to keep Maud at ease.

"I'm just a student, Maud, but I will try. Tell me everything you know. Do you have any idea why the Gestapo was interested in them?"

Maud's information was sketchy, but with the right questions from Erika a general scenario of what could have happened came forth.

Maud did not find out her friend's sad fortune until almost a week after the arrest. It all happened in late July. On Tuesdays, Maud and Sophie both worked as models at an art school. Sophie never missed; work was hard to come by and Sophie needed the money too desperately. When Sophie failed to show up one Tuesday, Maud, thinking Sophie must be ill, went by the loft to check on her. No one was home that night or the next day and Maud became worried. Like Erika, she finally found out from the old baker that Sebastian had been arrested and Sophie and Claude taken in for questioning. At first the old man would say nothing, but Maud kept coming back and making a pest of herself until he finally told her what happened. As far as why the Gestapo was so interested in Sebastian, Maud could tell Erika only about a conversation she had with Sophie one evening after work.

Sophie fretted about Sebastian getting into trouble. She told Maud that Sebastian now stayed out late several nights a week, something he

rarely did before, and a certain group of Sebastian's friends started visiting the loft more and more often. Their talk made Sophie nervous.

"Did she tell you what they talked about?"

Maud shook her head no. She was late for the next show. The other
cabaret girls had already returned to the dressing room and the show
was ready to start. A bartender was sent to fetch Maud. She told Erika
she had to do one more show and asked Erika to stay. It was the last
show of the night after which they could go to Maud's apartment and
talk more.

"You can stay with me while you're in Paris if you like," Maud added.
Maud told Erika she had a live-in lover at the time but she added, "I
change them often anyway. I'll tell him to leave for a few days."

Erika thanked Maud but declined the offer. The two women rose from
the table together. Maud kissed both of Erika's cheeks and made Erika
promise to get back to her if she found out anything at all about Sophie.
Erika skirted the back of the crowd on her way to the door as Maud again
worked her way through the crowd and the sea of groping hands.

Erika enjoyed the cooler and fresher air outside the nightclub and
paused for a moment by the curb. Because it was between shows, a sizable group of soldiers had amassed in front of the nightclub. A German
corporal approached Erika. The soldier thought the pretty blond was a
native Parisian (and possibly a prostitute since she was alone even
though she was not dressed like one). He offered her a cigarette in very
broken French. Erika smoked infrequently, usually only on assignment
when warranted by a social situation, but she took the cigarette and put
it to her lips. The soldier struck a match.

The man kept trying to communicate in French which he butchered.
He even produced a small German to French dictionary from a pocket
and attempted to look up a few words in the poor light from the cabaret
sign. Erika had other things on her mind and decided against letting the
man know she was German. She was not prepared for a long conversation

with a homesick soldier. Erika scarcely looked at the man; when she did it was with a quizzical mien—like she did not understand a word.

As she stood with her arms folded and her gaze directed to the street she felt the soldier's hand on her bottom. Erika ignored the hand as she thought about Sebastian. It was clear that Sebastian had gotten himself involved in something he should not have, probably some type of resistance group or underground organization. Until she finished the cigarette, Erika continued to ignore the corporal and his hand, then she dropped the cigarette butt into the gutter and walked away into the darkness of the City of Light.

✠   ✠   ✠

CHAPTER 20

Reinhard Heydrich was the hidden pivot around which the Nazi regime revolved. The development of a whole nation was guided indirectly by his forceful character. He was far superior to all his political colleagues and controlled them as he controlled the vast intelligence machine of the SD.

He was inordinately ambitious. It seemed as if, in a pack of ferocious wolves, he must always prove himself the strongest and assume the leadership. He had to be the first, the best, in everything, regardless of the means, whether by deceit, treachery, or violence. Untouched by any pangs of conscience and assisted by an ice-cold intellect, he could carry injustice to the point of extreme cruelty.

Heydrich's only weakness was his ungovernable sexual appetite. To this he would surrender himself without inhibition or caution, and the calculated control which characterized him in everything else he did left him completely. But in the end he always regained sufficient mastery over himself to prevent serious repercussions.

The decisive thing for Heydrich was always to know more than others, to know everything about everyone, whether it touched on the political, professional, or most intimate aspects of their lives, and to use this knowledge and the weaknesses of others to render them completely dependent on him, from the highest to the lowest. It was this that enabled him to hold and manipulate the balance of power in a milieu full of intrigue and crosscurrents of personal ambition, rivalry, and animosity, while he himself remained in the background. He was master at playing antagonists off one against the other, feeding each one, under an oath of strict secrecy, with detrimental information about his rival, and getting still more damaging information in return. Heydrich was, in fact, the puppet master of the Third Reich.

—Walter Schellenberg, SD Chief of Counterintelligence
The Labyrinth: Memoirs of Walter Schellenberg. 1956.

Paris—September 1940

Reinhard Heydrich had been signing papers for nearly thirty minutes. The fact that it was Sunday mattered not to Heydrich, who never took a day off. The paper on which he had just affixed his signature authorized a temporary curfew for the Latin Quarter of Paris. Anti-German graffiti had been found in an alley in that district. The Latin Quarter curfew would remain until the criminals were arrested. He handed the paper to an aide who placed it in a brown leather valise.

The last document mandated universities within the Paris city limits to turn over within five days a list of faculty who were Jewish. Heydrich did not have to read the papers. He had dictated them to a secretary yesterday.

Without a word between the two men, the aide, an SS captain, secured this last paper along with the others, closed and locked the briefcase, then found his own way out of Heydrich's suite in the Hôtel Ritz.

Heydrich rose from the desk and walked to a window. The square of the Place Vendôme below was mid-afternoon busy. High-ranking officers of both the Wehrmacht and Waffen-SS came and went from the lobby below, a fleet of staff cars lined up at their disposal. The Germans had requisitioned the Ritz for their Paris headquarters, and the world famous hotel now housed the doers and shakers of the Reich, both military and civilian. The Ritz was an adequate choice, Heydrich thought. The elegant suite reflected his station in the Reich, his accommodations equal to or surpassing those of any of the Field Marshals who billeted there.

A telephone rang which Heydrich ignored. He knew it would be answered by his valet in another room. Sitting back down at the desk, he resumed work on a speech he would deliver Tuesday at a luncheon for local authorities. He would offer an olive branch. Not all of Heydrich's colleagues agreed with the Führer's strategy of easy treatment for the French. Some would scorch the French countryside and turn Paris into another Warsaw, but Heydrich saw the wisdom in the Führer's plan—at least for now. It was a shrewd political move which had so far succeeded in making France, if not an enthusiastic, at least a submissive vassal. So Reinhard Heydrich, the *Blond Beast,* would pamper the French for now and let the local authorities have a say in running their city (as long as their agenda coincided with the Reich's).

The valet entered the room to inform Heydrich that the SS security people monitoring the lobby were on the phone. Someone had arrived at the hotel requesting to see Gruppenführer Heydrich and was being detained by Heydrich's personal SS body guards while they checked with their master.

"It is a Fräulein, Herr Gruppenführer," the valet said. The man then glanced at a small piece of paper on which he had written the information given him over the phone. "Her name is Erika Lehmann and her identification states…"

Heydrich stopped the valet with a raise of his hand. The guards downstairs were under strict orders to allow no one up without personal authorization from Heydrich himself. Heydrich picked up the receiver from the phone on his desk and issued orders to the man on the other end.

"Have the Fräulein escorted up immediately."

Heydrich dismissed his valet, left the suite, and walked down the hallway to meet the elevator. When the lift's door opened, she stood between two uniformed SS Sturmmanns (Lance Corporals). She saw him and smiled.

"Erika, what a wonderful surprise!" Heydrich was sincerely overjoyed to see her and offered his arm. "When my valet told me you were here I almost didn't believe it."

Erika took his arm. "It is nice to see you again, Reinhard."

Heydrich momentarily forgot about the SS men who followed them down the hallway. Finally aware of their presence, Heydrich ordered the men back to the lobby.

"My men were cordial, I hope."

"Oh, yes," Erika joked, "the body search by your men was great fun."

Heydrich looked chagrin. He had personally issued the orders to the sergeant in charge of his personal guard detail to search anyone unknown who called on him.

"I apologize, Erika. I will discipline them. They should have called me first." Heydrich was fully prepared to punish the men even though they simply carried out his orders.

"No," Erika insisted. "They were merely doing their job. Promise me you will let it pass."

"I will promise you anything," Heydrich responded. "You know this by now." When she smiled, Heydrich thought her even more beautiful than he remembered. It had been over a year since he last saw her.

Inside the suite, Heydrich instructed his valet to bring a bottle of wine. Heydrich knew, of course, that she had been in Lisbon on assignment for Abwehr. Her telephone call to him from that city seeking his help in releasing some Portuguese girl from Gestapo interrogation was a serious breech of security on her part. Perhaps this was something he could use to finally get her to leave Canaris and work for his SD. Reinhard Heydrich was never above a little blackmail.

"I see you arrived from Lisbon unscathed," Heydrich put on the charm. "The beautiful Fräulein Lehmann, more lovely than ever."

"The assignment went well, Reinhard. In no little part thanks to you."

"Don't say that. You'll have me thinking I'm working for Canaris!" They laughed together.

They talked of small matters for one hour during which they finished off a very expensive Sémillon; Heydrich considered himself a wine connoisseur and gave Erika a brief lesson on the white wine. He also told her about his duties in Paris. In the city for just a few weeks, it was Heydrich's job to oversee a few security matters. Erika filled him in on certain aspects of her Lisbon assignment including the story of the maid well aware she was breaking security. She had her reasons.

Finally she rose to leave.

"You have forgotten our agreement," Heydrich admonished. "Your promise from Lisbon to have dinner with me."

"I have not forgotten," she assured him. "I was wondering when you would remember."

Heydrich asked her where she was staying then told her:

"I'll call for you at eight."

✠   ✠   ✠

Looking into a mirror in her hotel room, Erika applied the finishing touches of her makeup. Her hair reflected the work of a salon one block down the Rue. Not having an evening dress (she left most of her more formal clothes behind in Lisbon), a stop was made at a boutique that afternoon. There was no time for custom alterations so Erika had to find a fit off the rack. The dress purchased was nice although not elegant. It would have to do on such short notice.

To beguile Reinhard Heydrich would not be difficult. He was obviously infatuated with her, and he would do practically anything to win her over; Lisbon had a maid who was still alive to prove that point. Enlisting Heydrich's help again was the fastest and only sure way Erika could think of to find Claude. The Paris Gestapo would release no information to anyone, especially not to an Abwehr agent, unless ordered to do so by 8 Prinz Albrechtstrasse—or Reinhard Heydrich. She briefly considered trying to enlist Abwehr's help for a records check, but she would have to concoct a false story to convince Canaris that finding the Frenchman was important to German military interests. Her attempts to secure the Admiral's help would be difficult, take time, and could very well be rejected in the end. The best strategy was obvious.

Bewitch the Blond Beast.

It would be a dangerous game. Heydrich was no lovesick fool. If he suspected she was using him simply to find an old flame, the scheme could backfire on both her and Claude; Heydrich's nickname was earned because of his capacity for brutal retribution. Instead, Erika would secure Heydrich's help to find Sophie. Finding Sophie would hopefully lead to Claude.

Eight o'clock brought a knock on the door. Expecting Heydrich, Erika was surprised to encounter a short, middle-aged Frenchman with a bald head and graying goatee. The man identified himself as Monsieur Lelonge, the chief concierge of the Hôtel Ritz. He said he had been sent from Monsieur Heydrich and assigned to attend Mademoiselle Lehmann.

"Whenever you are ready, Mademoiselle," the little Frenchman announced with a polite bow. Erika left the man in the hall while she went to find the light evening wrap purchased with the dress. She rejoined him and closed the door behind her.

Outside her hotel, a very large and very polished dark green Mercedes sat idling by the curb. Small swastika flags mounted on the front fenders hung limp in the absence of breeze. A uniformed SS sergeant, Heydrich's personal driver, stood beside the back door waiting to open it for his passengers. Erika slid into the seat ahead of Lelonge.

The limp swastikas suddenly stood erect when the car pulled away from the curb. Erika had expected Heydrich but was not offended or perturbed when he sent Lelonge. Powerful men do such things. Perhaps it was security, perhaps he had been momentarily called away on an

important matter; regardless, it gave Erika a few more minutes to collect her thoughts. She was baffled why a hotel concierge was sent instead
of simply sending an SS underling, but she said nothing to Lelonge as
the Mercedes sped down the Rue. The driver made a sudden turn
toward the Place Vendôme, steered the big Mercedes through the square
crowded with other German staff cars, and pulled over in front of the
Ritz. The SS sergeant exited, circled behind the car, and opened the
door for the two passengers. Lelonge offered Erika his arm and escorted
her into the lobby.

Instead of seeing her to one of the hotel's restaurants, Lelonge guided
Erika toward an elevator and instructed the operator to take them to the
second floor. This was not the floor of Heydrich's suite and Erika asked
Lelonge were he was taking her.

"Monsieur Heydrich has arranged a suite for your comfort,
Mademoiselle."

Halfway down the second floor hallway, Lelonge opened and held a
door for Erika. The first thing Erika saw when she entered the suite was
a group of people engaged in loud chatter. Several boxes, large and
small, were stacked on and near a table by the door. When Erika and
Lelonge entered, the room became immediately silent with everyone's
gaze directed intently on Erika. When Lelonge clapped his hands, the
group scurried.

"What is all this, Monsieur Lelonge?" Erika was baffled.

"Monsieur Heydrich ordered some gifts, Mademoiselle." Again
Lelonge turned and clapped toward the group of people. From a box as
long as a person a woman brought forth an exquisite dark red evening
gown while a man sat nearby extracting jewelry from an attaché case. It
was now evident to Erika why Lelonge was sent to fetch her.

"Make-up!" Lelonge barked and two women hurried toward Erika
then hustled her into the suite's bedroom where the women helped her
out of her dress. A man followed them, pointed to a bathroom door and
gruffly instructed Erika to remove her makeup. The women followed

her insisting they do most of the scrubbing. With makeup gone and still in her slip, Erika was taken back out to the bedroom where a station had been set up for the man's work. The man was Emile Lachaud, and he applied makeup as gently as a cowboy branded cattle. But Lachaud was renowned for his work throughout Europe and in demand by the richest and most famous actresses and socialites. Even queens gladly withstood his crotchety attitude and painful assault on their faces for the dazzling results. Lachaud was a wizard in his craft, the best and he knew it, and he suffered no suggestions or complaints from his subjects.

When Lachaud finished with his torture, he left the room while his two assistants gathered up his wares. Cued by Lachaud's departure, a male hairdresser entered and, from a photograph of a hairstyle chosen by Heydrich, redid Erika's hair. The women attending the clothes followed. They helped Erika out of her slip and into the strapless red dress. Shoes were chosen from a large trunk of many. The jeweler had waited patiently, knowing he was last. A choker necklace of sapphires encrusted with diamonds soon encircled her neck under matching earrings.

At nine thirty, an hour and a half past the time Erika thought she would be dining with Reinhard Heydrich, she was turned back over to Monsieur Lelonge. The fussy Frenchman looked her over like a mother checking her children after a bath. Erika's thoughts on the outlandish attention from all these people were ambivalent. If this is what Heydrich wanted, so be it. She had her own agenda for the evening.

Satisfied with his inspection, the Frenchman Lelonge escorted Erika Lehmann back to the elevator.

✠   ✠   ✠

"Well, give me your opinion." Erika stood in Heydrich's suite and removed the lace evening wrap from her shoulders, the expensive wrap another courtesy of Lelonge.

"Stunning," said Heydrich as he looked Erika up and down like a sculptor proud of his work.

"You certainly are full of surprises," Erika offered truthfully, referring to the makeover. "After this, I'm afraid to even guess about dinner."

Heydrich laughed. On a nearby table a silver bucket iced a bottle of Dom Perignon. Heydrich rocketed the cork and filled two crystal flutes. Erika was surprised by his attire. She expected more pomp and circumstance. Instead Heydrich's attire was civilian and almost casual: brown pants and a starched white shirt open at the collar.

"Where to dine was an easy decision," Heydrich said in reference to her remark about dinner. He offered her his arm and walked her to a set of double doors standing closed to another room of the suite. Heydrich opened a door and showed Erika in. A white-linened table with a golden candelabra sat in the middle of the room. Two French waiters in white jackets stood rigidly nearby. Heydrich nodded at one who immediately slid out one of the table's two chairs and held it for Erika.

"I took the liberty of ordering," Heydrich announced after both Erika and he were seated. "I trust you like *Médaillon de Mousse de Canard.*"

"Wonderful." Erika assured him. She had tasted duck before but not in this French style Heydrich referred to.

One waiter removed the candelabra to allow more room on the small table and an unobstructed view. He placed it on a stand alongside and lit the candles. The other waiter refilled the champagne glasses with more Dom Perignon and placed a small dish of pâté de foie gras in front of each diner. The pâté was followed by one large plate of escargots placed between Erika and Heydrich to share.

"So, Erika, what do you think of Paris?" Heydrich asked as he extracted a snail from its shell.

"I love it. It's perhaps my favorite city."

"Yes," Heydrich nodded, "I knew you would like it. It certainly has its offerings for someone like yourself…someone with a flair for the arts."

The talk remained idle while the waiters stood by. "Do you like the dress," Heydrich asked.

"It is very beautiful, Reinhard."

Heydrich smiled. "It would be an honor for me if you kept it...and the jewelry too, of course."

"Be careful, Reinhard. You might turn my head."

Heydrich laughed pleasantly.

He recalled when the two met. "I remember first seeing you at a dinner your father hosted for American journalists. Let's see...that would have been in '37."

"Yes," Erika confirmed, "I remember. My father asked me to attend as an interpreter."

"When I first saw you I thought you quite exquisite. The perfect Aryan woman. I still think that."

Erika smiled. "You're too kind to me, Reinhard."

Heydrich picked up his glass and offered a toast. "To Erika...to Paris...and to the Greater German Reich."

She clinked her glass with his.

When the pâté and snails had mostly disappeared the waiters cleared the table. The SS guard stationed in the hallway outside the suite let enter a French servant girl who delivered the entree. The pretty French girl pushed the cart into the room, turned it over to the waiters, curtsied at Heydrich and Erika then left without speaking. The champagne flutes were gathered up and replaced with wider crystal wine glasses. One waiter uncorked a bottle of Château Margaux and filled the glasses. No sampling was offered for Heydrich's approval and he did not expect it. The Blond Beast was a cultured man. He knew a wine as rare and elegant as a vintage Margaux was never subject to approval. It would have been an insult to Heydrich and to the wine.

With great flair, like magicians working an audience, the waiters placed the medallions of duck in front of Erika and Heydrich. Several wheels of cheese and *salade verte* were uncovered and arranged on the cart where they could be easily reached from the table. Heydrich then dismissed the waiters, ordering them to wait in the next room.

Surprisingly perhaps, little was said while the two Germans dined. Erika decided to let Heydrich dominate the conversation to see where it led, but, although he kept looking at her, Reinhard Heydrich spoke rarely. The SS and Gestapo overseer, second in command only to Himmler, simply studied Erika and ate his duck.

Heydrich finished first, then calmly sipped the Margaux and waited for Erika. When she finished, Heydrich summoned the waiters who brought forth another cart. This one contained the desserts. Erika chose the mousse au chocolat.

"I can see you have ulterior motives for this dinner," Erika said as she looked at the large dessert in front of her.

"What might those be?" Heydrich asked.

"You are intent on making me fat," she kidded. "Tell me, Reinhard, will you still think the same of me when I can no longer fit into this dress?"

Heydrich enjoyed the joke.

Eleven-thirty and dinner with Reinhard Heydrich ended.

"I would like to show you something, Erika." Heydrich walked her out to the sitting room where he donned a light jacket and grabbed a fedora. He handed Erika her wrap before picking up the telephone and ordering his car.

The same car and driver that delivered her to the Ritz earlier that evening now sped Erika toward the Champ de Mars, but instead of Monsieur Lelonge she now sat beside one of the most feared men in Europe. Heydrich preferred convertible automobiles and, at his insistence, the top was now down. The September night had cooled but Erika enjoyed the crisp wind after the long, hot summer in Portugal.

Ahead, the Eiffel Tower grew large as the car raced through the Champ de Mars. The famous park was all but deserted at this late

Sunday hour. Erika did see a young couple kissing on a park bench, love making everything around them oblivious, even the shiny Mercedes with the flying swastikas racing by. Erika's thoughts fell away one year to the Luxembourg Gardens and the little French boy who gave her a flower. She thought of Chi Chi dancing across his puppet stage. It now seemed an eternity ago. The SS sergeant finally pulled the car over at the base of the city's most famous landmark. He gunned the engine before turning it off then hustled around the car to open the door.

The immediate grounds around the Tower had been evacuated of locals hours earlier by a detachment of SS guards all of whom now stood at attention as Heydrich passed by with Erika on his arm. A skeleton crew of Frenchmen who worked at the Tower were on hand, ordered to stay late.

"Have you been to the top," Heydrich asked Erika.

"No." It was a little lie decided on in a split second. The top had seen her once before, during that other summer, but Erika felt it worthwhile to let Heydrich fascinate her. Heydrich showed her to the lift, the door held open by a nervous Frenchman who had no idea who in the world this man and woman were (both were dressed in civilian clothes) and why the infamous German SS had gone to all this fuss just for them. The lift had been giving the French operators trouble; it broke down three times in August stranding sightseers at various heights. The Frenchman was much relieved when the lift reached the top and the man and woman stepped out.

At a railing over nine hundred feet above Paris, the two Germans looked out over their country's recent conquest. Erika's previous trip to the Tower's zenith had been by day. The glimmering view at night inspired even greater awe. Even at midnight on a Sunday it was evident to Erika why the world called Paris the City of Lights. The war, which had dimmed lights in many European cities, had not diminish the glow of the French capital. Below, the world's largest diamond sparkled for as far as the eye could see.

"What's on your mind, Sonderführer Lehmann?"

"Beautiful seems a weak word," Erika answered, thinking Heydrich was asking her opinion of the view.

"You misunderstand," Heydrich turned toward her. "Why did you come to me?"

Erika looked at him then returned her gaze to Paris. The question caught her off guard. She knew telling him something about a promise of dinner made from Lisbon would be trite and ridiculous.

"I need your help again, Reinhard."

Heydrich turned back toward the lights. "Go on."

"Yesterday I attempted to find a friend—a French girl I met when I was here last summer on furlough. I spent almost two months here and she and I spent most of it together. We became quite close. When I went by her flat yesterday morning, someone else was living there. I talked to the landlord who informed me the Gestapo had taken her away about six weeks ago. I would like to find her, Reinhard." Erika paused. When Heydrich did not respond she asked outright, "Will you help me?"

Heydrich turned again to face her.

"No." He said it unemotionally but quickly enough to sound final. "I will do nothing to locate or help your friend." He studied her for a moment before adding, "But you can." Heydrich reached into a jacket pocket and brought forth a leather wallet. He nonchalantly handed it to Erika. There was sufficient light from the few incandescent bulbs lighting the platform walkway for her to inspect the wallet. On the outside face, burned into the hide, was a German eagle clutching a wreath-bound swastika in its talons. When Erika opened the wallet, her eyes immediately fell on a photograph of herself. She recognized it as the official photograph used for her OKW identification. On the other flap was a Gestapo credential card identifying Erika Lehmann as a "Special Investigator Executor to R. Heydrich."

"You would be the most powerful woman in the Gestapo…and in the Reich itself, Erika," Heydrich explained, "answering only to me. The

Gestapo would be at your unquestioned beck and call. You can travel about Europe or be stationed wherever you wish with your own car and driver. I know you love this city," Heydrich extended his hand toward the shimmering lights below. "I can give you this city, Erika. You want to find your friend? With what you hold in your hand, you can find her tomorrow. All you have to do is say 'yes', and this city is yours."

Erika looked again at the Gestapo credentials and then at Heydrich. His blue eyes burned a hole in her even in the dark. Like the story of Satan and the Christ, the Blond Beast had taken her up high and offered her the world. She closed the wallet and again looked out over the sweeping panorama of twinkling lights.

Unlike the Christ, Erika Lehmann said yes to the devil as the church bells of Paris tolled the witching hour.

✠   ✠   ✠

One hour later the Gestapo credentials lay on a chiffonnier next to the sapphire and diamond necklace and earrings. The elegant red evening gown lay across the foot of the bed. Back in her hotel room, Erika Lehmann soaked in a bathtub of steaming hot water thinking perhaps it was she, and not Reinhard Heydrich, who had just been bewitched.

In the suite at the Ritz a few blocks away Reinhard Heydrich poured himself a snifter of brandy. He handled her beautifully, he told himself and smiled. The prize was now his. He was sure she would serve him splendidly. She was intelligent, beautiful, and had already proved her competence. When they left the Eiffel Tower, she probably thought he expected her to spend the night with him, but he would wait. *She will come to me soon.*

Heydrich called down to an aide stationed in an office off the hotel lobby and issued orders concerning two attractive French women who had been picked at random off the street the previous afternoon. Forced into a car by the Gestapo under the pretext of routine questioning, the two frightened women had been held under guard in a hotel room on a lower floor. After ordering the man to have some guards bring the women to his suite, Heydrich entered one of the suite bedrooms, opened a bureau drawer, and extracted an assortment of handcuffs, leather straps, and a six-foot-long black whip.

✠   ✠   ✠

CHAPTER 21

God is alone—but the devil, he is far from being alone; he sees a great deal of company.

—Henry David Thoreau, 1854.

Berlin, 8 Prinz Albrechtstrasse

October 1942

Heinrich Himmler cursed his luck.

If it had been anyone besides Karl Lehmann's daughter, it would have been so easy. The girl would have had an unfortunate accident before she left Germany and the case closed.

But because she was the daughter of Karl Lehmann and because of the Führer's gullibility and misplaced sentiment, Himmler had been forced to let her leave the Reich. He now considered that a mistake. It had been almost two months since she boarded the U-boat on the west coast of France, and as yet, Himmler had been successful in finding out only that the submarine's destination was the United States.

The parameters under which he had to work were the problem. Great care had to be taken when requesting written reports or conducting interviews when it concerned the girl. It was imperative no one suspect Himmler had the slightest interest in Erika Lehmann. That huge obstacle greatly slowed the attempt to uncover the girl's mission and destination in America.

Many of the best leads could not be pursued. From the Quenzsee reports, Himmler assembled the names of the girl's Abwehr supervisors. But no one within the SS or Gestapo could detain and question these men without tipping Himmler's hand to Canaris, and eventually the Führer.

So the Reichsführer-SS sat waiting for Axel Ryker to check in. Ryker was several hours late. Ryker's orders were to report in twice a week to brief Himmler on the progress of the investigation. Himmler had given Ryker carte blanche. Not because he trusted Ryker. Heinrich Himmler trusted no one. Himmler chose Ryker because he was safe. Axel Ryker had no hidden motives for betrayal. Ryker was a simple man who did what he was told as long as it allowed him occasional fulfillment of his passion. Killing.

The intercom speaker on Himmler's desk came to life with a loud buzz. Himmler pressed the button and listened to Ursula Ziegler.

"Herr Ryker has arrived, Reichsführer."

"Send him in."

Ryker entered carrying a large envelope. He offered no "Heil Hitler" or greeting of any kind. Ryker never did. He dropped the envelope on Himmler's desk and sat down.

"You're late," Himmler admonished.

"Open the envelope," Ryker scowled. "I think you'll see it was worth the wait."

Himmler opened the envelope and extracted three 8" x 10" photographs. The photographs showed a middle-aged man on his knees performing a sex act on another man who looked to be in his twenties.

"What the fuck is this, Ryker?" Himmler asked disgusted.

"The photographs were taken with a concealed camera in a hotel room here in Berlin," Ryker offered. "The man standing worked for me when the photographs were taken. The man kneeling is an Abwehr training supervisor named Ernest Kappe. Kappe is an Abwehr administrator. He was one of the personnel in charge of Erika Lehmann's training for her current mission."

Himmler looked at an expressionless Axel Ryker, then back at the photographs.

The Reichsführer of the SS knew his luck had changed.

✠ ✠ ✠

CHAPTER 22

Little girl standing with her mother outside barricade watching reaction of the crowd to a Hitler speech in Nuremberg on Party Day, 1934:

> "Oh Mother, if I were not a Jew, I would like to be a Nazi."
> —*from **The New Order**, Time-Life*

Paris—September 1940

Early Monday morning William Stieff entered his office at 11 Rue des Saussaies, the address of Gestapo Headquarters "Region V" in Paris. Stieff had not had time to look over the week's agenda or even pour himself a cup of coffee before the intercom on his desk emitted its irritating buzz. He quickly pressed the button to quell the cacophony.

"What is it?" Stieff grumbled into the speaker.

"Someone to see you, Herr Stieff." It was the voice of Kurt Hoepner whose duties included checking people at the door and routing them to the appropriate official.

"Who is it, Dummkopf?" Stieff half-shouted, irked that the young Hoepner failed to supply a name.

"A special investigator from Gruppenführer Heydrich's office in Berlin," Hoepner answered quickly then paused for a moment as he read the name from the caller's I.D. "Erika Lehmann."

Stieff paused. During his brief stint with the Gestapo he had never heard of a female investigator. He knew a few women, *if you could call them that,* who sometimes served as interrogators. Stieff had seen some of the frumpy and usually obese Gestapo Fraus. One whom he crossed paths with in Antwerp, a Frau Klop, had three chins, a large black facial mole that one could not help but stare at, and more facial hair than he. But a female Gestapo investigator, never. *The idiot Hoepner probably misread the woman's identification.*

"Send her up," Stieff ordered.

Before the war, William Stieff toiled as a bookkeeper for a bank in Stuttgart. When the Wehrmacht began its impatient thundering across Europe, the various branches of the Reich military and political complex demanded additional personnel to man outposts and field offices in ever expanding territory. Stieff saw an opportunity with the Gestapo for an increase in pay and jumped at it. Now a low-level official in charge of record keeping, Stieff had been assigned to the Paris office in August after a brief stint in Belgium.

The young blond woman who entered Stieff's office was quite a surprise. The Gestapo keeper of records knew she would never be mistaken for Frau Klop. Stieff rose from his desk.

"Good morning, Frau Lehmann," Stieff greeted. "I am William Stieff."

"It's 'Fräulein', Herr Stieff," the young woman corrected him. "Good morning." Erika's Abwehr rank of Sonderführer was not used within the Gestapo.

"Pardon me, Fräulein. Please have a seat."

The woman handed Stieff her documents and waited for him to look them over. Along with her identification was an official letter signed by Reinhard Heydrich declaring she was indeed a Gestapo investigator attached to the Gruppenführer's office in Berlin and Heydrich's special envoy. She was to be given carte blanche and total cooperation from even the highest ranking Gestapo, SS, or SD personnel. The official raised seals of the Geheime Staatspolizei Berlin, the Schutzstaffel (SS), and Heydrich's Sicherheitsdienst, or SD, lined up across the bottom of the paper.

Stieff looked up at the woman who stared back at him. This was all quite new to him, but he had been Gestapo long enough to realize the woman sitting on the other side of his desk was someone he best cooperate with.

"What can I do for you, Fräulein Lehmann?"

"I am checking into a case conducted recently by this field office. I do not have an exact date, but the case was apparently initiated sometime in July. I can supply names."

"Very well," Stieff picked up a pencil and tore a piece of paper from a pad on his desk.

"I am looking for a French citizen, a female, named Sophie Somé. Resident of Paris. Age twenty-four. Apparently she was brought in for questioning along with two males of approximately the same age, also French."

Stieff scribbled the name on the paper and asked, "You said this was in July?"

"Yes."

"I'll see what I can find," the Stuttgart bookkeeper rose to leave the room. "I'll return shortly."

Erika knew several scenarios for what happened could exist. The worst: Sebastian had become involved in some sort of resistance movement which would subject him to a Gestapo interrogation of a sort she had witnessed in Lisbon. Erika recalled some of the communist and nationalist friends who visited Sebastian while she stayed in the flat last summer and feared this was the situation. If this proved true, things would not bode well for Sebastian. The landlord told her the Gestapo appeared looking for Sebastian and took Claude and Sophie in for questioning only after finding them in the loft, so those two were not originally suspects which was the good news. As Sebastian's roommates, both would have been questioned but released when their innocence determined.

The fact that they had not returned to the loft was not particularly disconcerting to Erika. It would be wise on their part to move on. Erika remembered Sophie telling her she was originally from Lyon. Lyon was now in Vichy France—a good place for Sophie to return to. Erika still hoped locating Sophie would lead her to Claude whose name she wanted to keep out of her inquiries if possible. And even if Sebastian was gone, she could still see Claude and Sophie to safety in a neutral country like Switzerland or Portugal. With her new credentials from Heydrich, getting them across a border should not be that difficult.

Stieff returned red-faced.

"Fräulein Lehmann, I found no records on a Sophie Somé. Are you positive about that name?"

"Yes, I am positive. She would have been brought in for questioning concerning a Frenchman—a Sebastian Delavenne. Check your records for that name, Herr Stieff."

Again Stieff departed.

Erika considered the absence of records on Sophie good news. Perhaps she and Claude were held just briefly and released. Surely, though, records existed on Sebastian. He had been the subject of the Gestapo's search. But maybe the news of Sebastian would be heartening as well.

Stieff returned much more quickly this time holding a folder in his left hand. He retook his seat, opened the folder, and thumbed through the papers.

"Yes," Stieff seemed pleased to report, "a Sebastian Delavenne was brought in on 25 July of this year on suspicion of subversive activities." Stieff looked at Erika and read her silence as an indication to continue. "According to this report, a member of an illegal French underground movement...a man, and a Jew no less, by the name of Jules Dumont, was captured. During interrogation, this Dumont named several co-conspirators; among the criminals the man named was Sebastain Delavenne, also a Jew. Delavenne was located and brought in on the date already mentioned. It says here that under interrogation this Delavenne refused to cooperate."

Stieff paused, then found the information Erika had feared. "On 28 July this Delavenne was turned over to the SS and his sentence carried out. He was shot for crimes against the Reich."

Even with the bad news expected, Erika had to fight to keep her feelings in check. She could not let Stieff suspect the reason she was here was anything but official Reich business.

Erika cleared her voice. "Any mention there of the woman I am trying to locate?"

Stieff shuffled more papers. "I do not find...wait, here it is...Somé, Sophie Somé. Yes, she was brought in and questioned about Delavenne." Stieff read quickly and to himself for a moment before continuing. "Also a Claude Vauzous was questioned." Stieff looked up.

"Go on, Herr Stieff." Now Erika did not try to hide her impatience. "Does it say where these two can be located?"

"One moment," Stieff said, rechecking the forms in front of him. "Here it is. When Delavenne refused to cooperate, it was naturally assumed this Vauzous and Somé were co-conspirators even though Delavenne denied their involvement. So they underwent further inter-rogation, of course."

Stieff again looked at the woman across the desk, but now a different person sat there. The pretty, soft facial features now seemed hard, and her eyes focused not on Stieff but at a point in another time and place. Erika knew what "further interrogation" by the Gestapo could entail. She remembered the maid in Lisbon. When Erika realized Stieff was looking at her, she again fought to compose herself.

"And...," she asked flatly.

"Both were determined innocent and released." Stieff further summarized from the papers: "Apparently both were in need of some medical attention after the interrogations, so they were taken to a local hospital and released from Gestapo custody there."

"I thank you for your efforts, Herr Stieff," the woman said as she rose to her feet.

"My pleasure, Fräulein. If there is anything else I can do to help, please call on me."

"Oh, I will, Herr Stieff. And I will take that dossier with me."

Stieff balked. "I cannot let the file leave the premises, Fräulein Lehmann. But I will be glad to have a secretary type a facsimile of whatever it is you want."

"I'll take the file, Herr Stieff," the woman repeated, then held out a hand and glared.

Perspiration bubbled on Stieff's forehead. He remembered the letter from Heydrich. He paused for a moment, then handed her the file.

"This is highly irregular, Fräulein," the overwrought Stieff cautioned. "There could be repercussions."

Erika looked at him.

"Yes."

Erika now had her own car and driver—another perk from Reinhard Heydrich. Both awaited her at the curb when she emerged from the visit with William Stieff. SS Sturmmann Ernst Zeller opened the back door for the quickly moving Erika Lehmann.

"Where to, Fräulein?" the young corporal asked.

"Just drive," Erika ordered, then ducked into the back seat.

This Mercedes was smaller than Heydrich's and sans the red flags, just another of many such vehicles that now cruised Paris streets. Since the occupation three months earlier, Parisians had grown accustom to the flood of Mercedes Benz and monstrous Horch automobiles now navigating their streets. The French scornfully joked (discreetly of course) that German big-shots gauged their manhood not on the size of their appendages but on the size of their chauffeur driven autos.

A gray sheet of clouds had moved in over the city and, as Zeller fired up the engine, the car's windshield ended the journey to earth for a few drops of rain. As Zeller guided the car away from the curb, Erika opened the file just commandeered from Stieff. The news of Sebastian's death was not a surprise. Erika had hoped for the best but she knew it would take much more than luck for Sebastian to have survived. A Jew suspected of subversive activities…no more needed to be said in the Third Reich.

Now, to find Claude and Sophie. Her eyes moved through the papers. There it was.

"Sturmmann Zeller," Erika drew her driver's attention. Zeller had been driving aimlessly around the Right Bank since leaving Gestapo Headquarters. "Hospital of the Holy Cross," she told him.

She would read the file more thoroughly later. Erika knew seemingly useless bits of information buried somewhere deep within a forgotten file sometimes turned the tide of a dead-end case. After Erika located the name of the hospital she quickly flipped through the rest of the contents. Under the papers, in the back of the portfolio, she found a manila envelope from which she plucked some photographs. Erika's face turned ashen. They were the Gestapo photographs of the "interrogations" of Sebastian, Sophie, and Claude.

"The Gestapo deposited them on the curb in front of the hospital on the 26th of July." The nun remembered the two young people but checked the papers in front of her for accuracy of date. "By 'deposited' I mean the Gestapo threw them out of the car and drove off. No one checked them in so it took some while to identify them. The man did not regain consciousness until the next day. The girl spoke only in babble."

"The extent of their injuries?" Erika asked the question reluctantly. She had seen the hideous photographs in Stieff's file.

"Both bled from multiple lacerations to the most sensitive areas. The man especially. Your people did a wonderful job," Mother Bernice said with obvious scorn. Erika had identified herself as Gestapo and the German-born nun made no attempt to hide what she thought of Erika and the Nazi regime in general. Born in Munich, Mother (then Sister) Bernice had been sent to France by her order during the first war. Mother Bernice considered herself not a citizen of either country but of heaven, and she had the absence of fear that people who burn with faith possess. The old nun was lean and hard from a lifetime of fasting; when spying sin or injustice, dark eyes ignited in their sockets like coals. Those coals now burned as she looked at Erika.

"Where are they now," asked Erika.

"Why do you ask? Did you forget to ask them something during questioning?" Mother Bernice said sarcastically.

"I am a friend of theirs, Mother. I met them when I was here last summer, before the war. I'm telling you the truth."

Mother Bernice glared at the young woman until finally something in the girl's manner convinced the old nun she was not being lied to. The dark coals softened slightly.

"Physically, Sophie recovered before Claude," the nun stated, "but she never recovered mentally from the torture. Finally, when Claude was able to leave the hospital, he took Sophie to our convent in Rennes where she is staying temporarily. Claude turned Sophie over to the sisters there and left. Sophie resides at the convent. I do not know what happened to Claude. No one has contacted Sophie since Claude left her with the sisters in Rennes."

The drive to Rennes took five hours so Zeller did not park the Mercedes at the front entrance to the Convent of Ste. Jeanne d'Arc until almost dinnertime that evening. Ste. Jeanne's was a large Romanesque structure of the French Norman style with plenty of ribbed vaults, pointed arches, and flying buttresses. Quietly located five miles outside Rennes, Ste. Jeanne's now served as a haven from war not just for the brides of Christ, but also for a certain number of the abused of the Third Reich.

It did not take long to locate Sophie. The number of women the convent could take in was limited, so all were known to the young nun who showed Erika into the dining room. Sophie sat near a window looking out, a surreal look in her eyes—that of a child's doll. Erika knelt beside her.

"Sophie."

No response.

"Sophie, it's Erika." Erika took her hand. The touch got a response. Sophie squeezed but still did not make eye contact. Erika held Sophie's hand for several minutes before speaking.

"Sophie, look at me…look at me, Sophie." Sophie did not turn her head, but tears welled in her eyes and one started down a cheek.

"Sophie, listen to me. I want you to stay here as long as you can. Do you hear me? Stay here as long as you can—as long as the war is going on if they will let you. If, after you get well, you have to leave, go back home to Lyon, not to Paris. Do you understand?"

Finally Sophie spoke: "Lyon?" Home sparked life somewhere behind the dead eyes.

"Yes! Sophie, Yes. Lyon. Go to Lyon when you leave this place."

Sophie turned and looked at Erika. Tears welled from both women and they hugged. Erika hoped she had somehow reached over Sophie's wall, and perhaps a conversation would follow, but a few brief seconds of lucidity for Sophie were avalanched by much longer moments of muddled thought.

Erika stayed for several hours and took over the task of feeding Sophie when the nun assigned to that job came by. Erika asked Sophie about Claude but, as Erika expected, the question drew nothing from the girl.

Before she left the convent, Erika asked to see the Mother Superior. Erika asked that Sophie be allowed to stay at the convent indefinitely and handed over a generous donation in Sophie's name with more to come later.

It was three in the morning by the time SS-Sturmmann Zeller dropped Erika off at her hotel unaware it would be the last time he would ever lay eyes on her.

Later that day, Erika walked into Reinhard Heydrich's hotel suite, tossed her Gestapo identification badge and papers on the table in front of him, and walked out.

✠ ✠ ✠

CHAPTER 23

The destiny of two great empires were tied up in some damn thing called an LST.

—Winston Churchill

Evansville, Indiana

November 1942

Joe Mayer turned right off of Ohio Street. Stopping at the security shed, he handed his identification card to a uniformed Navy Sea Policeman who checked the photo for a resemblance to the man behind the wheel. Even though the guard recognized Mayer, the official routine had to be followed. The sailor stepped into the small building, wrote something in a record log, returned and handed the government security clearance card back to Mayer. The young man nodded to another SP who leaned on a weight, raising the white wooden guard rail blocking the entrance. Mayer drove his car past the barricade and underneath a metal sign that read "U.S. Navy Auxiliary Shipyard at Evansville."

Mayer never failed to be amazed at the sight ahead. Before him was a massive jungle of concrete and steel. A garden of war with acres of crossing and twisting iron foliage casting lunatic shadows across the narrow drive ahead. Mayer guided his car through the alienesque landscape of belching smoke and fire.

This jungle of steel and concrete took root almost overnight. The Japanese planted the seeds on December 7, 1941. To Mayer, the scene served as testimony to the times. Innumerable tons of I-beams, rebar, and steel plating formed narrow metal canyons for trucks and forklifts. Ahead he could see the silhouette of one of the seven immense seacraft under construction. The place was a hub of activity even at seven in the morning. Workers scurried around the massive hulls. Scaffolding six stories high latticed its way around the sides of the enormous ships. Workers who could not find access via the scaffolds hung like spiders from cables. The constant loud banging and pinging of heavy rivets securing steel plates reminded Mayer of the sound of Hollywood machine gun fire.

Overhead, several enormous cranes stretched their cantilevered limbs high into the gunmetal November sky. Mounted on moving gantries, the cranes rolled along between the ships on train-like tracks rooted in four-foot-thick reinforced concrete. When the gargantuan cranes moved, they struck Mayer as looking like giant dinosaurs trudging their way through a dense primordial landscape. But in this jungle the rain was not water, but fire. Throughout this steel forest thousands of welders—mostly women—worked nonstop high overhead sending a constant shower of orange-hot sparks downward. The mist of this orange-hot rain, veins of bluish-gray smoke, whiffed slowly upward, like fleeing ghosts.

A good place for a metallurgist like Joseph Mayer.

Born and raised in Indianapolis, Mayer graduated valedictorian of his high school class. That accomplishment earned him scholarship offers from several prominent universities. His passion had always been the study of chemistry, his goal always to attend Harvard. But restrictions on the number of Jewish students allowed to enroll at the Ivy League school dashed any dreams he had of becoming a Harvard man. Finally, the University of Notre Dame came through with the best offer. Notre Dame had a respected chemistry department, so Mayer packed his bags and traveled the 150 miles from his parents' house in Indianapolis to South Bend. There he quickly became the top student in the chemistry program: the Jewish whiz kid at the Catholic university.

Mayer enjoyed his time in South Bend. He made friends among students and faculty. He even became somewhat of a favorite with the famous football coach, Knute Rockne, who himself had a degree in chemistry. Rockne invited Joe over to his house for dinner on a couple of occasions and they talked chemistry. Mayer respected the famous coach who had once been offered a job as a chemistry professor. And, although Mayer was himself quiet and studious, he also enjoyed the company of Rockne's fun-loving, sometimes raucous football players. He volunteered time as a compiler of statistics for Rockne and his team. Mayer was still an undergraduate when the coach was killed in a plane crash in 1931.

It took Joe Mayer only five years to earn both his bachelor's and master's degrees. He postponed work on his doctorate when Bethlehem Steel came calling with a lucrative job offer. He spent three years at the company with most of his work devoted to alloy development. Mayer quickly proved he was someone to be listened to in the company's research labs. Joe Mayer planned on happily spending the rest of his life in Pennsylvania finding ways to make car fenders lighter but stronger, and water heaters more rust resistant. But in 1936 he was contacted by the U.S. government and coaxed away from Bethlehem Steel with an offer to lead his own research team at a military research facility in New London, Connecticut.

Shortly after Pearl Harbor, Mayer attempted to join the Army and serve as an infantryman. The government quickly nixed that idea. A respected metallurgist like Joe Mayer could better serve the war effort working on improving metal alloys for tanks, aircraft, and submarines. Mayer spent six months assigned to a government research project at the Massachusetts Institute of Technology in Cambridge. There he worked with scientists from MIT and nearby Harvard (the school that thirteen years earlier felt it already had too many Jews). Mayer contributed greatly to a project that developed an unconventional anodizing process using a nickel alloy. When the project was completed, the Navy decided to use the process in its most recent high priority project: the building of a massive fleet of shore landing craft.

It was a project of immense proportion. Thousands of "Elsies," a play on the letters l.c. for landing craft, would be needed—boats of various sizes and purposes, from the small landing craft that could drop a platoon of Marines on the shores of Pacific Islands, to the goliath craft now being constructed on the banks of the Ohio River in a surprising place like Evansville, Indiana. These Landing Ship-Tanks, or LST's, were engineering marvels. Longer than a football field, they could cross the ocean, beach themselves on an enemy shore, disgorge dozens of tanks, heavy trucks, and scores of troops, then successfully retract from the beach and return to the sea. These amazing craft required more engineering skill and know-how than any destroyer or battleship ever would, so the United States assigned her top ship building masterminds to the LST project. Joe Mayer considered it no small honor, and a great responsibility, to be included.

When his assignment to Evansville came through, Mayer at first was surprised that such huge ocean craft were being constructed in the mist of the cornfields of the Midwest, but he quickly realized the astuteness of such a choice. Hundreds of miles from the Atlantic coast and two thousand miles from the Pacific, what shipyard was safer from enemy attack? After launching on the Ohio River, the craft simply made their way down river to the Mississippi, then south to the Gulf of Mexico.

Sometimes Joe Mayer felt guilty. He was stateside being well paid to do a job he loved, far removed from the dangers of Jap or Nazi bullets while many of his old high school chums served overseas. In August, Mayer's mother called from Indianapolis to tell him that Ralph Fielder, a boyhood friend with whom Mayer went through elementary and secondary school, had been killed on Guadalcanal.

And there were others.

The casualty lists in the newspapers grew longer every week. It seemed everyone knew someone who was now gone, and here Mayer was stateside and feeling his life had never been better. It was a feeling he was not sure he liked. With other young Americans of his age dying on foreign soil, he found himself feeling a little sheepish about his date tomorrow night.

His meeting with Sarah Klein was a memorable one, if not down right slapstick. It happened last Saturday, Halloween, at the worker celebration of the launching of the first ship, LST 157, earlier that day. The day was not a furlough from work. Nothing was allowed to slow the round-the-clock production of such a priority piece of war equipment as the LST, and work on subsequent ships began long before the launching of LST 157, but the first of anything is always special, and a day-long cookout was held near the launching docks. Shipyard employees could mingle and celebrate during their breaks or lunch hours.

It was a pleasant fall day. The chill earlier in the week had been bullied away by a sun not pestered by clouds. Mayer was standing by the red, white, and blue food tent talking to Howard Turnbull, an engineer from Baltimore who worked with Mayer in Building 11. When the gregarious Turnbull arrived at Building 11 six weeks ago, he and the quiet Mayer hit it off immediately. Although they had not bothered to buddy around away from the shipyard, at work the two men enjoyed each other's company. They were an unlikely pair. Turnbull was as outgoing as Joseph Mayer was introverted. This behavior reflected their dealings with the opposite sex. The handsome twenty-nine-year-old Turnbull had a flair for smooth talk and glib humor in the presence of women.

Mayer was different. Most women would judge him less handsome than the tall, blue-eyed Turnbull. Mayer's brown hair and eyes on a slim 5'10" frame qualified him as an average joe. Joe Mayer was not a wallflower, nor was he uncomfortable around women, but an inherent sincerity interfered with the slick opening repartee with the opposite sex that came easily to men like Howard Turnbull.

In addition to Turnbull's gifts for humor and insincere flattery, Mayer's new friend considered himself an expert on the female anatomy. In 1942, such shipyards as this one in southern Indiana offered an inexhaustible supply of subjects for a student of this discipline, so as the two men stood by the food tent talking, the engineer from Baltimore gave Mayer a private discourse concerning the figures of the abundant number of females who surrounded the two men.

With the majority of males between eighteen and thirty-five fighting a war oversees (or being trained to do so), many of the jobs in wartime industries were manned, and aptly so, by females in this age group. Thousands of young women from Indiana and adjacent areas such as southern Illinois and Kentucky had been hired and trained within the past year to become "Rosie the Riveters." But much to the dismay of Howard Turnbull, perusing the individual charms of any certain "Rosie" was not easy.

They all looked alike.

Rosies all wore their hair tied up in scarves or in the approved "military braids." For protection from hot sparks and steam, heavy denim overalls and baggy long sleeve shirts were standard. This apparel made it necessary for the male imagination to only guess at what lay underneath, so when Turnbull spotted an attractive blond in a tight green and white dress walking toward him and Mayer, he quickly turned his attention from the drably dressed Rosies.

The blond walked with a dark-haired woman who also wore a dress. Howard Turnbull, the authority on females, quickly concluded to Joe Mayer that these two were both secretaries: a deduction not exactly amazing, Mayer thought, since secretaries were the only female employees of the shipyard who wore dresses. The blond noticed the men staring. This embarrassed Mayer who quickly looked away. The two women stopped at another nearby food tent, and both came away holding a large paper cup filled with lemonade. The women stood and talked for a moment, then resumed walking their original course which would take them directly by the two men. As they neared, the blond smiled at Turnbull who remained unabashed in his staring. The lunch crowd around the tent was considerable and, as the two women passed Mayer and Turnbull, the two secretaries were jostled by the crowd and some of their lemonade ended up on Mayer's pant leg. Both women blushed and looked terribly embarrassed. Turnbull burst out laughing which only added to the their chagrin. Mayer showed the ladies that the damage was minimal and told them not to worry. Still, they apologized profusely while Turnbull grasped this golden opportunity to strike up a conversation.

Joe Mayer thought the raven-haired young woman to be as attractive as the blond but in a more virtuous way. She wore less makeup and a more conservative, looser fitting gray dress. Her black hair was tied back with a net as opposed to the spunky cut of the blond. Mayer looked at the name tag pinned above her left breast; it read "S. Klein - Building 23." She wore a blue armband; the color told Mayer she held only the low-level security clearance of most secretaries. Unlike the white armbands worn by Mayer and Turnbull, which allowed access to practically anywhere within the shipyard, blue and red armbands restricted the wearers to certain areas. The blond woman wore a similar blue, low-level armband.

Turnbull took charge of the brief encounter making sure everyone ended up being introduced. The blond's name was Carol Weiss. Her tag also specified Building 23. The dark-haired woman's name was Sarah Klein. The foursome chatted for a few minutes; Howard Turnbull and Carol Weiss flirted while Joe Mayer and Sarah Klein discussed that day's launching of the first LST. Sarah Klein looked at her wristwatch and reminded her girlfriend that their supervisor expected them back in a few minutes. As the women walked away both smiled when Turnbull warned them that he and Mayer would be in touch.

Turnbull kept his word. Yesterday he informed Joe Mayer that a double date was on for Saturday night.

Putting thoughts of Sarah Klein out of his mind, Mayer pulled his car into the parking lot that served a compound of long, narrow, Quonset Huts. The white structures were so alike new workers were often seen wandering around lost amid the maze of brick walkways separating the quickly constructed wooden buildings. The buildings were distinguished one from the others only by a small sign above each door that revealed its number. Adding to the dilemma of a worker's first day on the job was the willy-nilly numbering system that no one, including the mathematicians in Building 9, had been able to discern any rhyme or reason to. Just north of Building 11 where Mayer worked was Building 20; just south was 17; behind to the east 5; to the west, 8. These buildings were restricted access and located on the eastern fringe of the shipyard. They housed certain supervisory personnel, scientists and mathematicians, designers, engineers like Joe Mayer and Turnbull, and a small army of secretaries and female file clerks.

Mayer walked through a gate in a fence surrounding the Quonset Hut compound and showed his clearance card to the guard. His building, Building 11, sat near the middle of the compound so he had a short walk.

In addition to the guard who checked people entering the restricted Quonset Hut compound, each hut had a security guard assigned to further monitor access. As he did every morning when he walked through the dark gray steel door of the Hut 11, Mayer greeted guard Harry Krupsaw.

"Good morning, Harry."

"Morning, Joe," greeted the elderly guard who reached into an open file sitting on top of a dark wooden table. The old man quickly located a security tag with Mayer's name on it, handed it to him along with a key, and wrote Mayer's name and the time on a piece of paper fastened to a clipboard.

"How's the grandkids?" asked Mayer. Krupsaw had shown Mayer the pictures numerous times.

"Fine! Fine! The oldest one caught an eleven-pound channel cat the other day."

"Yeah? Where?" Mayer knew Krupsaw was referring to a fish.

"Pigeon Creek. Let me know when you're ready to go fishin' again. Found a great place loaded with bluegill just outside Boonville."

"Okay, thanks Harry." As he walked away, Mayer open his suit jacket and pinned the security tag next to the name tag above the left pocket of his shirt.

As was the case with the exteriors of these buildings, the interiors were also cloned. Immediately upon entering was a large, open area filled with the sounds of the ten to fifteen secretaries (depending on need) assigned to each building. It seemed like a large number to Mayer since each building housed only four to six methods personnel, but this was war and things needed to be done quickly. Papers for a project, major or minor, could not be held in limbo waiting to be typed, and dividing pages or reports between several secretaries added a certain security element—no single person typed an entire document. Secretaries and file clerks reported for work a half hour before the methods people like Joe Mayer, so activity was already well under way. Typewriters clicked, then pinged a warning when the end of a margin came dangerously near. File cabinet drawers banged loudly. Telephones rang and were answered by feminine voices. Of smells the room had two: the abundance of paperwork, wood flooring, desks and chairs gave it the musty odor of an aging library, a smell Mayer had always enjoyed; the second smell, best of all Mayer thought, was that of cleanly scrubbed and powdered females.

At the opposite end of this area was a smaller room separated from the secretaries' domain by a corrugated sheet metal wall with a locking, windowed door. Using the key that Harry Krupsaw gave him (a key he had to return whenever he left the building even if only for a break), Mayer passed through the door and removed his suit jacket. He walked over to a small, coffee-stained card table on which sat a coffee pot on a small electric Bunson Burner. On the table was a stack of paper cups, a bowl of sugar with a sugar-caked spoon someone had placed back into the bowl after stirring their coffee, and a can of evaporated milk which had two ice pick holes in the top. Mayer managed to procure only half a cup of the overcooked black coffee from the almost empty pot. Most of the time he drank his coffee black, but from the looks of what lay in his cup he figured it wise to cut it with a little milk.

This was the room where Joe Mayer had worked for the past six months. It was half the size of the secretaries' area and had portable partitions that separated the work areas of the designers and engineers. In Building 11, Mayer worked alongside four other methods people: a tool and die designer, a lubricant and fluids specialist, the jocular Howard Turnbull who specialized in stress analysis, and the boss of Building 11, Gary Delmar, a fifty-two-year-old hydraulic engineer from Cleveland who served as overseer for the work assigned their group.

Mayer and Turnbull currently worked together on a seam problem in the ship's rear pumping room. Ballast pumps in this room controlled the ship's center of gravity. After the LST grounded onto a beach and the armored vehicles, tanks, trucks, and its other matériel disgorged, the rear of the ship was flooded to realign the huge ship's center of gravity; this aided the ship in extracting itself from the beach. The problem that Mayer and Turnbull were currently trying to solve was the need for several hundred rivets along a seam where plates met at a critical weightbearing location of the ship's superstructure. Both Mayer and Turnbull wanted to eliminate these rivets in favor of welds. However, this critical junction point brought together metals containing several new alloys, and the degree of stress that the seam could bear when welded was not yet fully known. Testing and retesting the sturdiness of welds on these new metals had kept the two men busy for the past three weeks.

Mayer noticed that Turnbull was nowhere to be seen which was not unusual. His new friend was notorious for reporting to work late.

Mayer placed his coffee cup on a file cabinet beside his drafting board and rolled up his sleeves.

CHAPTER 24

Know, Christian, that next to the Devil thou hast no enemy more cruel, more venomous and violent than a true Jew. Their synagogues should be set on fire, and whatever does not burn up should be covered or spread over with dirt so that no one may ever be able to see a cinder or stone of it.

—Martin Luther, 1543

Evansville, Indiana

November 1942

Saturday evening. Joe Mayer drove his car slowly down a red brick street looking for the address on Riverside Drive that Howard Turnbull had written on a piece of paper. Because of the great influx of out-of-town workers, housing in Evansville was a major problem. Any basement, garage, or attic—practically any structure with walls and a roof—was prime rental property. This street had a long row of turn-of-the-century mansions, many of which had fallen into disrepair before the war but now were remodeled and turned into efficiency apartments. When Mayer spotted the address, he pulled over to the curb. He noticed two men sitting on the front porch: Turnbull and another man who looked to be ninety if a day. When Turnbull spotted Mayer he rose, said something to the old man, and walked to the car.

"Hey, old buddy!" Turnbull said with a mock salute as he got in the car and closed the door. "Do you feel lucky tonight?"

Mayer grinned as he looked in the rearview mirror before stepping on the gas and steering the car back out into the street.

"I feel lucky it's not raining. Is that what you mean?" Mayer replied tongue-in-cheek. The early-November evening was pleasantly warm for that time of year, but the forecast was for rain which had as yet failed to materialize. Yet from the looks of the gunmetal sky, it did not take a meteorologist to figure out there was a storm up there somewhere.

"Yeah, right," Turnbull answered sarcastically. "Well, I feel lucky. I'm going to get some tonight and I suggest you do the same."

Mayer ignored the remark and asked directions. Turnbull pulled a piece of paper out of his jacket pocket on which an address and some directions were scribbled. Carol Weiss, the object of Turnbull's wishful thinking, lived in a small boarding house on the far east side of town. Sarah Klein had agreed to be at Carol's at the appointed time, and the plan was to pick up both girls at Carol's place.

Turnbull looked around the vehicle's interior. "Nice car, Mayer. A Lincoln no less. What year is it?"

"Forty," Mayer responded. The car was a point of pride with Joe Mayer. The 1940 Lincoln Cabriolet convertible drew envious stares wherever Mayer went. He bought the car new, shelling out almost three thousand dollars, but with his salary as a high-clearance war shipyard engineer (almost a hundred and ninety dollars a week) he could afford the car.

"Engine is smooth," Turnbull remarked.

"Twelve cylinders," Mayer bragged.

Evansville was a middle-sized city founded in the early 19th century primarily for its proximity to the Ohio River which empties into the Mississippi. The city served as a convenient way station for trade up and down the mighty rivers. Cargo could be transported economically from as far east as Pittsburgh all the way south to New Orleans or north to Minneapolis and any point between.

The same geographical traits that made the location appealing to the early pioneers brought the war industries to town after Pearl Harbor. The city bustled. The LST shipyard where Mayer and Turnbull worked was the largest, but by no means the only, enterprise supplying war matériel. The U.S. Army Corps of Engineers had transformed the pre-war Chrysler and Sunbeam Manufacturing plants into the Evansville Ordnance Plant which quickly became the largest manufacturer of small caliber ammunition in the country.

And there were the Thunderbolts. Feeling that the East Coast was too vulnerable to attack, Republic Aviation of Farmingdale, New Jersey, chose Evansville as the site for a plant to produce the famous P-47 fighter planes. Early in '42 the company broke ground at a site just south of the airport, and in an astonishingly short time the Thunderbolts were rolling off the assembly line.

Although the bulk of the assembly jobs in these wartime plants were held by the scores of young women who converged on the city from farms and small towns in the surrounding states, the city held no shortage of men. Soldiers poured into the city on leaves from Fort Breckenridge in Kentucky, just forty miles away. Fort Campbell, also in Kentucky, was not much farther. Also to Evansville came Navy crews reporting for duty aboard their soon-to-be-launched LST's, and servicemen from all branches continually filtered through the city for stopovers during their travels to other locations. Like housing, the need to entertain these troops delivered yet another opportunity for local entrepeneuers, some who did not concern themselves with legalities. An area just east of downtown had acquired a reputation as Evansville's "red light" district where gambling could be found along with women who catered to the needs of servicemen on leave. As Washington Avenue took the two men through this area, Howard Turnbull made an admiring reference to this part of town, sounding like one who was familiar with its offerings. When Mayer just shook his head Turnbull looked at him.

"Don't tell me you have never been down here, Joe."

Mayer shrugged his shoulders.

Turnbull continued, sounding almost disgusted. "I swear I'm beginning to think you're one of those holy-rollers or something. What the hell do you do for fun, Mayer?"

Joe Mayer was not a saint. In college he had succumbed to the howls of male hormones with girls from St. Mary's, the woman's college in South Bend when, that is, on those rare occasions a St. Mary's girl with a sufficiently liberal outlook could be found. Then there was the lab technician at Bethlehem Steel, a woman ten years his senior who was separated from her husband. Mayer's liaison with her lasted several months, ending only when the woman and her husband decided to try it again for the sake of their young son.

Mayer felt no need to try to answer the question. "None of your damn business, Turnbull." It was said without rancor and when Turnbull looked at him both men chuckled.

Turnbull kept his attention on Mayer for a moment and then asked matter-of-factly, "You're Jewish, aren't you?"

Mayer glanced at him. "Yeah, that's right. Why do you ask?"

Turnbull shrugged. "I don't know. Somebody at work told me you're a Jew. Just thought I'd ask."

Mayer frowned at the thought that someone at the shipyard considered his background a subject for discussion—and gossip.

"Who told you that?"

Turnbull had already turned his attention to the piece of paper with the directions to Carol Weiss's apartment.

"Huh? Who told me what?"

"Who feels it necessary to go around work telling people I'm Jewish?"

Turnbull looked at him and searched his face. He could see Mayer was miffed.

"I don't know…I don't remember…who cares?"

"I care. I want to know who at work thinks it necessary to discuss the fact I'm Jewish."

"Hey, Joe, I'm serious, I don't remember. Don't get worked up about it. I don't give a damn what you are. All religions are the same if you ask me." Turnbull was watching street signs. "Turn right here. Carol lives down this block. She said it is the house with the birdbath in the front yard."

Mayer did not feel like dropping the subject but was forced to, at least for now. Turnbull spotted the birdbath and ordered, "Here it is, pull over."

Mayer parked on the street in front of the house. The two men walked up a few steps and across a front yard cluttered with toys (Carol told Turnbull she rented a room from a widow with four children). The men had to knock twice, but finally a plump, early-middle-aged woman in a flowered print dress and an apron answered the door. Two small children, a boy and a girl, clung to the woman's legs and stared up at the two men. Turnbull identified himself and Mayer and stated their purpose. The woman opened the door and directed them into a small sitting room off the entry way. She ordered the oldest child, the girl, to go upstairs and tell Carol she had company.

Mayer and Turnbull were kept waiting for fifteen minutes, but eventually the voices of the two women were heard coming down the stairs. Carol and Sarah Klein stepped into the sitting room and both men rose. Everyone exchanged greetings. Plans for the evening called for dinner and drinks at the swank McCurdy Hotel so formal attire was in order. The men wore suits and ties. Carol's dress was strapless and made of chiffon. The pale yellow color complemented her blond hair. A sheer, white lace evening wrap covered her bare shoulders.

Miss Klein wore a shining black V-neck dress surprisingly revealing for a girl who had impressed Mayer as conservative if not downright shy. It hugged her figure to the point where it drew Howard Turnbull's attention from the stunning Carol Weiss for more than just a quick glance. The dress reached nearly to the floor, but a strategically placed split rose enticingly up the front, offering a glance of a shapely leg. Like Carol, Sarah also brought along an evening wrap which she carried instead of wore.

Out by the curb, Turnbull held the car door and leaned the back of the front seat forward so Carol could get in the back seat. Turnbull was more than happy to be forced to squeeze himself into the small back seat beside the blond. Mayer and Sarah had more room in the front.

Turnbull was in top form.

"Carol, Joe is a terrible driver. You better find something to hang on to." Carol rewarded Turnbull's humor with a giggle.

"Is that true, Joe?" Sarah asked with a smile.

"I guess it depends on where you're sitting," Mayer smiled.

The sky was darkening fast. Mayer turned on the headlights as they drove back across town. Mayer and Sarah made quiet small talk in the front between interruptions by the spirited Turnbull who was having great success at keeping Carol Weiss laughing in the back seat. The rain was still on hold as Mayer turned the car into the parking lot of the McCurdy Hotel.

The lavish, U-shaped hotel was one of the Midwest's finest. Many of the choicest hotels in cities much larger than Evansville could not boast such opulence. A pink Tennessee marble floor below a towering lobby ceiling greeted the two couples. Massive crystal and gold chandeliers drew admiring comments from the women. The lobby reminded Mayer of the Brown Palace Hotel in Denver where he spent a week in a metallurgists' conference hosted by the Colorado School of Mines. Leave it to Turnbull. Mayer was as impressed as the girls who, like him, were seeing the McCurdy for the first time.

The hotel had several restaurants and the one Turnbull had reservations for, the Embers Room, was considered the swankiest. The Embers was a room of heavy oak columns that sported yet more brass and crystal chandeliers. When the foursome was seated, Carol removed her shoulder wrap, allowing the men a look at a revealing amount of cleavage. Drinks were decided on and the order given to an elderly black waiter in a black and white tuxedo.

"Waiter! Over here!" Turnbull shouted. "Champagne all around."

When the girls were ready to order dinner, Turnbull again summoned the waiter. Beef entrees were available but limited due to rationing. Sarah said the rainbow trout that Mayer decided on sounded good so Mayer placed a double order. Fish, unlike beef, was not rationed and was a popular entree in the better restaurants. At the nicer restaurants, Mayer usually found that non-rationed food was usually prepared with more flair to attract diners away from the hard-to-come-by rationed items such as beef. Carol and Turnbull also ordered from the non-rationed list, she the roast turkey breast and Turnbull the lamb chops.

During dinner, turns were taken relating brief autobiographies. Carol Weiss had migrated from Louisville, Kentucky, where in high school she had been a cheerleader and later a Belle Hostess at Churchill Downs one year for Kentucky Derby weekend. Sarah Klein was from Cincinnati. She had studied to be a music teacher but, after her father died and the war broke out, she, like so many others, put peacetime plans on hold to work in the war industries. Turnbull and Mayer took their turns and gave the girls a brief synopsis of their life's journey to Evansville. Sarah thought it interesting that Joe, despite his scientific and engineering background, had attempted to enlist as a G.I. after Pearl Harbor.

"What made you consider it?" she asked.

"I guess it was because of my father," Mayer answered after swallowing a bite of fish. "He was a doughboy in the Great War and I always admired him for that. I guess I felt that the guys with the rifles are the ones who really fight the wars, not guys like me and Howard who play with sliderules."

Turnbull overheard and interjected, "Hey, speak for yourself, Mayer! Somebody has to play with their sliderule!" Even Mayer had to laugh at Turnbull's foolishness.

After dinner Turnbull led them to the elevator and ordered the operator to take them to the Rose Room. On the eighth floor, the Rose Room was a large chamber of red and bone-white shades with a large dance floor. Tonight there was an orchestra. Despite the crowd, an attendant, motivated by a healthy tip from Turnbull, managed to find them a table. More black waiters, these wearing snow white suits trimmed in pink with pink bow ties, circled through the all-white crowd taking orders.

The girls decided to stick with champagne. Turnbull made sure the glasses stayed full, especially the one in front of Carol Weiss.

"Howard, a girl could get the idea you were trying to get her drunk," Carol half-slurred as she leaned over on Sarah and laughed.

Turnbull, faking a look of shock, shot back, "Why, doll, all who know me will assure you that thought...*is exactly what I have on my mind!*" Carol almost coughed up a half-swallowed drink of champagne and laughed loudly. Sarah and Joe grinned more at Carol's reaction than Turnbull's silly joke.

Carol cautioned Turnbull, "I feel I should warn you, sir. Back home I have a reputation of being a girl who, after one drink, she can feel it, after two drinks, anyone can!"

Mayer laughed; Sarah grinned and rolled her eyes. Turnbull countered, "Baby, there's only one reply to that." He turned around and shouted at the black waiter, "Boy! More champagne!"

The band played a very commendable rendition of Glenn Miller's *Moonlight Serenade*. Joe had been enjoying himself, but he thought a brief respite from the constant sexual banter between Howard and Carol might be welcomed by his date. Mayer considered himself a poor dancer, but he could fake his way through the slow ones. He asked Sarah if she wanted to dance and she seemed glad to accept. Sarah offered Mayer her hand and he guided her out onto the crowded dance floor.

Sarah Klein was an excellent dancer. This helped compensate for her partner's inadequacies. Although not as tall as the leggy Carol Weiss,

Sarah Klein's sling pumps brought her to within an inch or so of Mayer's 5'10". The glitter ball turned slowly overhead and flickered bright, quarter-sized dots of light on Sarah's creamy skin. As they danced, Mayer admired her inviting neck, exposed by the piling of her dark hair high on her head. They did not talk, but several times during their dance she looked at him and smiled. When the music stopped, they applauded the orchestra then returned to their table, where Carol Weiss was still doing what she had done for most of the night, laughing at some inane comment from Howard Turnbull. A cigarette girl with a camera suggested a photo was in order and the four smiled into the camera as the flash popped. Mayer paid the girl and gave her an address to send the photograph.

The four drank and chatted until the band struck up a fast paced swing number which attracted Carol's attention. She took Howard's hand and led him to the dance floor. Carol, despite her growing tipsiness, put on a show that drew the attention of most of the people in the room. She hiked her dress up brazenly high and set a standard in the jitterbug that none of the other women on the dance floor seemed tempted to try to match. Turnbull tired quickly, and Joe and Sarah both laughed at Howard's deteriorating attempt to keep up.

There were a few more dances left for the two couples. Joe danced with Sarah twice more and once with Carol while Howard partnered with Sarah. During Joe's dance with the drunken Carol Weiss, she brushed her thigh conspicuously hard against the front of his pants.

Shortly before closing, the crowd began thinning and the four decided to leave. As they stepped off the elevator into the lobby, Carol stumbled badly and only the quick reaction of the others kept her from falling.

Sometime during their time in the Rose Room the sky tired of supporting so much water. When they walked outside, the rain spanked the hotel's green canvas porte cochere in loud thumps. Mayer had brought an umbrella which was of course in the car. He secured his fedora, pulled up the collar to his trenchcoat, told the others to wait, and sprinted across the parking lot to the Lincoln. Mayer got in and slammed the door. He was soaked. He drove back to the entrance where the others completed the short dash to the curb and swiftly loaded themselves into the car. Everyone was wet. Sarah laughed and dried her shoulders and arms with her wrap. Mayer was not sure what the two in the back were doing. For the first time all night Howard and Carol were not talking. Mayer avoided looking.

Mayer was driving in the direction of Carol's house when Turnbull pulled himself away from whatever was distracting him in the backseat and boldly suggested they all stop by his apartment for a nightcap.

"It's only a few blocks from here," Turnbull assured the girls.

Sarah looked at Joe then turned around and looked at Howard.

"I'm not sure that sounds like a safe place for me," Sarah said with a smile. "What do you think, Carol?"

"Don't worry, honey, I'll protect you." Carol slurred the words and laughed.

Mayer parked in front of Turnbull's building then told Howard to hand him the umbrella which was somewhere on the floorboard in back. Mayer exited the car, opened the umbrella and escorted first Sarah then Carol to the covered front porch while Howard closed the car door and sprinted to cover. The girls escaped a thorough drenching, even if the men did not.

Turnbull's apartment was on the top floor of the three-story former mansion. While climbing the stairs, they heard music coming from behind a second floor door. Mayer could not tell if the music was from a radio or a phonograph, but at least everyone was not asleep. When they reached the room, Turnbull fumbled for his key like someone who, although not totally drunk, had taken one drink too many. With the key finally located, Turnbull unlocked the door, then reached in and flipped on a light.

It was a small, one bedroom apartment, but very nice compared to some places Mayer had heard about from other shipyard personnel. Off from the living room area was a small kitchen, and the apartment had its own bathroom with a small shower. The furniture was sparse. A table and one upholstered green chair sat across from a matching couch, but the place was surprisingly tidy for a bachelor's apartment. Only that morning's newspaper scattered on the floor seemed out of place. Turnbull tossed the key on a table and walked into the kitchen.

"Let's see, we've got bourbon and 7-Up and bourbon and 7-Up. What will you folks have?"

Mayer placed the orders. "How about bourbon and 7-Up?"

Sarah asked for a towel and Howard directed her to the bathroom. Carol was concerned that her last good pair of nylons, so valuable now that the war put a halt to their manufacture, would somehow sustain damage from her wet shoes. While either ignoring the presence of the two men or enjoying it, she kicked off her pumps, hiked her dress up past the garters that held up her stockings, unfastened the garters, then sat on the couch and rolled the stockings down off her legs. When Sarah returned, Carol rose from the couch, still unsteady on her feet, and took her turn in the bathroom.

Howard obviously felt it a higher priority to pour a round of drinks than to dry himself off, but after he had a drink in Sarah's hand and one awaiting Carol, Turnbull told Joe he would find them some clothes. Mayer followed him into the bedroom. Turnbull grabbed a shirt and pair of pants out of the closet for himself then another set for Joe. Turnbull was three inches taller than Mayer so Joe had to roll up the pant cuffs but at least the waistline was close and Mayer could use his own belt. Wasting no time, Howard threw his wet clothes in a corner and changed. He hung Mayer's clothes over the radiator to dry.

When the men returned to the living room, Carol was sitting in the green chair holding a glass which was already empty except for the ice. She handed the glass to Howard who promptly fixed her another drink. Sarah sat on the couch. An attractive leg, which had avoided proper viewing under the tables of the McCurdy, now presented itself from the split of Sarah's dress. Mayer sat down beside her while Howard plugged in a phonograph that sat on a short wooden bookcase against a wall. To free up an electric outlet for the record player, Turnbull was forced to unplug one of the two shaded lamps that lit the room. Doing so conveniently lowered the light level considerably. "Not enough outlets in this place," Turnbull informed. Mayer had to hand it to his colleague from Building 11. *This guy thinks of everything.*

Turnbull was a Marlene Dietrich fan. Several of the American née German singer's records lay stacked beside the turntable. Turnbull placed a record on the machine's spindle. In a moment the record dropped and the sounds of an orchestra lead by cellos filled the room. Dietrich's low, almost masculine voice rose from the spinning disk:

> ♪ *You've got that look, that look, between the lines.*
> *You with your let's get more than friendly designs.*
>
> *I should be brave and say, 'Let's have no more of it.'*
> *But, oh, what's the use when you know I love it.*

Howard seated himself on the opposite end of the couch from Sarah and Joe. When he showed Carol that enough room remained on the couch for her, she giggled and sat her glass down on the coffee table, spilling a little of the drink in the process. The blond rose unsteadily from her chair and joined the others on the couch, stumbling and almost falling again when she tripped over Turnbull's feet. The slick engineer from Baltimore and the agreeable blond secretary from Louisville wasted little time, immediately clasping hold of each other in a zealous kiss.

When Sarah, who sat next to Carol, saw the other couple's enthusiasm she turned to Joe and smiled. Taking this as encouragement, Mayer put his arm around her and drew her close. A second Dietrich record dropped on to the turntable. The voice of the sultry singer surrounded them, accompanied by sad violins and the rain rapping against Turnbull's window.

♪ *I've been in love before, it's true.*
Been learning to adore just you.
Some old romance taught me how to kiss,
To smile like that, to sigh like this.

Joe Mayer and Sarah Klein kissed.

Caught up in their own moment, Joe and Sarah's concern was not on the couple next to them, but progressively heavier breathing and a muted giggle from Carol drew a glance from Mayer after his lips separated from Sarah's. Turnbull's face was buried in Carol's neck, his right hand was inside her dress, placed over her left breast. Sarah's head lay on Joe's shoulder with her back to the other couple so she was unaware of the exhibitionism next to her. Turnbull removed his hand from Carol's breast and moved it down between her legs; he began slowly pulling up her dress. Carol noticed Mayer's glance and gave him a drunken smile. Carol glanced at the back of Sarah's dress, and, with Turnbull still burrowing his face in the side of her neck, Carol winked at Mayer then reached over and started unzipping Sarah's dress.

When Sarah felt her dress being unzipped, she thought the culprit was Joe. Sarah was about to whisper a soft warning for Joe to wait when the sheepish countenance on his face and the direction he was looking caused her to turn. When she saw it was Carol's hand that was unzipping her dress she sat back. Carol's drunken cackle forced the busy Turnbull to look up and pause.

"I guess you think we need some help?" Sarah joked, her humorous demeanor to some extent helping relieve the very embarrassed Joe Mayer. Turnbull, who was not sure what it was they were talking about and seemed impatient to resume what he had been doing, looked baffled.

"I just thought you guys were falling behind," Carol said and laughed wildly again.

"Well, Howard, you can't say you weren't warned," Sarah said, referring to Carol's joke earlier that evening about the effects of alcohol on her willpower. Carol continued to laugh and reached over to Turnbull, pulling him toward her.

"Yeah, I warned you!" said Carol.

Joe Mayer sat there feeling foolish and not sure what to do. He thought of asking Sarah if she wanted to leave, but he had also brought Carol and was expecting to drive her home. Sarah looked at him, and, as if sensing his disarray and reading his mind, took control.

"Carol, don't you think we should call it a night?"

"Let me think about it for a few hours," Carol answered as she made a clumsy attempt to unbutton Turnbull's shirt.

"Howard, you have a car don't you?" Sarah asked.

"Yes," Turnbull answered.

"I'm afraid I'm going to have to say good night," Sarah continued. "Would you mind terribly if you have to take my fun-loving friend home when she decides to leave?"

"Sure...er, that means no, I won't mind at all," Turnbull answered.

Sarah's cordial cancellation of the double date coincided with the other woman's declaration of the need to again use the bathroom. Carol wobbled as she stood, an occasion for more giggling on her part.

"Oops! Now see what you've done!" the drunken blond stammered at Turnbull as she started toward the bathroom.

Sarah told the men she would check on her friend and she excused herself. When she was out of earshot Mayer turned to Turnbull.

"Haven't you ever heard of a bedroom?"

"Hey, I couldn't help it," Turnbull stammered. "She wouldn't let me stop."

Mayer shook his head, stood up, and walked over and looked out the window through the rain. In a few minutes Sarah returned.

"Well, I assured myself that my sensuous friend has her wits about her, and she is quite emphatic in her wishes to stay. We are free to leave, Joe." Turning to the other man she said, "Howard, remember your promise to deliver her safely home whenever she wishes."

"You bet."

Sarah walked over to Mayer and turned around. "Joe, would you zip up my dress please?"

The long zipper was open down to the small of her back. Mayer felt like an idiot. He realized he should have helped her right away when she stood up. After her fumbling date got the zipper raised, Sarah walked over and kissed Howard on the cheek, thanking him for a "wonderful night." Even the ribald Turnbull recognized class; Mayer thought he noticed an uncharacteristically sheepish look on his colleague's face in the presence of such undeserved grace.

Sarah smiled at Joe and asked if he was ready to once more get wet. Sarah stepped out in the hallway and Mayer followed. Just before he shut the door behind him, Mayer caught a fleet glimpse of a naked Carol Weiss walking out of Turnbull's bathroom.

It was past three o'clock and the rain had let up only slightly, if at all. As Mayer drove away from Turnbull's apartment, his windshield wipers, which worked opposite one another, came together then spread apart like frantic oars on a sinking rowboat. As the rain tumbled on to the road ahead, the headlights turned a million tiny splashes into silver sparks.

"Sarah, I apologize."

She looked at him and put her hand on his arm. "If you're apologizing for Howard, you don't have to. It didn't look to me like Carol was having a problem with the way the evening was progressing."

"He shouldn't have plied her with liquor," Mayer added.

"She has a choice," she reminded him. "I didn't see Howard forcing it down her throat."

He looked at her. She smiled and continued.

"Don't think I'm an angel, Joe. Really, I'm not. You might want to watch out. Perhaps I'm not so innocent. Maybe I have a plan to make you think I'm virtuous but in reality am a wanton seductress, or a sly Jewish princess looking for a husband."

"I didn't know if you were Jewish or not," Joe said. "I thought you might be with that name, but I have met Kleins who are Gentiles. I'm Jewish too."

"I know. Carol told me."

There it was again—people from work discussing that fact about him. When he heard it earlier from Turnbull he felt an affront, but from another Jew, especially from her, he did not feel any ire. Turnbull must have told Carol and then Carol told Sarah. The subject was changed.

"Carol's quite a dancer," he said. "I'm glad for the sake of the jitterbug audience that she didn't forget her underpants."

Sarah could not hold back and neither could Joe. They both laughed loudly—she until tears almost fell. He was pleased with himself that he had made her laugh so completely. Sarah responded while still laughing and wiping her eyes. "I'm also glad for her sake that she doesn't have to work tomorrow."

As the car approached an intersection she instructed him to turn left. A few more blocks, then a right. They laughed some more, this time about their first meeting when the lemonade ended up on his pants.

Sarah's apartment was on North Main Street, on the second floor over a diner. She told Joe that an elderly couple owned both the building and the restaurant on the first floor. She said her apartment was small but private; it has a separate entrance and "it does have a bathroom" she added with a smile, noting that Carol and many other girls at work lived in boarding houses where lavatory facilities had to be shared.

With a few more directions from Sarah, they arrived and Mayer pulled into the diner's small parking lot. He turned off the engine and they sat for a moment listening to the rain rap on the car's roof. Mayer wanted to see this woman again and he decided, because of the lunacy in Turnbull's apartment, he would not make a pass but end the night as a gentleman and say goodnight at her door. He reached for the umbrella in the backseat, turning toward her as he did so. Suddenly she turned toward him, grabbed his shirt to help pull herself to him, and violently smashed her lips against his. After a long minute she withdrew and held her face just two inches from his. He felt her hot breath. She opened her eyes, staring into his. A ray of yellow light from a nearby streetlamp reflected a wild, almost crazed look in wolf-like eyes. Looking down at his lips, she again moved toward him. The bewitched Mayer sat frozen. Instead of an expected kiss, she placed her teeth around his lower lip and bit down hard, causing him to grimace. He might have cried out, but the breath wasn't there. Again she drew back to inspect his face. She smiled, an unnerving, savage smile, then she pushed herself from him and, without a word, exited the car and ran away into the rain, leaving her wrap behind.

Mayer wanted to tell her to wait, he would walk her with the umbrella, but the words would not come. His breath was gone. He saw her ascend, with a jaguar-like agility, a long set of wrought iron steps on the side of the building and, after a moment taken to unlock the door, disappear into the apartment. He sat with the passenger door of his car open. The rain, like his heart, pounding. He felt a moistness on his lips which he wiped with a knuckle. Blood. As he stared through a thin waterfall sliding down the glass in front of him, he could see a light come on in her window. It was several minutes before he leaned over, pulled the passenger door shut, and started the engine.

Inside, Sarah Klein turned on a light and walked into her bathroom. She placed a rubber plug in the drain of the white, claw-foot bathtub and turned the hot water on full. She did the same with the sink. She removed her clothing and tossed the wet dress and undergarments into a wicker laundry hamper. She let down her wet black hair which fell down over her ears. Naked, she stared into the mirror over the sink. She noticed a speck of Joe Mayer's blood on her lip and, without expression, she bent over and splashed her face with the hot water, washing the blood away.

She looked back in the mirror at the dark hair she felt made her look more Jewish. Before the rising steam in the room frosted the glass, she backed away so she could scan farther down her image. She looked at the real reason she was not still with Joe Mayer; the small patch of blond hair between her legs contradicted the dyed black hair on her head. She would have to do something about that.

She already knew blackmail was out; Joe Mayer was too much of a patriot. A scientist with a soft wartime job willing to give it up to join the infantry would never betray his country under blackmail. Joe Mayer would have to be handled differently. But no matter, the evening had worked out perfectly. She could see it in his eyes.

Over the toilet, along with other articles familiar to the bathrooms of females, sat a small leather pouch. After she opened the pouch and withdrew a razor, Erika Lehmann stepped into the bathtub.

✠   ✠   ✠

CHAPTER 25

What is America but millionaires, beauty queens, stupid records and Hollywood?

—Adolf Hitler, 1933

Evansville—November 1942

It was the morning after a restless night's sleep. The wristwatch lying on the bureau next to the bed told Joe Mayer it was 6:15. The rain had finally stopped around five; Mayer knew because he was awake at the time. The night had been a vain attempt at sleep. Mayer spent most of the night thinking about his first date with Sarah Klein.

His feelings were not happy but neither were they negative. He didn't know what he felt besides a strong attraction to this girl and—he didn't know what to call it—perhaps a strong curiosity. He had never met anyone like Sarah Klein. That was for sure.

She had been the embodiment of class the entire evening, always in control, and ever gracious even in the face of the fatiguing sexual banter of Turnbull and the silly drunkenness of Carol Weiss. And during the drive to drop her off at her place, she made him feel so at ease, like they had known each other much longer. But then, when he turned to get the umbrella from the back seat, the unnerving attack—and that's what it was, an attack, like a pouncing animal. That crazed look in her eyes Mayer remembered the most. That look.

And the kiss, if you could call it that. He felt for the cut on his lip with his tongue.

Mayer got out of bed, grabbed his watch, and went in the bathroom. In the mirror was the evidence. He could see the small cut on his lower lip.

He wanted to call her but he had no number to dial. What was the name of the people who owned the diner? Had she told him? He could not remember. Hell, he couldn't even remember the name of the diner. He looked at his watch again. 6:35. Too early in the morning to call anyway. She would think he was rude, or crazy. Besides, she might not even have a telephone.

Mayer lived in a two-bedroom house on the city's west side. A nice place, and a perk of his position as a lead engineer. The Navy people found the house for him and they paid the rent. It was perfect: only a five minute drive from the shipyard, yet private and quiet in an old neighborhood.

Mayer's usual Sunday morning routine included a newspaper and a cup of coffee at the Franklin Drug soda fountain which was also open for breakfast. After washing and dressing, he grabbed a light jacket and stepped out into a pleasant Midwest fall morning. The prodigal sun had returned; it was cool and pleasant. Fall had always been Mayer's favorite season, and he was especially enjoying the current weather after the sweltering southern Indiana summer.

Instead of wearing it, he threw the jacket in the back seat of his car and drove to Franklin Street, the Lincoln splashing through street puddles left behind from last night's torrent. On Franklin, he pulled over to the curb and bought a paper from a newsstand. But instead of parking and going into the soda fountain, on impulse he threw the newspaper on the back seat beside his jacket and headed to Sarah Klein's apartment.

Mayer parked the car in the small parking lot where he had dropped her off the night before. Empty then, now the lot was crowded with cars. Carrying the evening wrap Sarah left in his car, he climbed the black wrought iron steps and knocked on the door he had watched her disappear through the night before. Mayer was debating between a second knock or leaving when the door opened. He thought she would be surprised to see him and perhaps a bit amused, but Sarah Klein seemed neither. She smiled widely and said, "Come in, Joe," like she had been expecting him.

As he entered, he handed her the wrap. "You forgot this," he said as nonchalantly as possible.

"Thanks." She smiled again. "Have a seat."

Mayer sat in an upholstered wing chair and Sarah sat across from him on a small sofa. She wore a baggy sweatshirt, several sizes too large, which covered her upper body modestly and reached halfway to her knees. Her legs were exposed from that point down and she was barefooted. The makeup from the previous night's date was gone and her black hair, tied up high just a few hours ago, was down. Her hair had the look of recent sleep but was not messy. Mayer concluded Sarah Klein was one of those people who always looked good, no matter what, and he could not keep himself from wondering what she was wearing under the sweatshirt.

"I had a wonderful time last night," Sarah said with a smile. "I never knew getting drenched could be so much fun. Thank you again."

"I had a great time too," said Mayer.

For a moment there was silence. She sat expressionless, staring him in the eyes, like she was waiting for him to speak. It made him a little nervous. Mayer almost commented on the weather change but considered it too trite. Eventually a slight smile appeared on her face.

"Are you hungry?" she asked.

"A little," Mayer answered, relieved. "Mainly, I could sure use a cup of coffee. How about you?"

She nodded. "After that dinner last night, coffee is about all I have room for. We can go downstairs to the diner if you like; Emma makes the world's best coffee."

"Sounds great," Mayer replied.

"I'll get dressed." She got up and walked to the bedroom, closing the door only halfway behind her.

"I wonder how Carol and Howard are feeling this morning," she said with an amused tone, raising her voice so she could be heard from the bedroom.

"Probably not hungry," Mayer replied. "Unless food gets rid of hangovers." He heard Sarah laugh from the other room.

As he waited, Mayer looked around the small room. It was an older building, pre-turn-of-the-century Mayer guessed. A ceiling fan, the blades motionless, hung from a nine-foot-high ceiling. Mayer knew the room had to be a hotbox during the steamy summers, but now it was comfortable. Furniture and decor were sparse and aimed toward efficiency. A small radio and an electric clock sat on a table by the window. A couple of ceramic figurines sat on a small wall shelf. He saw no phone. The only picture on the wall was a department store print of a snow-capped mountain scene. He assumed the furniture and decorations probably came with the place. Most of the war industry workers who migrated to Evansville spent little energy decorating their temporary homes. In a city with such a severe housing shortage, most out-of-towners were happy just to find a place to sleep.

Sarah returned to the living room wearing a pair of light gray slacks and a yellow blouse. She followed Joe out the door, closing it behind her. As they walked down the steps she told him how lucky she had been to find this apartment.

"The couple who own this place are very nice. They treat me more like a daughter than a renter," she told Mayer. "They even feed me free at the diner. I tried for a time to pay for my meals but they won't take my money."

The restaurant was a typical "mom-and-pop" diner serving breakfast from six until ten, then twenty-five cents would buy you a good "home-cooked" blue plate special until closing in the evening at eight. Black and white checkerboard linoleum covered the floor; red tablecloths covered the tables. Sarah led Joe to a small table near the back. An elderly, heavyset lady approached.

"Good morning, honey," the lady greeted Sarah.

"Good morning, Emma," Sarah responded with a smile. "This is Joe. Joe, this is Emma." Mayer greeted the woman who smiled and greeted him in return.

Sarah looked at Joe and added, "Emma and her husband Ralph own this diner and are my landlords." Looking up at the woman, "Emma, Joe works at the shipyard."

"Seems like everyone does these days," the woman commented. "Either there or at the airplane factory. Honey, Ralph's in the kitchen, you just tell him what you want and help yourself."

Since they both wanted just coffee, Sarah rose and brought back two white cups and a pot from a nearby counter. She filled the cups at the table.

"Well, I imagine the pace at work will be picking up even more now that the first ship has been launched," Sarah remarked.

"Yeah, plans are to complete and launch several ships each month starting this spring," Mayer replied. "We knew the first one would be slow going—working the bugs out, so to speak. But now we can get in a groove and get things really moving."

"Your work must be very interesting," she said.

"I like it, but most people would probably consider it boring."

"Why is that?"

"Oh, I don't know," Mayer explained. "Working with math and chemistry all day. Not very glamorous to most people I'm afraid."

"I think your work would be exciting," Sarah offered. "What I mean is the type of work that you and Howard do—taking part in the design and solving problems as they arise, that sort of thing."

"Well, it's interesting to me, anyway."

Mayer took a drink of the black coffee and reached for a cigarette from a pack of Pall Malls he had laid on the table. He offered her one, which she took. Mayer had sat and listened to many seminars about not discussing work with anyone. In mandatory meetings held twice a month, everyone from the FBI to the Navy and Coast Guard reminded shipyard workers of the importance of discretion. Mayer was sure Sarah had sat in on similar meetings; all war industry workers, from janitors to top-level engineers, were required to attend such meetings. He lit her cigarette, then his. Almost as if the same thought had just crossed her mind, to Mayer's relief, Sarah changed the subject.

"What do you do on weekends?" she asked. Although the shipyard was a three-shift, twenty-four-hour-a-day buzz of activity, engineers like Mayer and many secretaries like Sarah Klein worked a standard business workweek.

"Oh, sometimes I'll go in and work if I'm bored or things are backed up," Joe answered. "Sometimes I go fishing with the guard in our building. He's an old, local guy and he knows all the best spots. Also, about once every six weeks or so I try to get back to Indianapolis and visit the folks. The Navy gave me a 'C' gas rationing card, so I'm not limited on the amount of gas I can buy."

"It must be nice," Sarah said enviously. She took a drag of the cigarette then added: "My 'A' card only allows me three gallons a week." (Erika Lehmann made sure she held her cigarette the American way between her index and second finger, and not with the thumb and index finger like many Europeans.)

"You have a car?" Mayer was curious and a little surprised. Not many women her age had an automobile.

"Yes, it's an older one my father left me but it runs okay." Then she joked: "On three gallons a week, it doesn't have to run very far."

Mayer laughed.

By now all the tables in the diner were occupied and Emma struggled to keep up. Four middle-aged men in overalls and caps sat at a table frowning and looking around, obviously impatient that they had not been waited on.

"Busy place," Joe stated.

"Very busy," Sarah agreed. "In fact, if you'll excuse me for a few minutes, I think I'll help Emma."

Mayer nodded as Sarah got up and walked to the front of the diner, grabbed an order pad and pencil from beside the cash register, and took the orders of the four frowning men. In a moment the mood of the men had changed and Mayer could see them smiling and chuckling. As Sarah walked back to deliver their order to the kitchen, she passed Emma who was at the table next to Mayer. Mayer heard her tell Emma: "See, Emma, I told you all you have to do is flirt a little." Sarah knew Joe heard and she looked at him and smiled.

Emma laughed, "Honey, you're forgetting. I think it also makes a little difference on the age and figure of the one doing the flirting."

Sarah took a few more orders, delivered some meals, and refilled several coffee cups. When things seemed caught up, Sarah returned and sat down with Mayer.

"Sorry, Joe," she apologized. "But Emma and Ralph are so nice to me, letting me eat for free and all, I try to help out if I'm here and they are busy."

"I think it's great you found this place," said Joe.

They chatted for a few more minutes. Finally, after two more cups of coffee, Mayer told Sarah he would like to see her again.

She looked at him. "I would like that, too."

"There's a nightclub here called the Trocadero," said Mayer. "I haven't been there yet, but Howard told me about it and I've heard from others that it's the place to go."

"Sounds like fun," Sarah said.

"Next weekend then?" Mayer suggested.

She smiled. "It's a date."

He walked her outside. It was now a grand fall day. A breeze, pleasantly cool, delivered a reminder of the season by propelling a red leaf across the sidewalk in front of them.

"Maybe I'll see you at the shipyard some this week," Mayer said, trying not to sound quite as eager as he felt.

"Maybe," Sarah nodded and looked at him.

When they reached the stairs to her apartment, Mayer paused for a moment, hoping she would invite him up. She didn't. Mayer leaned forward to kiss her, not knowing what to expect. Would it be tender, like the one in Turnbull's apartment or…. He placed his lips on her's, which she allowed for only a brief moment. She returned the kiss, but with just a fleeting brush of her lips against his.

"Until our date then," she whispered, then looked him in the eyes and grinned playfully. Sarah Klein then turned and walked up the steps, never looking back. And for the second time in less than six hours, Mayer watched her disappear through the door at the top of the stairs.

✠ ✠ ✠

CHAPTER 26

I saw, and behold, a pale horse, and its rider's name was Death, and Hades followed him; and they were given power over a fourth of the earth, to kill with sword and with famine and with pestilence and by wild beasts of the earth.

—Revelation 6:8

Boston—December 1942

It was cold and it was Christmas Eve. Despite both the temperature and holiday, Ruby decided to work. December had been a slow month and there were bills to pay. Age catches up to everyone Ruby knew (she had seen her fortieth birthday last summer), so she figured she should take advantage of every opportunity. A large Swedish freighter had docked that afternoon and Ruby knew many of the ship's men would drown their holiday homesickness at the Red Parrot, a popular place among both the local cargo workers and foreign merchantmen a block from the harbor.

Ruby had worked the docks for years. The business from the wealthy men of the Back Bay and Beacon Hill areas was not available to her. Those men preferred the younger and prettier girls, but Ruby did not mind. She preferred the less discerning men of the rough and tumble dock taverns near the Boston harbor. The dock workers and merchant sailors paid less than the high society types, but Ruby felt more comfortable with the former. And the docks had advantages: deals were struck more quickly with these hard working and hard drinking men who worked on or near the sea, and less conversation was expected, especially among the many non-English speaking merchant sailors who frequented the dock taverns on shore leave while their ships awaited unloading and loading.

The Red Parrot was a loud, dimly-lit place with a creaking wood floor. It was a floor never painted but nevertheless colored over the years by the spilling of oceans of beer, whiskey, rum, and not a small amount of blood from the numerous, almost weekly brawls and even a few stabbings. Ruby entered the tavern by way of a dark alley door (orders from Stuttering Moe the bartender). Inside, cigarette smoke permeated the air along with the curses of bearded men and the shrill laughs of low women. Both the cursing and cackling were expected in the Red Parrot. Ruby spotted three women who plied her same trade.

Stuttering Moe spotted Ruby and waved her over.

"Wa wa waa wa we've got e ee eeee ee enough whores in here already, Rr r r ruby," the bartender frowned. "Ga ga go on home."

Ruby dug in her purse and found her last two dollars. Without speaking she handed the bills to Stuttering Moe.

"Okay," the bartender said as he pocketed the money, "but da da don't be ta ta takin' em out of here til they've da da drank their fill. Ya hear?"

Ruby nodded, then sat down at the end of the bar. With no money for a drink, she lit a cigarette and scoured the dusky room for potential customers. Most, if not all, of the men were foreigners. The local dock workers were at home for Christmas Eve leaving the chairs tonight for the merchant sailors with homes an ocean away. Ruby could make out some English spoken, albeit with heavy accents, along with other languages she had heard before but never cared to understand. A card game occupied several men at one table; the money at stake prompted winners to laugh and losers to curse. A plump prostitute named Ethel— Ruby had seen her around the dock taverns and talked to her once briefly—held a man's attention at a small table along one dark wall by exposing a very ample breast. Ruby watched the man roughly grab the breast and heard Ethel squeal with feigned delight. Ruby also recognized the two other prostitutes (she did not know their names): one flirted with three men at a far table, the other hovered around the table of card playing men—her banter and attention changing swiftly to the latest winner. Not seeing any lone men, Ruby turned her attention to a table where two husky, bearded men sat drinking beer from large pitchers, then chasing the beer with swigs from a shared whiskey bottle. Failing to establish eye contact, Ruby rose from her bar stool and approached the men's table.

"Merry Christmas," Ruby said to neither one specifically. Her coat was open and her blouse unbuttoned just enough so the top portion of her brassiere was visible—a calling card so men would know. The men spoke a foreign language and abruptly halted their conversation to inspect her up and down.

"Buy a lady a drink?" Ruby asked. The men turned to look at each other then broke into laughter. Unintelligible words were spoken, then the closest man slapped Ruby's rear and waved her off. She continued walking, hoping a man, or a table of them, would signal her to join them. None did. As Ruby passed the prostitute working the table of gamblers, the woman glared at her until she passed. When Ruby had spanned the length of the dark tavern, she noticed a table in the farthest corner and the silhouette of a man sitting alone. Ruby made her way toward him. It was the darkest corner of the tavern and the man's features could barely be seen.

"Merry Christmas."

No reply and the man's head did not turn to look at her. Thinking it possibly her last and best chance since the man was alone, Ruby boldly took a seat at his table.

"Alone like me at Christmas, are you?" Ruby asked, seeking an answer only to acknowledge her existence. Again silence from the shadow but at least he had not refused her yet. Ruby felt in her purse for her pack of Chesterfields, wrested one from the crumpled and almost empty pack, then put it to her lips. "Have a light?" she asked.

Finally the dark head turned her direction, and after a long moment that made Ruby tense and ready to move on, a match was struck and held to her cigarette. In the flickering match light she made out the man's features, and she quickly diverted her eyes down to concentrate on lighting the cigarette. What she caught a fleeting glimpse of was not so much an ugly face as an alarming one.

"I am sure you would like a drink," the man said in heavily accented English.

"Thank you," Ruby smiled. "That would be nice."

The Red Parrot did not bother with waitresses. Stuttering Moe was shouted at from the tables or, if customers did not feel like waiting on the slow-moving bartender, patrons made a trip to the bar to pick up the drinks themselves. The man who offered Ruby a drink made no effort to summon Stuttering Moe or fetch the drink himself, so Ruby went to the bar, ordered a drink to be put on the man's tab, then returned to the table with drink in hand.

"My name's Ruby." She introduced herself as she touched a match to the wick of a small candle on the table. It shed enough light to at least see whom she was talking to. Ruby heard the man tell her his name was Ivan something.

"I heard there was a ship from Sweden. Are you from there?" Ruby tried to stoke a conversation.

"Russia," the man answered, then confirmed he worked as a cargo hand on the Swedish ship.

Ruby had not forgotten Moe's warning about taking his customers out of the bar prematurely, but she paid him two dollars and she had to make it up. She needed to make at least ten dollars tonight: that usually meant two customers so time was a factor. She would give Moe another dollar if he complained. Ruby unfastened another button on her blouse then pulled down her brassiere to show the man her breasts.

"Five dollars an hour for anything you want," Ruby talked business.

The man glanced at her breasts without emotion. Ruby felt she was in for another refusal when the man finally spoke.

"Agreed," he said matter-of-factly, like he had just settled on a price for tomatoes from an Italian street vendor.

Ruby knew the sailor had no place of his own. She would have to take him to her apartment which was a convenient three blocks away. A light snow dusted the ground as Ruby walked the man past a line of row houses with exteriors in dire need of repair. Her apartment sat on the ground floor of one of the row houses. With cold fingers, it took her a moment to find the key, but finally she opened the door and hurried inside.

"Come on in," Ruby beckoned so she could close the door on the inhospitable Boston night.

The apartment was just a room—no kitchen or bathroom. Ruby heated her meals on a hot plate and shared a toilet and tub down the hall with other tenants. But unlike some of the other apartments, and belying the drab neighborhood and the rundown appearance of the building's exterior, the inside of Ruby's apartment was clean and a small, decorated Christmas tree sat on a table in front of the room's only window. A small spill on the floor next to a cat's milk bowl Ruby noticed immediately. As she daubed the small puddle of milk with a towel, a calico kitten appeared and rubbed its flanks on Ruby's lower leg. Ruby picked up the kitten and scratched it behind the ears.

"Cats I like," the man said in broken English. Ruby smiled and handed him the kitten. The small animal almost disappeared in his large, square hands.

The room's light afforded Ruby her first clear view of the face that had startled her in the tavern. She finally judged it not an ugly face, just rare, appearing as if it was not made of flesh but rather stone or painted metal. It was a face that would take time to get used to, but that was not one of Ruby's aims. He would be gone in an hour, maybe two. If she could please him and convince him to pay for another hour it would save her the trouble of going back out and searching the night for a second customer.

The man rubbed the kitten while Ruby undressed.

It was a week later, New Year's Day, before someone missed Ruby and then only because the landlady sought the new month's rent. The old woman would never fully recover from the sight, and even the veteran homicide detective would be forced to deal with nightmares after he saw the naked body hanging upside down from a light fixture. Blood was everywhere. The handle of a kitchen butcher knife protruded from between the woman's legs, the blade buried in the vagina. A decapitated kitten's head was stuffed in the dead woman's mouth—the dead eyes of the cat staring out from Ruby's open mouth.

The Swedish freighter was five days out of port minus one hand. Axel Ryker was in America and heading to a place called Evansville.

✠   ✠   ✠

Southern Indiana—[that same night]

Ice crunched under the tires of the Ford as she slowed to negotiate a hairpin curve in the rural Indiana road. From this road Erika Lehmann turned off onto a remote path seldom used but by hunters and fishermen. It was Christmas Eve (actually Christmas Day, being it was two in the morning) and there would be no hunters or fishermen on this road tonight.

Erika found herself thinking of the night she and Henry Wiltshire drove the lonely stretches of roads through rural England and Wales. The last night Henry Wiltshire was a free man.

The dark and lonely Indiana road was similar to the road through Wales. Also, there was a big moon just like that night. If it were not for the facts she was alone, and the Ford's left side steering wheel was opposite the Bentley's, she might have thought it deja vu.

Erika had waited as long as possible. Shortwave transmissions were dangerous for enemy agents in hostile lands. Both sides monitored the airwaves. Transmissions were a double-edged sword that allowed critical communication with home but at the same time practically screamed "Here I am!" to the counterintelligence services of the infiltrated country.

But it could be put off no longer. She had to transmit.

One of the first conditions of Operation Vinland required Erika to establish contact with Abwehr by this date. Since the dismal failure of the last major Abwehr mission in America last June (Operation Pastorius), Canaris insisted on certain guarantees that *Lorelei* was alive and Operation Vinland still operational. Not knowing that *Pastorius* had been betrayed and the agents arrested, U-boats patrolling offshore kept *Pastorius* code links open weeks longer than necessary. It was a risk Canaris did not want to take again. So Erika had to establish contact by 25 December or Abwehr would consider her "broken" and the mission breached.

Unlike England with its proximity to Abwehr monitoring stations throughout France, communications from the American mainland worked differently. In England, Erika could use her transmitter whenever the need arose, but now, because of the great distances, contact could be made only when a U-boat was in range. Depending on atmospheric conditions, Erika's transmitter had a practical operating range of eight hundred miles. A U-boat within one hundred miles of the Virginia coast would be within that range. However, a U-boat could not simply sit offshore in one location for months awaiting a transmission. A time schedule for Erika's transmissions had been devised. The U-boats patrolling the American coast would swing into her transmission radius only at scheduled intervals.

If Erika did not transmit tonight, the scheduled U-boat positioning would be canceled and Erika's Enigma codes nullified.

Enigma.

It was the super secret and so far unbreakable German enciphering system. A set of spinning rotors within an encoding machine called Enigma assigned randomly selected letters to a plaintext[8] message typed into the machine. The rotor settings were changed often so the only chance an interceptor of a German cryptogram had to decipher the message was if he also had an Enigma machine. The interceptor typed the encoded message into his Enigma which deciphered the message back into plaintext.

The Enigma machines were guarded at all costs, and an agent on foreign soil would never be given an Enigma machine to take with them into an enemy country. Instead Erika used a crypt sheet with forty different codes based on Enigma principles. After each transmission, the receiver—in her case a U-boat cruising off the east coast of the United States—transmitted back a brief confirmation that her message was received and another message instructing her which of the forty codes to use for her next cryptogram. It was as close to the unbreakable Enigma code as one could get without an Enigma machine. This is another reason she had to establish contact tonight. If she failed to make the deadline, she would not know which code was chosen for her next transmission.

Failing to make contact tonight, Erika's only means of communication with Germany would be through letters addressed to a Luiz Antonio Gonzales at an address in Juarez, Mexico. The address and pseudonym were established by Abwehr for such purposes. After the letters were received, they would then be physically relayed to Germany

---

8   **Plaintext**—The original, intelligible text, as it was before encipherment, revealed after successful decoding or cryptanalysis. *A Lexicon of Cryptography* ("Most Secret," Bletchley Park, 1943). Harris, Robert. *Enigma.*

through the Bolivar network, or the message could be encoded and transmitted to a U-boat in the Gulf.

Letter drops could and should be used for certain types of communications, but a letter drop had its disadvantages. It was slow; with the war it might take a letter two weeks or more to reach Mexico. It was unreliable; unlike shortwave transmissions where a confirmation was received immediately, an agent never knew if a letter made it through. In some cases there was no choice but to transmit.

Erika knew her days were numbered once she started broadcasting. As in Germany or England, America had wartime monitoring stations listening in on all radio traffic with ears perked for any broadcasts of a suspicious nature. The first one or two transmissions might give the enemy only a vague idea where the signal came from. This initial area might encompass thousands of square miles. But with each additional signal the circle would tighten. This transmission tonight would start the clock ticking.

However, the mobile transmitter in her trunk gave Erika a measure of security. Certainly it was much safer than transmitting from an apartment where a snooping landlady might stumble across the radio when Erika was away, and changing locations provided obvious problems for the airwaves watchdogs attempting to pinpoint a signal's exact location.

The dirt road became increasingly bumpy and finally ended on a small wooded bluff overlooking the Wabash River. Across the river was Illinois. There had not been another car for miles and then only on the better road before she turned off. *This should do.* Erika turned off the engine and looked at her watch. It was 2:20 a.m. The U-boats off the coast monitored for transmissions for three hours each night—from 0100 until 0400 East Coast time.

Outside the car she stood listening. She saw her breath. The night was silent but for a slight breeze that gently rustled the more delicate branches. Cold but clear, the local sky should not cause any special atmospheric problems. Erika opened the trunk and removed the false panel hiding the transmitter, rolled out a fifty-foot coil of wire which was attached to the radio and served as an antenna, then threw the wire up as high as she could into the naked branches of a tall sycamore.

Seven hundred miles east of the bluff overlooking the Wabash River, U-314 cruised slowly on the surface forty miles off the coast of Norfolk, Virginia. The submarine had a twofold mission: sink unescorted merchant ships and, tonight, monitor the airwaves for possible communications from the American mainland. Below deck Radioman Hans Jost sat with a microphone headset covering his ears. The headset only partly drowned out four of his shipmates robust but out-of-key rendition of *Silent Night* coming from the galley two compartments aft.

♪Stille Nacht, heilige Nacht
Alles schläft, einsam wacht
Nur das traute hochheilige Parr
Holder Knabe in lockigen Harr
Schlaf in himmlischer Ruh,
Schlaf in himmlischer Ruh. ♪

As the lonely crewmen of U-314 tried to celebrate the holy day so far from home and the loved ones of Christmas past, Hans Jost noticed a faint but unmistakable tone coming through his headset.

✠　　　　　✠　　　　　✠

CHAPTER 27

I am weary with my moaning;
Every night I flood my bed with tears;
I drench my couch with my weeping.
My eye wastes away because of grief,
It grows weak because of all my foes.

—Psalms 6:6,7

Dachau Concentration Camp outside Munich

February 1943

It was the second *Zählappell* of the day. There were always at least two a day—more if the guards felt they had reason. Zählappell was roll-call and it drained the physical stamina and willpower of even the healthier inmates. Zählappell meant standing in lines of five—the SS did everything in fives—sometimes for hours in heat, cold, rain, or snow.

Ruth Mayer shivered. It was below freezing and she wore only the gown issued to all female inmates, her undergarments confiscated on her first day in camp. The Zählappell was now in its second hour. The old woman two rows over fainted nearly an hour ago and lay unattended where she dropped. People who collapsed had to be left where they fell until the count was completed. For the SS guards it was no harder to count a fallen body, alive or dead, than a standing one. Getting the count right was all that mattered.

Ruth felt pity for the old woman, but she did not move to help her; to move out of your spot was a serious infraction and she had her four-year-old son to think about. The child stood beside his mother shivering and whining. Ruth had to constantly hold him up, shush him, and encourage him to remain silent. During the winter she would place him under her gown which helped keep him a little warmer. Ruth was lucky David was only four. Four-year-olds were not officially counted on the roster at Dachau. These rules were arbitrary and subject to change at any moment depending on the mood of the SS masters,[9] but Ruth had been allowed to take care of David since they arrived almost a year ago. Other mothers, with more children, were not as lucky. More than two children and the mothers were forced to decide which two to keep. The others disappeared.

Five-year-old male children were separated from their mothers and sent to live in the male block. Ruth prayed daily that the war would end before David reached five. But a year was an eternity at Dachau where simply staying alive for one more day was every inmate's goal.

Ruth tried not to think of the unlucky turn of events that brought her and David to this hellish place, but standing at Zählappell for hours made it impossible for the mind to not sometimes wander back. With just a small turn of events here or there she and David would be in America now. In the end, she and her husband Saul simply waited too long. They chose to ignore the less serious harasses and taunts of the Nazis during the early years after Hitler was elected Chancellor. Even when the persecution got worse later in the thirties, Saul decided to ride out the storm and stay in Germany even though he had an American cousin who had volunteered to sponsor their immigration (and to be

---

9   Later in the war, rules concerning the younger children would indeed change for the worse at most of the camps, including Dachau.

fair she couldn't blame things on Saul, she too thought things would eventually return to normal in Germany).

Kristallnacht in November of 1938 was the killing blow to any hopes that Germany could remain their home. Saul's small engine repair business was burned to the ground. The family sold anything left of value to raise money for exit visas. Unfortunately, when the visas were finally obtained, the dates did not match, so Saul sent her and David on ahead. Saul would follow and had everything arranged: the train to Portugal and the liner passage to New York Harbor. Ruth thinks it was during a stop in France when the visas were stolen although she would not notice them missing until the next day when she was asked to produce them by an official at the Spanish border. Unable to return home or contact Saul who was in hiding in Germany until his visa became valid, Ruth and David were sheltered by a Catholic family in Dijon until a year ago when the Nazis swept the town of Jews.

The first few days at Dachau will be forever brazed into Ruth's mind and soul: the stripping naked in front of laughing male SS guards, the shaving bald of her head, the number tattooed into her arm, the retching at the first day's meal when she saw the little worms swimming in her soup. She was thankful David's age would prevent him from remembering most of it.

But she learned how to survive. The soup that she poured out on to the ground the first day was now consumed to the last drop; the worms were one of the few sources of protein. She learned how to distract David from looking at the soup as she fed him. She learned all the little tricks for remaining inconspicuous: don't talk any more than you have to, don't look the guards or their dogs in the eye, always be on time for Zählappell and work. Work hard without complaint, but do not work too hard; that also drew attention.

Finally, after almost two hours of standing at attention in freezing weather, the guards were satisfied the count was accurate and Zählappell ended. Relatives of the old woman rushed to her aid, but it was aid no longer needed and the body was left where it lay. The kapos would carry it away the next morning. Another woman who had swooned farther back in the formation—out of Ruth's view—was revived and helped back to the barracks.

Ruth hustled David inside her assigned barracks, one of a phalanx of unheated buildings where the crush of bodies would at least provide warmth.

Evansville [that same day]

Axel Ryker closed the door behind him and threw his coat across a chair. Since shortly after arriving in Evansville, Ryker had stayed in this dingy little cabin ten miles west of the city. The cabin was one of many down the shoreline of the Ohio River; most were abandoned this time of year. Locals called these places "river camps," and they were normally used only in the summer by boaters and fishermen. Ryker rented the shack for a pittance from a farmer who was happy to make any income, regardless of the amount, from the place this time of year.

The entire cabin sat on six-foot high stilts a few feet from the river. Bizarre-looking now, but extremely pragmatic when the mighty river decided to scorn its banks and flood the bottoms for miles around.

It was perfect for Ryker.

The shack was close enough to the city for access but far enough to keep Ryker's mingling with locals to a minimum. He struggled with his English and found interaction with the talkative and too informal Americans tiresome.

Ryker's phony but very official looking immigration papers identified him as Ivan Vasili Bazarov. To anyone who had to know, he was a former Russian landowner who escaped one of Stalin's *collectivization* purges in the thirties by fleeing to Finland. When the Russians invaded Finland in

1939, Ivan Bazarov was again forced to flee, this time to Sweden after which he eventually made his way to the United States. Complicated, but for all intents and purposes untraceable, and it was a perfect ruse for Ryker. Born in Lithuania, Russian was Ryker's native tongue.

Himmler's instructions were simple: kill Erika Lehmann. It would not be difficult. She had never seen his face; surprise would be total. Likewise, his escape would be uncomplicated. He would make his way to and across the Mexican border and hook up with German operatives of the Bolivar network who would transport him to Venezuela. A freighter out of Caracas (flying a neutral flag of course) would take him to Gibraltar. Once in Spain he was as good as home.

Rudimentary.

At least after the girl was found.

After arriving in Evansville, Ryker quickly realized that finding the girl would not be as simple as he once thought. Even though the hapless Abwehr training supervisor, Ernest Kappe, had been blackmailed into divulging the mission's location, Kappe was not privy to certain important facts such as the name of the target the girl would seek out, or what means she would use to infiltrate the facility. Ulrich von der Osten, the Abwehr's chief expert on America, handled that part of her training and, unlike Kappe, von der Osten could not be compromised.

So Ryker would be spending his time looking for the proverbial "needle in a haystack," and none of the Gestapo experts on America who took part in Ryker's preparation realized how big the haystack really was. The shipyard was much larger than he had imagined and with enough workers, Ryker thought, to populate a small country.

Another stumbling block for Ryker was the fact he had no hopes of infiltrating the facility himself. He did not speak English well enough to ever pass himself off as an American, and with a Russian cover identity he had no chance of being hired at an American war plant. The Americans hired no one for war production who was not a U.S. citizen and especially not a foreigner from a communist country. Ryker would have to find the girl from the fringes.

Ryker cut the lid off of a can of "pork 'n beans." It was something new he had tasted since arriving in America. Instead of pouring the beans into a pan for heating he placed the can on a small propane burner. From a satchel he pulled out several pictures of Erika Lehmann and a statistics sheet to study once again.

Subject:	Erika Marie Lehmann
Height:	170 centimeters
Weight:	61 kilograms
Hair:	blond
Eyes:	nußbraun
Build:	athletisch
Training:	Abwehrabteilung: Brandenburg/Quenzsee; Tegel

The report also listed as a distinguishing mark a five centimeter long knife scar on her inside upper right arm. Overall not a great deal that would distinguish the girl at a distance. Ryker picked up the pictures he had gazed at an untold number of times. At least the blond hair would help.

✠ ✠ ✠

PART 3

CHAPTER 28

There is a mysterious cycle in human events.
To some generations much is given.
Of other generations much is expected.
This generation has a rendezvous with destiny.

—Franklin Delano Roosevelt

Chicago—March 1943

It was the sixteenth ring, or maybe the seventeenth, when Charles Pulaski's eyes finally opened. At first he was oblivious to what awoke him. It took the fuzzy, liquor-championed twilight that cloaked his brain a few moments to clear before he finally recognized the sound as coming from a telephone. He did not move for several more rings, hoping the caller would hang up.

But in the end Pulaski knew the ringing would not stop. The only phone calls he received were from Harry Fallon, and *that son-of-a-bitch will let the phone ring until hell freezes over.*

Finally surrendering, Pulaski slowly sat up on the edge of the bed. That's when Thor's hammer hit him squarely between the eyes. Booze never made Pulaski nauseous, but the next morning headaches were a bitch. Reaching for the phone on the night table, he fumbled the receiver which fell with a loud thud against the peeling linoleum floor. The noise must have shocked the ear of the caller who Pulaski could hear ranting from the floor. He grabbed the cord, reeled in the receiver then threw it back to the floor, this time with an even louder bang. Again Pulaski heard cursing. He would have laughed if it were not for the drums pounding out a military parade march between his temples. This time after retrieving the receiver he held it to his ear but said nothing.

"Are you there, you goddamn stupid Polock?" the voice from the other end demanded. It was Harry.

"No." Pulaski scratched out as he rubbed his temples with his free hand.

"Where have you been, fuckhead?" Fallon asked. "I've been searching all over Chicago for your sorry ass since noon yesterday."

Pulaski's mind was still fogged. He tried to recall where he had been yesterday. He started bar hopping early…

"What day is it?" he asked Fallon.

"It's Sunday, dickhead, but you're on call seven days a week, remember. It's a good thing I finally got a hold of you. The boss is pissed. I'm supposed to call him as soon as I found you. Get rid of the bimbo, and meet us at headquarters in one hour. Don't be late, Charlie, or it's your ass this time for sure."

Pulaski heard the click then slowly returned the receiver to its cradle. He knew there was no woman in the bed behind him. There had not been one for a long time. Pulaski wanted desperately to lie back down, if just for a few minutes, but knew if he did he would be out for several hours. He stood up—much too quickly—which stoked the bonfire in his brain. He was sweating but not from the hangover. He had slept in his clothes and the room was hot. *It is always too hot in this fleabag hotel!* The room sweltered during the summer and stayed uncomfortably hot even during the cold Chicago winters thanks to a steam radiator that had a mind of its own, ignoring its thermostat despite how low it was set. Even though he made a decent living, Pulaski was forced to live in a rundown room in a cheap hotel: alimony and child support payments.

Shuffling to the room's only window, Pulaski struggled with the stuck crank but finally managed to open the window enough to let in a lifesaving blast of cold air. A week of pleasant spring weather had deserted the city—a brazen tease now turned away. Overnight a vengeful late-March cold wave that had lurked just north of the city moved in and now snow painted the avenue below. Usually loud and busy, the street was now early-Sunday-morning-lonely. Churchgoers rarely traveled this part of town and the hookers hated the cold. The only sign of life Pulaski noticed from his third floor window was a set of tracks in the snow left behind by a car that passed who knows how long ago. Even Frankie, the boy who hawked the *Tribune* in front of the hotel each morning, was AWOL. Pulaski retreated from the window to look for his watch. He finally located it on his wrist.

7:30 a.m.

What the hell was happening that occasioned a meeting with Harry and the boss this early on a Sunday? *Some major crap had to be stirring somewhere.* Pulaski removed his sweat-stained shirt, threw it on the bed, then went to the bathroom. His room was one of only three in the hotel with a private bathroom. *Must be one of the hotel suites* Harry Fallon joked sarcastically when he first saw the shabby room. Regardless of the sometimes vulgar name calling between the two, Harry was an old friend—probably Pulaski's only.

After relieving himself in the grimy toilet, Pulaski turned on the cold water faucet and splashed water on his face. Gazing in the cracked mirror, Pulaski ignored the bloodshot eyes and the two-day growth of beard. He stared at the paunch above his belt. He use to pride himself on being in shape but now, at forty-five, that, like his wife and kids, was something in the past. Pulaski smoked two packs a day and quit exercising several years ago. His diet was atrocious; lunch and dinner were more often than not a couple of dogs or brats from a street vendor. Thankfully, he was not an alcoholic; Charlie Pulaski could handle his booze, it's just that sometimes he handled too much of it, especially on weekends.

A razor was found but not a comb. He shaved quickly then settled for wetting his hands and running them through his hair. At least he had not lost that yet. Although some gray showed at the temples, he still had a full head of hair.

The pants he slept in were wrinkled but would have to do; they were the cleanest pair. The closet contained no clean shirts, so he picked the neatest looking one from a pile of dirty shirts on the floor. He grabbed a tie that was already tied and slipped it over his neck, adjusting it nonchalantly. Pulaski slipped on a brown leather shoulder holster that carried a Smith and Wesson snub-nosed .38 revolver, then grabbed a suit jacket and coat thrown carelessly across a chair.

After closing the door behind him, Pulaski walked down the hotel's poorly lit hallway and, almost as an afterthought, checked to make sure his FBI identification was in one of his pockets.

Just shy of 8:30 a.m. Pulaski walked into a drab, red brick building on 35th Street in the shadow of Comiskey Park. A young man who could pass as a teenager sat at a desk normally occupied by a female receptionist. On the wall behind the young man, a profile of J. Edgar Hoover seemed to stare at the official seal of the FBI hanging alongside. Pulaski ignored Hoover and the young man.

"Whoa! there old-timer," the young man objected to Pulaski's attempt to pass further into the building. "I'll need to see some I.D."

Pulaski stopped and looked at the kid.

"Who are you?" Pulaski demanded, irked at the kid's curtness. It was too early on a Sunday morning.

"Special Agent Saunders." The kid answered the question like he expected Pulaski to kowtow.

"Kiss my ass, Special Agent Saunders." Pulaski turned and continued down a hallway. Saunders mumbled an obscenity, rose from the desk and caught up with Pulaski as he entered Harry Fallon's office. Fallon sat behind his desk talking on the phone when Pulaski entered with the red-faced Saunders on his heels.

"Sir, this guy…"

"It's okay, Saunders," Fallon cut him off as he hung up the phone. Fallon then unceremoniously waved Saunders out the door. The young FBI agent shot Pulaski a scowl before leaving. Pulaski did not see it, but could not have cared less if he had.

"What, are we recruiting the high schools now?" Pulaski joked as he plopped down in a chair across from Fallon.

"He's twenty-four," Fallon remarked. "Just got out of the Academy, graduated top of his class."

"Where's Irma?" Pulaski asked, referring to the elderly receptionist who normally occupied Saunders station. Pulaski liked teasing old Irma.

"She's not here. It's Sunday, remember? Most of the secretaries are off. You look like shit."

Pulaski ignored the remark as he reached over and grabbed a folder of papers off Fallon's desk for no other reason than to get a rise out of his old friend. Pulaski opened the folder and began thumbing through the contents. Fallon stood up, leaned over the desk and snatched the folder out of Pulaski's hand.

"How much do you weigh now, Charlie?" Fallon had nagged his old friend about his weight for years.

"A hundred and eighty," Pulaski lied. That was his weight when he joined the Bureau in 1926.

"Horse crap."

"Two hundred and ten, maybe," Pulaski admitted unruffled.

"I bet it's more like two-thirty. You've got more chins than a Chinese phone book for Christ's sake. You're going to eat your way out of the Bureau," Fallon warned for the umpteenth time.

Fallon continued: "We're getting old. Guys like Saunders out there are circling overhead like buzzards. Past deeds only count for so much—

for so long. It's 'What have you done for me recently?' How long has it been now since Dillinger, Charlie?"

"I don't remember," Pulaski lied again. He knew exactly how long. July 22, 1934. 10:35 p.m. to be exact. In his mind it was like yesterday. Pulaski was younger and much leaner when he stood in a Lincoln Avenue alley on Chicago's Near North Side and watched John Dillinger walk out of the Biograph Theater with Anne Sage and Polly Hamilton in arm. Even though Pulaski was not among those who emptied their guns into Dillinger (Pulaski told Fallon years later that they could have taken Dillinger alive), it was Pulaski who started the rush toward Dillinger when the nervous Melvin Purvis could not get his cigar lit— the agreed upon signal. Pulaski sat beside Dillinger's body during the ambulance ride first to the Alexian Brothers Hospital for the death pronouncement, then to the Cook County Morgue.

"So why am I here, Harry?" Pulaski sought a subject change from both his weight and Public Enemy Number One.

"Strange happenings downstate," Fallon answered. "A couple of months ago, some insomniac HAM operator in a small town called Mount Carmel picked up a weird, middle-of-the-night Morse code transmission coming from somewhere down that way. The transmission was clear enough, but the words were a bunch of gobbledy-gook that made no sense. The guy more or less forgot about it until he picked up the same type of stuff a couple of weeks later. This time the guy wrote down part of the transmission and called the FCC. Like I said...weird stuff, obviously some sort of code. The boss will fill you in. But it looks like you'll be leaving Chicago for a while, old buddy." Fallon smiled devilishly. He knew Pulaski hated out-of-town assignments.

Pulaski groaned and looked at Fallon suspiciously. "Lord, not another rogue transmitter case! I've done these before and they've all been a huge waste of time, Harry. Whose idea is this? To send me I mean."

"Not mine." Fallon read his mind. "I had nothing to do with it. The old man chose you, Charlie, because you have experience with this type

of case. Like you said, you've chased down some of these rogue transmitters before."

"Yeah, and none of them turned out to be the bad guys," Pulaski
reminded Fallon. "All a waste of time. One time the FCC swore they
were intercepting secret coded messages every day at a certain time. Also
swore the signal was coming from across the Canadian border. Turned out
to be a Sioux Indian named Joseph Yellow Wolf who transmitted
weather reports in the Sioux language across a reservation in North
Dakota. I worked two months on that case, Harry. Scared the bejeezus
out of Yellow Wolf when we broke his door down in the middle of the
night. The crazy bastard threw a tomahawk at me...can't blame him
though."

Harry Fallon burst out laughing. "Well, hell, you'd throw a tomahawk
at somebody who broke down your door in the middle of the night,
wouldn't you?"

"You wouldn't laugh if you had a wicked looking thing like that stick
in the wall six inches from your face." Pulaski knew it was funny but was
good at remaining stone-faced when he told the story of his encounter
with Yellow Wolf. He knew the serious face made the story funnier.
"Another time a rogue transmission case in Milwaukee turned out to be
not a German or Jap spy but a pimple-faced teenage Romeo who was
using a HAM radio and a half-baked amateur code to send secret love
messages to his girlfriend across town."

"It doesn't matter, Charlie," Harry said. "They all have to be checked
out, you know that. Besides, maybe running around those corn fields
down there will burn off some of that blubber."

"Get me out of this, Harry. Tell him to send someone else. Send
Saunders out there; he'll love it. He can go around flashing his I.D. at the
young broads."

"No can do. This one will need experience, Charlie. Anything that
might be a wartime national security case is top priority for Hoover."
Fallon then rationalized: "Hell, it will be good for you to get away for a

while…and be thankful they still think enough of you to send you." The words were a not-so-subtle reminder that Pulaski's record over the past two or three years was not exactly sterling. Several cases he had worked on were still open with old leads dried up, and Pulaski had not endeared himself to certain superiors within the Bureau by an irreverent attitude toward their authority.

Fallon's phone rang. After a moment of listening, Fallon announced into the receiver that Agent Pulaski had arrived. "…and he'll be right in, sir." Fallon looked up at Pulaski as he replaced the receiver, "Go on in, Charlie."

The boss was Special Agent Preston Elliott, director of the FBI's Chicago field office. Elliott had been at the Bureau's helm in Chicago since 1935 when Melvin Purvis resigned. Elliott was a big-boned man who had to shave twice a day to combat five o'clock shadow. When Pulaski entered Elliott's office, the man sat flipping papers at his desk. Two men whom Pulaski had never laid eyes on sat across from Elliott, both also busy flipping papers. Both strangers looked up briefly when Pulaski entered; Elliott's gaze remained fixed on his papers. Pulaski unceremoniously took the last remaining chair in front of the desk, which sat him directly between the two strangers.

After a long pause, Elliott finally looked up over his reading glasses. "Gentlemen, this is Special Agent Pulaski." Even though he addressed the others, Elliott fixed his gaze on Charlie. "Agent Pulaski, these men are here from our Washington headquarters." Elliott pointed at the man on Pulaski's left. "This is Special Agent Dave Falasco." Pulaski and the man nodded to each other. "And," Elliott continued, "this is Mr. Stanley Mullen." More nodding.

Elliott cut to the chase. "There is some concern about some unusual Morse code transmissions originating from an area south of here. Mr. Mullen is with the Federal Communications Commission and is an expert on these matters and as such has served as an advisor to both the Bureau and our military. Mr. Mullen has C-1 security clearance so all matters concerning this case may be discussed in his company." Elliott turned to Mullen: "Mr. Mullen, I'll let you take over."

Stanley Mullen rose from his chair. A bald-on-top, mid-fifties man with thick spectacles, a stooped frame, and wrinkled suit, the frail looking Mullen looked to Pulaski like he should indeed be an expert on something—even if only God knew what it might be. Mullen handed Pulaski a small map of the United States on which a perfectly round red circle was drawn. A former college professor who apparently felt it necessary to stand while talking, Mullen pushed his glasses higher on his nose and looked at Pulaski.

"Agent Pulaski, I met with Agent Elliott extensively yesterday, and Agent Falasco has of course been briefed. Much of what I will relay to you will be redundant for them, so I'll try to stick to the brass tacks of the matter. There will be plenty of time later to give you a more detailed overview since we will apparently be spending some time together."

Pulaski glanced at Preston Elliott who ignored him.

"As you know," Mullen continued, "since the start of the war the Federal Communications Commission has devoted much of its time and resources to monitoring the air waves for national security purposes. Since Pearl Harbor, much of our manpower has been assigned to monitoring stations on both the east and west coasts for transmissions from sea, but we also have several substations farther inland to monitor any outgoing radio traffic that might prove of a suspicious nature. You might say the FCC has a twenty-four-hour ear tuned to radio, wire, and cable traffic across the entire continental United States and well out to sea." Mullen's glasses had again slid so he repeated the earlier push.

So far the FCC man had said nothing that Pulaski did not already know. Guys who say they will stick to "brass tacks" rarely do, Pulaski reminded himself. He knew the FCC monitored the coasts for enemy transmissions. All FBI agents were also aware that the FCC's ears pointed both directions. Radio transmissions from land were also monitored for any that might be covert messages from enemy agents at work in the States.

"When we get a 'hit' (Mullen thankfully did not stop to explain what a *hit* was, Pulaski knew it was reception of a suspicious transmission) we immediately go to work. By a technique called 'triangulation' we attempt to establish the location from where the transmission took place. Agent Elliott tells me you have worked this type of case in the past, so I'm assuming you are familiar with the term 'triangulation.'" Mullen paused and waited for Pulaski.

"I'm familiar," Pulaski assured the arduous FCC man. When it could be established that at least three separate monitoring stations, located far apart, had received the same suspicious signal, *triangulation* of the signal could determine within a couple of hundred miles its origin point. The strength of the signal received by each station would vary, after that the eggheads like Mullen could do the math. This original two-hundred-mile-radius-circle could be shrunk with each subsequent transmission to eventually pinpoint a location. During peacetime the FCC used triangulation to locate unlicensed radio stations. Since Pearl Harbor the technique was coming in useful for ferreting out those using the airwaves for much more sinister purposes.

Mullen: "Our monitoring substation in Dallas reported a suspicious International Morse Code transmission received on December 25 at 0330 hours, Washington time. The signal was obviously encoded and very brief—too brief to allow triangulation. On January 28 a second encoded signal, this one longer, was recorded by several of our monitoring stations around the country, and it was determined both signals shared the same fingerprint. (Pulaski knew *fingerprint* was radio operator jargon for the style and speed in which a person transmits Morse code. Like a fingerprint, each operator's style and speed varies). Fortunately, the length of this second signal was sufficient to allow triangulation between our Dallas station, a station in Kansas City and one in Wheeling, West Virginia. The map that I handed you is the initial triangulation area. We knew the signal had to originate somewhere within that circle."

Pulaski looked at the map and the red circle Mullen referred to. Inside the circle was an area encompassing St. Louis on the west, Indianapolis on the north, Cincinnati the east, and south to an area just below Nashville, Tennessee.

"That's a very big circle, Mr. Mullen," Pulaski said. "Can't this be narrowed down further? Agent Fallon mentioned something about a HAM operator downstate."

Mullen blushed at having to admit the FCC's major break had come from an amateur HAM operator from a small town who had trouble sleeping at night. "We were narrowing the area although the work proceeded slowly because of the infrequency of the transmissions. However, I will confess that the HAM operator Agent Fallon referred to was a stroke of luck. From his home in Mount Carmel, Illinois, this amateur operator twice picked up these signals. The real break comes from the fact that the second time the HAM operator received the signals he was in the process of moving his antenna and did not have it hooked up at the time. Taking into account the simplicity of the man's equipment, and atmospheric conditions on that night, to receive a signal as clearly as the one he recorded without an antenna could only mean the signal was coming from very close by—within a sixty to seventy-mile maximum radius I estimate."

Mullen walked over to an easel sitting in a corner of the room, picked it up and placed it closer to the sitting men. On the easel was a large map of Illinois and its bordering states. With a pointer he retrieved from the easel's tray, Mullen aimed at a point in the southwest corner of Illinois.

"Here is Mt. Carmel, the location of the HAM operator," Mullen said like a teacher addressing students, pausing as if he expected them to take notes. "We ran a search through government and military records to find out if any top secret installations or high priority wartime production facilities were located in that part of the state and came up empty." Hearing this from the FCC man was a surprise to Pulaski. Why would an enemy (if that's what this was all about) be sending coded messages from somewhere out in the sticks unless there was something important nearby? Mullen picked up a drawing compass and answered Pulaski's telepathic question.

"However," Mullen continued while drawing a circle on the map as intently as a surgeon making an incision, "if you draw a circle which represents a seventy-mile radius—the possible radius of our HAM's reception without an antenna—from Mount Carmel, Illinois, that circle leaves the state." Mullen stepped away from the map so Pulaski could see his work, and with pointer back in hand the FCC man pointed to the city of Evansville, Indiana, which lay on the circle's edge. "As I have already informed the other men in this room, Agent Pulaski, my theory is the signal is originating here. Evansville, Indiana, is a mid-size city currently playing an important role in our country's war effort. It serves as the venue for several high priority and top secret military projects. Although, as of this moment, this location is conjecture on my part, we are in the process of moving equipment into the area that will enable us to pinpoint the signal location if and when it resumes."

"Resumes?" Pulaski asked.

"No interceptions have taken place since the 28 January hit," Mullen admitted, "but this is not unusual with espionage transmissions."

Or with wild goose chases, Pulaski told himself before asking, "Why the six week delay in our response?"

Agent Falasco, the Washington man who had remained silent to this point, piped in. "Headquarters in Washington receives over a thousand reports every month from concerned citizens about suspicious activity. It's great that Americans are vigilant but at the same time the vast majority of the reports lead to dead-ends and tie up our manpower. That's it in a nutshell, Agent Pulaski. It comes down to manpower."

Pulaski had decided not to bring up wild goose chases, but Falasco opened the door talking about dead-ends. "I understand about dead-ends

Agent Falasco. I've been on these type of cases a few times. How sure are we that these transmissions are of a sinister nature?"

"Fair question. We've all done our share of running up dead-end alleys, Agent Pulaski, and none of us enjoy it. In answer to your question, it wasn't determined until last week that the code being transmitted from this area is remarkably similar to the German 'Enigma' code. When that determination was made, this case became top priority. Enigma was first used by the German submarine fleet and is now used by much of the German military. The Allies have not yet cracked the code, but Washington is working on it twenty-four hours a day and the British Secret Service has assigned most of its 'M' branch to the deciphering of the Enigma code. The British military has practically every college math professor in England squirreled away at a place called Bletchley Park working on the code. What makes it so tough to crack is the code changes every day with the use of a machine called Enigma that assigns word letters seemingly at random without any discernible pattern."

"What are the prospects for deciphering these messages as far as time frame?" Pulaski looked at Falasco.

"Not good," Falasco admitted. "We have only bits and pieces of each message and, like I said, we have not yet cracked Enigma. But I'll say again, Agent Pulaski, our people in Washington have earmarked this case as warranting investigation because of the similarities to Enigma."

Pulaski was unconvinced but remained silent. Although the Enigma code had never been brought up before, Pulaski had heard similar conjecture about "the high level of suspicion" during briefings on all the rogue transmission cases, but telling Falasco and Mullen about Yellow Wolf would serve no purpose. He doubted if the sour-faced Mullen would even find it funny. Pulaski looked at the map and bemoaned his luck. Evansville sat on Indiana's southern border; if it would just move itself a few miles south it would be in Kentucky and the Nashville office would have to handle this case. But as far as FBI districts were concerned, the state of Indiana was the jurisdiction of the Chicago office.

It was now Preston Elliott's turn to talk.

"Pulaski, you'll accompany Agent Falasco and Mr. Mullen to Evansville. Falasco here is in charge of the case. Those orders are from Hoover himself. The director is also sending any additional agents that can be spared from the Indianapolis and St. Louis offices. Agent Falasco has already visited those cities and met with the agents who will make up the taskforce."

Great, Pulaski mused, *I'm the guy who can be spared from the Chicago office.* Elliott made it sound like they were sending in the second stringers.

"The taskforce," Elliott went on, "can also draw as much help as needed from the military investigators and security people already stationed in the city. You'll drive down tomorrow with Agent Falasco. Be prepared to stay down there until the case is resolved. Any questions?"

"No, sir." Charlie Pulaski had resigned himself a half hour ago to the fact he would be packing his bags and shuffling off to the Hoosier State.

"Fine," Elliott said. "Good luck, gentlemen."

Pulaski sat in the passenger seat as Dave Falasco drove the government issued '40 Chevy south through Indiana. They left Chicago at nine that morning. The FCC man, Stanley Mullen, was not with them. Mullen had loose ends to tie up with the FCC in Chicago. Specifically, Mullen wanted to supervise the shipment of the monitoring equipment he would require—the equipment he promised would pinpoint exactly where the mysterious transmissions were coming from. Mullen and the additional technicians he needed to man the monitoring stations would follow the equipment truck down tomorrow.

Evansville, Indiana, was a seven-hour drive from Chicago, but they would not arrive until late that night because Falasco was expected in Indianapolis for what they both hoped would be a brief meeting with the FBI field office in that city. Professional etiquette required Falasco to brief the Indy field office of the goings-on, plus he wanted to check in with the agents from Indianapolis who were assigned to his taskforce in Evansville.

First impressions had left Pulaski skeptical of the Washington man, but during the drive through Indiana, Falasco took the initiative to establish some comraderie. The attempt succeeded in convincing Pulaski he might have been wrong in his initial appraisal of the man. Falasco was a tall and sturdy former tackle at West Point who had joined the Bureau after fulfilling his commitment to the army. He filled Pulaski in on his FBI background, admitting that his service to that point lacked a high profile case. This fact probably stoked Falasco's interest in Charlie Pulaski.

"Agent Elliott told me you worked the Dillinger case." Falasco offered the prompt as they passed through Lafayette, a town Falasco had never heard of but a place where Pulaski spent four days in '33 after Dillinger was reportedly spotted there. Indiana was Dillinger's home state and Lafayette only seventy miles from the outlaw's hometown of Mooresville. This area of central Indiana generated many Dillinger sightings in the early thirties—some false, some accurate. In April of 1934, during the height of the greatest nationwide manhunt for any outlaw in American history, Dillinger returned to Mooresville to visit his father and family for three days. The crafty Dillinger correctly calculated the law would never think him brazen enough to return home. (Pulaski was one of those tragically mistaken lawmen who reasoned that Dillinger could be anywhere but home in Mooresville.) Dillinger was right; that spring, as the FBI fanned out to search the country, Public Enemy Number One spent a long, peaceful holiday at home. The nation's most famous bank robber even posed playfully for photographs with old friends and neighbors while holding his Thompson machine gun.

"Yeah," Pulaski finally answered. "I spent ten months on the Dillinger taskforce." Falasco expected much more but Pulaski ended his remarks there.

Like a soldier with bad dreams from a war, Pulaski preferred not talking about John Dillinger. Pulaski had personally questioned Dillinger at the Lake County, Indiana, jail just a few hours before Dillinger broke out using the now famous whittled wooden gun. Pulaski was also present for what turned into every lawman's worst nightmare at the Little Bohemia Lodge in Wisconsin when the Dillinger gang was cornered (everyone, including Pulaski thought they had him dead to rights that time). Baby Face Nelson killed a friend of Pulaski's, and other FBI agents mistakenly shot three innocent bystanders—killing one. Dillinger, Baby Face, and the rest of the gang escaped.

The same storm front that frosted Chicago streets white over the weekend escorted the Chevy south. An icy rain greeted them as they drove into Indianapolis. Pulaski had a couple of hours to burn while Falasco took care of business with the Indy FBI and, on the spur of the moment, Pulaski took a cab to Crown Hill Cemetery, a place he had never been. It was the city's most famous residence for the dead. From a map near the entrance, Pulaski noticed that the remains of President Benjamin Harrison rested there along with a couple of vice presidents and the famous poet James Whitcomb Riley. From the same map, Pulaski found the grave he sought, pulled his coat tighter, then trudged through the cold drizzle over several small hills until he located the marker. A large tombstone bearing the name of Dillinger stood sentry over a smaller one marking the grave of Molly Dillinger, the outlaw's mother. There was no stone for Public Enemy Number One, but Pulaski knew John Dillinger was buried here alongside the mother who died when he was three. The ice cold rain waterfalled off the front brim of Pulaski's fedora as he stood at the grave. There for only a few seconds, Pulaski turned his back on the stone and walked away.

CHAPTER 29

The dawn of knowledge is usually the false dawn.

—*Bernard De Voto*

Evansville—April 1943

"Over medium." Charlie Pulaski answered the waitress then handed her the menu. Pulaski sat in the restaurant of Evansville's Sonntag Hotel across the table from Dave Falasco and Stanley Mullen. Falasco and Mullen had already ordered. All three men roomed at the Sonntag at the government's expense, the accommodations a definite improvement for Pulaski from his hotel in Chicago.

The trio had arrived in Evansville three weeks before. Falasco had spent most of his time initiating a series of background checks on workers. Mullen, the FCC man, had been supervising the setup of monitoring equipment that would allow triangulation of any shortwave transmissions from the area. As for his part, Pulaski had spent the past three weeks touring the various war plants in town and discreetly interviewing the higher-level security personnel.

Several teams of FBI agents now worked within the area, all under Falasco's supervision. The FBI agent from Washington met with each team at least twice a week for reports and to coordinate efforts, making sure work was not unnecessarily duplicated. Falasco's twice-a-week meetings with Pulaski and Mullen were always over breakfast at the Sonntag.

As soon as the waitress left, Agent Falasco opened the folder that had become quite familiar to the two other men at the table.

"Okay, guys," Falasco said, "background checks are ongoing and will continue for as long as needed. I think this is our best strategy for now. With over thirty thousand out-of-town workers hitting this town within the past year just for the war industries, the initial background checks were skimpy to say the least. Many of the security checks were simply checks for felonies from lists mailed from various out-of-town police departments. If the worker's name was not on the felony list from the hometown he claimed to be from, he was cleared for work. And as far as I can tell, few if any checks were made to verify if a worker was actually from that town. It would be a piece of cake for an enemy agent to get a low-level or perhaps even a mid-level clearance job at just about any of the plants in this town. Only with personnel in positions that demand the highest clearances were thorough checks made. However, Hoover still wants the high-clearance people checked first so we've got that in the works now. After we get done with these people, we'll work on the middle and lower-level workers."

"And, of course," Pulaski interjected, playing the devil's advocate, "our current round of checks are worthless if the person we are looking for is not a foreigner with an assumed identity but an American working for the enemy."

"Right," Falasco agreed. "We're going to need a break. Even if the checks do eventually turn up something, it might be months down the road. We're talking over thirty thousand security checks here."

Pulaski and Falasco sat silently for a moment and considered their predicament. Both agents knew a break in this case depended on one of two possible events: the bad guy would make a mistake, or the good guys would get lucky. Almost as if on cue both men looked at Stanley Mullen.

Like Falasco, the priggish FCC man had nothing of interest to report. "As you know, gentlemen, the monitoring equipment is set up and operational. It has been so for two weeks. I did have one of the units moved from Madisonville, Kentucky to Paducah; the elevation is more suitable. So our triangulation units are now located in Paducah, Kentucky; Vincennes, Indiana; and Louisville, Kentucky."

Mullen stopped talking when the waitress arrived with breakfast; she sat a plate in front of each man, then fetched a pot and refreshed their coffee. When she departed, Mullen continued.

"There has been no shortwave activity of a suspicious nature coming from within this region since we arrived three weeks ago, but I remain confident that the Enigma-type signals intercepted this past winter came from this immediate area."

"So it has been over two months since the last signal." Pulaski thought aloud as he cut his ham and eggs into bite-size pieces.

"Yes," Mullen confirmed just for the sake of having something to confirm. "Our FCC people around the country and the HAM operator in Mount Carmel, Illinois, picked up the last Enigma fingerprint in February."

All three men remained silent for a moment. There was still no confirmation that they were searching the correct area. The entire operation was being conducted on Stanley Mullen's educated guess that the dubious signals came from somewhere in this town or very nearby.

It was now Pulaski's turn to report.

"Since we got together last time, I have taken another turn around most of the factories, especially the P-47 aircraft plant and the shipyard. If Adolf sent one of his bad guys to this town, those two places would be the most likely targets in my opinion."

"What about the ordnance plant" Mullen asked. "I thought it was supposed to be the largest manufacturer of bullets in the country."

Pulaski looked at Falasco who grinned back. Both FBI men realized the Germans knew how to make their own bullets so that plant would hold few secrets for the enemy. And as far as sabotage, the Germans would never send an agent, or team of agents, this far inland to sabotage a small munitions factory, whatever its output.

"I think the more likely target would be the Thunderbolt plant or the shipyard, Stanley," said Pulaski patiently. "At this point they're much bigger fish than the bullet factory." Always ready to learn, Mullen, the professor, nodded excitedly like he had just been briefed on a new scientific discovery.

Pulaski continued: "By now I think I have met just about all of the higher-ranking security people at both places. As you know, Dave, the security people are in the process of compiling the lists we need."

"Yeah," Falasco interjected. "We have already started background checks on some engineers and design personnel, anyone with access to top secret information."

Pulaski: "Now that I've met the security people, I plan to get started with some of the engineers and high-clearance personnel this week. It's a start anyhow."

"Good," Falasco remarked. "Make sure you give me a list of the people you talk to, Charlie, so we don't waste time hitting the same people with multiple agents."

Pulaski nodded and finished off a biscuit.

"And as we all agreed, gentlemen," Falasco reiterated, "we want to keep all this as low-key as possible. No sense tipping off the bad guys that we are on to them."

If we are on to anything at all, Pulaski could not help thinking. Regardless, he agreed with the modus operandi, no need in letting an enemy (if there was one) know the FBI was sniffing around and put him even more on his guard.

"Keep up the good work," Falasco looked at both men. "Sooner or later things will go our way."

To Charlie Pulaski it looked like later.

Dave Falasco procured Pulaski a 1939 Oldsmobile from the military motor pool that supplied cars for VIPs and officers in town on official business. One hour after breakfast, Pulaski left the downtown Sonntag Hotel and drove north of the city on Highway 41 to the Republic Aviation plant.

One thing Pulaski liked about this town in southern Indiana was the spring weather. Winter had been left behind in Chicago. This morning's paper reported yesterday's high in Chicago of 49. In Evansville it was 68 and warming daily. Lawns in Evansville were green and people were already cutting grass. A friendly spring rain tapped lightly on the Olds' windshield.

Pulaski worked alone. They all agreed that for now the taskforce should remain low-profile; agents working in pairs or groups were avoided. One stranger wandering around did not command nearly as much attention as a gang.

The Republic Aviation factory was the home of the P-47 Thunderbolts. Unlike the LST shipyard where the ships sat outside during construction, the Thunderbolt factory was an enormous, enclosed structure of steel and green glass. The color of the glass was chosen for camouflage. Even here in Indiana this precaution was taken. From high altitude the green glass fooled the eye, giving the appearance of a lake.

Pulaski checked in with the plant's security chief—a short, stocky Army Air Corps Colonel named O'Connor—then for a little over an hour split time between two employee break rooms where he sat quietly in a corner drinking coffee and listening to the scuttlebutt. Surprising what one might hear from an informal gathering of workers. One woman in heavy dungarees, obviously a "Rosie the Riveter," sat at the table next to Pulaski's telling another "Rosie" about an affair between her married assembly line boss and a female forklift operator. In the next breakroom, Pulaski overheard a man wearing a white shirt and tie telling a group of male workers about some type of problem with a recent batch of hydraulic lines that ran through the aircraft's wing to the right aileron. Pulaski deduced the man was probably one of the plant's aeronautical engineers. Pulaski also knew the conversation was inappropriate; in wartime, design problems should be discussed with a confidentiality that this breakroom did not lend itself to. Pulaski could make out the man's name from the tag hanging from his breast pocket; he made a mental note and informed Major O'Connor of the man's improper conversation on his way out.

The morning rain had moved up river by the time Pulaski pulled out of the factory's parking lot. From a corner street vendor on Morgan Avenue he bought three hot dogs and a bottle of 7-Up. Eating as he drove, he cursed when a glob of mustard plopped on his shirt.

At the LST shipyard's main entrance, Pulaski showed his identification to a Navy Sea Policeman and drove his car through the gate. As with the aircraft plant, he had already visited the shipyard several times since his arrival in town three weeks ago. Pulaski guided the Olds through the dry dock area where several giant hulls rested, the car and driver dwarfed among them. Workers riveted, welded, hammered, cut, greased, and tightened. Like at the Thunderbolt plant, females were everywhere. Women held down many of the robust, hands-on jobs at the shipyard, and a small army of female secretaries worked within the shipyard's administration buildings and the compound of Quonset Huts that housed the ship designers, engineers, mathematicians and other high-clearance personnel. Most of the high-clearance personnel were men.

Pulaski parked in front of the main administration building, a large two-story white frame building that looked like a large army barracks. Inside, Pulaski passed by a guard after again showing his I.D., then proceeded to a large office on the main floor occupied by the naval personnel who were in charge of the shipyard's security. Pulaski passed by the desks of several warrant and petty officers. By now accustomed to seeing the FBI man, the men either ignored Pulaski as he walked by or nodded quickly while they spoke on the phone or typed.

Near the back of the room, Pulaski approached the warrant officer who served as secretary to the shipyard's chief of security. Seeing Pulaski, the warrant officer rose from his desk, disappeared into a nearby office then emerged and told Pulaski he could go on in.

Navy Commander Steven Forister stood at a file cabinet in his office and motioned for Pulaski to sit. Forister pulled a folder from the cabinet and returned to the seat behind his desk.

"Good afternoon, Agent Pulaski," the Navy man said as he opened the folder.

"Good afternoon, Commander."

"Here's the information you requested," Forister continued. "A list of all the high-clearance personnel is broken down by the jobs they perform. The building locations where these people work is there along with a list of the secretaries and security guards for those buildings, and you'll find in there the dates these people began working here at the shipyard."

Forister closed the folder and handed it across the desk to Pulaski.

"Thank you, Commander," said Pulaski as he took the folder.

"Cigar?" Forister took one for himself from a cedar cigar box on his desk, then turned the box toward Pulaski.

"No, thanks, Commander, but I'll have a cigarette if you don't mind." Forister shrugged, and Pulaski shook a bent Lucky from the crumpled pack in his coat pocket. He lit it with his Zippo, then clicked it shut.

"What's next on the agenda?" Forister asked as he bit off the end of the cigar and stared at the mustard stain on Pulaski's shirt. A career Navy man, Forister was under orders to cooperate fully with the FBI, and he knew the FBI's capability to run background checks was much broader than the Navy's. Forister insisted only on being kept up-to-date and the inclusion of his people in the investigation and any arrests, if ever it came to that.

"We have people currently running background checks on all the workers at both Republic Aviation and here at the shipyard. As you know, Commander, that process will take a while because of the num-ber of names involved."

"How long?" Forister still had not put fire to the cigar, seeming con-tent to merely roll it in his fingers.

"We could get lucky and one of the first few names checked could turn up a bogus identity, or it could take months if the name is one of the last ones checked. The *whites* will be checked first, then the *blues*."

(*Whites* was jargon for the high-clearance personnel—their identifica-tion cards and arm bands that color. Most shipyard workers—production workers, both skilled and unskilled, and secretaries—wore blue arm bands, indicating their lower level of security authorization.)

"While those checks are being processed, I will use these lists you just handed me to do a little snooping around myself—all low-key of course."

"Has your Mr. Mullen any news?" asked Forister. Stanley Mullen had accompanied Pulaski and Falasco to Forister's initial briefing when the FBI taskforce first arrived in Evansville.

"Mullen and his people have the monitoring equipment in place and operational. The air waves in this area are being closely monitored twenty-four hours a day, but to answer your question, no, there have been no suspicious signals since we arrived."

Forister nodded. Pulaski smashed out the Lucky in the ashtray on Forister's desk as he rose to leave. "Again, Commander, we feel it is very important that we keep all this under wraps. If there is someone in this town working for the enemy, we don't want them to know we are on to them. It's very important that routine procedures remain the same for the time being."

"I briefed only my top two assistants, Agent Pulaski, and you have their names. Otherwise it will stay business as usual around here."

"Thank you, Commander." The two men shook hands.

"Let me know of any developments right away," Forister ordered.

"I will."

Unlike the Thunderbolt factory, the shipyard had no breakrooms. A few open air canteens offered workers hot coffee during the cold months and lemonade during the hot. Workers on break remained outside or sought refuge from the elements inside one of the giant ships under construction. Also unlike the airplane factory which sat surrounded by cornfields, the shipyard rubbed shoulders with a residential area and nearby businesses. For meals many shipyard workers chose to walk the short distance to the diners and taverns of Franklin Street where business had boomed since the shipyard's opening just over a year ago. Many of these eateries now stayed open twenty-four hours a day to serve the around-the-clock shift workers. Pulaski decided to take a look.

Instead of walking, he drove his car and parked behind the Franklin Drug Store. Pulaski had never been there, but Forister told him that the store's lunch counter and soda fountain was a popular hangout for shipyard workers. When he entered, all the lunch tables were occupied and the counter stools taken. Pulaski was considering leaving when two young women at one of the tables called out almost simultaneously.

"You can sit here with us!" the women waved to draw Pulaski's attention. He walked toward the table.

"Hi there!" greeted one of the women before Pulaski had a chance to thank them for the invitation or introduce himself. "We're the Gambrel sisters from Flat Lick, Kentucky. I'm Bertha, and this here is my sister Hattie Emma." Both women smiled and extended their hands.

"Charlie Pulaski," Pulaski said as he exchanged handshakes with the two women. "Thanks for inviting me to sit with you." Both women shook hands with such enthusiasm the shaking almost became comical. When the Gambrel sisters finally finished their vigorous greeting, Pulaski sat down.

Both Bertha and Hattie Emma wore the heavy, masculine dungarees of a Rosie the Riveter which included a head scarf. Neither wore any makeup on their pleasant, pretty faces. Both smiled or laughed constantly. Both attacked colossal size banana splits, and both talked practically nonstop.

The Gambrel sisters confirmed they were both indeed Rosies. The shipyard had trained them both as welders. (Both women proudly showed Pulaski the little award pin from the shipyard's Mechanical Arts School that proved they had passed the training and were "certified, full-fledged welders, Charlie.") Their heavy clothing was soiled from a morning of hard work and sported numerous burn marks, evidence of the hot sparks spit from welding rods. The well-paying war industry jobs in Evansville lured the sisters away from their home in the poor hills of eastern Kentucky. Both were proud of their roots and not ashamed of the "hillbilly" label the city slickers bestowed on them. From each paycheck they sent money home to Mama and numerous siblings back home with still enough money left over to enjoy pleasures never before available—like banana splits.

"They pay us each $1.20 an hour," Hattie Emma whispered like it was top secret and a windfall that might end immediately if someone from the payroll department overheard her and realized their foolishness. "And time-and-a-half on Saturday and double-time on Sunday. Some weeks we each take home sixty dollars a week." The young woman looked at her sister and both bounced in their seats squealing with delight over their great good fortune.

"Where you from, Charlie?" Bertha asked right before she took another bite of ice cream.

"He's from Evansville!" Hattie Emma butted in. "Can't you tell he's from the big city and all from the suit?"

Bertha blushed. How could she have been so stupid?

"Actually, I'm from Chicago."

"Chicago, that's a big city." Hattie Emma again proved her sophistication. "Is it as big as Evansville?"

"A little bigger," Pulaski answered.

"Bigger than Evansville?" asked Hattie Emma astonished.

"Yes."

"Wow!" both sisters said wide-eyed.

"Did you come here for the pay at the shipyard like us?" Bertha asked innocently between another big spoonful of ice cream and toppings. It was a prying question that did not seem that way because of who asked it. Pulaski doubted that such genuine and delightful young women could ever intentionally be rude.

"No, not exactly. I'm a bookkeeper for the government, and they sent me down here for a while to help with some accounting."

"Wow!"

Pulaski had intended to sit quietly by himself and eavesdrop on those nearby like he had that morning in the breakrooms of the aircraft factory. That plan had to be scuttled when sitting with the Gambrel sisters, but the wholesome energy and exuberance of the sisters made it hard to regret sharing their table.

Pulaski ordered a 7-Up from the waitress.

"You're not having a banana split?" Bertha was astounded. Hattie Emma also looked at him strangely. Pulaski shook his head no, then noticed the sisters staring at him like he was off his rocker.

When the waitress delivered the 7-Up, Pulaski ordered a banana split. Only to prove to the Gambrel sisters from Flat Lick, Kentucky, that people from Chicago were not totally insane.

CHAPTER 30

My complaint against war is not that it kills men but that it kills the wrong ones, taking an undue proportion of the strong and adventurous and leaving too many weaklings and shirkers, thus working a perverse artificial selection of those who are least fitted to adorn or improve society.

—Sir Frederick Pollock, English jurist, in a letter to his friend
Oliver Wendell Holmes, 1908

Evansville—April 1943

"Okay, Charlie," Roy whispered, "I'll work my way up to the cars and then check things out from there. You cover my back in case he has someone outside."

"Let's stay here, Roy," Pulaski cautioned. "Purvis told us not to be seen unless they make a break for it out the back way. It's too exposed up there by the cars."

"It'll be okay; no one will see me."

FBI agents Roy McGuire and Charlie Pulaski were crouched behind a hedgerow eighty yards from the back of the Little Bohemia Lodge near Rhinelander, Wisconsin. McGuire rose and cautiously edged his way toward a row of five cars parked along a gravel drive leading to the back entrance of the resort. One of the cars was a 1933 Hudson Essex-Terraplane—John Dillinger's car of choice. The rest were Fords, also popular among the gang because of their new, powerful V-8 engines. Charlie Pulaski, Roy McGuire, and fifteen other FBI agents were spread out around the building's perimeter. Dillinger and his gang were inside, unaware that they were surrounded.

Pulaski thought Dillinger had to be the luckiest man on the planet. The outlaw eluded capture at the last moment time after time and even when captured somehow managed to escape. A legend had built up about the man. Children read comic books about Dillinger and his gang, but Pulaski considered Dillinger a common hood who left innocent people dead in his wake. Now it was payback time. Tonight Dillinger was going down.

Pulaski and McGuire had become fast friends since Pulaski joined the Dillinger taskforce six months ago. McGuire took Pulaski under his wing when the latter joined the group of agents assigned to find and bring in Dillinger—dead or alive. McGuire had tracked Public Enemy Number One for nearly a year and was even more impatient than Pulaski to capture the elusive bank robber.

Pulaski watched McGuire reach the nearest car, hunker down beside it, then look over the hood toward the lodge. McGuire repeated the process one car at a time until he was within a few feet of the building. *Dammit, Roy, where are you going?* A row of high shrubbery ringed the building. *He must be working his way to the shrubs for cover.*

Suddenly Pulaski thought he saw movement in the shadows beneath a covered walkway that joined two of the lodge buildings. He could not cry out to warn Roy and blow the whole operation; the movement he saw might not be Dillinger or one of his henchmen. Pulaski did the only thing he could do and that was to take aim at the shadow and try to cover his friend. His Thompson machine gun was a poor weapon for this situation. Though Pulaski was competent with the Thompson, at fifty yards it would be hard to hit anything with the jerking Tommy gun that bucked like a bronco. Pulaski wished he had a rifle.

The next several seconds lapsed in slow motion to Pulaski. As Roy McGuire reached the shrubs next to the building, a burning ball of white light spewed out from the shadows Pulaski had been concentrating on. Pulaski saw the white light before he heard the .45 caliber explosions that caused it. It was the unmistakable, hellish squawk of a Thompson machine gun just like the one in Pulaski's hands.

Pulaski watched in horror as the bullets slammed into Roy McGuire. McGuire's bulletproof vest did him little good at such close range. The bullets tore through the seams and found other areas of McGuire's flesh unprotected by the vest. McGuire remained on his feet for what seemed an incredibly long time as bullets found their mark forcing his body into an obscene dance of death. Walking out through the cloud of smoke still firing was Lester Gillis, better known to the American public as George "Baby Face" Nelson. Pulaski squeezed down on the trigger and sent a storm of bullets in Nelson's direction. A car window next to Nelson exploded and wood splinters and shavings shot out from the lodge wall behind him. Everything spattered except Baby Face Nelson who dove for cover behind the vehicle.

Pulaski's machine gun clicked quiet and he started reloading the awkward, round drum. Using the flash from Pulaski's weapon for a target, Nelson rose and returned the fire. It was Pulaski's turn to duck. The distance that had hampered the FBI agent's accuracy now did the same to the outlaw's fire. The bullets from Nelson's Tommy gun ripped through surrounding foliage, but none found Pulaski who lay prone on the ground behind the hedgerow. Pulaski knew he had to get closer; if the gang made a dash for it out the back, the inaccuracy of the Thompson at this distance would make the percentages of even shooting out a tire a bad bet.

Suddenly it was quiet. Pulaski knew Nelson's ammo was spent, so the lawman jumped up and ran toward the car nearest the hedgerow—the same car Roy McGuire first reached. When Nelson ran out of bullets, Pulaski saw him lower his head out of sight—a bad mistake. *Keep your target in view as you reload Baby Face—you should know that, you murdering son-of-a-bitch!* Losing sight of Pulaski allowed the FBI man to relocate without Nelson knowing.

The gravel drive curved as it headed into the Wisconsin wood. Although Charlie Pulaski and Baby Face Nelson were on the same side of the parked vehicles, the curve allowed Pulaski to work his way toward Nelson along the outside of the cars without being spotted. Now reloaded, Nelson's head was back up and looking in the direction of the hedgerow, his machine gun pointed skyward waiting to be lowered. Pulaski inched nearer, careful to avoid stepping on dry twigs. Suddenly Pulaski heard more machine gun and pistol fire coming from the other side of the complex. *All hell is breaking loose!* At last Pulaski worked himself to a position were he could get the jump on Nelson. The murderer's head was turned away still looking toward the hedgerow as Pulaski rose and aimed his weapon. Barely twenty feet separated the two men. From here Pulaski would not miss.

"FBI, Nelson!" Pulaski screamed. "Throw down your weapon, …Now!"

Nelson did not move. He remained hunkered down with the back of his head still to Pulaski. The FBI man lifted the barrel of the Thompson slightly and sprayed a short burst over Nelson's head. This convinced the criminal to cooperate. Nelson laid the machine gun gently on the ground then stood up and turned toward Pulaski. "Raise em up!" Pulaski ordered. The sweet-faced killer nonchalantly leaned against the car and raised his hands in the air. Other small arms fire could still be heard coming from other places around the lodge. Roy McGuire lay within view on the other side of Nelson. Pulaski thought of McGuire's wife and kids and a rage swept over him. His finger tightened on the trigger, and he was within a breath of forgetting about the arrest. The thought went through his mind that true justice would be better served by simply pulling the trigger and splattering Nelson's bowels on the paint job of the Ford he leaned against.

Pulaski never got the chance.

It was more of a dull thud than the sharp jab Pulaski had imagined being shot must feel like. The pistol bullet entered Pulaski's back at an angle one inch from the edge of his bulletproof vest. The bullet fractured then skipped off Pulaski's right shoulder blade and exited his torso just below his arm pit. Unfortunately his arm blocked the missile's departure so the same bullet ripped through his right bicep. Pulaski had been shot twice by the same bullet. The tearing of his bicep forced the Thompson down and it fired into the ground beside Pulaski's shoe. The recoil tore the gun from the G-man's damaged right arm, and he crashed to the ground at the feet of Baby Face Nelson.

"Good shot, Homer!" Nelson sang out with a laugh. Pulaski forced himself to remain conscious. When he opened his eyes he was on his back and looking up at Baby Face Nelson and Homer Van Meter, both of whom were on the nation's Top 10 Wanted List along with their boss, John Dillinger, at number one.

Nelson retrieved his machine gun and placed the end of the barrel on Pulaski's forehead as he told Van Meter: "Watch me make some scrambled eggs."

Pulaski did not want to give a mad killer who enjoyed his killing the satisfaction of seeing his victim's fear (although plenty was available). He thought of his three-year-old daughter and newborn son and tried to start a silent prayer for them. Pulaski felt the barrel of Nelson's gun, still hot from the killing of Roy McGuire, leave his forehead. He knew Nelson would not fire the gun with the barrel held tight against something to avoid backfire. When the barrel was drawn back, Pulaski knew Nelson was about to fire.

"Hold it!"

Pulaski heard the words among other shouts. He could hear men running and car doors opening and slamming closed. Engines roared to life. A third man's face appeared above Pulaski. It was the face of John Dillinger. Dillinger and Pulaski knew each other. Pulaski interrogated

Dillinger a few months earlier when the outlaw was in custody at the Lake County Jail in Indiana. The jail was just one more of the "escape proof" hoosegows Dillinger would escape from in short order.

"Charlie," Dillinger said, "you don't look so good." Other voices farther away pleaded with the three men to hurry up and get in the cars.

"Let's go." Dillinger ordered.

"Hold on," Nelson insisted. "I'm going to send this guy back to J. Fat-Ass Hoover minus his brains."

Dillinger grabbed Nelson's arm. "I said let's go!"

The distant gunfire grew louder and Pulaski thought he heard the voice of Melvin Purvis, the agent in charge, shouting something about "around the back."

Dillinger and Van Meter shoved the disappointed Nelson toward one of the idling cars (two of the Fords had been put out of commission by Pulaski's bullets). Three cars raced away with the gang firing wildly behind them as Purvis and other agents appeared from around the corner of the lodge.

The place looked like a battlefield. With no breeze to move it on, gunsmoke hung in the air, its sulphur smell stinging the nose, and dust kicked up by spinning tires settled over the scene like a lazy cloud. The back of the lodge sported numerous bullet holes, and two cars sat wrecked from machine gun fire, their windows spiderwebbed or missing altogether. The broken glass looked like diamonds sprinkled about the ground. A punctured radiator dripped.

Pulaski struggled to his feet and staggered toward the body of Roy McGuire. The adrenaline that had kept him going was quickly wearing off. Now weak from loss of blood, Pulaski fell and had to struggle to regain his feet. An agent was already bent over McGuire and another ran up to Pulaski and urged him to sit or lay back down. Pulaski waved him off with his left hand and continued toward McGuire.

McGuire had taken eight slugs from Nelson's Thompson, all in the torso except the one that entered the front of his neck and exited out the back taking a couple of vertebras with it. Just before Pulaski passed out beside his dead friend he saw Roy McGuire's dead eyes focus on him and the dead mouth utter: "You were supposed to cover me, Charlie."

Pulaski jerked and quickly sat up in the bed. The same nightmare again. He had not had the Dillinger dream in a couple of months and hoped it had left him. It always ended the same way with the dead McGuire admonishing Pulaski for not doing a better job of cover. It was not hot in the room but the bedsheets were soaked with perspiration. Pulaski turned on a night light next to the bed, rose, went into the bathroom, turned the cold water faucet on full blast and splashed cold water on his face and the back of his neck.

The shoot out at the Bohemia Lodge was not just a nightmare for Charles Pulaski. It was a public relations debacle for the entire Bureau. Not only had they lost an agent, but the gunfire Pulaski heard coming from the other side of the lodge was the FBI firing on three innocent bystanders fleeing the lodge in terror after hearing Nelson's and Pulaski's gunfire. The three innocent lodge guests did not stop running when ordered, and one carried a hunting rifle. Agents thought they were fleeing gang members and opened up. Two of the innocent lodge guests were wounded and one killed. It was every lawman's worst nightmare. And to crown it all off, Dillinger and his entire gang escaped. The only thing the Bureau had to show for the entire fiasco was three of the gang's molls whom the fleeing outlaws left behind. The press had a field day at the FBI's and Hoover's expense. A syndicated editorial cartoon appeared in newspapers around the country picturing Hoover and "G-Men" with dumb expressions on their faces spraying a crowd of bystanders with machine gun fire, then going around and asking the dying victims, "Are you Dillinger?" The caption read "Process of Elimination."

Hoover officially reprimanded every agent and reassigned everyone except Purvis and the wounded Charles Pulaski, who the press made out to be a hero of sorts since he was the only agent who exchanged gunfire with the gang. To Pulaski, his hero status was laughable. Three weeks in the hospital, then four more healing at home gave him plenty of time to replay his mistakes in his mind. Even though he did not know that McGuire was going so far in, Pulaski blamed himself for not following behind his friend so he could offer cover from a better vantage point. And he had let his rage at McGuire's death cloud his judgment when sneaking up on Baby Face Nelson. He should have known Nelson's gang members would come running when they heard the gun play. Homer Van Meter, who shot Pulaski, had skulked up behind him too easily.

Pulaski turned on a light over a table next to the bed and glanced at a small electric clock. It was 3:45 a.m. Throwing open a heavy curtain that covered the room's only window gained him only a view of the dark Woolworth's store across a deserted Main Street. At least it was not raining, something Pulaski had learned was more common than not during the spring in this part of the country. In the five weeks since he arrived in Evansville, Pulaski estimated over half those days had seen at least some rain.

Progress in the case was painfully slow. Charlie Pulaski had spent most of his time for the past couple of weeks interviewing engineers and design people at both the aircraft plant and the shipyard. That and sitting around in factory breakrooms and local bars and restaurants frequented by war industry workers eavesdropping on conversations. It was all that could be done until something broke. At times the enormity of the job was depressing. It could take a year for the taskforce to check out all the names. If there were an enemy agent, he might be finished with his mission and long gone before his name came around for the check. Moreover, checking out the names served a purpose only if a foreign agent were working undercover and had adopted a phony personae. If the spy was an American working under his real name, all their work was for naught.

Then there was Stanley Mullen. Nothing had changed there either. At the last breakfast with Mullen and Falasco, the bookish FCC man still professed confidence that his original hypothesis was correct: that last winter shortwave radio signals paralleling the German Enigma code emitted from the Evansville area. The professor spent every night at one of three triangulation stations he had set up around the area. One night might see him in Vincennes, Indiana, or just as likely in Paducah, Kentucky, or Louisville. The guy had to be logging a thousand miles a week, every mile so far fruitless. As far as dubious signals, only silence. All this meant that as of right now the FBI had constructed a large and very expensive operation in an obscure Midwestern city solely on the hunch of one stuffy ex-college professor.

Pulaski had enough experience with the Bohemia Lodge nightmare to know sleeping was history for the night. From a leather satchel, Pulaski pulled several pages of the paperwork Commander Forister handed over two weeks ago. The papers listed alphabetically the shipyard's high-clearance personnel (292 names) and gave the date they first reported to the shipyard. Thirty-seven of the people had not reported to the shipyard until after Stanley Mullen's last queer Morse code transmission, so Pulaski had put them aside for now. That left 255 engineers, nautical designers, metallurgists, chemists, mathematicians, and various other eggheads Pulaski had to meet and try to get to know. This is how he had spent most of his time for the past few weeks.

The same type of work was required at the aircraft plant and Pulaski had spent many hours there, but for some reason his main concentration was directed at the shipyard. Call it a hunch or deductive reasoning, but of the two places in town most likely to draw the attention of someone working for the enemy, the P-47 plant and the shipyard, Pulaski put his money on the shipyard.

Pulaski reasoned it this way: the first question that needed to be addressed was for which reason, espionage or sabotage, was an enemy agent infiltrating an American war material production facility. Pulaski believed everything pointed toward espionage, the stealing of secrets. Saboteurs usually worked quickly; they got in, did their damage, and got out fast. And they rarely sent a series of radio transmissions. The first transmission from this area was recorded in December and since then the only damage recorded at either the Thunderbolt plant or the shipyard had proved to be caused by uncontrollable accidents or worker carelessness. If a saboteur lurked, he had not done his job yet. Pulaski knew a foreign saboteur would never hang around for five months.

Espionage always required a much greater time investment than sabotage. As far as Pulaski was concerned, it had to be a spy. With that much established it was time to think about what in this town would a spy most likely be after. As would any good investigator, Pulaski put himself in the enemy's shoes.

The German Luftwaffe and the Japanese Air Force had fighter planes on par with the Thunderbolt. Many members of the U.S. Army Air Corps even considered the Luftwaffe's ME109 the most advanced fighter aircraft in the air on either side and the Japanese Zero as good as any fighter flying for the Allies. With planes in their arsenals as good as or perhaps better than ours, Pulaski could not see what purpose it would serve to steal secrets of our aircraft.

The shipyard, on the other hand, was producing something new. During Pulaski's briefings after he first arrived in town, the shipyard bigwigs bragged about the new, top secret alloys used in the LSTs and the radical engineering used to solve the problems faced by a ship the size of a destroyer that had to beach itself on a shore and then extract itself back out to sea. He might be right or he might be wrong, but after Pulaski added all those things up, the shipyard was the sum.

He looked over the names of the people he had already interviewed. Pulaski kept these interviews very low key, asking mostly mundane questions. Before questionning an individual, Pulaski found out something about the subject's background or hometown and subtly inserted one or two questions that might make a phony stumble. The questions were posed in a subtle and friendly manner and most people would not realize they were planned:

"Hey, it says here you graduated from Jefferson High School. My sister and her family live in that town and I think her boy, my nephew, goes to that same school. He's on the football team and I went to a game once when I was visiting. They are the 'Tigers.' Wear green jerseys, right?"

"Ah, no," the subject would disagree if clean, "my high school is the 'Saints' and the school colors are red and gray."

"Oh?" Pulaski would say surprised. "I guess it must be a different school my nephew goes to."

And "red flags" were zealously pursued.

Pulaski identified himself as FBI beforehand and kept an eye out for anyone who seemed unnecessarily nervous (a red flag) during the interview. Also, a few questions were asked about social lives, and interest in a subject's personal life was another reason Pulaski spent time at the local hangouts. Pulaski knew a spy could be of either gender. If a high-clearance scientist who looked like Jimmy Durante was suddenly seen around town with a young woman who looked like Betty Grable, that was a red flag. Pulaski would make a note to check out Betty Grable. Married men with a wife a thousand miles away were particularly susceptible to the advances of an enemy siren and therefore vulnerable to blackmail.

One middle-aged electrical engineer had been seen around town with a cute young waitress from one of the popular diners near the shipyard. Pulaski checked them out. He was a widower and a former doughboy of the first war who was awarded a bronze star and a purple heart. The girl was a local from a big family who had never been more than fifty miles from Evansville and had a brother fighting in the Pacific. Pulaski crossed them off the list.

Another red flag could involve previous travel. One of the shipyard's nautical propulsion experts had made several trips to Germany in the 30's, but after a check Pulaski discovered what the man told him was true; he was sent there at the request of none other than Cordell Hull, FDR's Secretary of State, to represent the U.S. Government in the monitoring of German Naval installations under provisions of the Versailles Treaty.

Pulaski had conducted seventy-six of these interviews so far. Keeping it simple he went in alphabetical order. He was just starting on 'K'. With the exceptions of the aforementioned red flags that had proved benign, the interviews so far had been run-of-the-mill. And nobody had come across as particularly uncomfortable during the questioning.

Pulaski had the personnel files of the next half dozen high-clearance workers on his list and had just opened the first one when someone knocked loud and long at his door. Pulaski glanced again at the clock. Who was knocking on the door at 4:30 in the morning? Mullen was out of town at one of his monitoring stations as usual. It must be Falasco whose room was in the same hotel. Maybe something had broken. *God, let's hope so!*

Pulaski went to the door in his boxers and sleeveless t-shirt. In the hall was a very excited Stanley Mullen. He looked pale and was so jittery he could not stand still. Pulaski waved him in.

"I drove two hours and just got back into town from our station in Louisville," gasped Mullen. "I've already been to Falasco's room." Mullen looked like he was about to faint.

"Sit down, Stanley," Pulaski pulled up a chair and the FCC man obeyed.

"Now, spit it out," said Pulaski as he sat down in the other chair.

"At exactly 2:04 this morning all three of our triangulation stations picked up the same shortwave International Morse Code transmission. The signal was loud and clear and displays to a tee all the characteristics of the German Enigma code. I computed the math and triple-checked it. I was right about location," Mullen seemed almost teary-eyed. "The signal was emitted from somewhere within a twenty-mile radius of where we now sit."

Chapter 31

We stand upon the brink of a precipice. We peer into the abyss—
we grow sick and dizzy. Our first impulse is to shrink from the
danger, and yet, unaccountably, we remain.

—Edgar Allan Poe, 1845

Evansville—April 1943

"The cipher runs congruent with the style of the Germans," Major
James Dabler of the Office of Strategic Services confirmed. Dabler, a top
military cryptanalyst for the OSS, had been flown in from D.C. later the
same day Stanley Mullen made his early morning visit to Pulaski's hotel
room. Dabler spoke to a group of six FBI taskforce members including
Dave Falasco, Stanley Mullen, and Charlie Pulaski. They now gathered
for a briefing in Falasco's room at the Sonntag Hotel after the OSS man
spent three hours listening to and breaking down Mullen's audiotape of
the previous night's transmission.

"Perhaps even more convincing," Major Dabler continued, "are the
'whispers.'"

Everyone in the room was by now aware that *whispers* was radioman
jargon for the sounds made by a wireless transmitter shortly before it
begins broadcast of a coded message.

"Listen."

Dabler cued the tape and turned up the volume. The room was quiet as a tomb before a few seconds of a low pitched hum was followed by a muffled squeal. A quiet pause followed which in turn preceded a short set of beeps.

"The low-pitched hum you first heard is very telling," said Dabler. "Sounds very much like the initial powering up of a radio that is using a special converter for the superheterodyne circuit popular with the Germans." When Dabler noticed his last statement left everyone in the room in his dust (with the exception of Stanley Mullen), he switched to laymen's terms.

"Sounds like German hardware." Dabler explained and everyone nodded.

"And that's not all." Dabler replayed the series of initial beeps. "QQVD QQVD—a standard test of transmitter strength before sending a cryptogram I've heard used for only two types of transmissions." Dabler stopped to light a cigarette which caused Dave Falasco's impatience to bubble over.

"Yes, Major," Falasco said rather loudly. "Those types of transmissions are?"

Dabler, unaware of the weeks of frustration already served by the men in the room, looked quizzically at Falasco, unsure why the FBI man was irritable.

"I've seen QQVD used as a prologue to communications only by German U-boats or by Abwehr—German Military Intelligence. Abwehr is run by a German Navy Admiral named Canaris and that's probably the connection."

"Don't sit down yet," Dabler cued the tape again, this time to near the end of the transmission. "This is the final validation," Dabler flipped the play button. A few beeps of Morse code could be faintly heard. The sounds were much weaker that the previous bulk of the transmission.

"VV XV—VV XV. Hear it, gentlemen?"

Several FBI men and Stanley Mullen nodded.

"Standard code used by the German Kriegsmarine—the Navy—that a message has been successfully received. Those beeps came from a German U-boat, probably just off the East Coast."

Charlie Pulaski felt the hairs on the back of his neck stand up.

"How about the message itself?" asked Falasco.

"It mimics most of the Enigma characteristics, although there are a few discrepancies. I'm sure those discrepancies are due to the fact a German agent this far inland would never be given an Enigma machine to use. It's about the size of a typewriter but a great deal heavier. The Germans would never allow an Enigma machine to be carted around the United States. Hell, U-boat captains have scuttled their ships and sent whole crews to the bottom just so their Enigma machine would not be captured. The person who sent these signals was probably trained in Enigma principles but is using something more portable."

It was Stanley Mullen's turn. "What about the transmitter? A unit is needed that is powerful enough to link up from here to the Atlantic. That's going to be a sizable unit and not very portable wouldn't you say, Major?"

Major Dabler pondered for a moment. "Yes, it certainly would take a radio more powerful than the briefcase units both sides currently use to send messages around western Europe. But radio technology has increased in leaps and bounds since the start of the war. We're talking about something the size of a medium suitcase."

"But heavy to lug around the country," Mullen pressed.

"Yes," Dabler took another moment. "But the unit could be assembled on location. The only parts our man would have to bring are the converter I mentioned earlier and the crystals. The other parts could be procured by stripping household radios by someone who knew what they were doing."

"What's the chances of deciphering the message?" Pulaski piped in.

"Hard to say right now," the major said. "Like I said, it's doubtful this message is pure Enigma, rather it's some sort of bastardized form of the

Enigma code since it is highly unlikely the person who sent the cryptogram is in possession of an Enigma machine. I'll have to take the tape back to Washington and have our people check it out."

"Make it a high priority, Major," Falasco ordered.

"Of course, I'll fly back tomorrow and get the E Street Complex on it right away." The *E Street Complex* was the cumbersome nickname for OSS headquarters in Washington.

"Thank you, Major," Falasco then turned to his FBI colleagues. "Gentlemen, no more maybes, no more doubts. We have a hunt."

Stanley Mullen's predawn visit to Charlie Pulaski's hotel room three days ago and the subsequent visit by Major Dabler of the OSS changed everything. Until three days ago, the official adjective used to describe the transmissions had been "suspicious." Overnight "suspicious" became "confirmed enemy" transmission. The new term alone picked up the spirits of the taskforce members, especially those of Charlie Pulaski who, until three days ago, was extremely doubtful he should even be in Evansville, Indiana.

It had been a very busy three days. Mullen spent the time moving his monitoring equipment; Falasco briefed and assigned the additional agents sent by Hoover, and Pulaski picked up speed on his interviews. Those changes were good; other changes were not so positive.

Hoover ordered Dave Falasco to brief the military security people assigned to the various installations, i.e., Commander Forister at the shipyard and Colonel O'Connor at the Thunderbolt plant. Against the recommendations and wishes of Falasco and Charlie Pulaski, the military immediately beefed up security when informed that an enemy transmission emanated from the Evansville area. Guards were doubled at both the Thunderbolt plant and the shipyard. Stanley Mullen's boss at the FCC showed up and brought more technicians with him. The low-key investigation that Dave Falasco had planned in order not to alarm the enemy was out the window. Whoever sent the transmissions now knew the United States government was aware of their presence and in pursuit.

Pulaski did not see much of Falasco or Stanley Mullen during these three busy days. Finally brought together again during one of Falasco's breakfast meetings, the three men exchanged quick greetings then discussed the changes. Stanley Mullen started the conversation.

"Our monitoring triangle has been reduced considerably. All three units are now within thirty miles of the Evansville city limits. With our equipment this close, the next hit should allow us to really narrow down a location. It can depend on a few factors such as atmospheric conditions at the time, but I'm hoping the next hit will allow us to pinpoint the location of the transmitter within a half mile or so."

The waitress delivered coffee and took their orders. Mullen, normally a finicky eater who sometimes ordered just coffee and toast, ordered a double helping of bacon to go with his scrambled eggs and biscuits.

Pulaski noticed right away that Stanley Mullen seemed more relaxed. Until the hit three days ago, the entire Evansville operation was conducted on a theory—Mullen's theory. Now Mullen had been proven correct and Pulaski knew that had to take a huge monkey off the professor's back. Pulaski had to give him credit, every guess the old boy had made so far had been confirmed.

"Let's hope it's not months before we hear from our bogey again," said Falasco before turning to Pulaski. "Even if it is, we can't sit around waiting on that to happen. How did the past three days go, Charlie?"

"Went fine, although, as you know, the cat's out of the bag. Forister doubled the number of SPs on guard duty day and night, which of course was noticed immediately by everyone. When I interview someone, they start asking questions before I get a chance to. Everyone wants to know what's going on."

"I know, I've run into the same thing. I tell them the extra guards are just trainees. What have you been telling them, Charlie?" Falasco wanted to know.

"I'm telling them it's just standard procedure before a VIP visit. It's pretty lame but some of them swallow it. Of course they want to know who the VIP is. I tell them Morgenthau or Admiral Halsey—whomever comes to mind. I told one guy Churchill."

Falasco and even Stanley Mullen laughed.

"One guy," Pulaski said with a straight face, "reminded me Morgenthau had already been here for one of the LST christenings. I told the guy he was coming back for the barbecue."

More laughter.

"But seriously," Falasco interrupted, "we should have coordinated our stories. That's my fault. I didn't realize the military would rush all these men in here overnight."

"I do have a suggestion." Pulaski was also serious now. "I would like to concentrate on one location. I feel running back and forth between the shipyard and the plane factory is counterproductive."

The waitress delivered breakfast.

"Sounds like a good idea," Falasco agreed.

"How about if I work the shipyard?" Pulaski requested.

"Done. With the extra men Hoover is sending in, I'll need a coordinator at each of the different facilities—someone to organize and monitor our work. You can be that guy at the shipyard."

Pulaski nodded.

"This is all getting quite exciting, gentlemen," Stanley Mullen announced. "All this detective work, I mean. Quite invigorating. Yes, quite invigorating!"

Pulaski and Falasco looked at each other. Pulaski had to kid.

"Your eggs are getting cold, Dr. Watson."

CHAPTER 32

The world cannot live at the level of its great men.

—*Sir James George Frazer, 1922*

Evansville—April 1943

Joe Mayer signed his name at the bottom of page 52 and closed the manual. The black leather cover read *Property of United States Government—Classified*. A Master Chief Petty Officer accepted the top secret manual from Mayer and logged the date and time of day that Mayer added the information. He handed the manual back to Mayer who walked it back to a safe sitting in the corner of the room, the security officer following at Mayer's heels. Mayer placed the manual inside the safe, then closed and locked the heavy door. When the Master Chief was confident everything was secured, he made another recording on a clipboard he carried with him, then left the room and closed the door behind him.

This routine was followed without exception when logging classified information. Mayer, Howard Turnbull, and the other engineers in Hut 11 had access to the classified documents stored in 11's safe, but whenever the safe was to be opened, the Master Chief had to be summoned, and he stayed in the room until any documents taken from the safe were returned and the safe door closed.

Page 52 of the manual, the page just signed by Joe Mayer, contained Mayer's latest entry on an ongoing experiment he was conducting using a semi-metallic element called tellurium. Mayer combined the specially processed silvery white crystals of tellurium with various alloys then "roasted" and "sintered" the alloy in a small laboratory blast furnace to remove sulphur and other impurities. Mayer was surprised, you might say shocked, when he found that roasting and sintering the crystallized tellurium alloy at different temperatures and for variable lengths of time produced what amounted to vastly different characteristics of the alloy. The anti-corrosion potential and strength of this new alloy were more than promising. It could amount to a major breakthrough and supply the allies with a lighter yet stronger metal for not only ships but tanks and aircraft. It was not hyperbole to argue Mayer's discovery could end up being one of the major technological developments of the war.

Four other engineers worked at drafting tables around the room separated by portable privacy partitions. Howard Turnbull was one of the engineers. His work station was closest to Mayer's and his partition rolled away. The partitions were not there for security and their use was optional; the men in the room often worked on problems together and shared ideas.

Turnbull specialized in stress analysis and was working on a problem with the LSTs' massive bow doors. After the ship beached on shore, the twenty-five foot high doors opened to allow the tanks, trucks, and troops to go ashore on dry land. A seal problem had developed between the bottom of the doors and the bow. The seals held up fine in warm or moderate weather, but after numerous openings and closings in extreme cold some of the seals tended to allow seepage. Joe Mayer suggested that a narrow strip of chromium attached to the bow underneath the seals might be a possible solution. The chromium expanded and contracted with temperature changes at a slower rate than the steel plates of the bow and could serve as an expansion joint. Turnbull's expertise was required to design a way to affix the chromium strip to the bow so it was not held rigid but could "float" and therefore expand and contract at a different rate than the other metals. Turnbull also determined the thickness and designed the shape of the chromium strip to assure it acted solely as a water seal and not as a fatigue-bearing component. During war, time is always a factor and Gary Delmar, Hut 11's lead designer, was pressing Turnbull to complete the specifications so the chromium shims could be mocked up and tested.

Mayer glanced at Turnbull who stood leaning over the angled drafting table working with a scale and protractor. Turnbull preferred to stand while working.

"How's it going, Howard?"

"Leave me alone, Mayer. I'm almost finished."

Joe Mayer smiled. Despite his friend's gregarious personality and sometimes obnoxious overbearance, Howard Turnbull was a topnotch engineer. Just last week Howard solved what had become known as "the riddle of the port screw whistle." A nerve-grating, high-pitched noise plagued the engine room crew of LST 327 during its maiden checkout voyage on the Ohio River. Everyone from lubricant specialists to hydraulic engineers to diesel mechanics went on board trying to find out what caused the vexing noise. Turnbull went on board and found a small dent in one of the port side screw shaft bearings. The dent, probably caused by an errant hammer blow when the bearings were set, was a weak spot where friction fatigue concentrated and in turn produced the high-pitched screech. It was not a problem that posed a danger, but the engine crew of LST 327 was so grateful that the nerve-grating noise was eliminated they took Howard out drinking with them that night and made him an honorary member of the engine crew when he won a drinking contest.

"There!" Turnbull exclaimed after several minutes with his sliderule. "A couple of minor changes to the mock up specs, which the genius from Baltimore—that's me—will make this afternoon, and Delmar can have it." Turnbull threw the sliderule on his table and walked over to another very important piece of equipment—the coffee pot.

"Want a cup?" Turnbull asked Mayer as he poured one for himself and scooped sugar using a spoon caked with the white grains.

"Yeah."

"Mayer, when are you going to wash this spoon?"

"I don't use the spoon, Howard. You know that. I take mine black."

"You could still wash it once in awhile. Don't be so lazy."

"I'll get right on it."

Turnbull brought Mayer the paper cup of steaming coffee. "Hey, I heard some more scuttlebutt." Turnbull did not have to explain what the scuttlebutt was about. Mayer knew Turnbull referred to the recent increase in military guards patrolling the shipyard and the presence of the FBI who were in the process of interviewing people. People like the men in this room of Quonset Hut 11. It was currently the major item of conversation throughout the shipyard.

"I know a fuel systems guy in Hut 23 who had his interview two days ago," Turnbull announced. "He said the FBI guy asked him all kinds of questions such as had anyone approached him asking questions of a suspicious nature. They're looking for a spy, old buddy."

"What?" Mayer responded surprised. "Two weeks ago you were ready to swear it was because Roosevelt was going to visit."

"And I was right,[10] wasn't I?"

"Yeah," Joe admitted. "You were right, but why this new theory?"

"That was before I found out what questions they were asking in the interviews," Turnbull explained matter-of-factly. "We have a spy in our midst, my boy."

Joe Mayer laughed out loud. "Howard, you're something else."

"What?" Turnbull warned. "You don't think we have anything here the Japs or Nazis might want? Think about it, buddy."

---

10 In April of 1943 President Roosevelt visited Evansville and toured the city's war plants.

Mayer thought of his recent classified experiments with tellurium and the Master Chief's routine with the manual. Similar top secret manuals rested in safes in other Quonset Huts.

"It's not that," Mayer argued. "It just doesn't seem likely to me. Those are probably standard run-of-the-mill questions they ask at every war plant in the country."

"Okay, Joe," Turnbull yielded the argument easily like someone who was confident he was right and could afford to bide his time until proven out. "Hey, your interview is coming up pretty soon, isn't it?"

"Monday."

"Mine's not for two weeks," said Turnbull. "They go in alphabetical order. Delmar had his a week ago but he's not talking. Said they told him not to discuss it."

"Your friend in Hut 23 should be as discreet. Tell him to remember the poster." Mayer pointed to a poster on the wall above the coffee pot that pictured two shipyard workers talking over drinks in a busy tavern. The large caption read: *"Loose Lips Sink Ships."*

Turnbull changed the subject. "Carol and I are going out Saturday night, why don't you and Sarah join us?"

"We already have plans. We're taking a drive to Indianapolis this weekend."

"Indianapolis?" Turnbull snorted then paused. "Hey, isn't that where your folks live?"

"Yeah, that's right."

"Oh, boy! Taking the little lady home to meet your parents. Is there something in the works here, Mr. Mayer?"

Mayer smiled. "Howard, you're an idiot."

"Yeah, we'll see. Sounds to me like old Joe's about ready to march down the old synagogue aisle."

The thought did not trouble Joe Mayer.

Indianapolis—Saturday, May 1, 1943

Joe Mayer led Sarah into his parent's parlor.

"Mother and Dad, I want you to meet my friend, Sarah Klein."

A late middle-aged man put down a newspaper, removed his reading glasses, then rose from his chair to greet the young woman. Noah Mayer, Joe's father, was a thin, balding man with a goatee. The mother, a short, silver-haired woman in a paisley print dress had been standing by the window. When the young couple entered the room, the wife walked over and stood beside her husband. Joe Mayer introduced his parents.

"Hello, young lady," greeted Noah Mayer as he extended his hand toward the girl. The mother smiled and nodded.

"Hello, Mr. Mayer; Mrs. Mayer." The young woman shook hands and took a seat in the chair offered her.

"Joseph tells us you are originally from Cincinnati, Miss Klein," Noah Mayer stated as he retook his seat. His wife excused herself to the kitchen to fetch refreshments.

"Please, call me Sarah, Mr. Mayer. Yes, I was born there; my father was a tailor and owned a small shop."

The mother returned with coffee and *kuchen*, a sweet pastry, which she had divided into handy portions.

"What took you to Evansville, my dear?" the mother asked as she poured coffee, obviously having overheard their chat.

"After I finished high school, my father enrolled me in a music conservatory in St. Louis. I became friends with a girl from Evansville who was also enrolled at the school. After my father died three years ago—my mother died when I was ten—I spent a great deal of time with my girlfriend and her family. She and I often made trips to Evansville to visit her family. When the shipyard opened I decided to try for a job there. I got on right away. My friend has since joined the WACS and shipped out, but I'm still there toiling away at the shipyard."

"I'm so sorry to hear about your parents," said the old woman sympathetically. "Such a young girl to be without a mother or father."

"Yes, we are very sorry to hear that, my dear," parotted the father. "So you are working in Evansville just for the duration and then returning to school after the war?"

"Yes, that is my plan right now," Sarah answered, looking at Joe and smiling. "I feel I am contributing to the war effort at the shipyard. I can always finish school later. My father fought and was wounded in the first war. I feel I am honoring his memory and helping my country." The first statement about her father was ironically true; she of course did not elaborate on which country he fought for when wounded.

Suddenly they heard the front door open. The elder Mayer addressed his son: "That will be your Uncle. Good! You can introduce Sarah to Saul."

A thin man with a thick, black moustache and heavy dark eyebrows entered the parlor. His work clothes were sweat-stained and dirty with grease. Sarah noticed a slight resemblance between the man and Joseph's father, the eyes were similar as was the shape of the chin.

"Uncle Saul, this is my friend, Sarah Klein," Joe said to the solemn, tired looking man. The man shook the woman's hand with the short, one stroke shake of the Germans.

"Hallo, madam." The man's greeting was courteous but without enthusiasm. The German accent heavy. "You will excuse me, please, I must clean myself."

"Saul, Miss Klein will be joining us for dinner," interjected the mother.

"Ja, gut," said the uncle as he abruptly turned and left the room.

To the mother, the young woman repeated the request made of Joseph's father, "Please, Mrs. Mayer, call me Sarah."

"Sarah, thank you," said the mother. "Please excuse Saul. He is not a rude person. He is just tired."

"He has a lot on his mind," added Mr. Mayer. "Saul's wife and son are still in Europe."

Joe Mayer and Sarah Klein sat alone on his parent's front porch. During the unusually warm spring days of 1943, American front porches were a popular place in the early evenings. Across the street, three shirtless teenage boys worked on the engine of an aging sedan. A few houses down, on the corner, young neighborhood children in swimsuits gathered to run through the cooling spray of a water hose, shrieking loudly at the delightful shock of cold water. Nearby, a neighborhood dog divided its attention between the children and scratching fleas.

Mr. Mayer had resumed his reading. The Mayers were in the habit of dining late during the warmer months. Appetites went up after the sun went down. Mrs. Mayer, who had the look of a woman familiar with cooking, cooked. Sarah offered to help, but the polite hostess insisted no, so the young woman now sat with Joe, gently rocking in a old wooden swing suspended from the porch ceiling by metal chains groaning in rhythm to the motion, a true Rockwellian scene reproduced on this spring night on myriad front porches across America. Only the young woman knew the severe aberration on this porch: a Jew with his arm around a daughter of Hitler's Third Reich.

"Joe, I didn't know you had a real German uncle," Sarah said casually, looking at him with a smile. A lie. Erika Lehmann had been briefed extensively on the Mayer family background, including the requests the family made in the spring of 1939 to the German government through the International Red Cross seeking help in locating Saul Mayer's family in Europe.

Joe nodded and replied, "He isn't actually my uncle. He is my father's cousin. It's a long story."

"We have time."

"Well, okay. Let's see…where to begin. To tell you the truth, I really don't know that much about Saul. My paternal grandparents immigrated from Germany shortly after they married. My father was born here in Indianapolis. Dad is a one hundred percent red, white, and blue American. He fought for this country in the first war—won a bronze star. After the armistice they kept him stationed in France for a few months, so he traveled into Germany with hopes of finding some relatives. Dad knew his parents were from Potsdam and he eventually found a few kinfolk there, including Saul. Here's the ironic part: Saul fought on Germany's side and after he and my father compared war stories—with the help of a neighbor of Saul's who spoke good enough English to translate—Dad and Saul discovered they had once actually fought in the same battle, on opposite sides. It was somewhere in Belgium. Who knows, they might have actually shot at each other! Anyway, after Dad returned home, he and Saul kept in touch over the years through occasional letter writing."

"Did your mother say Saul's wife and son are still in Europe?"

"Yeah, that's right," Mayer replied somberly. "Saul owned a small engine repair shop in Potsdam. On Crystal Night in '38 the Nazis tore up his place and set it afire. Previous to that, my father had written Saul letters for years trying to convince him to leave Germany and come to the States. My father and I both wrote letters to the German government, the Red Cross, and several other organizations and filled out a mountain of paperwork for the Immigration Service in the thirties volunteering to be sponsors which would allow Saul and his family to enter this country, but Saul brushed it all off. He always wrote my father that things would improve, that Jews had been persecuted on-and-off in Europe for centuries and it was silly to panic now. But after his business was burned on Crystal Night, Saul finally decided to leave."

The sun retreating over the western horizon painted the Indiana sky a riot of pink and orange. Joe Mayer took a drink of Coca-Cola from an eight ounce bottle and continued, "The trouble was, by then, it was becoming very difficult for Jews to get out of Germany. It took several months, and Saul had to sell everything he had, including his wife's wedding ring, to come up with enough money to bribe a couple of exit visas out of some crooked, small time official. But the visas had different dates so Saul and his wife could not leave together. Finally, in the spring of '39 it was time to leave, and Saul sent his wife on ahead with the child. They were to travel to Lisbon and then hop the first ship to the States. They never got here. We have no idea what happened. Saul followed a few weeks later. He arrived in New York thinking his family was already in this country. When he found out his wife and son—who was just an infant at the time—had disappeared, Saul tried to return to Europe to search for them but by then it was impossible. All we can do now is keep our fingers crossed and hope they are okay and that we'll be able to locate them after the war. So you have to overlook Saul if he occasionally comes up short in social graces. I can imagine some of the thoughts that have passed through his mind. Let's hope the horror stories we hear about the Nazi treatment of the Jews since the start of the war are exaggerations."

The pretty young woman he had his arm around nodded reassuringly.

"Sit here, Sarah."

The friendly order came from Mrs. Mayer.

Sarah sat down at the end of the rectangular dinner table. It was a place of honor afforded guests in the Mayer's modest home. Joe took the chair closest to her. Mr. Mayer sat at the end opposite Sarah, to his right was his wife's seat, to his left sat Saul Mayer. Although the house was still very warm, the setting of the sun and a large box fan made the room tolerable.

"Everything looks delicious, Mrs. Mayer," Sarah smiled at her hostess. Before her was a plate of baked cod, fried okra, sliced fresh tomatoes grown in the Mayer's backyard Victory Garden, boiled spinach, and a homemade biscuit. From a bottle labeled *Mogen David*, Noah Mayer poured glasses of wine and passed them down the table.

Pleasant chat accompanied the first few minutes of the meal. Mrs. Mayer embarrassed her son by telling Sarah amusing stories from his childhood. Thankfully changing the subject from Joe's point of view, his father commented that one of his co-workers, whose son had enlisted in the Marines shortly after Pearl Harbor and was somewhere in the Pacific, had recently received a letter from the boy. Apparently the boy was fine.

Joe's father then recalled for everyone the favorable reports in that day's newspapers about the Allied efforts in North Africa. Mr. Mayer looked at Saul, "The war news has been positive recently, hey Saul? We have Rommel on the run in North Africa."

Saul Mayer had been eating quietly and had seemed generally disinterested in conversation at the table, but he now retorted: "You cannot believe anything the government reports."

"This is America, Saul," Joe's father countered in an effort to cheer his cousin up. "The newspapers here are not run by the government. They are free to report the good and the bad. We do not have a Goebbels to control the newspapers here." A shrug from the morose German was all that was offered in reply.

Mrs. Mayer broke in, "The war, that is all you men talk about." Attempting to change the subject, she turned to Sarah. "Sarah, Joe told us you are a secretary at the shipyard?"

"Yes, ma'am. I type, take dictation, do filing…that sort of thing."

Sarah noticed that Saul Mayer was staring at her.

"Where did you learn that type of work?" Noah Mayer asked Sarah.

"Basically it was on-the-job training, Mr. Mayer. My experience was not all that impressive. I took a typing course in high school, and I had done a little secretarial type work for my father's business. Apparently they thought this was good enough. I feel lucky to have gotten the job."

Saul Mayer was still staring at her—aloof and lost in thought. Sarah ignored him. Finally, after a moment's lull in the conversation, the sullen German addressed her: "You do not look like Jew, Miss Klein."

Mrs. Mayer blushed and looked mortified. Joe laughed slightly and joked, "What is a Jew supposed to look like, Uncle Saul?"

Saul Mayer ignored his cousin's son and the embarrassed Mrs. Mayer. He continued, "Where is your family comes from, again?"

"Really, Saul," interrupted Mrs. Mayer. "We must not be rude to our guest."

The young woman did not avoid a reply. The question had been anticipated long ago, before she left Germany. In fact, it was a surprise to her that it had taken until now for someone to ask it. The irony was not lost on Erika Lehmann that it was asked, not by an American, but a German-Jew.

"No, that's all right, Mrs. Mayer," Sarah said. Turning to Saul Mayer, she answered him with a lie delivered quite easily and professionally. "Actually, I am only half-Jewish. My mother was a Gentile who converted to our faith after she married my father. My mother's paternal grandfather—my great-grandfather—was an Englander from Dover. She also had some Norwegian blood. I guess I look like her."

Joe looked at her with surprise and commented, "You never told me any of that."

"You never asked," she replied with a wink.

Saul Mayer added, "You know your blood lines very gut, Miss Klein. Strange for American." The young woman's eyes met Saul's before she looked away and took a sip of wine.

Noah Mayer looked at his cousin. "Saul, you sound like one of those Nazis you tell us about, questioning people about their ancestors."

Mrs. Mayer interrupted, obviously perturbed. "Oh, Lord! We are not going to sit here and talk about the Nazis and ruin another dinner! I told you two I do not even want that word mentioned at this table! And we are also not going to sit here and question a guest about her family background." She sent a piercing look in Saul Mayer's direction.

"It's okay, Mrs. Mayer," the young woman replied. "I thought nothing of it, really. It is very interesting to me…talking about ancestors, I mean. I've never been to Europe, but I would like to travel there some day and visit the places my family is from, maybe try to find some relatives."

Saul Mayer looked into Sarah Klein's eyes. They held each other's gaze for a moment, then both looked away.

✡   ✡   ✡

CHAPTER 33

When we were children playing together, my brother Adolf was always the leader.

—Paula Hitler

Evansville—Monday, May 3, 1943

When the lunchtime whistle sounded, Joe Mayer walked across the Quonset Hut compound to Building 23 where he spotted Sarah Klein leaving the building with Carol Weiss. As Mayer quickened his pace to catch up, the women noticed him approaching and stopped. They both smiled at Mayer as he neared.

"Can I buy you two lunch?" Mayer courteously offered both women hoping Carol would refuse.

"Sure," Sarah said. She took Mayer's arm with one hand and Carol's with the other.

"You two go ahead." Carol knew she would be a third wheel and pulled away from her friend. "I have some errands that won't wait."

"Are you sure?" asked Sarah.

"Honey," Carol tried to whisper. "Don't argue. Just go."

Mayer knew any place that served food within short walking distance of the shipyard would be crowded to overflowing so he drove to a place a couple of miles away called the Hilltop Tavern. It just so happened that the Hilltop sat atop a hill. Turnbull and Mayer ate lunch there occasionally. It was a comfortable, neighborhood tavern that had served good "homecooked" meals since the antebellum days. There was a local legend that Abe Lincoln, who grew up in southern Indiana not far from Evansville, stopped in at the Hilltop for a meal on his way to Illinois.

Mayer and Sarah hung their coats on a rack near the door then found a table. They had just taken their seats when a gray-haired waitress, who looked old enough to have served Abe, shuffled over to take their orders. Both Mayer and Sarah ordered the blue-plate special.

"Howard and I come here for lunch once in awhile," Mayer said as the waitress left. "The food here is really quite good."

"Great," said Sarah. "I usually walk over and eat lunch somewhere on Franklin Street. I'll tell Carol about this place."

Idle chat continued through most of lunch which was a thick breaded pork chop, mashed potatoes and gravy, lima beans, and bread. The daily specials at the Hilltop cost thirty cents, a nickel more than most of the other lunch specials in town, but most thought the extra five cents well spent.

"I enjoyed meeting your parents. They are very nice people, Joe."

"Yeah, that was fun. It was good to get out of town for a day. I'm glad you were with me."

Mayer took a bite of potatoes, then continued.

"This morning Howard asked me if we wanted to go out with him and Carol, but I told him we already had plans. If you like, we can meet them at the Troc for a nightcap."

Sarah nodded and smiled. "You know I enjoy our double dates with Howard and Carol," then she placed her hand on his and added, "as long as we get some time alone later."

Joe grinned.

"Speaking of Howard," she continued, "what's his latest theory about all the extra security at the shipyard. You told me a while back he was positive that Roosevelt was going to pay us a visit, then when Roosevelt actually showed up he couldn't believe it himself."

Mayer laughed and shook his head. "Now he's sure there's a Nazi spy running loose in Evansville, or maybe it's a Jap spy. I don't remember if he specified."

Sarah laughed with Mayer. "What makes him think that?"

"Oh, who knows with Howard? You know the FBI's been around interviewing people."

Sarah nodded. "Who doesn't? That's all some of the girls in my building talk about lately. They think most of the FBI men are good looking."

"Well, Howard knows some guy who went through one of the interviews a couple of days ago. According to Howard, this guy told him the FBI man asked him if anyone had been asking him inappropriate questions or acting suspiciously, that sort of thing. Howard thinks that means there's a spy lurking about. How's your lunch?"

"Good. They certainly give you enough to eat."

"Dessert?" Mayer asked.

"Tell me you're kidding, please!"

"My name is Joseph Mayer. I was ordered here for a two-thirty appointment with an Agent Pulaski of the FBI."

Mayer spoke to a petty officer second class who sat behind a desk just inside the entrance to the shipyard's administration building. The man checked for Mayer's name on a clip board.

"Okay, sir, go on back. Up those steps [pointing], make a right, down the hall, last door on the right."

When Mayer reached the room the door was open. A heavy-set man sat behind a desk reading papers in a folder. When the man noticed Mayer, he put the folder down, stood, then circled the desk with his hand outstretched. The man's tie was loose and the top button of his shirt unbuttoned.

"Hello," the man said with a big smile. "My name's Charlie Pulaski."

"Joseph Mayer." The two men shook hands.

"Thanks for coming. Sit down, Mr. Mayer, please." Pulaski pointed to a chair. Mayer took his seat while Pulaski circled back behind the desk and sat down.

"Mr. Mayer, I'm with the FBI and we are in town conducting a series of interviews with some of the war plant personnel." As he spoke, the man slid his identification across the table. Mayer glance at it without picking it up. "I'd like to ask you a few routine questions if you don't mind. There's nothing to worry about; it's just standard stuff we ask everyone."

"Fine, Agent Pulaski."

"Smoke?" Pulaski offered a cigarette from a pack on the desk.

"No, thanks."

Pulaski lit one for himself. "Tell me about your background."

"Well, ah…I'm a metallurgical engineer, originally from Indianapolis. I received both my bachelor's and master's degrees from the University of Notre Dame; began my doctorate work at MIT but suspended it to take a job at Bethlehem Steel; worked there three years until I went to work for the government conducting alloy research; tried to join the army when the war broke out but they sent me here instead; been here since last June." Mayer paused. "That's about it, I guess." As he spoke, Mayer was sure the heavy-set man behind the desk already knew this information.

"Do you like it here at the shipyard?" Pulaski asked pleasantly.

"I like it a great deal. I feel I'm contributing something to the war effort."

The FBI man asked several generic questions about Mayer's current work; questions that were not of a classified nature, then suddenly Pulaski fired out this one: "How are the experiments with tellurium going?" The question surprised Mayer.

"I can't answer that, Agent Pulaski."

Without a hitch Pulaski moved on. "Do you see your father much?"

"My father?"

Pulaski nodded.

Mayer was again surprised but answered the question. "I saw him just this past weekend when I visited him and my mother in Indianapolis."

"You must be proud of him. I came across his war record and saw he won a bronze star in 1918." Pulaski looked at Joe and waited for a response.

"Yes, that's right, and yes, I'm very proud of him."

"My dad served during the Spanish-American war," Pulaski announced with a grin. "Shows how old I am."

Mayer smiled politely.

"I think I recall reading in your dad's war record that after Germany surrendered, he applied for permission to travel into Germany?"

"Yes, that's right."

"Sightseeing?"

"No, he went there looking for relatives. My dad's parents immigrated to the United States from Germany and he figured he had some relatives there somewhere."

"Did he find any?"

"Yeah, my father knew his parents were originally from Potsdam, and he found a cousin and his family there."

"Hey, that's great. I have some relatives in Poland my mother used to exchange Christmas cards with. Did your dad ever hear from his cousin again?"

"He lives with him."

It was the first pause in the FBI man's rapid-fire questioning. Mayer got the sudden impression that what he just said was the first piece of information that was not in the file on the FBI man's desk.

"Your dad brought his cousin back from Germany with him?"

"No. Saul, my dad's cousin, immigrated in the spring of '39. My dad and I both applied to the Immigration Service and, through the Red Cross, to the German government for sponsorships for Saul and his family. To make a long story short, the visas that Saul finally obtained had different dates. Saul left a few weeks after his wife and child; Saul got out but his family is stranded somewhere in Europe, maybe still in Germany."

Mayer awaited the next question, but Pulaski just sat and looked at him across the desk. Suddenly the FBI man seemed ready to wrap up the interview.

"Mr. Mayer, contact me if you ever see anything suspicious no matter how insignificant you feel it might be." This was the way Pulaski ended all the interviews. "You can get hold of me here, or if it's after hours I'm staying at the Sonntag Hotel. Here's a card I've written my phone number on."

Mayer took the card.

"Just one more question, Mr. Mayer," Pulaski finally declared. "What can you do for fun in this town?"

Mayer looked at him—probably strangely. *What kind of FBI guy is this?*

"There's the movies of course," Mayer said. "And the canteen dances if you don't mind fighting your way through a battalion of soldiers. And you see a lot of the shipyard people at the Trocadero."

Pulaski's last interview of the afternoon was over by four—a navigation expert named Mitchell. He closed Mitchell's folder and tossed it on the desk, discovered his pack of cigarettes was empty, crumpled the pack and tossed it toward a small waste basket without looking to see if it went in, then sat back and rubbed his temples. The rubbing failed to ease his headache.

After a moment Pulaski pulled his chair back close to the desk, opened a drawer and pulled Joseph Mayer's folder which he had kept separate. If Pulaski had discovered on his own that Mayer had known relatives in Germany, he would have tagged his file just for that reason, but Mayer offered the information himself. That, and the information on line fourteen of his personnel sheet stating Mayer is Jewish, made him a poor candidate to be a Nazi spy.

But Pulaski saw red flags immediately. Mayer was a Jew with Jewish relatives in Germany. Everyone knew about the harsh treatment of Jews by the Nazis before the war, and most suspected the plight of the Jews had worsened since the start of the war. If the Nazis could somehow connect an American engineer, who did top secret work for the United States Navy, to relatives under the Nazis' heavy thumbs in Germany, then two plus two equaled four as far as having a potential blackmail victim. The Nazis had that connection when Mayer and his father applied to the German government for immigration sponsorship for those relatives. Tracking Joe Mayer's whereabouts would, unfortunately, not be that difficult for the Germans. Everyone leaves paper trails: driver licenses, phone records, paperwork concerning real estate purchases, easily accessed information that any American citizen could obtain without raising suspicion. And unlike the general public, the FBI was well aware of the Bund.

The German/American Bund was an organization of American citizens with ties to Germany or German sympathies. The organization was legal—anyone's next door neighbor might be a member. Before the war the Bund had been very public and vocal in its support for Germany, and its members worked fervently to keep the United States neutral. Bund membership dropped off after Pearl Harbor for fear of reprisals, but the FBI had an ongoing investigation into Bund activities and knew it was still out there. Cincinnati, a city not far up the Ohio River, had a large number of ethnic Germans and one of the most active underground Bunds in the country. Tracking Mayer's whereabouts would not take a trained spy. Any American citizen, like a Bund member for instance, could track Mayer by legally accessing his paper trail. Sending that information on to Germany would be treason, but acquiring it would not be that difficult.

During the interview, Mayer impressed Pulaski as very sharp-minded. Mayer quickly recognized Pulaski's attempt to trick him into divulging classified information with the tellurium question, but at the same time

Mayer did not impress Pulaski as someone who could remain totally cool during FBI questioning if he were being blackmailed into handing over secrets to the enemy. Mayer did not seem inordinately nervous, so the blackmail scenario was weak if Pulaski went by first impressions. But despite how calm Joseph Mayer had been during questioning, the red flags were there and this was a wartime national security issue.

Charlie Pulaski picked up the phone and asked the operator for the Sonntag Hotel. A desk clerk answered and Pulaski asked for David Falasco. "If he's not in his room, try the FBI conference room." Falasco had permanently reserved the conference room for taskforce meetings and briefings and he could often be found there whittling down a mountain of paperwork. It took a few minutes, but Falasco's voice finally came through Pulaski's phone.

"Falasco here."

"Dave, this is Charlie."

"Yeah, Charlie."

"I need a surveillance team."

Thursday, May 6, 1943

Joe Mayer sat in the kitchen of the house the Navy graciously paid the rent on, thumbing through a large stack of mail. Notoriously lackadaisical about checking his mail, Mayer sometimes ignored letters for weeks before even bothering to glance at the return address, let alone open it. (This frustrated his mother to no end when she asked about a card or letter she sent two weeks past and found he had not opened it yet.) This quirk sometimes caused him problems with colleagues. Important communications from universities and research labs received tardy responses. Mayer knew this was unprofessional, and lately he had made a deliberate effort to respond to his mail more regularly.

Last weekend Joe Mayer and Sarah Klein returned from the visit to his parents home in Indianapolis. The visit eased Mayer's conscience; the drive was less than four hours from Evansville, but it was early March when Mayer had last dropped in for a visit. Mayer always enjoyed seeing his folks, but the best part of the trip was the hours alone with Sarah during the drive. They spoke of things new, things they had never discussed in the months they had known each other. Mayer felt he knew her even better now, and his feelings toward her were growing very strong.

The stack of mail contained a few bills; a trade magazine called *Modern Metals Journal;* a postcard from the Red Cross addressed to *Resident* that avowed the importance of donating blood; and a hand-addressed envelope postmarked Indianapolis. The envelope had no return address and the poor scribble looked like neither of his parent's handwriting. Mayer opened it.

It was a note from his father's cousin, Uncle Saul. Mayer smiled. He had never received a letter from Saul. The two men were not that close; Saul struggled speaking English and writing it even more so, and Saul knew Joe did not speak or read German. However, the note was in English which Joe knew had to have been quite a struggle for Saul. It began in the familiarity Saul addressed Joe with—*Nephew Joseph*—with Joe's name spelled in the manner most common in Germany.

Neffe Josef,
My English forgive. Woman you bring lies. No Jew. Danger.
Saul

What was this all about? Mayer shook his head bewildered. He remembered Saul staring at Sarah during dinner and his uncle's questions about her background that at the time seemed amusing to Joe and rude to his mother. *Saul has gone over the edge.* Why would someone claim to be a Jew if they were not? Usually, if people lied, it was timid

Jews claiming they were not for social or business reasons to a still sometimes biased public, a certain segment of which held onto the old stereotypes about Jews. Besides, at dinner Sarah told everyone that she was only half-Jewish.

Mayer looked at his watch and figured his parents would most likely be home. He picked up the telephone and asked the operator for long distance, "Indianapolis, please, Belmont 70776."

Mayer knew Saul was under pressure. What Jew wouldn't be with a wife and child missing in Nazi Europe? That pressure had gotten to Saul, Mayer feared.

The phone connection took about two minutes. Finally, Joe heard the rings and then a familiar voice.

"Hello." It was Joe's father.

"Hi, Dad."

"Joe! What's up, son? Miss your mom's cooking already?"

Joe laughed. "Sure I do. I can smell the Matzo balls over the phone." Joe heard his father laugh in Indianapolis. "Hey, Dad, I got a note from Saul in the mail."

"What?...what kind of note?" Joe could hear the surprise in his father's voice.

"I'm worried about him, Dad. He sent me a note about Sarah."

"Oh, boy," the surprise in his father's voice was no longer there. "What does it say?"

Joe read Saul's note to his father.

"Don't pay any attention to it, Joe," his father suggested. "Saul's been driving your mother and me batty ever since you left saying stuff like that about Sarah. Your mother is about ready to kick him out of the house. He wanted me to write you a letter warning you about Sarah. I think Saul thinks she might be some kind of gangster's moll on the run or something."

"What???"

"Yeah," Noah Mayer chuckled. "Sorry to laugh, Son. It's not funny. I refused to write any crazy letter, of course, so he obviously wrote it himself."

"Why does he think all this stuff, Dad?"

"Saul says Sarah is not Jewish, half-Jewish, or any part Jewish. He's convinced she is not who she says she is so he thinks Sarah has to be hiding some dark secret. He thinks she might have been in some sort of trouble or something."

"How in hell can he know if she is Jewish or not?" asked Joe.

"I asked him that. He says he can just tell. He said it was some little things she said or did. He claims she called her great-grandfather an 'Englander' instead of 'Englishman.' Now who in the heck would pay any attention to that except Saul. He also mentioned something about the way she laid down her silverware when she finished eating, said she laid down her silverware like a Catholic. Crazy stuff. Like I said, Son, don't pay any attention to him. Just forget about it and try to cut him some slack. You know, if I were here and you and your mother were in Europe, I would be nuts too."

"Maybe you need to get him some help, Dad. A psychiatrist or someone."

"Maybe. I'll keep an eye on him. Tell Sarah hello from your mother and me. Your mom's crazy about her, you know."

"Is Mom there?"

"Nope. She took the bus downtown to shop with a couple of women from her sewing circle. Saul's out back in the garage sharpening the lawnmower blades."

"I'll guess I'll let you go then."

"Okay, Son." Noah Mayer tried to relieve his son's concerns about Saul's mental health with humor. "Hey, if Sarah turns out to be Bonnie Parker, I guess that makes you the new Clyde."

"Funny, Dad."

✡   ✡   ✡

CHAPTER 34

Report by Prof. Dr. Holzlöhner, Dr. Rascher, and Dr. Finke regarding human low-temperature experiments at Dachau, 10 October 1942.

If the experimental subject was placed in the water under narcosis, one observed a certain arousing effect. The subject began to groan and made some defensive movements. In a few cases a state of excitation developed. This was especially severe in the cooling of head and neck. But never was a complete cessation of the narcosis observed. The defensive movements ceased after about five minutes. There followed a progressive rigor, which developed especially strongly in the arm musculature; the arms were strongly flexed and pressed to the body. The rigor increased with the continuation of the cooling, now and then interrupted by tonic-clonic twitching. With still more marked sinking of the body temperature it suddenly ceased. These cases ended fatally, without any successful results from resuscitation efforts.

—Trials of War Criminals Before
the Nuremberg Military Tribunals—Washington, U.S. Govt.
Printing Office, 1949-53, Vol. I, p. 226-243

Dachau Concentration Camp

Friday, May 7, 1943

A narrow escape this morning, and Ruth Mayer cautioned herself to never let it happen again.

Dachau served the Luftwaffe as a center for hypothermia research. The objective was to supply the German Air Force with new and better ways to combat the effects of hypothermia on pilots downed in frigid waters. Male inmates at Dachau served as test subjects for SS-Untersturmführer Rascher's hypothermia chamber. Subjects were immersed in water, the water gradually cooled to the point the subjects lost consciousness, then experiments were conducted to find the most efficient means to return body temperatures to normal. Everything from experimental clothing to Gypsy women were used as warming mediums. Unfortunately, Dr. Rascher had lost several subjects lately to unsuccessful revival attempts so he stepped up the experiments: the next report was due on Göring's desk by week's end.

A middle-aged woman who had befriended Ruth learned her nineteen-year-old son in the male block had been chosen for one of Rascher's experiments. The mother lost control and ran shrieking at a group of SS guards standing near the motor pool. The woman's actions were tantamount to a suicide attempt, and indeed one of the guards was reaching for his pistol when Ruth ran over, begged for the woman's life, then hustled the woman back to the barracks.

Later, when Ruth had time to think about what she had done, she shook uncontrollably. It might have cost her her life, then what would happen to David?

Never again. *Do nothing to draw attention to yourself!* It was the first rule of staying alive at Dachau, and Ruth broke that rule today. The only way she could protect David was to remain alive.

She looked down at David who slept snugly against her holding tight to his constant companion—a little clown doll. David had been running a fever for over a week, a fact Ruth hid from the guards. She had seen sick children disappear. The bunk where mother and child lay resembled more a wooden shelf than a bed. No mattresses or pillows. Other women, some with small children like Ruth, crowded the shelves straining them to the breaking point. The stench of bodies gave Ruth a constant headache.

She stroked David's forehead and knew she would not sleep tonight.

Evansville—[that same day]

The bath water was hot enough to frost the mirror and fog the air. Erika Lehmann soaked. Her wet hair dripped.

When the FBI showed up and began questioning the shipyard's high-clearance personnel, Erika knew her time in Evansville was drawing to a close.

The clock started ticking when she made her first transmission last December. Unlike England where so much encoded radio traffic bounced back and forth to and from France, the Low Countries, Scandinavia, and countless ships at sea making the sorting out of what came from where sometimes impossible, suspicious transmissions from the American mainland were uncommon and chasing them down was top priority for the Americans.

Erika knew that with each transmission the Amis[11] closed the gap, so she used her radio sparingly, kept her time on-air brief, and transmitted from a different location each time. So far she had made only four transmissions since U-260 delivered her to the Carolina shore in August. This allowed her to ride the mission out in relative safety. Until now.

---

11 Common German slang for Americans during WW II.

Obviously, the FBI planned to check the high-clearance personnel first, but it was only a matter of time before they finished and moved down to the mid and low-level clearance personnel which encompassed the secretaries. When she first applied for work at the shipyard last September, her cover identity had been sufficient to get her past the hasty and haphazard scrutiny of the civilian and low-ranking military liaisons who manned the personnel offices. Those harried people had been forced to hastily assemble a shipyard workforce that would eventually total over 19,000 workers. Under those circumstances it had not been hard for her to slip through the cracks and get a secretary's job, but her cover would never hold up to a full-fledged FBI background check. Time was now a factor. Her time table would have to be condensed and moved up.

It had not been a particularly difficult mission so far.

Her original strategy had been to use the predicament of Saul Mayer's stranded family to bribe information from Joe Mayer. She would promise their release from the concentration camp in exchange for just a tiny tidbit of information. Once Joe Mayer supplied even the smallest piece of information, he was hooked. Treason had been committed. She could use that to blackmail more important details out of him.

Saul Mayer's wife and young son were located last summer, before Erika left Germany. Canaris assigned three Abwehr investigators to the difficult task—the family had disappeared several months before the start of the war in 1939—but eventually they were located at the Dachau concentration camp outside Munich. Since the family failed to make it out of Germany before the war, they were being housed there for their own protection, Erika was told. Hidden in an envelope taped inside her transmitter was a photograph of the woman and boy taken at Dachau; the mother held a July 1942 *Time* magazine to prove the timeliness of the photo. The three-year-old boy stood beside his mother tightly gripping his mother's leg with one arm and a ragged clown doll with the other. The photo would be used to prove to Joe Mayer that the woman and child were alive. When Erika first saw the photograph, she was shocked at the emaciated condition of the people, but she was told their condition was caused by a typhoid fever epidemic that had recently swept through the camp. In the report given her, the official word was that the disease had been eradicated, and mother and child were now regaining their health.

But all the work to find the family was for naught. She abandoned the bribery/blackmail scheme soon after meeting her American target. Erika Lehmann was by necessity an excellent judge of character, and after getting to know Joe she had quickly come to the conclusion that the bribery strategy would be fruitless. A highly paid engineer who would give up a cushy wartime job to enlist in the infantry, which Joe had attempted to do, was not a good candidate to betray his country. Joe Mayer would sacrifice himself, and her, before committing treason. Besides, in the end, her original strategy was not needed. Luck had again interceded on Erika's behalf. Luck by the name of Howard Turnbull.

During double dates between Mayer and *Sarah Klein* and Turnbull and Carol Weiss, the gabby Turnbull unwittingly supplied Erika with a wealth of information a tidbit at a time. Tiny bits of information here and there that, to others, went unnoticed helped Erika immensely: a complaint here; a boast there; kidding Joe about something that happened at the shipyard; repeating rumors; small indiscretions that even the careful Joe Mayer often failed to perceive as dangerous. On those occasions when Mayer realized Howard was saying too much and admonished him, by then the damage was already done.

Then the night at *Sarah's* apartment.

Erika had checked Joe's wallet hoping to find the combination to the safe in the Quonset Hut where he and Turnbull worked. It was forbidden to write down the numbers—all high-clearance personnel were under strict orders to memorize the combination—so she was not surprised when she came up empty. Joe Mayer was not one to break the rules.

So one evening, after a double-date movie with Howard and Carol Weiss, *Sarah* suggested everyone stop by her place for a nightcap. Fulfilling her role as the gracious hostess, she took everyone's coat and placed them in her bedroom. Erika knew Howard kept his wallet in his coat's inner pocket. A quick rifling of Howard Turnbull's wallet produced the combination of the safe in Quonset Hut 11.

Besides listening carefully to Turnbull's indiscreet chatter, simply keeping her eyes open at the shipyard allowed Erika to gather other important information such as how many ships were being launched and the draft of the ships, which Erika could calculate by watching the ship's test run on the river. The latter information was critical for Wehrmacht plans to keep the ships from assailing the beaches. She relayed the information to Abwehr through radio communication or letter drops. The letters, sent to an address in Juarez, Mexico, were relayed through the *Bolivar* network to South America and then to Germany. This system was not as efficient as encoded transmissions, but it allowed her to cut down on transmission time and slow the FBI's hunt.

It was all important and useful information but incomplete.

The most important, and most dangerous, part of her mission still lay ahead.

CHAPTER 35

In wartime, truth is so precious that she should always be attended by a bodyguard of lies.

—Winston Churchill

Evansville—Friday, May 14, 1943

It was Friday evening and Joe Mayer's mood was high. He had just finished reading Ernie Pyle's syndicated column reporting on the Axis surrender in North Africa. Besides the good news from Ernie Pyle, something else boosted Joe Mayer's spirits. Love.

Mayer turned on the radio. Something lighthearted was in order. He spun the tuning dial on the Emerson until he found one of his favorites, *The Jack Benny Show.* Jack and Rochester quipped about a five-cent child's pencil sharpener the miserly Benny had just given Rochester for his birthday. Rochester was getting the best of the wisecracks, of course, although only the audience realized it—not Benny.

> *Rochester: Thanks for the pencil sharpener, Boss.*
> *Benny: You're welcome, Rochester.*
> *Rochester: Now I can sharpen that pencil you gave me for my birthday last year.*

Mayer was heading to the kitchen for a beer when the telephone rang.

"Hello."

"Oh, good, you're there." It was Howard Turnbull hollering into a telephone from somewhere with a very loud crowd in the background. "Hey, we're down here at the Trocadero and you'll never guess who's here."

"Who's 'we?'"

"What?" shouted Turnbull even louder. "Speak up I can't hear you."

"You said 'we' are down at the Troc." Mayer shouted now also. "Who's 'we?'"

"Carol's with me. Who do you think? Do you want to know who's here or not?"

"Roosevelt?" Mayer was having fun aggravating his friend.

"Very funny, smart ass. William Powell and Myrna Loy!"

"You're kidding." The film stars, famous for their roles as Nick and Nora Charles in the popular *Thin Man* movies, were passing through town with several other celebrities on a cross-country war bond drive. Mayer had seen the movie stars' pictures in that morning's newspaper.

"No joke," assured Howard. "I bought them a drink, Joe, and Carol and I both got autographs. Carol and I are sitting at their table!"

"Man, that's great, Howard."

"Is Sarah there?"

"No."

"Go get her and bring her down here. Hurry up, I don't know how long they'll be here."

"I don't know, Howard. This afternoon I took her to lunch and she said she was feeling ill and would probably stay home tonight."

"What? Speak up!"

"Okay, okay. I'll swing by her place and check on her and see if she feels up to it."

"Yeah, just hurry up!" Turnbull started to hang up then pulled the phone back to his ear. "Hey, Joe, still there?"

"Yeah."

"Bring a camera."

"Okay."

Click.

Sarah had no phone so Joe would have to drive over. He found his camera but barren of film and not wanting to stop for any, he left it and headed to Sarah's apartment. He arrived in the diner parking lot just before ten. Her windows were dark, but he thought the chance to meet the famous stars a sufficient one to rouse her out of bed. If she felt too ill to go out, at least he could check and see if she needed something. Mayer parked the Lincoln, then walked up the wrought iron steps to her door. After knocking loudly, waiting, then knocking loudly again several times with no sign of life, Mayer descended the stairs. He noticed Sarah's car was not in the parking lot. The diner closed at eight but the lights were still on. Maybe Emma, the elderly lady who ran the diner with her husband and was Sarah's landlord, would know where Sarah was. Mayer tried the diner door which was unlocked. He found Emma scrubbing pots in the kitchen.

"Oh, Joe, are you two back already?" Emma seemed surprised.

Mayer paused for a moment. "Uh…I don't follow you Emma. I came by to see Sarah. She wasn't feeling well earlier…"

The old woman looked at Mayer perplexed. "Oh, she didn't tell me. That's just like her. She probably thought I would worry. Now I am worried. When she packed to leave, I just figured she was going somewhere with you."

"Packed?"

"Yeah. Well, I don't know if you would call it packing. I saw her load a duffle bag or something in the trunk of her car earlier this evening. I didn't get a chance to talk to her, but I thought she might be going with you to Indianapolis again to visit your family."

"No," said Joe, "but she must feel better so don't worry. I'll, ah…check back later. Thanks, Emma."

"I'm going to have a talk with her about not letting me know she was sick. Ralph and I consider her a part of our family; she's such a sweet thing. But no wonder she's under the weather. Poor thing is probably worn out with you keeping her out til the wee hours every night this week and all." Then the old woman added with a twinkle in her eye, "But I was young once, believe it or not, and I remember how love is."

Mayer made no reply except to absentmindedly thank the woman again before leaving. "...*keeping her out til the wee hours every night this week.*" Mayer took Sarah out three times this past week but only for dinner. He had dropped her off at her apartment no later than eight on any given night.

In his car Mayer tried to think of obvious possibilities: *Late night runs to do her laundry? That might explain the bag. No, that was ridiculous—not every night and so late. Had she been called out of town tonight when someone in her family had taken ill? No, her parents were deceased and she told him she had no other close relatives, and that didn't explain the other nights.*

Suddenly Mayer caught himself. What was he doing? He was not the girl's father. They were not engaged, and had no "understanding." If Sarah Klein was dating someone else it was none of his business. Mayer tried to fight off the feeling of a heart growing heavy with more noble thoughts: she obviously felt better which Mayer was happy about. He would swing by the Trocadero and check back for her later.

When Mayer walked in the Trocadero, he quickly spotted the hubbub. There, surrounded by a throng of patrons standing around their table, was Howard Turnbull and Carol Weiss sitting across from William Powell and Myrna Loy. Joe Mayer had to grin. *Leave it to Howard to be one of the chosen. He probably elbowed his way in and told someone else sitting at the table they had an emergency phone call at the bar!* Mayer made his way through the crowded nightclub. Howard, acting like he had known the famous screen couple for years, introduced Mayer to the movie stars and a press agent who accompanied the stars on the war bond tour. Howard had Joe pull up a chair and squeeze in between Carol and Myrna Loy.

"Where's Sarah?" Howard asked.

"She wasn't home. I'll check back later."

Myrna Loy sipped her drink but Powell belted them down much like the character he portrayed on screen. Howard bought another round while the stars signed a few more autographs.

"I really enjoy your work," Mayer finally said to Myrna Loy, then regretted it immediately thinking it sounded hackneyed.

"Thank you," the actress smiled. She was a beautiful woman with snow white teeth and blue-green eyes. Mayer tried again.

"How long are you in Evansville?" It was a little better.

"We leave tomorrow for Columbus, Ohio, then on to Cleveland…I think. To be honest, we've been to so many cities I'm losing track of where we've been and where we're going."

"It must be tiring," Mayer said.

"Yes, but when I start feeling sorry for myself, I just think of our boys overseas sleeping in wet foxholes and that straightens me out quickly."

Powell said something funny that Mayer did not hear but which succeeded in breaking up the others around the table. Joe hated it that Sarah was missing this.

"What do you do?" Myrna Loy asked Mayer.

"I'm a metallurgical engineer assigned by the government to the naval shipyard."

"Wonderful. That has to be some valuable work."

"Thanks."

Howard, who by now was calling William Powell "Bill," turned to Joe and asked about the camera.

"No film." Mayer said, then told Howard he would again try to round up Sarah. He excused himself.

The drive from the Trocadero to Sarah's apartment took fifteen minutes. Her car still was gone and her windows still dark as were the windows of the diner. Having no other options he again knocked on her door. *Maybe she had car trouble and someone brought her home,* but again there was no response to his knocking. By now it was approaching midnight.

Within a few hours, Joe Mayer's mood had gone from elated to deflated. Mayer started the Lincoln and headed home under a thin sliver of moon.

✠   ✠   ✠

This was the night of the waxing crescent: the day after the new moon. Always a dark night. The same tiny sliver of lunar silver that guided a melancholy Joe Mayer home less than an hour ago now did a poor job of illuminating the Kentucky river bottoms across the Ohio River from Evansville.

The car crept slowly down the secluded dirt road, the headlights offering a movie screen view through the windshield—vision straight ahead, blackness to both sides.

In the latter part of the nineteenth century, this road allowed access to a ferryboat dock on the Kentucky side of the river. Kentucky Colonels, riverboat gamblers, and fine ladies in frilly dresses were conveyed across the river to Evansville to await departure on the Delta Queen, Memphis Belle, or other riverboats docked on the Indiana side.

Nature now threatened to reclaim this backwoods road so forgotten by man. The car's tires crushed weeds and the bumper bent tree saplings, some as high as three feet. After the bumper kowtowed the saplings, the malleable young trees snapped back up, seeking their revenge against the car's belly.

The sapling's ancestors, large beech, oak, and sycamore trees, stood guard along both sides of the overgrown road. These trees reached across the road and joined hands. This formed a leafy canopy that might have been beautiful by day, but eerie tonight. The trees formed a wall along both sides of the road, so the driver could not steer around the numerous craters——hence the car's snail's pace.

After the rains earlier that spring, the adult trees had for a while been up to their knees in water and the road completely submerged. ("The Ohio's banks are as fickle as a woman's moods," locals like to say, "always changing.") Years of this unkind treatment succeeded in dissolving some of the old road completely. The path now ended almost a half mile from the river's edge. The ground became increasingly spongy as the car approached the end of any useful part of the road, so the driver thought better of going any further.

Erika Lehmann guided the car into a small break of trees, turned off the headlights and killed the engine. She exited the car, closed the door quietly and listened. A symphony of bullfrogs, quite loud, croaked in the nearby murk, but she heard no sounds generated by humans. Good. She expected as much; this was an area she had explored well.

Erika opened the trunk, took off her clothes and threw them in by the spare tire. She unzipped a canvas rucksack and dumped the contents out in the trunk. Using a small penlight to locate a small tin of black grease paint from among the contents of the bag, Erika liberally smeared the black grease on her face, arms and neck, then threw the tin into the forest. The other contents of the canvas bag were a t-shirt and a pair of lightweight cotton pants that already had a belt threaded through the loops. At the back of the pants, a zipped bag, also with belt loops, was attached. Both the t-shirt and pants were black. Erika quickly slipped on the clothes, closed the trunk, and began working her way through the thick underbrush of the Kentucky river bottoms.

Working at the shipyard these past months afforded Erika Lehmann ample time and opportunity to observe security, both from inside while she worked and from outside on her own time. The high school parking lot that loomed over the shipyard just a few blocks west of the facility gave Erika an ideal vantage point to observe the area at night.

From there she learned that the Navy Sea Patrol concentrated on securing the fenced outer borders of the facility. It would be extremely risky to attempt entry by going over one of these fences. The enormous lights that enabled production of the LSTs to continue twenty-four-hours-a-day flooded the surrounding residential neighborhood with light for blocks. Might as well go over the fence during the day!

But fences are on land.

To Erika's surprise, even with the recent increase in the number of guards on patrol, the security overseers practically ignored the river. Although the shipyard lighting illuminated several blocks of land on three sides, *none of this lighting was directed toward the water!* At night, only one Coast Guard runabout occasionally putted up and down the river's edge, sometimes remaining docked for an hour between patrols. Besides the boat, the only other attention given the river was by a lone Navy Sea Policeman who patrolled the shipyard's dark shore.

And dark it was. Another pleasant surprise for Erika Lehmann. Erika knew that if this facility were in Germany, several towers would constantly sweep the river with spotlights. Guards with dogs would continually patrol *both* shores. A small flotilla of boats, all with searchlights, would constantly chop the water. But this was not the case here, and it was the Achilles' heel Erika would exploit. There would still be one fence to climb, the fence that surrounded the Quonset Hut compound, but it was smaller and less secured than the main perimeter fence.

Erika paused when she reached the edge of the Kentucky forest. A narrow beach strewn with dead branches dropped a few feet to the water. She chose to enter the water at the wide bend of the river, north of the shipyard. The current would take her down river as she swam. Across the river, the lights of Evansville glimmered. Down river to her left were the brighter lights of the shipyard. She checked her waterproof wrist watch.

It was 12:50 a.m.

Erika Lehmann covered her hair with a black swimming cap and adjusted her eye goggles, both had been in the waterproof bag attached to her belt. Quickly and quietly she slipped into the dark waters of the Ohio River.

The river was nearly three quarters of a mile wide, but because Erika entered up stream from the shipyard her swim would be double that—almost a mile and a half. She allowed plenty of time when planning because instead of a front crawl which would propel her across the river quickly (but make noise and frothed the water), she used the slower breast stroke which was silent and did not disturb the surface.

The spring had been very warm, in fact the past two weeks had been uncomfortably hot and humid. However, the river had dragged its feet and fell behind the season. The water was still very cold. But the chill water of high Alpine lakes had never kept Erika out of the water, plus she knew the exertion of the swim and the adrenaline rushing through her veins would keep her warm enough.

Halfway across she was still well up river from where she wanted to come ashore. She slowed to allow the current to take her down river.

Twenty-five minutes after entering the water, Erika was within two hundred yards of the Indiana shore. The shipyard itself was operating at full steam and Erika could hear the familiar banging, hissing, and grinding noises. The Coast Guard runabout was docked farther down the shore, its crew nowhere to be seen. Staying low in the black water Erika scanned the shore looking for a patrolling guard.

At a hundred yards offshore, Erika finally spotted the guard. He stood by a crane smoking a cigarette. *Very nonchalant, these Americans, to be smoking on guard duty.* She stopped and treaded water, not moving closer to the shore until she had time to observe the guard. He never once glanced at the water, not that he could see anything in the blackness anyway. When the guard resumed his rounds, he walked west along the top of the river embankment—away from Erika.

Quonset Hut 11 was her target. The huts sat at the far eastern edge of the shipyard. Erika had planned her swim well; she was now directly offshore of the huts and still up river of the well-lighted docks. Staying low in the water, she headed to shore.

The riverbank was steep. Erika was within six feet of shore before her feet felt the bottom. At water's edge she knelt, removed her goggles and swim cap, and placed them in the waterproof bag attached to her belt. She looked up and down the shore, then lithely scurried up the steep ten-foot embankment.

The Quonset Hut compound sat behind a chain-link fence a hundred yards from the river. In the area between sat material recently unloaded from river barges. Erika weaved her way through a maze of oil barrels, bundles of rebar, and stacks of wooden and metal crates. Near the fence, Erika crouched in the shadows behind a forklift.

This was the compound chain-link fence within the main fence of the shipyard. Erika had avoided dealing with the heavily patrolled outer fence by entering from the river. The fence that now separated her from her objective was eight-foot high and topped with three rows of barbed wire. This area was where the recent increase in security was most noticeable. Through the fence, Erika counted at least six Navy Sea Policemen making their rounds, crisscrossing through the rows of Quonset Huts.

The huts were dark and empty: the scientists, engineers, and secretaries were home in bed (or at the Trocadero, it being the weekend). Light from the shipyard flooded the area but the buildings cast large, dark shadows. The shadows, unchecked by the weak light of the waxing crescent moon, would obliging conceal.

But this fence was dangerous.

Not in the climbing. Erika had scaled a similar fence at the Quenzsee obstacle course dozens of times. She could be over it in a matter of seconds. What made the fence risky was the light from the shipyard—way too much of it, but there was a possible solution. While scouting from the hill west of the shipyard, she had paid close attention to the movement of the giant crane gantries that rolled back and forth between the ships' massive hulls. Through her binoculars, Erika had observed the gantry closest to the Quonset Hut compound move into a position that cast a shadow on the fence. The shadow lasted only a few seconds but that would be long enough. The main problem was the lack of any discernible schedule to the gantry movement. It might move three or four times one hour and not at all the next hour.

But it was too dangerous to go over the fence under the bright light from the shipyard utility poles. She would have to wait. Perhaps for the best, Erika thought. This would give her clothes, which were still dripping and clinging to her skin, time to dry. Now perhaps she would not drip water all over the hut floor. Erika found the most secure spot possible among the maze of stacked crates and sat down in the shadows.

Forty minutes passed and the gantry in question still had not moved. She looked at her watch. It was 2:15. Erika had to make it back across the river before first light at 5:00. Time was now a factor. There were only two options. She could take a huge chance and go over the fence in the light, hoping no one saw her, or she could abort the mission and return to the water. If she aborted she would have to wait three weeks for the waning crescent. She was pondering her choice when she heard the hellish groan. The sound was similar to that of a heavy metal door with rusty hinges slowly opening, only magnified a hundredfold.

The gantry moved.

Erika knew it would take several minutes for the sluggish behemoth to cross in front of the fence. The shadow of the fifteen-story-high machine moved toward the fence like a solar eclipse. Finally, the shadow reached out and buried the fence in darkness. Erika sprinted to the fence, scaled it rapidly without any objection from the barbed wire, then dropped to the ground on the other side. Staying low she ran to the nearest Quonset Hut and ducked into the shadows behind the building. A patrolling Sea Policeman passed between buildings, two rows away. Still in the shadows, Erika lay on her stomach until the guard passed. She checked both directions then began working her way to Building 11 which sat near the middle of the phalanx of huts. Checking carefully for guards, she moved from the shadows of one building to the next. When a guard came into view, she would drop and hug the ground next to a building always careful to remain in the shadows.

Finally at the back of Building 11, she dropped to a knee and opened her bag. Inside the bag, underneath her swim cap and goggles were a few assorted screwdrivers, a set of lock picks, a small roll of tape, and a microcamera. Erika retrieved a screwdriver and quickly extracted four screws from a small metal gridiron in the hut's foundation. The gridiron fit tightly, forcing Erika to jimmy it with her screwdriver. Once free, the grate was set aside and Erika swiftly snaked her way through the small opening. She was now under the Quonset Hut in a crawlspace accommodating plumbing pipes, heating ducts, and electrical wiring. She reached back out through the opening, grabbed the gridiron, and from inside fitted the grate back into the frame in the foundation. The tight fit insured the gridiron would stay put; she would not need the tape.

It was a two-foot-high crawlspace. Not enough height to kneel or even sit up, but it provided her the most safety since she left the water. Foundation gridirons on three sides of the building, like the one Erika just removed, allowed ventilation and workmen access to the utilities. These gridirons now served German intelligence. The grates let in just enough light to allow Erika to move around, and she could monitor the patrolling guards without being seen.

Erika located the largest of the heating ducts and followed it through the crawl area, crawling on her belly over pea gravel. The gravel was rough on her elbows and knees but she was thankful for it. Her clothes were still damp; crawling over dirt would have caked her clothes with mud which would become evidence left behind on the floor above. Reaching the end of the duct, she used the penlight to locate the screws in the large, rectangular sheet metal elbow. The screws fastened the elbow to the duct. Erika took a Phillips screwdriver from her bag and removed the screws. She loosened and pulled away the metal straps holding the elbow to the above floor then pulled the fitting free. Once the elbow was removed, the heat register was easily pushed up and out onto the wood floor above.

The screen was fourteen inches by eighteen, the same size as the grate in Erika's building (for planning, it was her fortune that the Quonset Huts were clones). She knew it would be tight, but she squeezed through the opening and was now inside the dark building.

Erika was now in the room that housed the secretaries. A locked security door separated this room from where Joe Mayer and the other engineers worked. Erika knew the key was in the security guard's lock box which hung on the wall over his desk. This lockbox had a rudimentary lock; opening it with her lock picking tools was a simple matter. Once she had the door key, Erika crossed the room, checking out the windows for guards along the way. A sign on the door read: *Engineering—White Card Admittance Only!* The key turned easily. Erika left the key in the lock as she step into the room.

The safe sat in a back corner of the room. Erika knelt and opened the safe door with the combination from Howard Turnbull's wallet. Inside were an assortment of folders of various thicknesses, loose papers, blueprints, *and* the top secret engineering manual. She flipped rapidly through the manual photographing each page. This took some time and she had to load fresh film before she finished. She especially looked for pages detailing Joe Mayer's work with tellurium, something Howard Turnbull had been foolish enough to mention one evening after one drink too many. When she finished with the top secret manual, she photographed any papers from the folders she thought might be important, concentrating on documents containing engineering details. To accomplish this Erika laid the papers on the floor and, holding the penlight beside the Leica microcamera, clicked the shutter. After photographing a document, she was careful to place each back in its original order. Occasionally she would pause for a glance outside.

When she finished and began replacing the documents, she noticed a small round container in the back of the safe. The container was no larger than a lipstick tube, and she nearly missed seeing it altogether. With her penlight she read the label: *Tellurium—Property of United States Government—Top Secret*. Opening the container revealed a silvery white substance in crystal form. Erika could scarcely believe it; she was not expecting to find a physical sample of the top secret substance in the hut! It was an unbelievable stroke of luck. Erika considered taking the entire container, but decided instead to take just a portion. She poured what she estimated to be a couple of grams of the crystals into the empty film canister.

Erika returned the tube to the safe along with the rest of the documents, careful to arranged them as they were found. She closed the safe door and turned the dial to thirty-one, the number it was on when she arrived.

The drafting boards that sat around the room were quickly checked, but nothing of interest was found. *Even the Americans aren't that careless.* She checked her watch.

3:15.

She locked the engineers' room behind her, crossed the secretaries' room and returned the key to the lockbox. Once again she squeezed through the heat vent opening and dropped into the crawlspace. Reaching back up through the opening, Erika replaced the heat register then went about the slow work of reinstalling the sheet metal elbow.

3:50

She belly-crawled to the gridiron she had entered through and peered out. A guard walked past on the brick walkway ten yards away. She waited until he disappeared around the next hut then pushed on the gridiron which did not budge. She turned and kicked it out, the noise drowned out by the twenty-four-hour cacophony coming from the shipyard.

Once out of the crawl space, and with the gridiron screws quickly replaced, Erika began working her way back to the fence. An early morning ground fog had moved in off the river. These morning river mists were common to the area but unpredictable. No way could Erika have relied on one when planning, so the fog was more good fortune. Now she might not have to wait for the erratic movement of the gantry to shadow the compound fence. Finally arriving back at the hut closest to the fence, Erika paused in a shadow and peered out toward the shipyard. The fog was heavy and moving across the shipyard like cannonsmoke across a battlefield. Visibility was fifty feet, and only because of the effulgent light of the shipyard. The blurry forms of the giant hulls could be scarcely discerned; the workers were completely shrouded from view. *But don't get in too big a hurry,* she reminded herself, *that's when mistakes are made.* If someone spotted her, all hell would break loose.

4:10

Erika checked behind her one last time for the Quonset Hut guards, then again to the shipyard for workers. No one could be seen in the fog. She sprinted to the fence, jumped half way up, and shot to the top. *Just like Quenzsee.* Grabbing the top wire between two of the sharp barbs, she flipped over the wire, free fell to the ground on the other side, and darted into the oblivion of the crates. Checking, things appeared okay: there was no commotion to indicate she had been seen.

Now she just had to work her way through the relative safety of the crates and storage drums to the water. She reached the stack of drums closest to the river embankment and paused to check for the shore guard. She knelt and peered around a drum, but had to jerk back quickly. The shore guard was twenty feet from her and walking her direction. While he walked, he talked to the two Sea Policemen in the runabout slowly putting along at walking speed a few feet out in the water.

The SPs would have to be waited out. To stay out of sight, Erika worked her way around the drums as the walking guard passed within a few feet. At the end of the concrete pad, the guard, now faced with walking in the mud of the embankment, stopped, waved to his buddies then turned and headed back down shore. The boat continued up river.

4:40. Erika knew she could not wait much longer. These shallow to the ground, early morning river fogs were burned off quickly by the rising sun, and first light was twenty minutes away.

With the Coast Guard runabout disappearing into the mist to her left and the shore guard walking away to her right, Erika slipped on her goggles (no time to bother with the cap), and crept down the embankment. Just before returning to the waters of the Ohio River, Erika heard the deep moaning sob of a tugboat horn coming from somewhere out in the mist of the river.

Erika used the breast stroke to stay low in the water until she was sure she was far enough out to be beyond any residual light from the shipyard. Then she broke into a full crawl. She would not have to breast stroke all the way across the river, another advantage of the fog. With the crawl, she would traverse the river in a third of the time it took her to cross earlier. The one negative aspect of the fog, which on the river was even thicker, was insuring her swim took her in the right direction. The river current now ran from her left to right; the current, and keeping the sounds of the shipyard to her back for as long as she could hear them, would be her bearings. She should be okay, she thought, all-in-all fortune had been very good to her tonight.

But luck is a fickle flirt.

As Erika continued to swim, she again heard the tugboat horn. It was much louder this time. She stopped and treaded water for a moment. Still she could see nothing in the pea soup fog, so she resumed her swim.

Suddenly a blurred white light illuminated the fog to her right. Erika knew it was the tug and, turning her head, saw the rusting hulk of a barge plowing toward her through the mist. Less than thirty feet away from the barge's wide, flat bow, the only thing Erika could do was dive.

It was after she had gone deep in the water that the undertow seized her. The powerful cross-current dragged her under the barge.

She fought against the undertow, trying to swim from under the barge but, like a powerful underwater wind, the undertow pulled her back. In the murky blackness, Erika could not see the barge overhead but could hear and feel it rumble the water. She didn't know how deep the cross-current ran, but she realized her only chance was to get underneath it. She flipped over and dove deeper into the inky water. Visibility was zero but she had no choice but to keep swimming downward. After what seemed an eternity her hand felt the mud of the riverbed. Erika hugged the bottom and used it to help propel herself in what she hoped was the right direction. She could see nothing but could feel the silt from the riverbed being kicked up as she fought her way across the channel. Her lungs were on fire. Finally, after being submerged for over a minute, she could hold her breath no longer. With no visibility, she could only hope she had cleared the barge. She stopped, righted herself, and marshaled all her strength for the push off the bottom.

She broke the surface gasping. After her battle with the river gods, providence blessed her again. She had surfaced on the Kentucky side of the barge.

She could now see it was not one barge but an assembly of barges as they passed just a few feet from her: coal barges running low in the water. Erika treaded water for a moment, content to suck in several deep, sweet breaths of air, not caring that the wash from the giant craft bobbed her up and down in the water like a liquid trampoline.

Suddenly the running lights on the starboard side of the pushing tug appeared. From atop the pilothouse a spotlight swept left to right vainly trying to pierce the fog. Another red light spun frantically in all directions. At water level Erika spotted the row of donut shaped life buoys roped over the side of the ship. Concerned about being sucked into the froth of the tug's giant screws, Erika kicked toward the ship and grabbed hold of a buoy. She could at least catch her breath and evaluate her situation.

Erika was exhausted. She decided to hitch a ride on the tug. She held onto the donut shaped life buoy and let the tug drag her through the water.

The tug took her around the big bend in the river. Once around the bend, Erika pushed hard off the side of the ship and with all the strength she could muster dived to the river bottom to avoid the suction of the tug's screws. She stayed submerged as long as possible, then surfaced. It was still dark and the fog thick, but the tug allowed her to get her bearings; she knew it headed up river. With the ship a safe distance, she turned in the water and swam toward the Kentucky shore. First light dissolved the fateful fog, and Venus, the morning star, was still bright in the east as Erika Lehmann exited the water, climbed a short embankment, and melted into the Kentucky wood.

Shortly after dawn Joe Mayer was back in his car and once again driving to Sarah's apartment. During the night he might have slept for an hour or so. Fitfully. When Sarah was not home last night after earlier telling him she was ill, and then Emma's surprise announcement about Sarah's other nocturnal disappearances, what was he to think?

Poor thing is probably worn out with you keeping her out til the wee hours every night this week…

Joe's first thought was Sarah was seeing someone else. If that were the case he could live with it. He had to live with it; he had no choice. All she had to do was tell him.

Then other thoughts crept into his brain.

Mayer had forgotten about the strange letter from Saul with the cryptic warning that Sarah was not who she claimed to be. He had called his father out of concern for Saul's mental state and not because of any suspicions about Sarah. Joe had not thought about the letter since, but now it returned to haunt him.

What if she were in trouble?

What if she *had been* in trouble? Maybe some trouble with the law. What if crazy Uncle Saul was right? What if her real name was not Sarah

Klein? Surely she should feel like she could trust him with the truth; maybe he could help.

It was six a.m. and the diner was just opening when Mayer turned into the parking lot.

Sarah's car was still not there!

Back at her car, Erika quickly stripped off her wet clothes and threw them in the trunk. Before she could dress in dry clothes, she had to remove the black grease paint. From the rucksack she removed a jar of cold cream and began briskly rubbing it on her face and arms. Erika was naked and still wet from the swim, and the surge of adrenaline that had allowed her to ignore the cold river was wearing off. She began shivering in the cool dawn air when the stubborn grease paint took several minutes to remove. She checked her arms, then her face, in a small mirror and when the black makeup was suitably removed she toweled off and dressed.

Erika started the engine, but while attempting to back out of the stand of trees where she hid the car the tires spun in the soggy earth. She was stuck. Only after gunning the engine and quickly shifting from reverse to first gear several times did she finally rock the Ford free.

The abandoned river road had also turned muddy from the morning dew, and Erika had to be careful not to get stuck again. She was relieved when at last she reached the paved road which would take her to the bridge.

At a few minutes past seven she pulled into the diner parking lot from a back alley. She always used the alley because it could not be viewed from inside the diner. This made it harder for Emma, who fretted over her like a nanny, to monitor her comings and goings. Erika immediately spotted the Lincoln.

What is Joe doing here!

She parked in the rear of the lot and raced up the steps to her apartment.

At seven-thirty Joe Mayer was on his seventh cup of coffee. He had not seen Sarah's car return and was surprised when she walked into the diner. She looked freshly scrubbed.

"Joe, I saw your car," said Sarah. "Feel like buying a girl breakfast? I'm starving."

"Sure," Joe responded slowly. Sarah felt the tiredness in his voice.

"I'll go tell Ralph so Emma doesn't have to wait on us. What would you like?"

"Nothing."

Sarah walked to the back and returned momentarily.

"How are you feeling?" Joe asked.

It had slipped her mind that yesterday at lunch she told him she felt ill when he offered to buy dinner. "Much better, thanks. I don't know what was wrong with me."

"Guess who I met last night?" Joe asked.

"Who?"

"William Powell and Myrna Loy."

"Really?"

"Yeah, they were in town yesterday for the War Bond drive."

"That's right," Sarah nodded. "I remember seeing their picture in the newspaper. Where did you meet them?"

"Howard called me last night from the Trocadero. They dropped in there and Howard had them cornered."

"Leave it to Howard," Sarah laughed.

Mayer paused for a moment to light a cigarette. He offered Sarah one and lit it for her.

"I came by last night to see if you felt up to going with me to meet them."

Sarah took a drag, then turned her head and blew the smoke to the side. She looked at him.

"And you are wondering where I was." She said it in a way that made Joe feel embarrassed and dictatorial, but he had to know.

"Sarah, if you are seeing someone else that's your business, but if there is some problem you're having, I hope you feel you can confide in me. Maybe I can help. Emma told me you've been out late almost every night this week. She thinks we were together."

Good old Emma. Using the alley doesn't work after all. When she saw Joe's car, she knew an explanation would be needed for last night but now, thanks to Emma, she had to explain the entire week she had spent reconnoitering the shipyard. Thankfully, Emma now proved useful by delivering the breakfast. It gave Sarah a moment to think.

"Are you feeling okay, honey?" Emma asked as she placed a motherly hand on Sarah's forehead feeling for fever. "Joe told me yesterday you weren't feeling well."

Sarah smiled. "I'm a lucky girl to have so many people worry about me. Thank you both. I felt a little under the weather yesterday but I feel fine now, Emma. I think I'm just tired. A friend of mine is pregnant. She's due soon and having problems. Her husband works nights so I've been at their apartment just about every night this week sitting with her."

Emma immediately began a lesson in the art of delivering a baby, but was interrupted when Ralph hollered for her from the kitchen. The old woman promised Sarah she would continue the lesson later.

"Why didn't you tell me?" Joe asked as Emma went to see what her husband wanted.

"I should have. I'm sorry I worried you, Joe." She patted his hand.

Exhausted from lack of sleep, Mayer sat quietly and watched her devour a huge breakfast of scrambled eggs, bacon, hashed browns and biscuits like someone who had not eaten in days.

Joe Mayer felt almost ashamed of himself but he could not avoid doing it. When Sarah finished her meal, Mayer found himself watching the way she laid down her silverware.

He walked her out to the parking lot. They both needed sleep badly.

"Do we still have a date tonight?" Sarah asked.

"Sure. I'll pick you up at seven."

Before they parted, Sarah kissed Joe and apologized again for causing him needless worry. As he walked to his car, Mayer noticed Sarah's Ford parked near the back of the lot, the tires and fenders caked with mud.

Inside her apartment, an exhausted Erika Lehmann collapsed in the nearest chair. She had not slept since Thursday night, and then only for four hours. She spent half that night in the Kentucky wood peering through binoculars across the river at the nighttime activities of the shipyard. It was amazing that she could even think straight enough to come up with the quick lie to Joe and Emma. She thought it sounded feasible, and Joe had no reason not to believe it. All in all she felt things were holding up reasonably well.

She had done her job.

Although only Wilhelm Canaris decided when a mission was successfully completed, Erika had fulfilled all of the mission objectives. Now she had to make contact, let them know her original objectives were completed, and await instructions. There was always a chance that something could be added to the mission, but she would inform Abwehr that the FBI had moved in so there was little chance of Canaris keeping her here. There was only one glitch. Originally, she planned on breaking into the shipyard in June or perhaps even waiting until July. Those months had dates when the right moon was followed the next day by a possible transmission hook up. She could enter the shipyard one night, radio the next night, then be on her way. But the arrival of the FBI forced her to moved up her timetable to May when the most favorable moon, last night's waxing crescent, was not followed by a possible transmission date for five days. It would be Thursday night before she could contact a U-boat.

Thursday she would radio that her mission objectives were obtained, and she fully expected to receive her *Wotan invites you to Valhalla*. She would make her way back to the East Coast—this time she would drive—and use the radio one last time to establish a rendezvous with a U-boat. It would be good to get home. Erika received a certain thrill from the danger of operating undercover, but at the same time it was extremely stressful. Her guard could never be down. A slip could never be made regardless of how tiny. A noose awaited.

Now, with her job done, it was important to be as careful as ever. She had to make sure not to change anything, any routine, any habit, while she awaited recall. That is why she asked Joe about the date tonight. Life had to go on as normal until she earned her *Valhalla*.

Joe.

She was sure he had fallen in love with her, and perhaps she had even grown fond of him. In another life, another time and place, who knew? But of course they were mortal enemies: an American and a German; a Jew and a Nazi, escorted on the arm of Hitler himself. Joe would hate her if he knew, and she held no silly misconceptions about love keeping him from turning her over to the authorities.

Just a few more days. By Friday she would be on her way home.

CHAPTER 36

If I cannot bend heaven, I'll stir up hell!

—Vergil, (ca. 20 B.C.)

Evansville—Saturday, May 15, 1943

Charlie Pulaski already had two surveillance teams at work, and he had not yet finished interviewing all of the "white" clearance personnel at the shipyard. One team was assigned to a metallurgical engineer named Joseph Mayer; the second to a mechanical engineer by the name of Thomas Cole. An extensive background check of Cole turned up a skeleton. The man had been charged (but not convicted) of embezzling funds from a former employer in 1934. Also, a look at Cole's current financial status revealed he was heavily in debt.

Red flags.

Dave Falasco agreed the surveillance teams were justified, but Falasco's lead investigator at the Thunderbolt plant, an Agent Turpin, had also requested a surveillance team when a check of a petroleum specialist at the aircraft factory revealed the man was a relative, although distant, of Antonio Grosso, the editor of *Il Popolo d'Italia*, Mussolini's official propaganda newspaper. Three around-the-clock surveillance teams stretched thin Dave Falasco's manpower. Hoover had classified this case top priority because of its national security implications and honored Falasco's request for more agents. But often where much is given, much is expected in return. Falasco told Pulaski that Hoover expected results.

Across from Pulaski sat an energetic, but at the same time tired looking, young FBI agent named Chris Singleton. Singleton headed one of Pulaski's surveillance teams.

This was Agent Singleton's first real assignment and he wanted to do a good job. The young FBI man from Salt Lake City was ordered to Evansville and assigned to Special Agent in charge Falasco's taskforce three weeks ago. Last week Falasco ordered him to take charge of a surveillance team and report his information to an Agent Charles Pulaski. Because Singleton wanted so badly to do a good job his first time out, he had worked too much of the surveillance himself and the lack of sleep showed on his face. He was nervous and talked too formally for Pulaski.

"As you know, Agent Pulaski, we started round-the-clock surveillance of the subject last week. To recap that first day of surveillance, the subject left the shipyard that afternoon at 4:30 p.m. and went home where he stayed until 6:04 p.m. at which time he left his domicile and drove to a location on North Main Street where he picked up a young woman."

"Relax, Agent Singleton," Pulaski said. "Here, have a smoke, and do me a favor, don't use the word 'domicile' again." Pulaski leaned over the desk and lit Singleton's cigarette. "I've read all your daily reports except the one from yesterday which I assume you have with you."

"Yes, sir."

"Let's start there." Pulaski kept track of Joe Mayer through Singleton's daily reports which had so far only convinced Pulaski that Mayer was a boring guy. Mayer had gone nowhere during the past week but to dinner with a woman two or three times and then home early, and alone, for the night.

Singleton shuffled his paperwork and read last night's surveillance report to Pulaski. It was all there: Mayer's trip to the woman's apartment where Mayer received no response to his knocking; Mayer briefly entering the diner below; the drive to the Trocadero; a return trip to the woman's apartment (still not home), then the drive home late last night. Singleton paused for a moment and Pulaski thought him finished.

"Do we have the woman's name?" Pulaski asked.

"No, sir."

"The woman's description," Pulaski ordered.

"Caucasian, dark hair, medium build. Keep in mind, sir, I've only viewed her from a distance and usually through binoculars."

"Then this morning at 5:52," Singleton started again, "Mayer left his domi…, home and returned to the address on North Main. The woman still did not answer, so Mayer went into the diner apparently to wait for her because she arrived by car at 7:09. Before going into the diner to rendezvous with Mayer, the woman ran up the stairs to her apartment like she was in a hurry; I got the impression she was running late. Mayer and the woman left the diner together at 8:17, spoke briefly in the parking lot where the woman kissed Mayer. Mayer did not follow the woman to her apartment; he drove home and was still there when I left the surveillance one hour ago to report here to you. Agents Teague and Stuart currently have Mayer's house under watch."

Pulaski took a moment to think. "Do we know if the girlfriend returned home last night after Mayer's last visit." Pulaski was curious to know if the woman came home late and then left again in the morning before Mayer (and the surveillance team) returned.

"I don't know, sir," Singleton seemed worried. "I was not instructed to surveil the woman…"

"It's okay, Singleton. You've done a fine job." Pulaski paused again to think. "We need to identify the woman. But that's not your job. I'll handle that. I don't want you doing anything that might tip off Mayer that he's being followed." Another brief pause. "Here's what I want you to do. Tell your people watching Mayer's house if he goes anywhere tonight with the woman—dinner, a show, a bar, whatever—to call me at the Sonntag Hotel right away. Got it?"

Singleton nodded, "Yes, sir."

"Then go home and get some sleep this afternoon."

"Yes, sir."

"Keep up the good work, Singleton."

"Yes, sir. Thank you."

When Singleton departed, Pulaski put fire to another Lucky and ruminated on Mayer's surveillance. Nothing there really. Apparently Mayer's girlfriend forgot about their date last night and took off. Either that or they never had a date and Mayer went over on the spur of the moment. The morning rendezvous was a little odd since the woman was not home when Mayer got there. Had she spent the entire night out? Singleton said she ran up the stairs like she was running late. Was she late for a planned breakfast date, or was she surprised to find Mayer's car in the parking lot? It sounded like Mayer's girlfriend had someone on the side. Was it a lover, or something more sinister like a contact who was blackmailing Mayer. Could the woman be the go-between?

Probably none of the above. Singleton said they kissed in the parking lot so there was obviously a relationship there, not simply meetings between a blackmailer's message girl and a hapless stooge being pumped for information.

Nevertheless, it was time to identify the woman so a check could be run. Pulaski considered ordering Singleton, who had seen the woman's car, to return and get her license plate number, but Pulaski did not want Singleton or one of his men wandering through the parking lot. If the woman was someone they should be worried about, and she looked out the window and saw a man in a suit writing down her license plate number, the jig would be up. She would disappear before they could run the plate.

But if the truth be known to Agent Singleton, Pulaski figured he was putting the earnest young FBI man and a great many other people to chore for nothing. Pulaski figured he was fishing a dead lake when it came to Mayer. Odds were Mayer was just a boring egghead whose good-looking girlfriend had more than one stud in the barn. But Pulaski could not ignore the fact that Mayer, in trying to obtain an immigration sponsorship for his relatives, had contacted the German government before the war and identified himself and what he did for a living. It was the red flag that demanded Pulaski stick with it until he could cross Joseph Mayer off his list.

☆   ☆   ☆

"Hi, Mom."

"Joseph, is that you?" Joe Mayer's mother rinsed a breakfast dish as she held the telephone to her ear by squeezing it between the side of her face and shoulder.

"Yeah, Mom, it's me. Hey, is Saul there?"

"Yes, he's here. When are you coming home for a visit?"

"I'm going to try to get up there during the Memorial Day weekend."

"Good, and bring that nice young girl, Sarah, with you. You are still seeing her I hope."

"Yes."

"Good. Hold on, I'll get Saul."

Mayer waited a long time for Saul to pick up the phone. Mayer knew he was probably out back. When not at work, Saul spent most of his time in the garage tinkering with anything that needed fixing. Joe's father told him it helped keep Saul from just sitting around crying about his lost family. Finally Joe heard Saul's thick accent.

"Hallo."

"Uncle Saul, this is Joe."

"Yes."

"Uh…I'm calling about that letter you sent me about Sarah."

"Yes, Josef. I was right, yes?"

"No. I mean I don't know. You wrote she was lying about who she is. I wanted to ask you why you think that."

"She lied."

"What do you mean she lied?" Mayer's voice got loud and he made a conscience effort to lower it. "That's what I'm asking you, Uncle Saul. Why do you think she lied?"

"She said she ist never been to Europe. She ist from Europe and a Roman...a Catholic."

"What??? How do you know that?"

"When she finished her food she made sign of cross."

"She didn't make the sign of the cross! I was sitting right there."

"She made sign of cross, Josef."

"Uncle Saul," Joe was more than frustrated. "She didn't cross herself. I didn't see it, and I'll guarantee you Mom and Dad didn't see it."

"She did not cross herself. She crossed plate."

"Okay, Uncle Saul, she crossed her plate. What does that mean? She crossed her plate."

"She crossed her plate, Josef."

Pulaski was in the shower when the phone rang. Water dripped on the braided rug as he picked up the receiver.

"Pulaski here."

"Agent Pulaski, this is Chris Singleton."

"Yes, Singleton."

"You said you wanted to be notified if Mayer and the girl went somewhere."

"Yes, that's right."

"They just went into a night club called the Trocadero. It's just off the highway..."

"Yeah, I know where it is. You said they just got there?"

"Walked in two minutes ago."

"What time is it?" Pulaski was thinking aloud now and looking for his watch, but Singleton answered the question.

"Quarter til nine."

"Okay, Singleton. I want you to stay there and keep a watch on the place in case they leave before I get there. If that happens, stay with them. Got it?"

"Yes, sir."

"Hey," Pulaski remembered something. "How come it's you calling me and not one of your men? I thought I told you to get some sleep."

"I grabbed a couple hours this afternoon."

"You're a good man, Singleton, but get some sleep tonight. You're not the only FBI guy on the planet. You have to trust your team."

"Yes, sir."

Pulaski left the Sonntag at 9:05 and drove to the Trocadero. A saying among the Ute Indians is that those who hunt are the easiest to track. As Pulaski pulled out of the hotel parking lot, he failed to notice the headlights of the car parked down the street come on and the car pull away from the curb.

The Trocadero nightclub sat in a no-man's land of disputed border territory between the states of Indiana and Kentucky. To blame for the dispute were the shifting banks of the Ohio River. The river bank served as a natural border between the two states, but the banks sometimes failed to cooperate with the state legislatures. Years ago the banks underwent a major shift, and now the nightclub sat on land that used to be under Kentucky rule but now was north (the Indiana side) of the great river. Neither state could decide which one had legal rights to the no man's land, so the club owners enjoyed a unique advantage in that law enforcement agencies of both states generally ignored jurisdiction of the area. Hence the Trocadero was a very popular night spot offering a variety of entertainments (not all legal) to a wide range of wartime patrons.

On any given night, and especially on weekends, one might run across a soldier, a sailor, a congressman, a gambler (if you could squeeze into the crowded parlor in the back), a movie star in town for a war bond drive, a worker from the Thunderbolt factory, a prostitute, a sheriff from Kentucky (who bothered neither the prostitute nor the patrons of the smoky gambling parlor the sheriff had been known to frequent himself), a doctor, a shipyard engineer, and a German spy. Now an FBI man could be added to that list.

Charlie Pulaski was lucky to find a stool at the crowded bar. The bar sat off from, but open to, a large dance floor ringed by blue linen-covered tables. The dance floor and tables absorbed most of the club's floor space. Couples packed the dance floor responding to a six-piece band crowded on to a small stage. Pulaski lit a cigarette and ordered a beer from a large and villainous looking bartender who was six-foot-five if an inch.

Despite the crowd, it did not take Pulaski long to locate Joe Mayer. Mayer sat at a table near the dance floor beside a dark-haired woman— Singleton's dark-haired woman. Also at Mayer's table Pulaski recognized Howard Turnbull whom Pulaski interviewed just two days ago. Turnbull schmoozed with an attractive blond. The FBI man picked up his beer and walked over.

"Hey, Mr. Mayer, Mr. Turnbull," Pulaski acted surprised to run into them, "I was at the bar and I saw you over here. How are you?"

"Agent Pulaski," it was Mayer who responded first. "I see you found the place." Joe Mayer remembered Pulaski asking about the local night life.

"Yeah, thanks for telling me about it. Seems like a heck of a place."

Turnbull spoke up. "Have a seat?"

"Well," Pulaski acted coy, "okay, thanks. I'm supposed to meet someone, but I'm early." Pulaski pulled up a chair. Mayer made the introductions.

"Agent Pulaski, this is Sarah Klein."

"How do you do, Agent Pulaski?"

"Nice to meet you," Pulaski replied to Sarah then looked around the table. "Call me Charlie, please, everyone."

Mayer continued. "This is Carol Weiss. Carol, *Charlie* Pulaski." Pulaski and Carol nodded at each other before Mayer said, "And I think you and Howard know each other."

"Right," Howard confirmed. "Girls, Charlie here is an FBI man."

"No kidding?" exclaimed Carol. Pulaski shrugged and swallowed some beer.

Turnbull had not finished. "We have a spy in town and Charlie's going to find him."

Everyone looked at Pulaski. Turnbull's security check turned up no red flags, but Turnbull's subsequent interview convinced Pulaski that the man was someone whose mouth outran his brain. Pulaski was now doubly convinced.

Carol Weiss had heard Howard's theory before, and, being a lover of excitement, she hoped it was true.

"Is that right, Charlie?" Carol asked with a look of yearning. "How exciting. Tell me it's true, please!"

Pulaski was aware of the shipyard scuttlebutt. Any sensible person would know that the arrival of an FBI taskforce and the doubling of military guards held a reason. Pulaski knew it would be fruitless to deny. He was ready for the question. Perhaps he could use it to his advantage.

"I can only speak for myself. I doubt we have anything so intriguing as a spy in our midst," Pulaski lied. "Somebody seems to think there is a problem here, but I think we are wasting a lot of taxpayer money and I told my supervisor exactly that."

"I told you!" Howard said loudly, sounding triumphant. "He just said someone at the FBI thinks there is a spy. What did I tell you, Joe?"

Joe Mayer sat silently staring into his drink. Mayer's reaction was watched subtly but closely by Pulaski. Pulaski then carefully turned his attention to Sarah Klein. Pulaski found her already looking at him. When Pulaski caught her gaze, she smiled.

"Chasing spies must be exciting work, Charlie," Sarah Klein said matter-of-factly, then took a drink of her champagne cocktail.

"To tell the truth it's usually quite tedious."

The band struck up Benny Goodman's *Stompin' at the Savoy,* and Carol wanted to dance. She jerked on the always-reluctant-to-dance Turnbull who could never keep up with Carol, but, as always, Turnbull knew his fate and rose from the table and followed Carol to the dance floor.

"Joe, let's dance," Sarah said as she rose from her chair.

"Maybe later."

The young woman looked at Pulaski, "Charlie, let's dance."

From the bar across the room, Axel Ryker watched Charles Pulaski. Ryker had been following Pulaski on and off for the past three weeks. Ryker knew finding Erika Lehmann would take time, but he never imagined three months would pass without a sign. So instead of worrying when the FBI arrived last month, Ryker considered it an act of providence. He knew why they were here: eventually the FBI would intercept her radio transmissions and pinpoint her location.

Pulaski had not been difficult to spot. From outside the shipyard, Ryker observed the comings and goings; Ryker tagged Pulaski as FBI right away. His calculations proved correct when he followed Pulaski to the Sonntag Hotel and discovered the place swarming with FBI. So Ryker's plan changed from looking for Erika Lehmann to following Pulaski. Ryker would let the FBI find the girl for him.

Ryker thought for a moment his search was over when he saw the blond woman at Pulaski's table. The woman (or anyone else at the table) might simply be an acquaintance of Pulaski's, but on the other hand the FBI man might be playing cat-and-mouse with a suspect. If the latter were the case, Pulaski had led Ryker to the girl. But a hard look at the blond revealed she was not Erika Lehmann. Ryker had studied the photographs for months. He knew his prey's face.

"Hey, bub." The burly bartender tried to get Ryker's attention. Ryker had sat at the bar for twenty minutes without ordering a drink.

"Hey, bub. If you're not going to buy a drink, you need to move your ass off that stool so a paying customer can sit down."

Ryker ignored the man and continued to watch Pulaski.

Growing angry at being ignored, the giant placed a huge hand firmly on Ryker's shoulder to get his attention.

"Hey, buy a drink or get…" The man never finished. Ryker reached up, ripped the man's hand off his shoulder, and twisted it until the man grimaced in pain. Ryker took hold of a finger and was going to snap a bone for good measure, then thought better of it. With Pulaski present he should not draw attention, and others sitting at the bar were already watching. Ryker released the man's hand.

"Vodka," Ryker growled.

The bartender inspected his hand for damage. Embarrassed and angry, the bartender thought of throwing a punch. It would not be the first time he punched a customer who got out of line, but when he looked at the man he changed his mind. The man had twisted his hand as easily as if it were a child's, and something in the man's eyes convinced the bartender to back off. He turned and reached for a bottle of vodka.

Ryker returned his attention to Pulaski's table. Only one man remained at the table. The blond and her date danced as did Pulaski and the other woman. When the song ended the men returned to the table as the two women walked toward the restrooms which were near the bar.

As the two women walked past the bar, Ryker looked first at the blond then the dark-haired woman. The eyes of the two Germans met as Erika Lehmann walked directly past Axel Ryker.

✠   ✠   ✠

CHAPTER 37

The fiend in his own shape is less hideous, than when he rages in the breast of man.

—Nathaniel Hawthorne, 1835

Evansville—Saturday, May 16, 1943

From his car Axel Ryker watched Erika Lehmann and the man leave the nightclub. The man opened the car door for the woman, started the engine, let it idle for a moment, then guided the car out of the parking lot. Ryker suspected the FBI man might have a surveillance team on the woman so he patiently waited another moment. Ryker guessed right. Shortly after the car carrying the woman left, another car pulled out of the lot. Ryker started his engine and joined the clandestine caravan, staying back a safe distance. When the woman's car pulled into a parking lot on North Main Street, the FBI car pulled over a block away while Ryker drove past, turned the corner and parked on the next street. On foot, Ryker watched from a dark alley until the man left the apartment and drove off. Ryker almost laughed when he saw the surveillance car follow the man's car away. They were following the man, not the woman! The Fates had again smiled on Ryker, but he had to act quickly.

When Joe departed, Erika turned the bath water on full, disrobed, then stepped into the tub with the water still running. It had been an interesting evening. She knew bumping into the FBI agent was not an accident when she spotted the trailing car in the Lincoln's passenger side mirror. But she knew the FBI was not sure about her or she would already be in custody. When Joe left, she watched through a crack in the blinds from her dark apartment as the car followed Joe away.

They had Joe under surveillance.

Erika knew it was time to leave. The FBI must have found out the same things about Joe that prompted Abwehr to make him a target, so they decided to keep him under surveillance. She would pack up and be gone before daybreak. Best to leave in the dark when the headlights of a tailing car would be easily noticed. She would head east and lay low until Thursday night when she could radio the U-boat.

The running water prohibited Erika from hearing the clicking at her apartment door as the lock was jimmied open. She continued to mentally analyze her situation as she splashed water on her face. When she sat up to reach for a sponge, she saw the face in the bathroom mirror. It was the face of a man standing just outside the half-open bathroom door leering at her in the mirror. Erika sprang from the bathtub, her wet feet slipping on the linoleum floor. She regained her balance and attempted to burst through the doorway where the man blocked her path. Erika swung a twisting backhand and delivered a blow to the side of the man's face. He barely reacted to the blow—a blow she had used to drop men at Quenzsee—and he even smiled at her as she tried to run past. The man was surprised at her quickness, and, since she had on no clothes to grab, he managed only a partial grip on a quickly moving arm. She managed to slip the wet arm out of his grip and get past. Erika had a Beretta in the bedroom—her only hope. She raced toward the bedroom with the man close behind. Erika dived across the bed and managed to get the drawer open and her hand on the gun when his body crashed into hers and smashed her against the wall, the gun still in the drawer. The man slapped her viciously across the face several times, then grabbed her hair and bashed her head into the wall knocking her unconscious.

Not knowing how long she was unconscious, Erika came to as the result of a blast of cold water thrown in her face. When she awoke, she was lying on the bed with the man nearby. He grabbed her hair, dragged her off the bed, and threw her face down on the floor. He placed a heavy boot against the small of her back then, still gripping her hair, lifted her head and upper body off the floor. The pain of having her hair nearly ripped out cleared her senses in time to hear the man speak in German.

"Good evening, Sonderführer. Reichsführer Himmler sends his regards."

Ryker took his foot out of her back and used the boot to flip her over on to her back, this time placing the boot on her chest between her breasts. He reached behind his back and under his jacket to bring forth a Smith & Wesson .38 revolver with a silencer. Ryker looked at Erika with his dark, lifeless eyes and cocked the pistol. He aimed it at Erika's left eye.

"Now, Fraülein," Ryker paused to enjoy the moment, a sardonic smile on the menacing face. "You may get up." Ryker withdrew the gun from Erika's face and his foot from her chest.

She laid there for a moment dazed; a second ago she had been quickly preparing herself to die. When she did not respond to his instruction to rise, he kicked her hard in the ribs.

"Get up!"

Erika rolled over and struggled to her feet. Ryker walked behind pushing her out into the living room where he again grabbed her hair and roughly jerked her down on to the couch. She grimaced in pain but fought off the urge to yell out. Ryker sat in a wing chair facing the couch and placed the gun on the small lamp table beside the chair. He lit a cigarette from a pack he produced from his jacket pocket.

"Who are you?" Erika said in English. The pain in her ribs felt like electrical shocks pulsing through her chest.

"A comrade. May we speak in German? I would feel more comfortable."

Erika switched languages. "Why are you here?"

"Ah," Ryker remarked upon hearing German again. "Yes, that is much better, friendly to the ear. This English, such a crazy language, don't you agree?"

"You were at the nightclub."

"Very good, Sonderführer. Such a brief glance. I see they have trained you well at Quenzsee. Clever also changing the color of your hair. This slowed my quest to find you considerably. Stupid of me not to have considered it."

"May I get dressed?"

Ryker thought about it. "For what reason."

"Modesty."

"No. Later. Do you have anything to drink, Fraülein? Some vodka perhaps?"

"Whiskey or brandy." She kept the whiskey on hand for Joe, Howard, and Carol. Erika enjoyed an occasional brandy.

"Where is it?"

"In the kitchen."

"You may serve me whiskey."

Erika did not move, instead she stared at the man. He took a drag on his cigarette and waved his hand to signal her to get moving. When she rose from the couch, another stinging pain shot through her chest. Limping toward the kitchen, for a moment she considered attempting another dash for the gun in the bedroom, but she now did well to walk, and the gun was most likely no longer there. He did not follow her to the kitchen, allowing her to leave his sight which surprised her, but on reflection she realized what he already knew. There was nothing she could do to escape him. She was a German spy in a town swarming with FBI agents here on the hunt for her. She was injured and any dash for freedom would be a comically slow one. A naked woman fleeing down the street!—wouldn't that scene be lovely for an enemy spy? Or trying to smuggle a butcher knife back to the living room—where would she conceal it? She was helpless.

She returned with the bottle and a glass, placing them both on the table beside him. The gun lay within arm's length, but Erika knew the man was daring her to reach for it.

"You may sit now, Fraülein." Erika returned to the couch and sat down gingerly.

"The name is Ryker. I work on special projects for the SD and the Gestapo. I was sent here to kill you, Sonderführer Erika Lehmann."

"Why?…and on whose authority?"

"Conspiracies against the Reich," Ryker answered flatly, "and by the Reichsführer-SS, of course."

"Himmler has no authority over me whatsoever. I answer only to Admiral Canaris, the Wehrmacht High Command, or the Führer."

"I am aware of that and so is the Reichsführer. Why do you think you were allowed to leave the Reich?"

Erika stared at the man while she assembled the facts before speaking. "So, while I am on a high-priority mission, designated by the Führer himself as of the utmost importance, Himmler sends you here to eliminate me to settle a personal grudge." She paused as another pain shot through her chest. She bled from the lip and from somewhere on her forehead, and her face was swelling from his slaps. "Some top secret information that is critical to our war effort is in my possession, Herr Ryker. That information has to get back to Germany." She took a belabored breath. "Do you know what will happen to the Reichsführer if the Führer finds out about this?"

"I suppose the Reichsführer would have a bad day."

"Do you know what will happen to you? You know once this is done Himmler can never afford to let you live."

"Of course not, Fraülein," Ryker agreed. "That is why you are still breathing."

At least Ryker was not a fool, Erika thought. The man realized he could never return to Germany if he killed her.

"That is why we will work together, Fraülein, let us say for the benefit of the Fatherland." Ryker paused and downed a shot of whiskey.

"Please listen carefully," Ryker stressed. "You will contact your people at Abwehr and inform them that you have been successful in convincing your American target to cooperate in exchange for 200,000 American dollars. You will instruct your people that this money is to be wired immediately."

Ryker poured himself another drink.

"How rude of me. Would you like a drink, Fraülein?"

Erika did not respond.

"No? The Americans know how to make whiskey—not quite as good as the Scots but better than the Irish."

Ryker took a sip and continued.

"When you deliver the money to me, I will hand this over to you, then you can deliver it to the Fatherland." From his jacket pocket Ryker produced Erika's microcamera, film, and the film canister containing the tellurium sample.

"I stumbled across this while you were resting. Clever, Fraülein, but unfortunately a false plumbing pipe under the kitchen sink is vintage Quenzsee. I assume this is the important material you referred to?"

Ryker paused to allow his total control of the situation to sink in. He did not care that Erika did not respond. He could see in her face that what he had in his hand was valuable.

"Fraülein, I assume you know the authorities are following the man who brought you back here tonight. I presume he is your mark?"

Again Erika said nothing.

"I suggest you leave this place tonight while you still have the opportunity. I assume you have an auto and that is where your transmitter is located since it is not in here. Travel somewhere where you will feel safe while you make your contacts. I will allow you two weeks to return with the funds. There is a telephone number on this paper." Ryker tossed the paper beside her on the couch. "Two weeks from this Monday call me at that telephone number at exactly one o'clock in the afternoon local time. If I do not answer call back at exactly two o'clock the next day, three o'clock the third day, and repeat each day adding one hour to the time until you contact me. When we speak, I will inform you where we will meet to make the exchange. When you call, if someone else answers, do not ask for me, simply hang up and try again, one hour later, the next day. Do you understand?"

Erika nodded and Ryker placed the film and canister back in his pocket. He tossed the miniature camera on the couch beside Erika.

"Any questions?"

"What if I have trouble with the money."

Ryker smiled.

"Come now, Fraülein Lehmann, you insult my intelligence. The game is over. You know the procedure—a simple transfer by wire from one of the international banks in Switzerland your Admiral at Abwehr keeps accounts at for just such purposes. For you I am confident this will be accomplished with little problem."

Ryker moved the gun from the arm of the chair to his lap.

"I'm not a greedy man. Two hundred thousand dollars—not so much for such important information. Don't you agree? I would prefer Swiss marks, but that would raise suspicion—your American target would of course want American currency. Just remember to tell them the money is to purchase information from your target, otherwise they will not send it. If that happens I will migrate to South America a poorer man, and you will return to Germany without the information you risked your life for. Information that, like you say, is vital to the Fatherland. Now, Fraülein, you may get dressed."

"Why did you agree to take this assignment?"

"Agree? Fraülein, let us not be naive. As soon as our illustrious Reichsführer briefed me on this assignment, I was a dead man, and if I carried out the assignment, you would now be dead. Instead you still have the opportunity to fulfill your mission and return to Berlin a hero and sport another dagger on your chest at Quenzsee."

"Now I suggest, Sonderführer, that we both depart this place."

✠   ✠   ✠

Evansville—Sunday, May 16, 1943

Charlie Pulaski thought Joe Mayer seemed sullen last night at the Trocadero, but then again anyone would be if he knew his girlfriend was catting around on him. Pulaski sat at his desk with the form Sarah Klein filled out when she applied for a job at the shipyard. Dated last September, she stated on the application that she was born in Cincinnati and had also lived in St. Louis. Father a Frederick Klein, mother a Josephine Klein née Steiner—both deceased. She listed her faith as Jewish.

Normally Pulaski was not at his desk at six a.m. on a Sunday morning, but today he wanted to assemble all the information he could on Sarah Klein. Before Pulaski left the Sonntag this morning, he woke up Dave Falasco so Falasco could get the ball rolling on a background inquiry on the girl. Being Sunday, Pulaski knew county clerks and other record keepers would be hard to run down, so it would probably be tomorrow before the Cincinnati and St. Louis FBI offices could access the records and get back to him.

Pulaski's reason for hurrying along the background check on Mayer's girlfriend was more pragmatic than investigative. Falasco's manpower was stretched thin so Pulaski had decided if the girl checked out, he would pull the surveillance team off Joe Mayer, at least for now. Regardless of the red flags swirling around Mayer, after a week of having the man tailed nothing seemed dubious enough to warrant the man-power it took for around-the-clock surveillance.

A couple of Jews were not likely to be in cahoots with the Nazis.

✠   ✠   ✠

Every time Erika shifted gears, a stabbing pain shot through her chest like a flaming arrow. She knew ribs were at least cracked, maybe broken. A nasty cut on her lip, another in her right eyebrow, and a welt on her forehead were only partial evidence of her first meeting with Axel Ryker. Also, the left side of her face was swollen from the savage slap-ping. As she drove south through Kentucky, first light appeared and she was thankful for it. The sooner this horrible night was over the better.

Time to leave Evansville, Ryker was certainly right about that, although it was a conclusion Erika came to before she saw his gruesome face in the bathroom mirror. If only she had left yesterday!—right after the shipyard entry. She should have had everything packed in the car and never gone back to the apartment. The film and sample would be with her instead of in Ryker's hands. She cursed out loud.

Erika knew Ryker had no intentions of letting her live. Ryker was wily in the ways of his perverted world. He would never leave her alive to inform on him later or possibly hunt him down herself in South America. She glanced at the speedometer; she was speeding so she let up on the pedal.

I can't get stopped by the police!

She was exhausted but she had to keep a clear head and assess her sit-uation. What would happen first? Emma, or Joe, would be the first to discover her missing. The local police would be notified and the FBI would soon know. Because Joe was already under a cloud of suspicion (evidenced by the surveillance), his girlfriend, *Sarah Klein,* would become the number one suspect of the spy search and an All Points Bulletin would be issued for her and her vehicle. She had wisely chosen the '36 Ford because it was a common make and model. Wise also when she pilfered the extra dealer tags from the desk of the salesman in St. Louis. To avoid suspicion from driving around for months with temporary tags, Erika had eventually licensed the car in Indiana; all it took was her address and her forged birth certificate. The FBI would have that plate number. But because she had stolen the extra temporary stickers, she could now discard the permanent plates and go back to using the temporary dealer tags which were almost impossible for authorities to trace. Still, she would have to get rid of the Ford as soon as possible.

Physical and mental fatigue gripped her, and her thoughts rambled.

There was something incredibly wrong in the Third Reich. Erika had suspected it for sometime. She had no doubt about it now. A man like Heinrich Himmler left unchecked—a cancer to eat away the flesh of the nation—signified doom for Germany. Arguably the second most powerful man in the Reich, Himmler would disregard the best interests of his country to gain personal revenge. How could Hitler, so adept at spotting conspirators in the past, not see what type of man Himmler was? Or did Hitler know? Was the malignancy within the Third Reich not centered at Prinz Albrechtstrasse with Himmler and his Gestapo thugs, but on a mountaintop above Berchtesgaden?

Erika thought about the torture of Claude and poor Sophie, neither of whom would hurt a fly. The execution of Sebastian. The beating and raping of the innocent maid in Lisbon under the facade of being an interrogation.

And the Jews. Germans were told the European Jews were given land and jobs to relocate in the east. But could the horrible rumors be true?

Erika never understood the thing about the Jews. Why so much hatred for these people? Oh, she had heard the litany of reasons why the Jews were no good: the Jewish bankers in Berlin sold out Germany in the first war was a common complaint voiced in the *Völkischer Beobachter* or Streicher's *Der Stürmer,* and she had read *The Protocols of the Elders of Zion* that revealed the worldwide plan of the Jews to assimilate into and undermine various cultures and eventually gain dominance. Was it all true or black propaganda? She had blindly accepted it as fact. Now after all she had seen...

Had Ryker slapped her awake?

A deer picked a bad time to cross the road forcing Erika to jerk the wheel hard and almost roll the car. She pulled over and stopped on the side of the road. Suddenly overcome with nausea, she opened the car door and vomited on the shoulder of the road. The effort it took her body to vomit caused her excruciating pain in her chest. Her heart pounded and she felt she was about to faint. She fought to remain conscious. *How much farther?* Totally spent, Erika slowly put the Ford back in gear and drove on.

✠   ✠   ✠

Joe Mayer came to Sacred Heart Church because, after asking around, he had been told the priest was from Germany. Mass had just ended. It was not the first Catholic mass attended by the Jewish Joe Mayer. Mayer served as a statistician for the football team while attending Notre Dame, and priests were always around. Mass was said before every football game. Mayer even prayed along, although with his own prayers and always foregoing communion.

"May I see you for a moment, Father?" Joe Mayer asked the tall priest after the man shook the last hand of the departing faithful. The priest extended his hand while attempting to identify Mayer from among his flock.

"You don't know me, Father. My name is Joe Mayer. I was hoping to have just a few minutes of your time."

"John Imesch." The two men shook hands. "What can I do for you, Mr. Mayer?" Mayer was happy to hear the German accent.

"I was told you're from Germany, Father. Is that right?"

"No, my son. Switzerland."

"Oh?" Mayer did not know whether to be disappointed or not.

"Let's walk back to the vestibule," the priest said and turned. Mayer walked with him. "What's your question? Something about Germany?"

"I'm trying to find out something. I don't even know what you would call it: a custom perhaps, or a tradition among Catholics. I think probably among German or European Catholics. Something to do with crossing your plate with your silverware after finishing a meal." Mayer looked at the priest hoping he would not see a baffled look.

"Oh, yes. Started by monks in a Spanish cloister centuries ago. Spread among Catholics throughout Europe. It used to be commonly used, now not as much."

"What does it look like exactly?"

"Follow me, I'll show you." The priest led Mayer past the altar and through a door. Using a piece of paper to represent a plate and two pencils for a knife and fork, Father Imesch placed one pencil over the other to form an X, or cross. "That is all it is, my son. When finished with the meal the utensils are laid on the plate as you see there. Just a simple little way to honor Christ. Unfortunately, I'm afraid to the few who still hold to the practice today it has become a thoughtless habit—something learned in childhood and just repeated without thinking."

Mayer looked again at the crossed pencils. Yesterday morning in the diner, Sarah Klein laid her utensils on her plate just so.

"Father, where would you guess someone was from who crossed their silverware like that after they finished eating?"

"Well, I would probably think they are from somewhere in Europe."

"And Catholic, of course?"

"I've never seen the practice used by Protestants. Yes, I would imagine they were a Catholic from Europe."

On his way out Mayer's attention was suddenly drawn to a symbol in one of the church's stained glass windows. The site stopped Mayer dead in his tracks. The priest, who walked alongside, noticed Mayer's face go suddenly ashen. He asked Mayer if something was wrong.

"Is that a swastika, Father?" Mayer pointed to the symbol in the stained glass.

"Yes. It is an ancient symbol used by the Church for centuries, my son. Sacred Heart was built in 1928 before Hitler came to power and made the symbol infamous."

The thoughts in Joe Mayer's head made him feel ill.

✠   ✠   ✠

Saturday nights were always the busiest in a barmaid's life, and when she finally arrived home Sunday morning, she was too tired to sleep. *Too tired to sleep*—ironic she thought. The sun rose and still she had not been to bed, choosing instead to drink coffee and read. First read was yesterday's newspaper someone left in the bar, then it was a new edition of poetry from Edna St. Vincent Millay. Her favorite Millay poem was "I Think I Should Have Loved You Presently" though the message of love delayed too long made her sad.

> *A ghost in marble of a girl you knew*
> *Who would have loved you in a day or two.*

One of Millay's poems was written very recently. *I Forgot for a Moment* lamented the destruction Hitler currently wreaked in Europe and dreamed of days before the war.

> *It seemed that all was well with Holland*
> *not a tank had crushed the tulips there.*

Someone knocked on her door but she ignored it. It's the juvenile delinquents again, she told herself. A woman with two young sons she could not control moved in down the hall two months ago. The bratty kids delighted in running up and down, knocking on doors, and raiding the shared refrigerator in the hallway.

The knock again. Usually the hooligans knocked once and ran off. Dorothy Nolan tied her robe, went to the door and gasped when she opened it.

"It's that bad, huh?" the woman in the hall said. "It's me, Dorothy. It's Helen."

Recognition finally. "Helen!" Dorothy closed the door, quickly removed the chain and flung the door open. "My god, Helen! What happened?" Dorothy helped her to a chair then rebolted the door.

"Could I have some water?"

Dorothy raced to the sink and brought back a glass of water and a wet towel. The injured woman quickly finished off the water with several long, deep gulps, then Dorothy used the towel to begin wiping away some dried blood in Helen's eyebrow.

"I'm okay, Dorothy. Nothing that a little time won't heal."

"What happened?"

"My boyfriend beat me up. He got mad when I broke up with him."

"I'm calling the cops on the son-of-a-bitch!"

"No. I already did. It's taken care of, and it didn't happen here in Nashville anyway. I just need a place to stay for a couple of weeks where he can't find me and I was hoping I could stay here."

"Yes, of course." Dorothy continued to nurse Helen's face. "What's with the hair?"

"My boyfriend wanted me to dye it black. I'm changing it back as soon as I can."

"I liked your natural color better anyway. I didn't recognize you with the new hair."

"That and the new face, right," Helen tried humor to lighten the mood.

"Well, yes, but you said it not me."

The humor was a mistake. The laugh caused Helen to grimace in pain.

"What is it?" Dorothy gasped.

"He kicked me in the ribs."

"I'm taking you to the hospital!"

"Dorothy, I'll be okay. I just need a few days. A little sleep will do me a world of good."

The bed was already pulled down from the wall. Dorothy helped Helen undress. After two more glasses of water, the injured and exhausted woman fell asleep almost immediately. Dorothy decided to sleep in the chair so she would not accidentally bump one of Helen's injuries.

Dorothy watched her sleep. She had thought she would never see her again. It had been nine months.

✠ ✠ ✠

CHAPTER 38

One of the first duties of man is not to be duped.

—*Carl Becker*

Evansville—Monday, May 17, 1943

Yesterday, Joe Mayer stopped by Sarah's apartment twice; the second time he checked with Emma. She must be with her pregnant friend, Emma had reasoned. Mayer wanted to believe that. He had forced himself to believe Sarah's story about her strange nocturnal routines of the past week being the fault of a pregnant friend, and, even after the visit to the priest Sunday, Mayer chose to ignore the cryptic warning from Saul. But when Sarah failed to report for work Monday morning, and did not call, Joe Mayer had to finally admit to himself something was seriously wrong. She never missed work. Ever.

Later Monday morning came the final blow.

The Master Chief recorded the time as 1013 hours when Mayer opened the safe. Joe Mayer's heart broke at 1015 when he opened the vial of tellurium. He knew immediately that some of the top secret substance was missing, and he was afraid that he knew who took it.

Mayer reported the missing tellurium to his supervisor, Gary Delmar, and left Quonset Hut 11 escorted by the Master Chief.

Mayer was immediately ushered in to Charlie Pulaski's office. The Bureau man sat at his desk smoking the omnipresent Lucky Strike.

Mayer reported the missing tellurium to Pulaski, then told the FBI man everything: the strange warning from his German uncle about Sarah Klein, her strange nighttime disappearances of the past week, and her failure to show up for work that morning.

"When did you meet this woman?" Pulaski asked Mayer.

"Last fall."

"At the shipyard?"

"Yes."

"Tell me about your first meeting with her."

Mayer put his thoughts together. "I was with Howard Turnbull. I remember it was the day of the first LST launching, and Howard and I were outside at one of the food booths. Sarah walked by with Carol Weiss and she, Sarah, got bumped and accidentally spilled lemonade on me."

The FBI man slumped in his chair and shook his head tiredly. "She accidentally spilled lemonade on you." It was not a question but a weary echo, like it was the last thing Pulaski wanted to hear. The FBI man put two fingers to the bridge of his nose like he was rubbing a sudden headache.

"Agent Pulaski, I still am not convinced Sarah is at fault here. We need to find her. Maybe it is all coincidental and she has some problem…" Mayer was abruptly cut off when the telephone on Pulaski's desk rang. Pulaski picked up the receiver and spent three minutes listening, speaking rarely. When he hung up, Pulaski leaned back in his chair and stared at Mayer for a long moment before speaking.

"Mr. Mayer, I had a background check done on Sarah Klein. That phone call was from our FBI field office in St. Louis where, according to her personnel file, she claims to have lived for a time. Miss Klein has a problem; you're right about that. You'd have a problem too if you died in 1934."

Charles Pulaski, along with Dave Falasco and two other FBI agents, interrogated Joseph Mayer for four hours, then placed Mayer under security watch. Pulaski stopped short of charging Joe Mayer with treason, at least for now. Mayer could have easily covered up the missing tellurium but instead reported it immediately, plus he had voiced his concerns about his wayward girlfriend. Pulaski concluded Mayer was most likely innocent of all except being a patsy, but Pulaski agreed with Falasco that Mayer should be placed under a security watch. An FBI agent was assigned to live with Mayer to insure that Mayer could communicate with no one without an FBI overseer. Mayer was relieved of his duties; he would not go back to work at the shipyard until he could be exonerated. Pulaski assigned Agent Daniel Engler, a member of Chris Singleton's surveillance team, to be Mayer's overseer. Engler would live with Mayer twenty-four hours a day: staying in Mayer's house, accompanying Mayer to the grocery store, doctor's office, anywhere Mayer went when he left his house. And there was one other very important reason Pulaski agreed that Joe Mayer be placed under a watch—Chris Singleton's phone call.

During Mayer's interrogation, Pulaski sent Singleton to check out Sarah Klein's apartment. Singleton called to report a bathtub full of water, specks of blood on the bedroom wall, bed, and floor, and a jimmied door.

Another bombshell in a day of bombshells.

Now Pulaski's best guess was a third party had worked with the girl. Perhaps the conspirator spotted the surveillance on Mayer, got scared and, not trusting the girl to keep her mouth shut if arrested, decided to eliminate "Sarah Klein" and dispose of the body.

This changed everything.

When Mayer's interrogation was finally over late that afternoon, both Pulaski and Dave Falasco accompanied Agent Engler and a mentally exhausted and very despondent Joe Mayer to Mayer's house. Pulaski wanted to acquaint himself with the surroundings and give last minute instructions to Engler. When Pulaski and Falasco were satisfied, they left Engler in charge of babysitting the hapless Joe Mayer and left to begin the hunt for the girl (if she were still alive, which Pulaski doubted) and the mysterious third party.

✠　　　　✠　　　　✠

Nashville—Thursday, May 20, 1943

On the day Erika Lehmann returned to Dorothy Nolan's apartment the exhausted and damaged woman slept for twelve hours, rose for an hour, then returned to bed and slept several more hours. When Erika, a.k.a. Helen Gray, finally arose she felt invigorated mentally, but her body was extremely sore and stiff from Ryker's beating. Especially causing her discomfort were the ribs Ryker kicked while she lay on the floor, and the left side of her face, still swollen from his vicious slaps. But the physical pain would have to be dealt with. There was work to do.

On Monday, the day after Erika arrived in Nashville, she took bus rides around town until she spotted a car with a for sale sign parked at the end of a driveway. At the next stop, she exited the bus, walked back to the house, knocked on the door, and without haggling paid an old man what he asked for the 1937 Chevy. That night, while Dorothy worked tables at the Excelsior, Erika used blankets to conceal what she transferred from one trunk to the other. She then promptly drove the Ford to the train depot parking lot where she abandoned it, then caught a cab ride back to within a few blocks of the apartment, careful not to have the cabby drop her off at her exact location. Ditching the car at the bottom of a remote lake would have been preferable, but she was in no condition to hitchhike back to town.

The next day's chore was easier. It was time for the black hair to go. Dorothy bought the dye at Woolworth's. It turned out a half-shade darker than her natural color, but it was blond, and it would do until her natural color grew out.

Now it was Thursday night and the Chevy bounced its way over a dirt road twenty miles northeast of Nashville.

Erika would requisition the $200,000 from Abwehr even though she knew Ryker would kill her when the money was his. With her dead, the articles he stole from her would never make it to Germany, so the money was useless as a tool for purchasing the tellurium and film. She would have to deal with Ryker on her own to get back the stolen secrets.

Besides the money there was another, very different, request Erika would make to Canaris.

The message was enciphered yesterday while Dorothy was at work. It was a lengthy message and the encoding process took Erika three hours. Now, from a high point in the forsaken road where she could spot approaching headlights a mile away, Erika began tapping International Morse Code on her transmitter key.

QQVD QQVD QQVD

These letters were not coded and simply a signal to a U-boat that an encoded message was to follow. She waited for a reply.

Nothing. She tried again.

QQVD QQVD

She waited. After a moment she heard it.

KXK KXK

The U-boat was listening. It took Erika nearly twenty minutes to key the long message twice, which was standard procedure. Erika included nothing in her coded message about the presence of Ryker or that her mission was compromised. To do so would insure the special request she just made would not be honored. As far as Abwehr knew, Operation Vinland was going smoothly.

When she finished she signed off and waited impatiently for the short signal that indicated the message had been received. It took what seemed an eternity, but the acknowledgment—*VV XV*—that the sub received her transmission finally came back. Erika ripped the headset from her ears and threw it in the trunk.

✠   ✠   ✠

Evansville—Saturday, May 22, 1943

Charlie Pulaski's nightmare returned. Again his mind was forced to watch in horror as Baby Face Nelson riddled Roy McGuire with bullets from the Thompson. Again Pulaski saw McGuire do the gruesome dance as the bullets tore through his body. Again Pulaski said a prayer and tried to hide his terror as he lay at Nelson's feet waiting to die. Again the voice of John Dillinger haunted him as the outlaw called off Nelson and spared Pulaski's life.

As always Pulaski awoke drenched in sweat. Dark outside. The clock said four. Pulaski wanted no part of trying to return to sleep, so he rose and went to the bathroom. He splashed cold water on his face and thought of Preston Elliott's phone call. Pulaski had been sending his boss in Chicago frequent updates on the status of the Evansville case. With the disappearance of both the tellurium and the main suspect, Elliott considered the case over. Elliott shared everyone's opinion that it now boiled down to the nationwide manhunt now ongoing to try to keep whoever had the tellurium from leaving the country.

Immediately after Joe Mayer's interrogation, a nationwide All Points Bulletin was issued for the girl's car, and for the girl (who Pulaski figured was dead). If they found the car, they might find the girl's accomplice, but Pulaski doubted that anyone would be stupid enough to still use the car. It was not much to go on: a description of a car that was probably at the bottom of some lake, and a black and white shipyard personnel photo of a woman whose real name they did not know, and whose body probably lay inside the trunk of the car at the bottom of that lake.

The epicenter of the hunt was now in Tennessee. Early Friday morning, Stanley Mullen reported to Dave Falasco that a "hit" with the familiar "fingerprint" was intercepted the night before. The transmission was lengthy compared to the earlier hits from the Evansville area, but it was undeniably keyed by the same hand. The length of the transmission allowed Mullen's colleagues to narrow the origin location to an area approximately 150 miles south of Evansville. It was as everyone expected; the suspect was now a fugitive. Copies of the girl's shipyard I.D. photo were forwarded to the Nashville FBI field office, the Nashville Police, surrounding sheriffs's offices, and the Tennessee State Police.

With the manhunt now coordinated in Washington, Preston Elliott recalled Charlie Pulaski. Elliott ordered Pulaski to use the weekend to tie up any loose ends in Evansville, then report to him in Chicago for reassignment on Tuesday.

Pulaski fired up a Lucky Strike and poured a double whiskey from a pint bottle stashed in a drawer. He had drunk little since Preston Elliott assigned him to this case, but now his involvement was over. He leaned back on the bed, but the bed made him think of the nightmare, so he moved to a chair. Would Dillinger forever haunt him? Pulaski thought of the rush toward Dillinger on Lincoln Avenue in front of the Biograph Theater. Other agents opened fire. Pulaski remembered thinking "Hold your fire!" but he never uttered the words. In his mind Pulaski again saw the bullets spin Dillinger around. Before the outlaw's death their eyes met for the briefest instant—his and Dillinger's. The killer who spared Pulaski's life seemed to smile in recognition at Pulaski even as the bullets ripped into his flesh.

Pulaski shouted an obscenity and threw the glass of whiskey in disgust, smashing the glass and splashing the alcohol against the opposite wall. This case was another failure. Just one of several in the past few years. He remembered Harry Fallon's words: *Be thankful they still think enough of you to send you.* He was washed up. The cat-and-mouse game at the nightclub was his big mistake. He should have brought in the girl for questioning and held her until her background check was complete, or at least put a tail on her, then he would have had men on the scene when the unknown accessory showed up that night at her apartment. He picked up his FBI badge from the bureau and stared at it. He should have buried it with Dillinger.

Dillinger.

Suddenly the thought flashed across his brain. Could it happen again? Could he be making the same mistake again? Could he be overlooking the obvious as he had once done with Dillinger? During the next thirty minutes, things fell in place for Charlie Pulaski. It was as if Dillinger spoke to him from the grave.

Pulaski did not wait for a decent hour, instead pounding on Falasco's door before dawn—pounding hard enough to summon Falasco after just two knocks despite the time of day.

"Dave, I have to talk to you," Pulaski said to the sleepy-eyed man in boxer shorts and an untied robe. Falasco turned on more lights as he led Pulaski into the room.

"What is it, Charlie?"

"I want to stay on this case…stay in this town a little while longer."

"Why?" Falasco asked. "Washington is running the show now. I'd be pulled out of here myself by now if it wasn't for the security watch on Mayer, and that will end as soon as they decide what to do with him. The case is over, Charlie, as far as this town is concerned. You know our bogeys are long gone from here by now."

"I don't think so," argued Pulaski. Falasco stared at him for a moment and wiped sleep from his face with his hand.

"Don't stop there, Charlie, keep going."

"I can't prove it, Dave, but I have this feeling the game is not over yet…in this town I mean."

"You have a feeling? Would this feeling happened to be based on anything?"

"I and a lot of other people made a mistake once that cost some people their lives. We overlooked the obvious." Pulaski paused. "You asked me once about the Dillinger case. I'm sure you've heard that Dillinger spent a weekend at his father's farm while we conducted the most massive nationwide manhunt in the Bureau's history."

Falasco nodded and Pulaski continued.

"We overlooked the obvious and it cost lives. If we would have had someone keeping an eye on the family home, we would have had Dillinger, and the people who ended up getting killed in the following months— before we finally got him—would still be alive." Pulaski stopped.

"Okay, Charlie," Falasco humored Pulaski. "But I'm lost about what, if anything, that has to do with this case."

"I don't want to overlook the obvious again," Pulaski stated emphatically. "If some foreign agent successfully completed a mission, she would be breaking her neck to get out of Dodge, right?"

Falasco reminded Pulaski about the transmission from Tennessee the previous day.

"That's exactly what bothers me, Dave. Tennessee is less than 150 miles from here and the transmission took place Thursday. The tellurium was discovered missing Monday morning. That means it was stolen over the weekend. Why, after almost a week, is the suspect only 150 miles away?"

Falasco did not answer.

"If it was me," Pulaski kept stressing his point, "I'd be a helluva lot farther away than 150 miles. I'd already be across a border or at least on the East Coast by now if I were waiting on a U-boat."

"Charlie, maybe the agent has no plans to leave the country," Falasco thought aloud. "Maybe it's an American and they just got out of town while the heat is on. Maybe the classified information they stole was relayed by the transmission; Mullen said it was a long one. Or maybe a dead letter drop was used, and this person was just notifying the Krauts the information was on the way."

"We have a physical sample here Dave, the tellurium. A physical sample cannot be relayed over the air, and no foreign agent in their right mind would send such an important sample via a letter drop—way too undependable. It would have to be hand-delivered whether the agent was American or not, and remember what Mayer told us about his German uncle telling him the girl was from Europe. That and her taking the identity of a dead girl. She probably got the name from a cemetery. That's vintage foreign agent procedure, Dave; you know that. She is a German, Dave, probably Abwehr from what the OSS man told us about her use of Enigma principles. She would be looking to get as far from here as possible as quickly as possible if her mission was over. She's not fleeing, just lying low a couple a hundred miles away. That makes sense. It puts our triangulation attempts back to square one. The area circle the FCC gave us for this last transmission is a broad one just like the first circle we had to work with when she was transmitting from this area. Hell, if it wasn't for that HAM operator in Mount Carmel, we might not even be in Evansville yet. Now Mullen has to move his equipment and wait for another transmission before the location can be narrowed."

"Couple of big problems here, Charlie," Falasco announced as he rubbed his temples. "You keep using the word 'she.' We have another culprit here and we don't know the gender. And we don't know who made the transmissions: Mayer's girlfriend, or the person who apparently accosted her in her apartment. By the way, all week you've been of the mind the girl is probably dead."

"The girl made the transmissions and she's still alive," Pulaski said confidently. "And the unknown accessory is a man and he's still in this town—or close by."

"How do you know all that???"

"It's the girl, *Sarah Klein,* who made all the transmissions including the one Thursday night in Tennessee. The new bogey in this case, Mr. X, is completely unknown. There's no reason for him to feel like he has to leave town and lie low. We have no idea who he might be and he knows that. He could be a bellhop at this hotel for all we know. His cover is secure. Mullen said the radio fingerprint from Tennessee is the same as from the previous transmissions. The girl is the one whose cover was compromised. She is the one who had to leave town, so the transmission fingerprint is the girl's."

Falasco so far was following Pulaski's reasoning. "But what business could she still have here?"

Pulaski knew the question was coming. "We have two bogeys: the girl and Mr. X. If they were working together, they would both be long gone but the evidence suggests they are at odds: the blood in the apartment, the radio transmission from too close to make sense. It's obvious Mr. X has plans that don't coincide with the girl's. The girl is German; it's Mr. X we don't know about. He could be American, maybe an underworld figure hired to help the girl in some way who double-crossed her and stole the tellurium. Maybe he plans to sell it to the highest bidder unless the girl comes up with some money. I don't know. But she knows he is still here, he has the tellurium, and the girl wants it back. The girl is alive and remaining too close to Evansville to be logical unless she plans to return. It's the only scenario that pans out. If the girl had the tellurium she would be long gone. She's coming back, Dave."

Pulaski paused and searched Falasco's face.

"Call Elliott and keep me on the case, Dave, just another week or so. We're still in the game here if we can get any kind of lead at all on Mr. X. I know it's far-fetched but I need to see this out. I couldn't take another

Dillinger. I don't want the Bureau to be searching all over creation for Dillinger while he's at home in bed."

Falasco remained silent for several moments. "Your right about one thing, Charlie. It's far-fetched all right." There was another pause. "You never explained why you're so sure Mr. X is a mister."

"Mayer told us the girl was athletic and strong for a woman. Doesn't sound likely she would be overpowered by another woman. So that makes the blood in the apartment hers. If the blood was from the other person that would mean *Sarah Klein* got the best of the fight, which in turn would mean *Klein* would still have the tellurium. No, it was a man. He surprised her in the bathtub; it was still full of water two days later. Mayer said the tellurium in the safe was undisturbed Friday when he left the shipyard; he found some of it missing that next Monday. It looks like, from Singleton's surveillance reports on Mayer, the girl was gone from her apartment all night Friday. Somehow the girl entered the shipyard that Friday night and took the tellurium. Mr. X took it away from her the next night."

"Charlie, how could the girl enter the shipyard, gain entry to a locked Quonset hut, break into the safe, and walk out without anyone seeing her?"

Pulaski had wondered that himself.

"Got me there, pal, but I can tell you one thing, she's a good one. I know from meeting her at that nightclub she's a cool customer. She knew I was FBI and she asked me to dance, for Christ's sake! Smiling and flirting with me on the dance floor. My reason for being there was to find out her name for a background check; I should have at least had her watched until her check came through. I thought I was being smart with the accidental *bump* at the nightclub and she turned it around—put me off my guard. She's a pro."

Falasco hesitated. He had no idea if any of Pulaski's deductions were worth the time of day, but at this point he had no leads and nothing to lose.

"I'll call Elliott."

Nashville—Saturday, May 23, 1943

The crowd was large in the Excelsior Hotel lounge, even for a normally busy Saturday night. It was ten, halfway through Dorothy Nolan's shift before she took her first break. Despite the crowd and the rushing it took Dorothy to keep everyone waited on, the evening had gone smoothly, and the last week had been a good one (Helen was back). But Dorothy's feet still ached, and she looked forward to her day off tomorrow.

With her cup of coffee in hand, she sat at a small table in the corner of the adjoining restaurant's storeroom. Surrounded by boxes of can goods, napkins and other paper goods, shelves of assorted food stuffs, and a large commercial vacuum cleaner, Dorothy opened that morning's newspaper.

Dorothy borrowed the newspaper from a small stack kept at the bar for customers. It had been read several times, and one section was wet from a spilled beer. Having lost its virginity, the paper was out of order and a few pages AWOL. Dorothy always looked for the page with the weather forecast first. She walked home each night, so checking the forecast was pragmatic. *Rain tomorrow night.* That was okay; she was off work.

Dorothy checked the ads. The Excelsior was advertising the Ray Kraft Orchestra currently playing in the hotel's Emerald Room: dinners starting at $1.50 cents—no cover. A radio store on Woodmont Boulevard advertised Philco radios for $13.95, and Woolworth's had pajamas on sale, prices starting at $3.95 a set.

Dorothy skipped the sports pages and picked up the front page section lying out of order near the bottom. The headline reported another Allied bombing raid on Berlin. She scanned farther down the front page until her eyes locked on a photograph. It was a photograph of Helen with her dark hair! Dorothy read the bold heading over the photo: *SPY SUSPECT.* The caption beneath read: *Woman suspected of espionage. Wanted by FBI. Believed to be in Nashville area.*

CHAPTER 39

There is not, there was not, and there never will be any romance about the spy trade. The silent war of the spy is mean, cold and bitter. It is the dirtiest side of war.

—Erich Gimpel, Abwehr spy captured in America during the war,
released in 1955.

Evansville—Sunday, May 23, 1943

Charlie Pulaski got his wish and was out of bed early.

Preston Elliott acquiesced to Dave Falasco's request to keep Pulaski in Evansville at least through the next week. So just after dawn, Pulaski was in his car heading to Sarah Klein's apartment. Why, he was not sure. Pulaski and a team of Bureau investigators had already combed the place for clues or evidence. This would be Pulaski's fifth trip to the apartment since the phone call from the St. Louis field office last Monday.

Pulaski parked in the diner lot, ducked under the chain strung across the bottom of the stairs with the sign that read *Off Limits by Orders of the FBI,* climbed the stairs and used a key to unlock the FBI padlock sealing the residence. Not even the elderly man and woman who owned the property were allowed inside the apartment.

Pulaski had questioned the landlords, but neither the man nor his wife had seen or heard anything the night *Sarah Klein* disappeared. They lived downstairs but at the back of the building. The girl's apartment was in the front over the diner. The elderly couple was told nothing except the girl was missing, and Pulaski felt sorry for the old woman who fainted when she heard the news. Apparently the girl had endeared herself to the old lady.

On this fifth visit the apartment was unchanged from the first: drops of dried blood in the bedroom, the bathtub still with water although some had evaporated, an empty bottle of whiskey and a glass on a small light table beside a living room chair, cigarette butts in the ashtray beside the whiskey bottle. Fingerprints all over the place with no attempt to wipe them away. He sat in the chair beside the whiskey bottle.

The fingerprints.

One set of prints matched those in Sarah Klein's shipyard file. A few of Joe Mayer's prints were found and a set matched the old woman, Emma, who with her husband owned the place. But on the whiskey bottle and glass a strange set of fingerprints was lifted.

An unknown set of prints.

Those prints bothered Charlie Pulaski.

Pulaski had theorized to Dave Falasco that perhaps Mr. X was an underworld member hired to work with the girl. It was not uncommon for enemy agents to solicit the help of the mob, black marketeers, or Irish Republic Army members, some of whom would do anything to battle British interests including side with the Nazis.

But the unknown fingerprints weakened that theory. Any of the above people would likely have a police record with fingerprints on file. They would have taken care to wear gloves or wipe the place clean before they left. Here was no such attempt, and that bothered Pulaski. Mr. X did not care that he left his prints behind. Although the mysterious prints were still being run, so far there had been no match in the massive FBI fingerprint archives in Washington.

Pulaski was also bothered by a stumbling block in another part of his theory, the part about the relationship between Sarah Klein and Mr. X. If the two were co-conspirators, why was the door lock jimmied? Why would a partner have to break in? The jimmied lock did not make sense unless they had their falling out prior to that Saturday night. But the girl was a pro. Pulaski knew if the girl was worried about Mr. X, she would not have been surprised so easily—not with the tellurium in her possession. If relations between the girl and a co-conspirator had broken down before that night, the girl and the tellurium would have disappeared immediately. Yet she stayed in town.

So it was the only conclusion that worked in Pulaski's mind: Mr. X was a complete surprise.

A surprise who did not care about the FBI finding his fingerprints.

Monday, May 24, 1943

Over the course of the past three days, his office at the shipyard saw more of Charlie Pulaski than his hotel room at the Sonntag Hotel. In fact Sunday night Pulaski was seen not at all at the Sonntag, instead sleeping in his office on a camp bed requisitioned from the shipyard quartermaster.

Monday afternoon, when Pulaski finally checked back in at the Sonntag front desk, a message awaited.

Charlie, Important news. See me immediately. Dave.

Pulaski found Falasco in the taskforce conference room.

"Come on in, Charlie," Falasco waved and put his hand over the receiver, "better sit down for this one." When he hung up, Falasco turned to Pulaski.

"Charlie, you need a shave," Falasco grinned.

"That's why I'm here. I slept at the shipyard last night. What's up, Dave?" Pulaski parked himself in a Windsor chair beside the table where Falasco sat.

"One hour ago I got a call from a friend of mine in Washington. He works in the fingerprint section, and he and his crew have been pulling all-nighters trying to match the John Doe prints from the girl's apartment."

"Mr. X?"

"Right. They came up empty last week in the Bureau print files on known felons, but they kept looking. Friday they began cross-matching prints from unsolved felonies from municipal police files. They worked around-the-clock all weekend. They came up with a match on Mr. X."

Falasco was right. It was a good thing he was sitting. Pulaski stopped short of letting out a war whoop; nevertheless, his elation at the announcement must have shown in his face.

"Before you get too excited," Falasco warned, "Mr. X is still Mr. X. The match is still a John Doe." Falasco extended the papers and Pulaski quickly took them. The case file had been flown in from Boston. "The prints were found in the apartment of a prostitute who worked the Boston docks," Falasco summarized. "Grisly business, this one. Our Mr. X is a bad apple. I'll let you read the details. The woman's body was found on New Year's Day. Coroner reports she had been dead about a week."

Pulaski turned to the page containing the investigation reports from the Boston detective assigned to the case. Falasco knew what Pulaski was looking for so he continued his narration.

"The Boston P.D. detective assigned to the case asked around some of the dock taverns the prostitute was known to frequent. The last anyone saw her was Christmas Eve when she was seen leaving a local dive with a man who the bartender figures was off a Swedish freighter that had docked that afternoon."

"Why does the bartender figure this guy was off the freighter?" Pulaski interrupted.

"It's a good bet. The bartender had never seen the man before that night and never saw him again. It was Christmas Eve and the local dock workers were all at home. The bartender told the detective the only people in the place on Christmas Eve were men off the Swedish freighter, all foreigners, and two or three local 'ladies of the night' who worked the dock bars. The bartender remembers the guy because he sat off by himself, apart from the rest of the men. The description is sketchy. Around six-foot, dark hair, 'tough looking guy' the bartender told the detective. The description is at the bottom of page four. When the guy ordered a drink the bartender said he had a heavy accent and struggled with English."

Pulaski's attention was perked even further. "What type of accent?" he asked as he flipped through the papers looking for the answer. Pulaski knew nationalities of merchant sailors ran the gamut on most ships; a freighter flying a Swedish flag might have no Swede crewmen on board.

"Next page," Falasco helped. "The bartender didn't know. He told the detective every man in there that night had a heavy accent and spoke little or no English."

Pulaski lowered the papers and assembled his thoughts. "Of course the Boston P.D. assumed their killer left on the boat."

"Right," Falasco confirmed. "The body wasn't found for a week. The coroner's estimate fits in with the last time the woman was seen alive on Christmas Eve. The freighter left port December 26. The ship was half way across the Atlantic by the time the body was found, if, that is, it made it through the U-boat wolfpacks. The police had no name, a piss-poor description, the victim was a prostitute, and the suspect believed to be on a ship heading back to a continent at war. You can guess where that investigation was quickly headed."

"The dead-end file," Pulaski answered.

"Exactly."

"But now we know he missed the boat," Pulaski said lost in thought, not intending a pun.

Later that day, Charles Pulaski sat on a barstool at the Hilltop Inn with his thoughts, a fish sandwich, and a Wild Turkey on the rocks to keep him company.

Pulaski's theory that Mr. X might be an American underworld figure or an IRA sympathizer was out the window and he was glad. Mr. X was a foreigner with limited English skills. It was a break; the man would be more conspicuous.

Who is this man who had followed the female German agent to America? And why?

Pulaski drew a blank on why the man followed *Sarah Klein* to the USA. Was he sent to help or supervise her? That scenario did not pan out since the evidence suggested his arrival on the scene was a sur-prise—and a painful one—to the girl. But in reality the answer to why Mr. X was here was not paramount. Right now the only thing that mat-tered was finding the man.

Pulaski did not like the Bureau's chances of locating the girl on the lam. She was a pro and the search encompassed too large an area. Finding Mr. X, Pulaski felt, was the best chance of finding the stolen tel-lurium and eventually *Sarah Klein.* He asked the bartender for some-thing to write with and was given a stubby pencil with no eraser. A napkin served as document. Putting himself in Mr. X's shoes, Pulaski began scribbling.

—*Mr. X.*
—*limited English skills*
—*hard to converse with locals so avoid them as much as possible, stay in background, lie low, stay out of trouble*
—*avoid suspicion*

Pulaski stopped after the last line to consider Mr. X's accent. This was an area where a German accent was not all that uncommon among a few old-timers, but a *stranger* with a German accent would stick out like a sore thumb when trying to rent an apartment or a hotel room. Maybe. Pulaski resigned himself to the fact it would take some time to check the town thoroughly. Everyone with a spare room in an attic or over a garage was now a landlord because of the huge influx of out-of-town workers.

Pulaski threw some money on the bar, swigged down the rest of the Wild Turkey, and left the half-eaten sandwich. Chris Singleton and his surveillance crew now had a new job and the work would have to start tonight. Pulaski's entire hypothesis was a gamble based on Mr. X still being in town and the girl returning.

He had to find Mr. X.

Nashville—Tuesday, May 25, 1943

Dorothy Nolan sat at a small coffee table in her apartment sharing a lunch of fried bologna sandwiches, applesauce, and coffee with Helen Gray. Helen returned over a week ago and had healed quickly. The swelling in her face was gone and only remnants of the facial cuts remained. Her ribs, although still sore, did not bother her nearly as much as when she first appeared at Dorothy's door.

It had been two days since Dorothy came across the shocking picture of Helen on the front page of the newspaper. Those two days passed while Dorothy avoided asking Helen about the photograph. No question remained in Dorothy's mind that the woman in the photo was Helen, and, surprising to Dorothy, she was not scared. She was not sure why she had not confronted Helen until now, but, as they ate, Dorothy laid the page of the newspaper on the table between them.

"I was afraid you would see it," admitted Helen. "I saw it at a newsstand when I went grocery shopping the other day. I'm glad I went back to blond, aren't you?"

"What does it mean, Helen? Why would they put your picture in the paper and accuse you of being a spy?"

Helen looked at Dorothy then used a drink of coffee to give herself a moment.

"Because I am a spy, Dorothy. And my name is not Helen Gray. It's Erika Lehmann."

Evansville—Wednesday, May 26, 1943

"All the hotels, motor courts, and apartment buildings of any size in Evansville or within an hour's drive have been checked for anyone with a foreign accent, sir."

Agent Chris Singleton sat in Pulaski's office in the shipyard administration building. "It went quickly," Singleton continued. "Luckily, there doesn't seem to be many foreigners in this area. We came across only five people with an accent noticeable enough to have come to the attention of the staffs at these places. Mr. X isn't among them. All five are registered with the Bureau of Immigration, and none remotely fit the description from the Boston bartender. The only one of the five who is not a U.S. citizen is a fifty-year-old Italian woman from Little Rock staying in a little motel across the river in Henderson, Kentucky. She's here visiting her daughter who works at the Thunderbolt factory."

Pulaski sat back in his chair and reached for a cigarette. He too had beat the local bushes since Monday, and Singleton was right—not many foreigners in this part of southern Indiana. Although a German heritage was common among the local citizenry, the number of German language speakers who would have an accent when speaking English was comparatively small.

As always, Singleton did his job well. But checking hotels and apartment buildings was the easy part. Now the real grunt work lay before them: finding and knocking on the doors of the myriad locals who supplemented household incomes by renting an extra bedroom, basement room, or jerry-rigged attic apartment in this housing-starved city. Pulaski knew it would prove exhausting and time-consuming.

Pulaski had no doubt a front page story asking locals to call the FBI if they knew the whereabouts of a stranger with a heavy foreign accent could bring a lead from the patriotic locals, but it was out of the question. The only card Pulaski held was the fact Mr. X did not know he was hunted.

"Okay, Agent Singleton. Agent Falasco has cleared four more agents to work with you. He's pulled them from the background check team. That should help a bit. Let's stay hard on this one. Time is critical, as you know. You have the lists of locals who are known to be renting a room in their home?"

"Yes, sir."

"If you run across any potential suspects, take them in for questioning immediately. Tell your men to be careful; this guy is no one to fool around with. Be sure your men work in pairs and one keeps an eye on the back of the dwelling while the other knocks on the door."

"Got it. You can count on us, Agent Pulaski."

"I know I can, Singleton. So if there aren't any questions, might as well get back on it."

After Singleton walked out the door, Pulaski pivoted his chair around to face a window drummed by rain. Between streams of water falling to the sill he looked out to the shipyard still busy, the mighty river chopped by rain, and the Kentucky wood on the far bank. He stared long enough for the forgotten Lucky between his fingers to burn a long ash that broke off and fell to the wood floor.

Am I right? Are you still out there? What could I be missing? Where in the hell are you, you sonuvabitch?

One hour later, Pulaski knocked on Joe Mayer's door. Mayer answered with a rubbernecking FBI Agent Dan Engler standing over his shoulder.

"Mr. Mayer…Agent Engler," Pulaski acknowledged both as he stepped in from the rain. Mayer nodded silently and held the door open. Engler also nodded, plus he conveyed a "Hello, Agent Pulaski" to acknowledge his supervisor.

"Things okay, Mr. Mayer?" Pulaski asked for etiquette's sake.

"Swell," Mayer intoned with mock enthusiasm. Pulaski ignored Mayer's sarcasm and turned to Engler.

"Engler, have cabin fever yet?"

"No, sir. Doing fine. Agent Fleck relieves me twice a week during the daytime."

Mayer cut in. "Agent Engler and I get out quite often. We can both quote all the prices at the local grocery by heart. I plan to get a job there bagging groceries when the war's over."

Pulaski smiled.

"Have patience, Mr. Mayer," Pulaski advised. "For what it's worth, I personally believe you'll be exonerated before long and returned to work at the shipyard." Pulaski believed what he said. Although other metallurgists had been brought in to continue Mayer's experiments with the specially processed tellurium, the government knew the child needed the father. Unless new information surfaced to implicate Mayer in a conspiracy to aid the faux Sarah Klein, Pulaski would give odds Mayer would be cleared as soon as the case was resolved.

The three men moved to the kitchen and sat around a table; Pulaski laid his wet trenchcoat on the spare chair. Everyone filled his own cup from a coffee pot on the stove.

"So, Mr. Mayer," Pulaski again did the talking, "anything more come to mind about what we talked about the other day? I asked you if you remember ever seeing anyone hanging around in the background when you were out with the girl. Any stranger that you might have noticed more than once?"

"No," Mayer seemed confident. "I've given it more thought, as you asked, but my answer is the same. I don't recall ever noticing a stranger lurking about when Sar…the woman and I were out together."

"And it was usually just you and the girl, or the two of you with Turnbull and Miss Weiss?"

"Yes, Sarah—I guess I'll have to call her that for lack of anything else—liked going out with Howard and Carol."

Pulaski could see why. After meeting Howard Turnbull, Pulaski cringed at the thought of the indiscreet Turnbull blabbing away in the presence of a German spy.

"And you mainly frequented the places you told me about last time."

"Yes. The restaurants I named, the Trocadero, the Loew's Theater for a movie—the places I listed the other day. Then the time she went fishing with me and Harry Krupsaw, but I told you all of this during my questioning."

"Oh, yeah, the old door guard at your hut," said Pulaski. "He took you and the girl out on the river in his boat but she was nervous because she couldn't swim?"

"That's right," Mayer verified. "So we docked it at Harry's river camp and fished from the bank."

"Catch anything?" Pulaski asked to keep things low-key and to keep Mayer talking, but the FBI man was thinking ahead and not paying attention to Mayer's answer.

"No. As I recall a lightning storm moved in so we went inside Harry's cabin to get away from the water."

"The old boy has a cabin at his camp? Must be nice being rich." Pulaski was still just being polite.

"Well, I don't know if I'd go as far as to call Harry rich. The cabin is rustic to say the least—pretty much like all the others."

"Others?"

"Yeah, the other camps up and down the river. I said Harry's is much like the rest."

"Do many of the camps have cabins?" Pulaski's attention no longer wandered.

"Yeah, about all of them do. I told you about going with the girl to Harry's river camp in the deposition, Agent Pulaski."

"Yes, but I assumed a river camp was just a place where you pitched a tent or something. You say these cabins run up and down the river?"

"Yeah, for miles each way once you get out of the city."

"So the owners keep them locked up and just use them for fishing?"

"Some keep them locked up, but some people live year around at their camp according to Harry. Harry used to rent his out but stopped doing that a couple of years ago."

"Why was that?"

Mayer had to think. "Harry said something about too hard to find decent renters. His last renter tore up the place. Harry wanted a married couple; he says a couple takes better care of the place. But Harry's camp was pretty isolated and no women wanted to live there—the women thought it was too spooky, especially at night. So Harry quit renting it out, just keeps it locked up now."

"But some of the other camps are rented out?"

"Yeah, I guess."

Forty-five minutes later, Harry Krupsaw had been summoned from Quonset Hut 11 and now sat giving directions in the passenger seat of Pulaski's Oldsmobile. The rain had stopped and a thick bright rainbow spanned the river, its pot of gold somewhere in the Kentucky wood.

The old security guard pointed. "Turn here."

Pulaski turned the wheel to the left and guided the car down a narrow farm road that mimicked the twists and turns of the river that flowed no more than the length of a football field away. As was common in spring, the river ran high, and here or there spilled its banks to submerge the country road. At low spots along the way, Pulaski was forced to slow the Olds to a crawl and pilot through three or four inches of water.

Krupsaw was an enthusiastic tour guide.

"Most of this good bottom land belongs to farmers. It's all good land for watermelons and cantaloupe, lots of corn too as you can see over there." The old man pointed to the right. Pulaski glanced at the acres of young corn stalks, but his interest lay to the left, to the narrow forest along the river where the camps were.

The distance between cabins varied greatly. Some were as close as thirty yards, others too far apart to be aware of one another. Some sat elevated on pillars to compensate for the river when it ran amok; others sat on the ground.

"How far down river do these camps go?" asked Pulaski.

"Oh, way down, as far as the river goes, I reckon."

"And some people live in these places full time?"

"You bet," said Krupsaw. "Some of the cabins are really nice: electricity, indoor plumbing, the works. Some are just shacks. Some folks who own them live in them; some rent them out to other folks. Most owners would rather have them occupied—at least in the winter when they're not using them. Keeps out burglars and unruly young-uns who break in looking for hooch. I use to rent mine, but the last guy just about ruined the place, so I just lock it up tight now and take my chances. Besides, I'm down here almost every weekend, even in the winter."

Six miles west of town, Krupsaw pointed out his camp and Pulaski turned in. The cabin sat on pillars seven feet off the ground and no more than thirty yards from the river; Krupsaw and Pulaski walked directly under the structure. A homemade wooden raft with attached empty oil drums to increase flotation sat on dry land beside the cabin. A fifteen-foot johnboat sat chained to a tree just out of the water.

"This is where you brought Joe Mayer and Sarah Klein to fish?" It was the first time Pulaski had mentioned the names.

"Hey, that's right! How did you know that?"

"Joe Mayer told me."

"Hey, what's going on with Joe? I haven't seen him at work for over a week now."

"He's been sick. Bad case of the flu."

"That's too bad. Nice young feller. Joe and me went fishin' down here pretty often."

"What can you tell me about the girl, Sarah Klein?" asked Pulaski.

"I only met her the one time but she seemed real nice. I think Joe's real struck on her. She didn't like the boat though," the old man chuckled, "said she can't swim a lick."

Pulaski had seen enough. These places would be perfect for a foreign agent with poor English like Mr. X. The river camps were close enough to town for frequent access, yet remote enough to keep mingling with locals to a minimum. Back in the car, Pulaski drove a few more miles down the river road, then turned around and headed back. Singleton and his crew were starting to check small-time landlords in town, and that work had to continue. If Singleton came up with no leads in town, Pulaski decided checking out these river camps would be next on the list.

On their way back to town they drove by a tavern Pulaski had noticed passing earlier from the other direction. The sign read *Dogtown Tavern* and the place sat lonely on the road—the only road to the river bottoms.

"Ever stop in there, Harry?"

"Sure. Good food there and it's the only place in the bottoms. Great fiddlers."

"Fiddlers? They have a band there?"

Krupsaw snorted loudly at the city-slicker from Chicago. "No, son. Fiddlers are breaded catfish fried in oil or lard. Don't tell me you've never had fiddlers."

"Nope, sorry to say I've never had fiddlers." Pulaski drove on for a moment as he thought about the Dogtown Tavern. Krupsaw said the place was the only eating establishment in the area. Pulaski slowed the car.

"Why don't we try some now," Pulaski suggested as he turned the car around on the narrow road and backtracked.

Pulaski guided the Olds into the gravel parking lot. As the two men walked toward the tavern door, Harry Krupsaw pointed to a water line stain about six feet up the exterior wall.

"The big flood of '37," said Krupsaw.

Inside, Krupsaw led Pulaski to a table the old man considered his favorite, then greeted the middle-aged waitress by name as she delivered beers to three men nearby. The waitress returned the old man's greeting then moved to his table.

"What will it be, Harry?"

"A mess of fiddlers, Hazel. My friend here's from Chicago, and he's never had fiddlers." Harry smiled at the waitress like what he said was almost unbelievable. Hazel cast a suspicious eye at the weird man who had never eaten fiddlers. "What to drink?" she asked.

"Pabst Blue Ribbon," Pulaski ordered the beer.

"We've got a special on Sterling."

"That's fine," said Pulaski. Krupsaw ordered the same.

The catfish dish was a popular one at *Dogtown* and was delivered to the table in short order.

"Joe caught a twenty-five-pound flathead catfish one time," Krupsaw told Charlie as they dug in. Pulaski had fished little since he was a kid and had a hard time visualizing a twenty-five-pound fish.

"That's big," Pulaski remarked.

"Not bad, but about five years ago a friend of mine pulled a fifty-pounder out of the river near Mt. Vernon. Pulaski thought the old man might be telling him a fish story until Krupsaw pointed to a picture hanging among many on the wall. A man in the photograph stood cradling the leviathan in his arms like a giant newborn. Other photos showed more catfish, some even larger, alongside proud sportsmen.

The fiddlers of the Dogtown Tavern were delicious, and most were consumed by the time Harry Krupsaw excused himself to the restroom.

"The beer and an old bladder," Harry explained unnecessarily, but it was a good time for Pulaski to flag down the waitress. If by chance Mr. X was staying in one of the river camp cabins, he would have to pass by this place every time he drove to and from town.

"Everything, okay?" Hazel said as she responded to Pulaski waving her over.

"Fine, Hazel," answered Pulaski pleasantly. "Say, I'm looking for an old friend of mine. Foreign fellow, talks with an accent. Loves catfish, and I thought he might have stopped in."

Hazel frowned. "You mean Ivan?"

Pulaski almost dropped his fork. He felt the hair on the back of his neck bristle.

"Yeah, Ivan." Pulaski tried to say the name like he was happy to hear it.

"He's a friend of yours?" Hazel sounded surprised.

"Yes, an old buddy from way back. Why do you ask?"

Hazel shrugged. "He doesn't seem like the type to have many friends. Sits off by himself. He gives me the creeps."

Good Lord! Pulaski's mind raced. *Could it be? Ivan*—a Russian cover; it would make sense.

"When was the last time he was in?" Pulaski asked excitedly. "And please think carefully."

"Don't be so nervous," Hazel admonished. "You'll have one of those heart attacks. He's still around. He was in this afternoon, left no more than half an hour before you and Harry pulled in."

CHAPTER 40

Often an entire city has suffered because of an evil man.

—*Hesiod, ca. 8th century B.C.*

Evansville—Wednesday, May 26, 1943

The day Charlie Pulaski walked into the Dogtown Tavern would be Hazel the waitress's last day on the job for a while. Hazel's *Ivan* was currently the top candidate to be Mr. X (right now the only candidate), and, if Ivan were his man, Pulaski could not take the chance that the waitress might let something slip the next time Ivan stopped in. Hazel underwent questioning at Pulaski's shipyard office, a description of Ivan taken, then she was sent on her way with instructions to go nowhere near the *Dogtown* and speak to no one about her questioning—or about Ivan. Before she left, Pulaski promised the worried woman her lost wages would be reimbursed by the Bureau.

The *Dogtown* opened from eleven a.m. until nine and not at all on Sunday. The stakeout would be full-time during the tavern's open hours. During questioning, Hazel told Pulaski that Ivan stopped in irregularly. He might be in two or three days in a row, at various times of the day, then not be seen for a week or more.

Checking for leads in Evansville should continue, there was no guarantee Ivan was Mr. X, but Falasco would have to come up with another team to take over that task. Pulaski planned to pull Chris Singleton and his crew off that detail and have Singleton assign some of his men to check land deeds and identify owners of the river camps, then locate and question them to see if any had rented a cabin to a man with a foreign accent. In addition, Singleton and the remaining members of his team would serve as backup to the stakeout at the Dogtown Tavern.

Before the day was out, Pulaski returned to the Dogtown with a new waitress, a twenty-six-year-old Navy WAVE named SuzAnn Miller. Yeoman First Class Miller was the only female member of Commander Forister's shipyard security crew. Pulaski gave the tavern's owner a few sketchy details about the Bureau looking for a bank robber suspected of being in the area. The owner was a salty old cuss who was happy to do his civic duty, and the fact the old man's tavern would for a while have a pretty young waitress he would not have to pay did not hurt Pulaski's cause. When employees or regular customers asked about Hazel, Pulaski coached the old man to tell them Hazel was called away to nurse a sick relative and SuzAnn was a temporary replacement. Other than those basics the old man was told no more and his employees told nothing. Hazel seemed sure the old man, who spent most afternoons behind the bar until the night bartender went on duty, could point out Ivan, but Pulaski decided against getting the old man involved further. If Ivan was Mr. X they were dealing with a killer; people could get hurt if the old man was not discreet. It should not be hard for SuzAnn Miller to recognize Ivan: Hazel had supplied a decent description and confirmed that his English was rudimentary and his accent thick.

Pulaski hated stakeouts. Like most lawmen he found the endless hours of waiting for something that might never happen arduous. In this case, however, the leads had been so scanty, Pulaski felt like he operated more like a sleepwalker than an investigator, going about business in the dark with only hunches to guide him, so he now welcomed anything concrete even if it took a stakeout.

Let the waiting began. 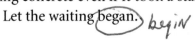 begin

In dungarees and with fishing hat complete with hooks and fishing flies, Charlie Pulaski spent Thursday afternoon and evening in the Dogtown Tavern sitting at a small table near the back. Chris Singleton, also in outdoor wear, occupied a barstool near the front door.

The tavern presented several logistical problems for a stakeout, the most problematic of which was the flat farmland and wide-open spaces surrounding the establishment. Outside were no places of concealment near enough for additional agents to supply prompt backup. Since Pulaski could not risk loading up the inside with agents (Mr. X, a quasi-regular customer and a professional at his trade, would notice any abnormal number of "customers"), it would be up to Pulaski, Chris Singleton, and SuzAnn Miller.

All day Friday they waited.

Saturday the same. No sign of Ivan, but Pulaski was getting well acquainted with fiddlers, and SuzAnn Miller was getting great experience at honing her waitressing skills.

Sunday the place was closed, and Falasco called Pulaski in for a meeting. When Pulaski entered the Bureau's conference room at the Sonntag Hotel, Harry Fallon, Pulaski's old friend from the Chicago office, sat in a chair across from Falasco.

"Hey, Charlie," Fallon greeted loudly. Both men smiled and exchanged a handshake.

"Harry, what brings you down this way?" Pulaski already had a suspicion why his old friend was here.

"Elliott sent me down to check your weight," Fallon joked and everyone laughed. "Looks like you've picked up a few pounds."

"I've been eating too many fiddlers."

Fallon had no idea what kind of food that was but saw an opportunity for a laugh. "Well, don't eat them all, leave a few for the philharmonic."

A tired looking Dave Falasco took over. "Charlie, Agent Elliott has sent Agent Fallon down for a first hand appraisal of our situation and particularly your involvement in the taskforce operation here in

Evansville. I've briefed Agent Fallon on your stakeout and our other efforts to this point." Falasco paused and loaded some papers into a briefcase, "I've put in another request to Agent Elliott that he allow you to remain on the case indefinitely. So far I have received no reply, but maybe you and Agent Fallon here can settle the matter."

Two hours later Pulaski and Harry Fallon had both finished a mutton stew in the restaurant of the Sonntag. The waiter refilled their coffee cups.

"Not bad," Fallon testified as he scraped the last bit of stew from the bottom of the bowl.

"Good food down here," said Pulaski. "Some of it's kind of weird. A local favorite is brain sandwiches."

Fallon stared at Pulaski. "What do you mean, 'brain'?"

"Brain," Pulaski repeated. "You know, that thing you don't have any of."

"Whose brains?" Fallon ignored the joke.

"Cow, I think."

"Ugh!"

"You can also get squirrel and possum meat at some of the barbecue joints down here," Pulaski added.

"You're crappin' in my hat, Pulaski."

"Nope."

"Get me out of here," Fallon quipped.

Pulaski chuckled. "The place kind of grows on you after a while. Good, salt of the earth people down here."

"Man, I need to get you back to Chicago." Fallon paused, then said seriously: "Which is exactly what will happen, Charlie, unless you can convince Elliott you're pursuing something solid down here. Falasco has you only on loan, Charlie. Elliott has the final say. Don't forget that. The only person that can overrule Elliott concerning your involvement in this case is the big dog in Washington. Charlie, your last four cases have been goose eggs, and with the FCC report about the fingerprint transmission leaving the area, Elliott figures you're involved in another bust. He thinks you're riding shotgun for another wild goose chase. As far as what Hoover thinks, who knows? It's always hard to get a line on Washington, but I know for a fact the only reason Falasco and some of his men are still here is for mop up."

"Falasco said he briefed you on my stakeout. Tell Elliott about that."

"Charlie, you're not paying attention. Think about it. The transmission you were sent here to investigate is now coming from two states away. You've been sitting on your ass at a bar, or restaurant—whatever the hell that place is out in the sticks—for three days now because a waitress told you one of her customers has a foreign accent. How am I supposed to keep Elliott off your ass with that, for Christ's sake?"

Pulaski stared across the room and rubbed a stubble of beard. He had refrained from shaving for the past couple of days because he thought he looked more fishermanlike. Pulaski said nothing.

Fallon: "Give me something solid to take back to Elliott, Charlie. It's either that or I have to take you back to Chicago with me."

Pulaski went through his list of hunches. He explained to Harry why he thought the case should not be closed in Evansville, about why he thought Mr. X was still in town and why *Sarah Klein* was coming back.

Fallon looked away and slowly shook his head. "Charlie, I'll call Elliott tomorrow morning and say what I can, but I think you better start packing."

Henderson, Kentucky—Tuesday, June 1, 1943

The shabby room in the fleabag motel called the Betz Motor Inn was perfect. Henderson, Kentucky, was just across the river from Evansville, and none of the down-on-their-luck motel residents, or the drunkard who assigned the rooms, was the least bit curious about the young woman who registered last night.

Gazing in the cracked mirror over the rust-stained lavatory sink, Erika Lehmann wondered how much the different hair would help. Her *bob* was gone in favor of a cold wave, and Sarah Klein's raven color was now blond. Stodgy was the desired look so she had darkened the blond color a bit more until now it was what the Americans called *dishwater* blond. She tried on a pair of horn-rimmed glasses—the frumpiest-looking pair Nashville had to offer. She thought for a moment: a scarf should help. The look should fool strangers if Sarah Klein's shipyard picture had been published in the local newspaper, but for anyone who knew her, the disguise would probably work only from a distance. It was the best she could do.

Finding out the location of the phone whose number Ryker had given her was a simple matter of dialing the number and waiting until someone answered. Erika knew Ryker would not use a phone where he was staying; it would be a pay phone or a phone in a restaurant, bar—a public place. Shortly after arriving in Nashville Erika dialed the number. It rang for a long time, but eventually a waitress answered and Erika had the location. The phone was in a tavern and she wanted to check the place out. Risky but necessary. Erika did not want to meet Ryker in a place she had never before been.

✠   ✠   ✠

Evansville [that afternoon]

Last night had been another restless one for Pulaski. Dillinger did not visit, but Pulaski spent most of the night in a chair gaping out the window. Earlier that day, Preston Elliott ordered Pulaski off the case and gave him until Wednesday to report back to the home office in Chicago. Dave Falasco kept Pulaski at the hotel all day Monday writing reports;

Falasco told him to use Tuesday to clean out his office at the shipyard and tie up any other loose ends. So that was what Pulaski did. After thanking Steven Forister, the shipyard security chief, for his cooperation, Pulaski loaded a box of odds and ends from his desk into the trunk of the Olds and drove out of the shipyard. As simple as that it was over.

Pulaski had not been back to the Dogtown Tavern. The stakeout was canceled. Falasco thought the lead on Ivan was credible enough to pursue, but he redirected the efforts from the stakeout to locating and questioning owners of the river camps. So Chris Singleton and his men had spent the past two days at the downtown courthouse pouring over land deeds, then fanning out to call on the landowners. Pulaski was glad Singleton had been left on the case; Singleton was a good man. Tonight, after Singleton returned to the Sonntag, Pulaski would look up the young agent and say goodbye.

Harry Fallon was probably right, Pulaski told himself as he turned the Olds into the Sonntag's parking lot. His reasoning for the stakeout and his entire speculation that Mr. X was still in town was likely crocked. This would be Pulaski's fifth case in a row that came up bust. Maybe it was time to retire. He had three weeks of vacation time built up and had already decided that when he got back to Chicago he would take some time off and mull things over. *Be glad they still think enough of you to send you, Charlie. Past deeds only count for so much, for so long.* Fallon had said it that day in Chicago and he was right.

The sooner I'm out of this goddamn town the better, if for no other reason than to get some sleep, Pulaski told himself. It would be good to get back home to Chicago.

That evening, just before closing, Hazel stacked chairs upside-down on tables so the floor could be mopped. She was glad to be back at work at the *Dogtown*. A young FBI man she had never seen before came by her house Monday morning to tell her the bankrobber was not Ivan. The real criminal had been apprehended in Ohio and she could now return to work. When the last customer walked out the door, Hazel retrieved a key from behind the bar and was about to lock the door when it opened from the outside.

"Is it too late for a quick drink?" It was a woman.

"Ah...I guess not," Hazel stammered then stepped aside so the woman could enter. The *Dogtown* did not count very many lone females among its clientele.

Hazel had never seen the woman before but she had seen enough "Rosie the Riveters" to know this woman was one who had obviously just gotten off work: glasses, a scarf covering most of her hair, smudges on her face, the heavy masculine clothing.

"The kitchen is closed, ma'am," Hazel said. "What would you like to drink?"

"Schlitz."

Hazel placed the order with the bartender who was busy cleaning behind the bar. She delivered the beer to the woman, then went about her business. Hazel gave the woman's restroom a quick cleaning, and when she emerged the woman was gone: the glass of beer half full, the money left on the table. Hazel locked the door.

Close to ten that evening Pulaski dropped by Chris Singleton's room. The two men took the elevator to the lobby, then walked to the hotel lounge. They sat at the bar.

"What time are you leaving tomorrow?" Chris Singleton asked after beers were ordered.

"Late morning. I have to turn in the car at eleven, then Falasco is driving me and Harry Fallon to the airport," Pulaski then turned to the bartender who had just sat down two tall glasses of draft beer. "Put them both on my tab." Pulaski took a long quaff of beer, sat the glass down, then began cracking peanuts from a bowl the bartender sat between the two men.

"Agent Pulaski," Singleton hesitated.

"Call me Charlie."

"Charlie, I'm glad my first real case was under you...you've taught me a great deal and I appreciate it. For what it's worth I think they're making a mistake pulling you off the case."

Pulaski cracked another peanut before turning to Singleton.

"Chris, you remind me of me when I first joined the Bureau—only you're smarter. I'm glad the Bureau still has young men like you who want to sign up."

There was an awkward moment as is typical between men when they find themselves in a situation where sentiment is mandated.

"Well," Pulaski broke the uneasiness, "enough of that bullshit." Both men laughed. "How did your day go?" Pulaski regretted the question immediately; the last thing he wanted to hear about was the Sarah Klein case.

"I had most of my men checking out owners of any land where one of those river camps might be found. We've been finding that quite a few of the owners live out of state; getting in touch with them is time consuming. Most of them employ locals to manage their property but there is no record of whom that is so we have to contact the person whose name is on the deed. We came across one who lives in Florida, another in Missouri—you get the picture. Several others, who are locals, have not been at home after several phone calls or visits—that sort of thing. You know how it is. Finding Ivan this way is going to take some time I'm afraid."

Pulaski finished his beer then ordered another round even though Singleton had barely touched his. Then he tried to change the subject. "The paper today said the Limeys plastered Cologne with 900 bombers. Something new. *Saturation bombing* they call it. Instead of concentrating on a specific military target they just head to a city and try to blow up everything and everybody."

"Yeah, I saw that," Singleton replied. "I hate the thought of women and little kids being blown up, but the lousy Krauts started it—bombing London and all."

Pulaski nodded absentmindedly, glad he had redirected the flow of the conversation. But Singleton was not finished and abruptly pulled a U-turn.

"I went by the Dogtown Tavern for a few hours this afternoon while my men were running checks…yesterday, too."

"Oh, yeah?" Pulaski fidgeted with his glass. "Why?"

"I don't know," Singleton did not want to admit it was because of respect for Pulaski and he went there hoping he might get lucky and Mr. X, a.k.a. Ivan, walk through the door. "Habit, maybe. You and I sat in there last week for so long maybe my ass was having withdrawal pains."

Pulaski laughed at the joke.

Singleton continued: "I was there for the lunch crowd both days but I had to leave by three to meet my men back here for daily reports."

"I bet SuzAnn Miller is glad to be done with that assignment," Pulaski quipped. "I think she was getting tired of propositions from toothless farmers."

Before continuing, Chris Singleton swallowed some of his first beer as the second sat warming on the bar in front of him. "Charlie, you know how you told me to pay close attention to deviations, even very minor ones, when I'm on a case?"

"Yes."

"This is probably nothing, but today when I was in the Dogtown the phone in that phone booth in the back rang for a long time." Singleton looked at Pulaski, "Do you know the one I'm talking about? The customer's phone in the back of the bar."

Pulaski remembered. It was a booth with a folding wooden door. "Yes."

"Do you remember it ever ringing last week when we were there?"

Pulaski thought for a moment. "No."

"Right. I don't remember it ringing last week either. I remember the other phone, the one at the bar, ringing last week. That's the business number; I checked it out. But the phone booth phone, never. I even asked the waitress, Hazel, and the owner. They both told me that phone never rings. People in the bar use the phone booth to call out on, but no one ever calls that number."

"What's your point?" Pulaski asked.

"The phone rang yesterday at one o'clock. The only reason I know the time is because I had just walked in the place and I recorded the time in my log as 1256 hours when I got out of my car to go in the place. Anyway, I probably wouldn't have paid any attention to a ringing telephone but the bartender made a big deal out of it. He seemed real surprised. When he answered it, he slammed down the receiver and cursed because whoever was on the other end hung up without saying anything. Then today the same thing happened—the call and the hang up when someone, this time Hazel, answered it. Today the phone rang at exactly two o'clock. I looked at my watch this time. Yesterday at exactly one; today at exactly two. Then a hang up when it was answered."

Singleton stopped and waited for Pulaski's reaction. Pulaski gazed into his glass.

"It's probably nothing," Singleton finally admitted.

Evansville—Wednesday, June 2, 1943

"Where in hell is he?" asked Harry Fallon as he looked at his watch.

"I don't know," Dave Falasco answered.

Both men referred to Charlie Pulaski. Falasco was supposed to meet Pulaski and Fallon at eleven in the lobby of the Sonntag Hotel, collect the keys to Pulaski's government issued car, then drive the men to the airport for a flight to Chicago. It was a quarter to twelve and Pulaski had not showed. Nor was he in his hotel room or at his shipyard office. Falasco had checked.

It would be late that evening before Charlie Pulaski allowed himself to be found.

Just after noon, perhaps twelve-thirty, Pulaski took a seat near the back of the Dogtown Tavern. During yet another night of sporadic sleep, he had tried to disregard what Chris Singleton told him about the ringing telephone, but in the end it was impossible to ignore. So here Pulaski sat. Singleton's account of the phone calls—Monday at exactly one o'clock, Tuesday at two—was a curse Pulaski had to break. Knowing what Falasco and Harry Fallon would say to any request to remain in town and on the case, Pulaski did not bother asking.

When Chris Singleton walked through the Dogtown door a few minutes before two, Singleton was more surprised to see Pulaski than vice versa. Pulaski had a feeling the plebe agent from Salt Lake City would show. Singleton was a born cop; Pulaski realized that the first time they met. Only a good investigator would have questioned the ringing telephone. Pulaski waved Singleton back to his table.

"Agent Pulaski," greeted Singleton, "I see you changed their minds," obviously referring to Falasco and Preston Elliott.

"Yeah," Pulaski lied.

Both men knew why the other was there. With good luck Ivan might drop in; with great good luck Ivan would be Mr. X and arrive to answer the phone. If neither happened, they were there to at least find out if the phone rang mysteriously on schedule.

The phone booth was at the back of the tavern and just a few feet from Pulaski's table. Customers left and came. Singleton briefed Pulaski on the latest.

"For a brief moment this morning I thought we might have a lead," Singleton told Pulaski. "One of my men came across a farmer who owns some land by the river and rents out two separate river camps. My man reached this guy on the phone and the farmer confirmed that he rents to a foreigner. He said the renter and his family work his fields. When he mentioned 'family' I figured it was a bust, but we checked it out and found a family of nine Mexican farm workers living in a one-bedroom cabin with an out house. Terrible conditions."

Time passed. Lunch finished. Hazel came by to pick up plates and refill glasses of iced tea. When first Pulaski and then Chris Singleton had walked through the door, Hazel was understandably inquisitive but Pulaski assured her they were there for the fiddlers and nothing more. Pulaski had his glass upturned when the telephone in the booth rang.

The glass went back to the table quickly. Pulaski looked at his watch: two minutes after three. Singleton's watch read three sharp, no *Ivan* types in the place, the mid-afternoon crowd sparse. Three men, all very American and sufficiently loud to assure the FBI agents the only accent among them was Hoosier, sat at a table. A man who was seventy if a day sat at the bar. No one else. Hazel started toward the phone booth but was intercepted by Pulaski.

"Hazel, don't answer it yet," Pulaski ordered quickly. "Have a seat with us for a minute, would you please?"

Hazel looked bewildered but obeyed.

The two FBI men and the Dogtown waitress sat in silence for several long moments as the phone rang. Aware that Hazel's Ivan was not among the Dogtown clientele, Pulaski was curious to determine the commitment of the caller. He let the phone ring at least thirty times: so long that the old man at the bar griped to the bartender. Finally, Pulaski instructed Hazel to answer the phone, and he followed her to the booth.

"Pick up the phone, Hazel," Pulaski coached, "just say 'hello.' Don't identify yourself or the tavern, then hand the phone to me." Hazel did as she was told then Pulaski quickly snatched the receiver from her and put it to his ear.

Silence at both ends. Pulaski guessed—no, in his heart he *knew*—that the woman, *Sarah Klein,* sat listening at the other end.

A long moment passed.

Finally, at the other end, Erika Lehmann hung up the telephone.

CHAPTER 41

I do not mean to deny that there are varieties in the race of man, distinguished by their powers both of body and mind. I believe there are, as I see to be the case in the races of other animals.

—*Thomas Jefferson, 1784*

Evansville—Wednesday, June 2, 1943

There were fewer repercussions for his disregard of Preston Elliott's orders than Charlie Pulaski expected. Pulaski was expecting at the very least an official reprimand and perhaps even being asked for his badge. To counter he would request the three weeks of vacation time he had coming and stay in town on his own.

None of those scenarios came about.

That evening, shortly after he arrived back in his hotel room, Pulaski answered the knock on his door. In the hall stood Dave Falasco alongside J. Edgar Hoover and another man Pulaski had never seen before. All three walked into Pulaski's room without waiting to be invited. Hoover lowered himself into a chair; Pulaski and the other two men stood.

"Sit down, gentlemen," Hoover gave the order like it was his room before directing his attention to Pulaski. "Hello, Agent Pulaski, it has been a long time." Hoover did not offer his hand.

"Hello, Director Hoover. Yes, it has been a while."

Pulaski had not seen Hoover since shortly after Pearl Harbor and then only for a quick handshake and the pep talk Hoover delivered to a large gathering of agents in Washington. Hoover's speech was on the importance of the Bureau's role now that the country had entered the war. The last one-on-one conversation Pulaski shared with Hoover took place shortly after Dillinger's death in 1934.

Hoover emphasized he was in town incognito: the press were not to be notified and conversations concerning his visit were not to leave the room.

Pulaski knew Hoover had not made the trek from Washington solely to chastise him. That business would not draw J. Edgar Hoover to Evansville. Agents were ordered to Washington and Hoover did his ass chewing from behind his massive desk. Besides, Pulaski had not disobeyed his orders until today. Hoover would not be here this soon.

Hoover told Pulaski that he had followed the case closely from Washington with regular updates from Falasco. Included in those reports was Pulaski's theory that Sarah Klein would return to the area. The woman's trail had cooled since the transmission from Tennessee, so Hoover was ready to listen. For the next thirty minutes Pulaski had the floor and finished with the story of the mysterious ringing phone at the Dogtown Tavern. Hoover stood and paced the floor for several moments after Pulaski finished talking.

"Gentlemen," said Hoover. "Here's what we'll do."

Yeoman First Class SuzAnn Miller's waitressing days were not over after all. With a dead trail and no other leads to work with, Hoover put Pulaski back on the case. The first thing Pulaski did was place Hazel back on waitress sabbatical and SuzAnn back on the job. Pulaski and Chris Singleton would not be inside the tavern. Hoover reasoned that if Mr. X had Sarah Klein under his own surveillance, X might recognize

Singleton from the surveillance on Joseph Mayer, and Pulaski from the encounter in the Trocadero.

SuzAnn Miller would be on her own inside the Dogtown Tavern. Her job: to identify Mr. X and give the agreed upon signal if he appeared. Pulaski, Singleton, and two other agents would monitor the building with high power binoculars and photographic equipment while concealed in a wooded area a half mile away. With flat farmland surrounding the tavern it was as close as they could get.

Mr. X would be allowed to receive his phone call undisturbed. The phone would be tapped, and if a meeting between the spies was arranged the taskforce would know where to pick up Sarah Klein. Regardless, no more chances would be taken with Mr. X. He would be allowed to leave the tavern—confronting the killer inside the tavern could prove dangerous for innocent onlookers. Teams of agents hidden at strategic spots down the road would set up road blocks and intercept Mr. X after he left the Dogtown. The remoteness that made the Dogtown advantageous for Mr. X's purposes would now aid the FBI—only one road passed by the tavern.

All was ready hours ahead of time on Thursday. SuzAnn Miller waited tables and Pulaski and his men stared through large binoculars and fought off mosquitos in the soggy wood across the cornfield while other agents sat hidden in cars just off the road two miles away ready to respond to Pulaski's radio call. Thursday came and went with no sign of Ivan. The only consolation was the phone in the Dogtown phone booth ringing at exactly four o'clock.

✠   ✠   ✠

Friday, June 4, 1943

Axel Ryker walked into the Dogtown Tavern at ten minutes past four. If the Abwehr girl followed instructions she should call at five. Ryker sat at a table near the back of the bar—next to the telephone booth.

Ryker had not been in this place in almost two weeks, but he noticed the new waitress immediately as she approached his table.

"What can I get you?" she asked.

"Beer and a vodka," Ryker ordered. Not many locals drank straight vodka but Ryker had no need to adjust his ordering in an attempt to fit in; his Russian accent made any attempts to pass himself off as a local impossible. "Where is the other waitress?"

"Oh, Hazel? She had to take some time off to care for a sick relative." SuzAnn Miller moved quickly and returned in a moment with Ryker's drinks.

Always suspicious, Ryker was wary of any deviations to routine (the same advice Pulaski had not long ago given Chris Singleton). Ryker watched the new waitress closely. She made no suspicious moves and went about her business, stopping to laugh with a group of men at a nearby table. Ryker scanned the room. He remembered some of the faces.

Ryker drank slowly and by the end of his second round the telephone rang. Five o'clock. Ryker glanced around the room one more time, then rose, entered the phone booth, and closed the folding door behind him.

Through his binoculars Charlie Pulaski watched the window shade lower. When a man walked out of the front door, the window shade went back up; Pulaski was proud of the young WAVE who had obviously remained cool under extreme pressure. Pulaski watched the man get in his car, then waited until he saw which way the car headed. The FBI men broke and ran (Singleton and the other agents ran, the overweight Pulaski huffed and puffed) through the woods to Pulaski's car.

It took the FBI men a minute to get to Pulaski's car, then another half-minute for the car to reach the road from its hiding place in a grove of trees. Pulaski floored the Olds and sped down the road while Singleton radioed his men that Mr. X was driving a dark green 1938 Chrysler and instructed them to set up the roadblocks. Pulaski knew Mr. X would be in custody by the time he and the other agents reached the road block a couple of miles down the winding dirt road. Pulaski churned a dirt cloud as he steered the Olds around a curve. He spotted the road block up ahead, but not the green Chrysler. Pulaski skidded the Olds to a stop just feet from one of the roadblock vehicles.

"Where's the car?" Pulaski shouted at agents still hunched for cover behind their cars with guns drawn.

"Yours is the first car to come this way since you radioed!" a young agent, one of Singleton's men, called out. Pulaski slammed the gear shift lever into reverse and spun gravel as he turned the car around. They sped back passed the Dogtown and toward the road block at the other end thinking Mr. X must have turned around while they ran through the woods to Pulaski's car. The story was the same at the other end. Mr. X, and his car, had apparently vanished into thin air. Pulaski ordered the agents to maintain the road block and he had Singleton radio the other road block the same instructions while he again turned the car around. This time he drove slowly. To the left were stands of trees and the Ohio River within a few hundred yards, to the right mostly open farmland stretching for miles. The sharp eyes of Chris Singleton were the first to spot the Chrysler parked down by the river, almost hidden from view by the trees.

Pulaski turned off the road and bumped and scraped the bottom of the Olds across the washboard terrain until he had to slow so much that travel on foot would be faster. The four men quickly exited the car and Singleton lead the way, sprinting the remainder of the distance with his gun drawn. The winded Pulaski pulled up the rear.

The car was abandoned. On the river, in the far distance, the men spotted a johnboat heading toward the Kentucky shore just before it disappeared around a bend.

"Damn it!" were the first words issued by Pulaski when he got the news. The tape-recorded telephone conversation between Mr. X and Sarah Klein was in *Russian!* Pulaski could only pray that by the time the recording was translated it was not too late. *What if the meeting is tonight?* There was no time to fly a Bureau translator in from Washington. Someone had to be found locally. Inquiries were made and a professor from the local college was unceremoniously shanghaied from his home dinner table by Chris Singleton and raced with sirens screaming to the Sonntag Hotel.

While they waited for Singleton to return with the professor, Falasco just had to mention he was glad Hoover had returned to Washington that morning—before Mr. X was allowed to escape. Pulaski ignored the remark; he had no time to worry about that now. Any pride Pulaski might have felt because he was right about the woman returning to Evansville (the phone call placed to the Dogtown was a local one) was totally negated by the newest predicament they were now in, a predicament that Pulaski would take the heat for.

When Singleton's car skidded to a stop in front of the hotel, the college professor and over a dozen FBI men crowded into the conference room and shut the doors behind them. Two more agents guarded the doors from outside the room. Silence was absolute as the tape played and the professor scribbled notes. The voices were obviously one male and one female; Pulaski felt a shiver go down his spine. When the professor heard the hang up clicks, he asked for the tape to be played again. This time he ordered the tape stopped several times as he checked his notes.

Finally the nervous professor, overwhelmed by the events of the past hour, began. "As you can tell we have a man and a woman. The man speaks the language as if it is his own. The woman's Russian is acceptable, but it's obvious to me it is not her native language." With that the professor ceremoniously cleared his throat and narrated what was said over the phone at the Dogtown Tavern:

Man: *Yes.*
Woman: *It is I.*

"This is where they switch to Russian," the professor interjected unnecessarily.

Man: *We will speak Russian. I know you are qualified.*
Woman: (in Russian) *Continue.*
Man: *Was your task a success?*
Woman: *Yes.*
Man: *Good. Then I assume you have my package.*
Woman: *Yes.*
Man: *I am sure you have visited this place to where you have been calling.*
Woman: *Yes.*
Man: *You will meet me here tomorrow at nine o'clock for the exchange. My package for yours.*
Woman: *No. I will not meet you there.*

"Here is one of those pauses I'm sure you noticed," said the professor. "The man says nothing so the woman continued."

Woman: *I would not feel safe there. I will choose the place. We will meet at the nightclub Trocadero.*
Man: *You will meet where I say if the return of your merchandise is important to you.*
Woman: *I repeat: the Trocadero.*

Professor: "Here is where you hear the second silence, the longer one."

Man:　　　*As you wish. Nine o'clock. Do not be late.*

"That's it, gentlemen," the professor concluded and looked at Pulaski with anticipation.

"Are you confident of a complete translation, Professor?" Pulaski asked. "Nothing left out, or anything you are not sure of?"

"I'm sure. The conversation is quite rudimentary really."

"Thank you, professor," said Pulaski. "I hope it won't be too much of an imposition but this is a highly classified matter, and we will be placing you under what we call a security watch until this is resolved. Hopefully, it will last only a day or two. A security watch simply means we will monitor phone calls to and from your home, and one of our agents will be staying with you and accompanying you wherever you go. I'm sure you understand. It's for your safety and in the nation's interest."

"Staying at my house?" asked the professor.

"It's either that or we can take you in to protective custody here at the hotel. This is wartime, professor, and you now have information of a top secret nature. I'm sorry, but it's a security watch or protective custody. Your choice."

The security watch seemed the much lesser of two evils to the professor, and he was escorted out by one of Chris Singleton's men.

Pulaski sat down and dissected the events of the past three hours. There would be a meeting and a package exchange. Obviously Mr. X had the tellurium which he stole from the woman that night in her apartment. Pulaski had been right on that score too. But what did she have that he wanted? Other information? Money? In the end, it made no difference. The only thing that now mattered was capturing the enemy agents and making sure the tellurium did not leave the country.

Pulaski worried and wondered if Mr. X spotted the surveillance at the Dogtown Tavern earlier that afternoon. No, Pulaski wanted desperately to assure himself, he could not have spotted the road block. X turned off the winding river road before he could have seen the FBI cars. But what if X *had* spotted the FBI or for some reason grown suspicious? Did X have a way to contact the woman for a change of plans? Pulaski doubted it from the elaborate contact scheme; it was obvious Sarah Klein and Mr. X did not trust each other. The johnboat had to be just a cunning precaution by X, probably done to insure that he was not followed by the woman.

It was Charles Pulaski's only consolation.

The only hope.

CHAPTER 42

Great deeds are usually wrought at great risks.

—*Herodotus (ca. 424 B.C.)*

Evansville—June 5, 1943

Joe Mayer was not sure what woke him, especially when his wristwatch on the nightstand told him it was not yet four in the morning. He thought he heard a sound from the living room where Agent Engler slept. Engler probably woke him, Mayer reasoned; Engler was a light sleeper and usually arose once or twice during the night.

Mayer was sleeping better. Charles Pulaski assured him the investigation into his involvement with Sarah Klein was nearly complete and that the FBI was confident he did not knowingly aid the German spy. Yesterday Pulaski told Mayer that it was probably a matter of only a few days until he would be allowed to return to work at the shipyard.

Sometimes Mayer still found himself refusing to believe that Sarah was a German spy. He had loved her and had considered asking her to marry. Then a sudden shame would wash over him. He had let down his country, his family, himself. Then he would hate her. These thoughts accompanied Mayer as he rose from bed and walked to the bathroom.

Mayer stood in front of the toilet, relieved himself, then flushed. Moving to the sink he splashed water on his face and squinted into the mirror. He had not shaved in a couple of days and needed one badly. He turned off the bathroom light, a relief to eyes still accustomed to the night, and returned to the bedroom. Mayer did not see the shadow sitting in the chair in the dark corner until he heard the voice.

"Hello, Joe."

Mayer reeled backwards and probably would have fallen back out the bedroom door if not for banging against a dresser. The start was so sudden, for a moment Mayer felt light-headed from the sudden jump in heart rate. He immediately recognized the voice of Sarah Klein.

For a moment, Mayer could not decide what to do, then he remembered the gun in the dresser. He spun around and jerked open the drawer. As Mayer frantically ripped through underwear and socks, she turned on a small writing lamp on the desk next to her chair.

"Is this what you're looking for?" She threw the gun on the bed and made sure he saw her toss the bullets into a small waste can next to the desk. "Surely you haven't forgotten, darling, I've been in this room a few times."

She was dressed in dark clothing but normal pants and blouse, nothing that would draw attention. The hair was now blond.

"How did you get in?" Mayer demanded.

She reached in a pocket, pulled out a key, and placed it on the desk. "A key, of course. You gave it to me. Luckily it also fits the back door. I think your chaperon would have heard me come in the front."

Mayer suddenly remembered Engler. "What did you do to him?"

"He'll be fine. Just a slight tap on the head before giving him something to make him rest comfortably. Nembutal leaves few side effects. He'll awake in a couple of hours with a slight hangover, nothing more." Nembutal was the drug Erika placed in Henry Wiltshire's brandy on the beach in Wales. Because it worked quickly and came in oral as well as intravenous form, Nembutal was Erika's favorite tool for rendering a subject comatose.

Mayer turned and raced out of the room. Engler was sprawled on the living room floor. An empty syringe lay discarded on the coffee table.

Mayer looked behind him and discovered she had not followed him out of the bedroom. He sprinted into the kitchen, found a butcher knife and made no effort to conceal it as he ran back to the bedroom where she still sat, an unlit cigarette now in her lips. She glanced at the butcher knife, made no comment, then struck a match and held it to the cigarette.

Mayer was now giving orders. "Don't move out of that chair, Sarah—or whatever your name is. I'm calling the FBI." Mayer moved toward the phone on the nightstand and picked up the receiver. The phone was dead. With an eye on the woman, Mayer banged hard on the cradle several times attempting to raise a dial tone.

Nothing.

Mayer cursed and threw down the receiver which crashed against and broke a glass ashtray sitting next to the phone. He looked back at the woman who calmly sat and watched him in his frustration. She crossed her legs and exhaled a cloud of smoke.

"Okay," Mayer said. "We're going to walk out of here together, get in my car, and drive to the cop station. You're driving." Mayer made the knife very visible as he spoke.

"That might look rather startling, don't you think?" she said. "A man in his underwear forcing a young lady to do his bidding at knife point. Yes, it would look very naughty I'm afraid."

"I don't give a damn what it looks like," said Mayer as he reached for and put on his pants, all the while controlling the knife and watching the woman.

"Sit down, Joe. We have business to discuss."

Mayer buckled his belt. "The only business I have with you is to get you turned over to the authorities, *Sarah!*"

"My name is Erika."

Mayer paused and looked at her for a long moment, then located his car keys. "Let's go."

She remained seated. "Joe, I really think you should sit and listen to what I have to say."

"Not interested, let's go." He moved over and grabbed her arm to lift her out of the chair. Erika Lehmann knew Joe Mayer would never use a knife for more than a bluff. She stood and turned toward him, grabbed his hand that held the knife and placed the knife point against her chest.

"You have three seconds to use the knife, Joe, either that or sit down and listen to what I have to say." She began counting.

"One..." Mayer's red face was a combination of anger and embarrassment.

"Two..." She made sure she kept eye contact.

"Three..."

Mayer threw down the knife and attempted to grab her, but she had anticipated something of the like and used a move that had served her well at Quenzsee against the bigger and less agile males. As Mayer tried to lock his arms around her, Erika dropped to the floor and pulled him off balance and to the floor with her. Before he could turn over, she maneuvered on top of him like a wrestler, pulled a handgun from behind her back and held it to his throat, making sure he could both see and feel the gun.

Instead of feeling fear, Mayer suddenly found himself beyond caring. "You gave me three seconds to use the knife. Now you have three seconds to use that gun, Sarah, before I kick your ass."

Erika Lehmann's bluff worked no better than Joe Mayer's had and, wanting no part of a wrestling match on the floor, she quickly jumped up.

"I told you my name is Erika...get up!" She held the gun on him. "You're right, Joe," she admitted as Mayer rose from the floor and sat on the end of the bed. "I won't kill you, but I will shoot you." She turned the gun toward the useless telephone across the room, squeezed the trigger and shattered the phone. The exploding telephone made more noise than the silenced weapon. "A round through a kneecap makes a terrible mess."

Mayer ignored her as she moved the chair far enough away from him so she could react if he rushed her. She sat down and lit another cigarette with one hand while holding the gun on him with the other.

"You were a bad influence on me, Joe. I've smoked more cigarettes in the past few months since meeting you than I have in my whole life."

Mayer did not look at her and showed no reaction to her small talk. "Why are you here?"

"You'll have to be more specific. Do you mean 'Why am I in this town?' or 'Why am I sitting here tonight?'"

"Why did you come here tonight? There is nothing more you can take from me. You've taken everything."

"Maybe I've come to give some of it back, Joe," she said seriously. He laughed. She reached into a pocket, pulled out some folded pieces of paper, and tossed them on the bed beside Mayer. He ignored the papers.

"I came here tonight because by this time tomorrow I will be either dead or gone from here forever." Mayer finally looked at her. She continued: "On one of those papers is the name of a bank in Nashville, Tennessee. There is $200,000 being held in an escrow account at that bank with Saul Mayer's name on it. The account number is on the paper. I would have delivered the money to you here tonight, but I know that would have looked very suspicious and you would have to turn it over to the authorities. You can still tell the authorities about the money of course, that's your prerogative, but the money is meant for Saul, so I think that should be his decision. Tell Saul it's repayment for his business being destroyed on *Kristallnacht*."

Mayer laughed bitterly. "What is this, a Nazi with a last minute surge of conscience? This is supposed to repay Saul for everything?—for his wife and son being God knows where and probably living in one of your hell-hole concentration camps—if they're still alive, that is. Yeah, I've seen the reports. The New York Times ran an interview article last week with some guy who escaped from one of them. I hope you read it. Makes you want to puke!"

"Propaganda," replied Erika. Her heart still would not allow her to believe the worst. "The camps are there to house criminals and enemies of Germany. You have your prisons and, since your country entered the war, your camps where the Japanese-Americans are concentrated."

"You said 'enemies of Germany.' How can that label be applied to Saul's wife and four-year-old son? They are discriminated against solely because they are Jews. Admit it."

"Yes," said Erika. "Like your Japanese-Americans and your Negroes. When I arrived in this country, one of the first things I witnessed was a Negro soldier and his pregnant wife being forced to stand in a train station because all the seats for Negroes were taken when there were rows of empty 'white only' seats. It is the same, you must now admit that."

"It's not the same. Starving and working men, women, and children to death is not the same as refusing someone a seat in a train station! Neither is right, but it's not the same. There are different levels of evil."

"Propaganda," she said again.

Both stopped talking for a moment. Finally Joe Mayer picked up and looked over the paper with the bank information. When Mayer spoke it was slowly. "So this is the price you place on a man's family. Are you expecting a 'thank you'?"

"Saul's wife and son are no longer in Germany," Erika announced. "Last week they were transferred across the Swiss border and are now at an International Red Cross refugee camp just outside Zurich. All the information you'll need is on one of those papers. It should not be difficult to bring them to the United States now." In her transmission from Tennessee, besides the money, Erika informed Abwehr that the release of Saul Mayer's wife and son were part of the deal to purchase the tellurium.

Mayer quickly found the paper. He looked at Erika and was about to ask why she was doing this, but it caught in his throat. Mayer gathered all three papers. The last one was written in German. "What is this?"

"It's a note to Saul's son. He may read it when he's older."

Mayer looked at her strangely.

"Now, I must go," Erika announced as she rose from the chair.

Mayer's mind raced. *He had to stop her!* Before he got the chance to try, she pointed the gun and fired a single shot through the outside of his left thigh. Mayer shouted out in surprise more than in pain and slipped off the bed on to the floor.

"Sorry, but you needed that. You're the hero type, Joe, and would try to stop me. Besides, I'm sure you want to return to your duties at the shipyard. I already have you under undue suspicion, and this night would just add to it if you came away without a scratch when the FBI man out there in the living room was drugged. The wound is minor, there are no major arteries in that area outside the femur, just get some pressure on it and you'll be able to get to a neighbor's house or the FBI man's car and radio for help."

"Good bye, Joe."

Erika Lehmann stepped around Joe Mayer and was gone.

✠   ✠   ✠

CHAPTER 43

Bravery is half victory.

—*Tacitus, (ca. 100 A.D.)*

Washington, D.C.—Wednesday, June 9, 1943

Forty minutes, maybe fifty, Chris Singleton waited until J. Edgar Hoover and an entourage of six men entered the room: three wore gray suits, the others military uniforms. Besides Hoover, the only person Singleton recognized was General William J. "Wild Bill" Donovan, the director of the OSS. Singleton rose and stood while Hoover introduced the others: two military intelligence supervisors, another OSS big shot, and a couple of FBI higher-ups. Singleton had written the reports and related the story of last Saturday night ad infinitum, but Hoover insisted on hearing it in person so Singleton was flown to Washington.

Hoover took the middle seat while the others divided up equally on the long side of the oval table. Young Chris Singleton sat conspicuously alone, opposite and facing the men.

"Of course I have read your report, Agent Singleton," Hoover began. "The other men here have done likewise, but I ordered you to Washington because I wanted you to be on hand to personally answer any questions about the events of this Saturday past."

"I understand, sir," Singleton said.

"To begin, give us your rundown of what happened last Saturday." Hoover looked at the papers in front of him. "Start from the time the principals arrived at the meeting location."

Singleton began: "Agent Pulaski, myself and two of my men, Agents Stuart and Buecher, were stationed inside the nightclub. Agent Pulaski felt more men than that might be too obvious to the suspects. Outside the club was a different matter. Agent Falasco had assembled a large contingent of agents to established road block capability both directions on the highway that passes by the premises—out of sight, of course—including a team of agents on the Kentucky side of the bridge that crosses the Ohio River south of the club."

"Agent Pulaski, myself, and my two men took our places inside the club. We all sat separately. The male suspect, we refer to him as 'Ivan,' entered the nightclub at 2010 hours, fifty minutes before the scheduled rendezvous. Initially, Ivan took a seat at the bar but after a few minutes moved to a table. The woman agent, we're calling her 'Erika' now, arrived at 2035; she spotted the man and joined him at his table."

Hoover held up his hand to stop Singleton. "The name 'Erika' comes from the woman herself?"

"Yes," Singleton nodded. "It is the name she claimed was her's during the break in at the engineer's home the previous night."

"Wild Bill" Donovan broke in. "I saw that in your report. That certainly is a strange kettle of fish. In your report you state this engineer, Mayer, claims this German spy broke in and drugged an FBI agent just so she could tell this Mayer guy that she had succeeded in getting his relatives released from a concentration camp?"

"That's Mayer's story, General," Singleton confirmed.

"Then she shoots him for good measure?"

"She knew the engineer would try to capture her, sir."

The men behind the table looked around at each other.

"Go on, Agent Singleton," Hoover ordered.

"Agent Pulaski preferred to not make the arrest inside the nightclub if possible. The place was crowded and Pulaski worried about innocent bystanders. The two suspects talked for fifteen minutes before they rose and left the nightclub. Agent Pulaski gave us the signal to follow them out. It was outside in the parking lot where we attempted to make the arrest." Singleton paused for a moment to see if there were any questions. None were asked so he continued.

"As it states in my report, I was the first to approach the suspects along with Agent Pulaski who was a half-step behind me. I withdrew my identification and showed it to the suspects. The male immediately produced a handgun and pointed it in my direction." Singleton paused for a moment and collected himself.

"I had my gun drawn but everything happened so quickly. Agent Pulaski knocked me out of the way, and he himself was hit by the bullet. Ivan fired two more shots in our direction but we—Stuart, Buecher, and myself—were able to find shelter behind some parked cars. I raised my gun and was about to return the fire, when Ivan grabbed a bystander—a young woman who had just walked out of the club. He used the woman as a shield. We held our fire; Ivan forced the hostage into an automobile. The female suspect, Erika, also jumped into the same car. They sped from the parking lot with the man behind the wheel."

"This is when you radioed the road blocks?" Hoover asked.

"Yes," replied Singleton. "The first thing I did was check on Agent Pulaski, of course. He sustained a gunshot wound to the abdomen and was bleeding profusely but was conscious. I then ordered Agent Stuart to alert the road block people, and I ordered Agent Buecher to call for an ambulance. But Agent Pulaski insisted we help him into a vehicle and take out after the suspects. With the nature of Agent Pulaski's wound, I didn't think this was a good idea from his standpoint. I told him we had notified Falasco and the road block people and they would pick up the suspects. But Agent Pulaski would not calm down. He kept insisting his wound was not that bad, and he ordered us to pursue the suspects."

"What was the time frame," one of the military people asked, "from the gunshot to the time you pulled out in pursuit?"

"Less than one minute," Singleton answered the inane question, "probably forty-five seconds."

"The suspects headed south, away from the city and toward the bridge that crosses the river to Kentucky. Buecher drove our car and quickly closed on the suspect's car. By the time we were on the bridge we were no more than one hundred yards behind them. I knew we had them when I saw the flashing red lights at the far end of the bridge. The Kentucky side of the bridge was completely barricaded with cars while Falasco, who was with the men north of the nightclub, ordered those cars to follow and set up a barricade at the Indiana side on the bridge. The suspects were completely trapped on the bridge."

"So," Hoover interrupted, "let's make sure everyone is picturing this correctly. It ended up being just your car, and the car driven by the suspects, on the bridge with both ends of the bridge blocked from escape."

"That's right, Director." Singleton confirmed. "Agent Pulaski, who I was trying to attend in the back seat as best as I could, ordered Buecher to radio that there was a hostage situation and to maintain the barricade but not to pursue onto the bridge."

"I have a question, Agent Singleton," grilled the OSS man who accompanied Donovan. "We have no eyewitness reports on the events that took place on the bridge from Special Agent in Charge Falasco or any of the other men from the Bureau. Why is that?"

"The bridge is a mile long, sir," Singleton remarked, "and it was after dark."

"Go on, Singleton," Hoover nodded.

"Again, I estimate we were about a hundred yards behind the suspect's car, both doing about ninety miles an hour on the bridge. When the suspect spotted the barricade at the other end he slammed on the brakes and spun to a stop. That's when the door opened and the hostage was thrown out."

Hoover shuffled through papers until he found what he looked for. "I see from your report the hostage claims the female suspect—this Erika—opened the car door and threw her out of the automobile?"

"Yes, Director, that is what the hostage claims."

Singleton: "After the hostage was ejected from the car, the car headed back in our direction. I guess they were hoping the north end of the bridge wasn't blocked yet. With our headlights on bright, and shining directly on the car as it came toward us, we saw what we thought was the female suspect fighting with the male as he tried to drive the car. That was just before the car swerved violently and crashed into the bridge guard rail."

"The car door opened and the man and woman fell out of the car. I could see then that they were indeed fighting. The man punched the woman and she flew back against the guard rail. This is when he picked up a gun one of them had apparently dropped during the fight. We were all out of our car and had taken cover by this time. When I saw the man level the gun at the woman I fired two shots. The guy staggered for a second and dropped the gun but he didn't go down. Instead he went after the woman again."

"Where did you hit the suspect?" Hoover asked.

"I hit him with two solid shots in the torso," answered Singleton. "It was unbelievable the guy didn't go down." Singleton took a breath and went on.

"Erika began climbing the outside metal work of the bridge and Ivan went after her. I ordered them to come down and surrender but both ignored my orders. She went up much more quickly than he did and I got the impression she purposely slowed a couple of times to allow him to catch up, staying just high enough over him to stay out of his reach."

Donovan interrupted, curious about how Singleton could see all this in the dark.

"Stuart kept the car's spotlight trained on them," Singleton stated.

Donovan nodded and Singleton restarted.

"When they were finally near the top of the bridge's metal work, the woman produced a dagger then jumped down on to the back of the man. From where we stood it looked like she then buried the knife in his throat. He lost his grip and they both fell off the metal work. Together they plunged passed us and down to the river. It was a long fall—over one hundred feet, but there was enough moonlight to enable us to watch them hit the water. The woman still clung to the man's back when they disappeared into the murky water. We saw neither suspect surface, but within thirty minutes Agent Falasco had a Coast Guard runabout and a couple of Sheriff's Department motorboats conducting a searchlight sweep of the river."

"No bodies were found that night?" Donovan asked.

"No," confirmed Singleton. "Dragging operations began at dawn on Sunday. The man's body was dragged up Monday afternoon a mile down river. The autopsy report confirmed that two .38 caliber bullets from my weapon entered his chest area, and his jugular vein was severed by the woman's knife. The knife wound was the mortal one."

"Any news on the woman's body?" Hoover jumped in.

"An hour ago I called Agent Falasco in Evansville for the latest. We still have not retrieved the woman's body."

Donovan: "What are the chances, in your opinion Agent Singleton, that the woman could have survived the fall?"

"Not likely. First she had taken a beating from the man, and from interviews with Joseph Mayer and a security guard at the shipyard who took Mayer and the woman fishing, it seems the woman could not swim and held a fear of the water. Even if that were a fabrication on her part, it would be hard to survive the fall. After a fall from that height, they would have entered the water at over sixty miles an hour."

"But still it could be possible to survive," Hoover frowned.

"Yes, anything is possible," Singleton conceded. "That's why we still have an APB out for the woman. The local police tell me bodies of drowning victims in that river are sometimes not recovered for weeks or even months. With undertows, cross currents, and underwater debris that can entrap a body and hold it under, I'm told bodies are sometimes never recovered. Nevertheless, the APB will remain in effect."

When Singleton finished, some of the men looked down at papers on the table, others looked at Singleton. Apparently no one had any more questions. Hoover spoke to the committee.

"Despite some rather bizarre happenstance to accompany this case, gentlemen, I feel we must count our blessings. The stolen tellurium and several roles of microfilm were recovered from the trunk of the male suspect's automobile. These highly classified materials were in the hands of the enemy for three weeks. To have recovered them is certainly reason for celebration." Hoover turned to Singleton. "Agent Singleton, you have every reason to be pleased with your work."

"Thank you, Director, but it was Charlie Pulaski who should get the credit for this case. Pulaski was the only one who felt the woman would return to Evansville. Pulaski's the one who uncovered the leads that eventually cracked the case." Singleton paused to collect his thoughts.

"Not to mention he saved my life by taking a bullet intended for me."

"Of course, Agent Singleton," Hoover agreed. "What are the plans?"

"I'm flying back to Evansville this evening and accompanying Charlie's body to Chicago tomorrow for burial Friday."

"It was a shock when Falasco called last night to tell us Agent Pulaski passed yesterday," Hoover said. "We were all praying he'd make it."

Singleton said nothing.

"I will be there for the funeral in Chicago on Friday, of course," said Hoover. The FBI director asked the other men if there were any more questions for Singleton. When there were none Singleton was dismissed.

"Just one last reminder, Agent Singleton," said Hoover as Singleton made his way to the door, "none of this reaches the newspapers."

Chris Singleton nodded and closed the door behind him.

A warm rain fell gently on Chicago when the body of Charles Pulaski was lowered into the ground. The contingent from the FBI was there: Hoover and his entourage from Washington and Preston Elliott and others from the Chicago office. Chris Singleton and Harry Fallon were among the pallbearers. The ex Mrs. Pulaski stood by the grave with the two children who had not seen their father in over a year. Hoover assured her she would receive Charlie's death benefits and pension for the children.

The body of Erika Lehmann was never found. The All Points Bulletin for the German spy would stay in effect for twelve months and the case remained open until well after the end of the war. Finally, on September 18, 1946, the case of the break in at the United States Navy Auxiliary Shipyard at Evansville was officially closed.

EPILOGUE

February 2001

Readers who contend there are gaps in this story will get no argument from the author. Why did Dorothy Nolan not report Erika Lehmann to the authorities after she saw her picture in the Nashville newspaper? What was Reinhard Heydrich's reaction when Erika Lehmann returned her Gestapo identification? I attempt to answer none of these questions when the truth is not before me.

Although David Mayer and I spent countless hours applying for access to, and then poring over, literally thousands of pages of government documents (U.S., British, and German), some of which have become declassified only within the past few years, in an account such as this one an author has to rely heavily on eyewitnesses if the story that evolves is to become more than an antiseptic documentary.

Consequently, it goes without saying that when attempting to piece together a series of events that took place over a half century ago, the completeness and accuracy of the story will depend on if the participants are still living and are willing and able to tell their story. And, of course, nearly sixty years will mean that many participants will no longer be with us. Others were never found and their fates unknown.

So the success in finding a few of the key players in this story was critical, and without one of these participants the events that took place in Evansville, Indiana, would have never seen the light of day.

Chris Singleton is alive and enjoying a healthy retirement with his lovely wife, Alice, in Tucson, Arizona. Chris retired in 1978 after a thirty-seven-year career with the FBI. At eighty-two, Chris Singleton can still be found on the links around Tucson. When he is not golfing, Agent Singleton spends most of his time attending the high school athletic events of his and Alice's four grandchildren—fine athletes each. Chris Singleton spent countless hours with me in person and on the telephone reconstructing the events in Evansville.

In late 1995, one year after I began chronicling the events of this story, I created a web page in the hope it might generate contacts from people who took part in the events or who could share information about events or participants. The web page paid off in a big way in 1996. I received an email from a woman in Birmingham, Alabama, whose aunt in the story I call Dorothy Nolan (not her real name, changed at the niece's request, and the only name in the book that has been changed). *Dorothy Nolan* died in 1981 but her niece kindly allowed me to read and take notes from her aunt's detailed diary. From Dorothy's diary I filled some large gaps in the story.

As far as the fates of some of the shipyard people, Howard Turnbull died in Baltimore in 1990. I never located Carol Weiss.

There was great good news from Europe in 1998 when Sophie Somé was found. Sophie recovered from the Gestapo interrogation, made it through the war, and eventually returned home to Lyon where she married and bore three children. Sophie is now a great-grandmother and supplied most of the facts surrounding Erika Lehmann's life and times in Paris.

From Sophie, I learned that after Sebastian Delavenne's death, Claude Vauzous became an active member of the French Resistance. He was severely wounded on June 7, 1944, outside St. Lo while attempting to delay movements of Rommel's panzers in Normandy immediately after the D-Day invasion. Claude survived the war but suffered with liver complications brought on by his wound and died in 1952 at the age of thirty-five.

Well documented are the fates of historical figures who played a part in the story such as Heinrich Himmler and Reinhard Heydrich, as is the ultimate demise of Admiral Wilhelm Canaris, the head of Abwehr, who was hanged by the SS on April 9, 1945, in Flossenberg Concentration Camp.

Details are not as clear concerning the fate of Karl Lehmann. By some accounts he was captured by the Russians and was never heard of again, but strangely there are no records of Lehmann's detainment by the then Soviets now Russians who took great pains to document such things and were very cooperative with records from the war years. Finding out what really happened to Karl Lehmann would be an interesting and worthwhile task.

Henry Wiltshire, the unfortunate Englishman taken captive by Erika Lehmann, sat out the war in Stalag Luft 2 outside Barth, Germany, near the Baltic Sea. The Russians liberated Stalag Luft 2 at the end of the war, and Wiltshire returned home to England where he died of complications from a stroke in 1971.

And of the Mayer family.

On August 4, 1943, two months after Erika Lehmann's last, fateful visit to Joe Mayer, Ruth Mayer and her four-year-old son, David, stepped off a French Moroccan freighter-turned-refugee-ship on to a dock in New York Harbor. There to greet them was Saul Mayer, his cousin Noah Mayer, and Joe Mayer. It was a joyous reunion.

Of the Mayers mentioned in this story only David Mayer remains with us. Saul died in 1978 and his wife Ruth in 1993. Noah Mayer and his wife (Joe's parents) both died in the 1960s.

The FBI exonerated Joe Mayer of any wrongdoing, and he returned to work at the Evansville Shipyard where he worked until the war's end.

After the war, Joe Mayer took a research job with Alcoa Aluminum in Pennsylvania. Joe married in 1948 and by all accounts led a happy life with his wife and two children. Joe Mayer died in 1990.

David Mayer graduated from Northwestern University (he turned down a scholarship offer from Harvard, the university his Uncle Joseph was denied admission to in the late twenties because of Jewish quotas). David became a corporate lawyer and just recently retired in 1998. He lives in the Denver suburb of Wheat Ridge with his wife Elizabeth. A son, Pete, is a high school math teacher in the Denver area. Pete and his wife have a son.

The Mayers of Dachau survived.

The real puzzle for me was what happened to Erika Lehmann. Like that of her father, the fate of Abwehr's *Lorelei* remains a mystery. Did she survive the fall from the bridge? The absence of a body is little proof that she did not die with Axel Ryker. Police, and people who reside near mighty rivers such as the Ohio, will attest to the many cases of drowning victims never found. But still....

A few artifacts concerning Erika Lehmann exist. Joe Mayer's widow gave David Mayer most of her husband's wartime effects after Joe's death. In an old cigar box, along with ragged wartime gas rationing cards and shipyard identification tags, David Mayer showed me a photograph of four nicely dressed people sitting around a dinner table. The photo is dated Nov. 7, 1942; *McCurdy Hotel* is written under the date. The names written on the back of the picture are Howard Turnbull, Carol Weiss, Joe Mayer, and Sarah Klein. All four people are smiling into the camera. This picture served as the basis for my scene in the book depicting the first date between Joe Mayer and Erika Lehmann.

Sophie Somé has in her possession in Lyon, France, some paintings by Claude Vauzous and sculptures by Sebastian Delavenne. Luckily those possessions, left behind in the loft, were stored by the baker who owned the property. Sophie claimed them after the war. Sophie showed me a painting dated '39 and signed *Vauzous*. The picture is of a young blond woman in a yellow summer dress holding a flower to her nose. The French words across the bottom of the canvas translate to "The Flower of Germany." Sophie did not have to tell me it is a painting of Erika Lehmann; I immediately recognized the facial resemblance between the woman in the painting and the *Sarah Klein* of the Hotel McCurdy photograph.

And then there is the note, handwritten in German. Joe Mayer gave it to David after the young man's bar mitzvah. It is a note from the perpetrator to the victim: from the epitome of the perfect Aryan—a woman who had walked on the arm of the Führer—to a Jew. With his German long lost, David did not bother having the note translated until years later.

> *Dear David,*
>
> *If the worst is true there will be no need for an apology. Such words would be insults to you. The blind hatred for your people will become the downfall of mine. We should have welcomed your people, as fellow Germans, to join us in the fight against Bolshevism, instead we chose to make you the enemy and with that destroy ourselves.*
>
> *I myself have allowed the worst. I offered my life to a leader undeserving. For years I forced myself to blame the smaller men under him for the wrongs I saw with my own eyes. Now I realize none of it could have happened without his approval or at least his knowledge. So I have handed over my honor as a German. Everything for me is in vain.*
>
> *You however, David, have your honor. Use it more wisely than I used mine.*
>
> *Shalom Little David and Grüss Gott.*
>
> *Your countryman,*
> *E. L.*